SLEIGHT OF CRIME

FIFTEEN CLASSIC TALES OF MURDER, MAYHEM AND MAGIC

BY ELLERY QUEEN, STEPHEN LEACOCK,
CLAYTON RAWSON, WALTER B. GIBSON,
DOROTHY L. SAYERS, PHILIP MACDONALD,
GRANT ALLEN, MANLY WADE WELLMAN,
CONWAY LONSTAR AND OTHERS.

HENRY REGNERY COMPANY·CHICAGO

Library of Congress Cataloging in Publication Data

Main entry under title:

Sleight of crime.

    CONTENTS: Leacock, S. The conjurer's revenge.-
Rawson, C. From another world.—Allen, G. The
episode of the Mexican seer.—Novotny, J. A trick
or two. [etc.]
    1. Detective and mystery stories, American.
I. Clute, Cedric E II. Lewin, Nicholas.
PZ1.S6376 [PS648.D4] 813'.0872   76-6261
ISBN 0-8092-8081-7
ISBN 0-8092-7978-9 pbk.

Published by Henry Regnery Company
180 North Michigan Avenue, Chicago, Illinois 60601
Manufactured in the United States of America
Library of Congress Catalog Card Number: 76-6261
International Standard Book Number: 0-8092-8081-7 (cloth)
                                     0-8092-7978-9 (paper)

Published simultaneously in Canada by
Beaverbooks
953 Dillingham Road
Pickering, Ontario L1W 1Z7
Canada

Acknowledgments

"The Conjurer's Revenge" and "A Model Dialog" reprinted by permission of
Dodd, Mead & Company, Inc., and the Canadian Publishers, McClelland and
Stewart Limited, Toronto, from *Literary Lapses* by Stephen Leacock.

"From Another World" by Clayton Rawson. Reprinted by permission of Mrs.
Clayton Rawson. This short story originally appeared in *Ellery Queen's Mystery
Magazine.* Copyright 1948 by the American Mercury, Inc., renewed 1976 by Mrs.
Clayton Rawson.

"A Trick or Two" by John Novotny. © 1957 by Mercury Press Inc. Reprinted by
permission of the author from *The Magazine of Fantasy and Science Fiction.*

Special thanks are due to Dean and Shirley Dickensheet, Jack Leavitt, Tom Whitmore, Debbie Notkin, Jeff Busby, Bart Whaley, Don Simpson, and Quinn Yarbro; to Bill and Milt Larsen for the generous use of the Magic Castle's library; to Pete and Judy Clute and Turk Murphy for keeping the spirit of Carter the Great alive and well in The Magic Cellar.

Special thanks in Los Angeles to Jean Cantor for the unlimited use of Magic Castle stationery; Susan Lewin; and Julian Portman, our agent; without his efforts this book would not have been possible.

For Ken Brooke,
  who made me
    a magician,
      and Milt and Bill Larsen,
        to whom I owe so much.
          —Nicholas Lewin

To Jan, my wife,
  the greatest
    magician
      of them all.
        —Cedric E. Clute, Jr.

Contents

Introduction

"Secutoris, foremost stage magician and escape artist of his day, flashed white teeth between spiky beard and spiky moustaches at his guests. Full bodied, vigorous, ungrayed despite his fifty-odd years, in the flame-colored evening suit he affected, he dominated the living room of Magic Manor."

Thus begins "Murder Among Magicians," one of fifteen magical mysteries intended to deceive, and by the skillful use of misdirection, deception, trickery, and bluff, lead you on a very crooked path. In these tales you will meet the great magicians and criminals of fiction, as they engage in battles of wit that employ each of their unusual talents.

Consider this—who has more in common with the master magician than the master criminal? After all, the main tool-in-trade of both the magician and the criminal is the little known art of "misdirection," that illusive ability to make the audience, or the victim, look "here" when he should have looked "there"; the illusion as well as the crime is carefully planned and rehearsed before execution, and the conditions under which the "game" will be played are studied to the last detail.

And this, necessarily, leads to the most important question of all—can it be pulled off successfully?

Of course it can! The ability to believe totally and unwaveringly in his talent is the prime requisite for both the magician and the criminal. They will never ask themselves if it can be done; they will simply ask themselves how to do it.

In fiction there have been many detectives involved in the occult sciences—John Silence, Carnaki, Miles Pennoyer, and Jules de Grandin are the most famous, but tales involving magicians, mystery, and murder are much harder to find. The question is why, and the answer, like the purloined letter in Poe's famous story, is right under your nose if you take the time to look for it.

Simply stated, most writers of crime fiction don't have the patience or the desire to study the art of conjuring and stage illusion in all its complexity, and a partial knowledge of the field would hinder rather than help. On the other hand, the professional magician, with five thousand years of recorded magical history at his fingertips, would much prefer the manipulation of coins to the manipulation of words.[1]

But sparse as they may be, the tales are there. And finding them is the sport.

We began to dig through old files of *Weird Tales* and *Black Mask*, collections of early detective stories, and faded copies of *Ellery Queen's Mystery Magazine*, and six months and a couple of thousand volumes later we discovered with delight that Lord Peter Wimsey dabbled in magic, that Ellery Queen solved a magical circus murder, and that

---

1. The honor of being the "first known magician" belongs to an Egyptian by the name of Dedi. Five thousand years ago he performed by royal command before the Pharaoh Cheops, builder of the Great Pyramid. An account of this performance was recorded in the Westcar Papyrus and is now housed at the State Museum in East Berlin.

Walter B. Gibson, creator of "The Shadow," was also a magician of the first rank.

The pieces came together slowly, but finally a complete picture began to take shape and our magician friends took an interest. They would whisper into our collective ear and make suggestions. "Let's have a locked-room murder!" or "Have you found any funny ones?" or the inevitable "Hey, how about a magician murdering a magician!"

They provided us with hard to find general publications, rare magicians' magazines, and lots of talk, and one bright day we found "From Another World" by Clayton Rawson, two deadly humorous pieces by Stephen Leacock, and a murderous yarn by Manly Wade Wellman that had appeared in an early detective pulp.

Later we discovered gems of mayhem and misdirection by such masters as Philip MacDonald, Grant Allen, and Conway Lonstar, and the magical mystery puzzle was complete.

So sit back and relax, as criminal meets conjuror in confrontations designed to baffle the astute, observant reader. As The Great Carter once said, "Enjoy these myriad modern masterful mysteries that paragon description!"

Cedric E. Clute, Jr.
San Francisco, California

Nicholas Lewin
Los Angeles, California

1

Stephen Leacock (1869–1944), world-famous wit, economist, and parodist, sets the stage for our first excursion into the realm of magic and mystery.

The author of such acclaimed works as "Maddened by Mystery; or, The Defective Detective" from *Nonsense Novels* (New York: Lane, 1911) and "Murder at $2.50 a Crime" from *Here Are My Lectures and Stories* (New York: Dodd, Mead & Co., 1937) takes careful aim at the most aggravating enemy of the magician—the wise guy—and finishes him off in a manner that would please the most ruthless conjuror.

The Conjurer's Revenge

by Stephen Leacock

"Now, ladies and gentlemen," said the conjurer, "having shown you that the cloth is absolutely empty, I will proceed to take from it a bowl of goldfish. Presto!"

All around the hall people were saying, "Oh, how wonderful! How does he do it?"

But the Quick Man on the front seat said in a big whisper to the people near him, "He—had—it—up—his—sleeve."

Then the people nodded brightly at the Quick Man and said, "Oh, of course"; and everybody whispered round the hall, "He—had—it—up—his—sleeve."

"My next trick," said the conjurer, "is the famous Hindostanee rings. You will notice that the rings are apparently separate; at a blow they all join (clang, clang, clang)—Presto!"

There was a general buzz of stupefaction till the Quick Man was heard to whisper, "He—must—have—had—another—lot—up—his—sleeve."

Again everybody nodded and whispered, "The—rings—were—up—his—sleeve."

The brow of the conjurer was clouded with a gathering frown.

"I will now," he continued, "show you a most amusing

trick by which I am enabled to take any number of eggs from a hat. Will some gentleman kindly lend me his hat? Ah, thank you—Presto!"

He extracted seventeen eggs, and for thirty-five seconds the audience began to think that he was wonderful. Then the Quick Man whispered along the front bench, "He—has—a—hen—up—his—sleeve," and all the people whispered it on. "He—has—a—lot—of—hens—up—his—sleeve."

The egg trick was ruined.

It went on like that all through. It transpired from the whispers of the Quick Man that the conjurer must have concealed up his sleeve, in addition to the rings, hens, and fish, several packs of cards, a loaf of bread, a doll's cradle, a live guinea-pig, a fifty-cent piece, and a rocking-chair.

The reputation of the conjurer was rapidly sinking below zero. At the close of the evening he rallied for a final effort.

"Ladies and gentlemen," he said, "I will present to you, in conclusion, the famous Japanese trick recently invented by the natives of Tipperary. Will you, sir," he continued, turning toward the Quick Man, "will you kindly hand me your gold watch?"

It was passed to him.

"Have I your permission to put it into this mortar and pound it to pieces?" he asked savagely.

The Quick Man nodded and smiled.

The conjurer threw the watch into the mortar and grasped a sledge hammer from the table. There was a sound of violent smashing. "He's—slipped—it—up—his—sleeve," whispered the Quick Man.

"Now, sir," continued the conjurer, "will you allow me to take your handkerchief and punch holes in it? Thank you. You see, ladies and gentlemen, there is no deception, the holes are visible to the eye."

The face of the Quick Man beamed. This time the real mystery of the thing fascinated him.

"And now, sir, will you kindly pass me your silk hat and allow me to dance on it? Thank you."

The conjurer made a few rapid passes with his feet and exhibited the hat crushed beyond recognition.

"And will you now, sir, take off your celluloid collar and permit me to burn it in the candle? Thank you, sir. And will you allow me to smash your spectacles for you with my hammer? Thank you."

By this time the features of the Quick Man were assuming a puzzled expression. "This thing beats me," he whispered, "I don't see through it a bit."

There was a great hush upon the audience. Then the conjurer drew himself up to his full height and, with a withering look at the Quick Man, he concluded:

"Ladies and gentlemen, you will observe that I have, with this gentleman's permission, broken his watch, burnt his collar, smashed his spectacles, and danced on his hat. If he will give me the further permission to paint green stripes on his overcoat, or to tie his suspenders in a knot, I shall be delighted to entertain you. If not, the performance is at an end."

And amid a glorious burst of music from the orchestra the curtain fell, and the audience dispersed, convinced that there are some tricks, at any rate, that are not done up the conjurer's sleeve.

In 1938 The Great Merlini took his first stage bows when he solved the murder of Eugene Tarot, "The King of Cards." The novel was *Death from a Top Hat,* and it instantly catapulted The Great Merlini and his creator, Clayton Rawson, to the top of legerdemain's ladder.

Two more Merlini novels quickly followed, both based on the assumption that things are not always what they seem—especially where magicians are concerned—and where every move has been planned to deceive.

Then, in 1940, a rival appeared; *Red Star Mystery,* a typical pulp magazine of the period, published the first amazing adventure of Don Diavolo—The Scarlet Wizard. It was "Ghost of the Undead," and it was written by Stuart Towne. Now the mystery reader's voracious appetite could be satisfied by not one, but two, masters of magic and mystery; so while The Great Merlini was solving the cases of "The Footprints on the Ceiling" and "The Headless Lady," The Scarlet Wizard was applying all his cunningly contrived conjuring conceits to untangling the baffling cases of "Death out of Thin Air" and "Don Diavolo Goes to the Circus."

One more Scarlet Wizard novel appeared, and then, as later happened to all the pulps, *Red Star Mystery* folded, and Don Diavolo had given his last performance.

But The Wizard went out in true magical style when it was revealed that Stuart Towne, creator of Don Diavolo was, in reality, Clayton Rawson.

The final Merlini novel, *No Coffin for the Corpse,* appeared in 1942, and as the years passed it was feared that the great magician had "laid down his wand."

Then, in the June 1948 issue of *Ellery Queen's Mystery Magazine* a prize-winning story by Clayton Rawson was published. It involved a perfectly-impossible-situation and a perfectly-possible-solution and—The Great Merlini.

It was . . .

From Another World

by Clayton Rawson

It was undoubtedly one of the world's strangest rooms. The old-fashioned roll-top desk, the battered typewriter, and the steel filing cabinet indicated that it was an office. There was even a calendar memo-pad, a pen and pencil set, and an overflowing ashtray on the desk, but any resemblance to any other office stopped right there.

The desk top also held a pair of handcuffs, half a dozen billiard balls, a shiny nickel-plated revolver, one celluloid egg, several decks of playing cards, a bright green silk handkerchief, and a stack of unopened mail. In one corner of the room stood a large, galvanized-iron milk-can with a strait jacket lying on its top. A feathered devil mask from the upper Congo leered down from the wall above and the entire opposite wall was papered with a Ringling Bros. and Barnum & Bailey twenty-four sheet poster.

A loose-jointed dummy-figure of a small boy with pop-eyes and violently red hair lay on the filing cabinet together with a skull and a fishbowl filled with paper flowers. And in the cabinet's bottom drawer, which was partly open and lined with paper, there was one half-eaten carrot and a twinkly-nosed, live white rabbit.

A pile of magazines, topped by a French journal,

l'Illusioniste, was stacked precariously on a chair, and a large bookcase tried vainly to hold an even larger flood of books that overflowed and formed dusty stalagmites growing up from the floor—books whose authors would have been startled at the company they kept. Shaw's *Joan of Arc* was sandwiched between Rowan's *Story of the Secret Service* and the *Memoirs of Robert Houdin*. Arthur Machen, Dr. Hans Gross, William Blake, Sir James Jeans, Rebecca West, Robert Louis Stevenson, and Ernest Hemingway were bounded on either side by Devol's *Forty Years a Gambler on the Mississippi* and Reginald Scot's *Discoverie of Witchcraft*.

The merchandise in the shop beyond the office had a similar surrealist quality, but the inscription on the glass of the outer door, although equally strange, did manage to supply an explanation. It read: *Miracles For Sale*—THE MAGIC SHOP, *A. Merlini, Prop.*

And that gentleman, naturally, was just as unusual as his place of business. For one thing, he hadn't put a foot in it, to my knowledge, in at least a week. When he finally did reappear, I found him at the desk sleepily and somewhat glumly eyeing the unopened mail.

He greeted me as though he hadn't seen another human being in at least a month, and the swivel chair creaked as he settled back in it, put his long legs up on the desk, and yawned. Then he indicated the card bearing his business slogan—"Nothing Is Impossible"—which was tacked on the wall.

"I may have to take that sign down," he said lazily. "I've just met a theatrical producer, a scene designer, and a playwright all of whom are quite impossible. They came in here a week before opening night and asked me to supply several small items mentioned in the script. In one scene a character said, 'Begone!' and the stage directions read: 'The genie and his six dancing girl slaves vanish instantly.' Later an elephant, complete with howdah and princess, disappeared the same way. I had to figure out how to manage all that and cook up a few assorted miracles for the big scene in heaven, too. Then I spent thirty-six hours in bed. And I'm still half asleep." He grinned wryly and added, "Ross, if you want anything that is not a stock item, you can whistle for it."

"I don't want a miracle," I said. "Just an interview. What do you know about ESP and PK?"

"Too much," he said. "You're doing another magazine article?"

"Yes. And I've spent the last week with a queer assortment of characters, too—half a dozen psychologists, some professional gamblers, a nuclear physicist, the secretary of the Psychical Research Society, and a neurologist. I've got an appointment in half an hour with a millionaire, and after that I want to hear what you think of it."

"You interviewed Dr. Rhine at Duke University, of course?"

I nodded. "Sure. He started it all. He says he's proved conclusively that there really are such things as telepathy, mind-reading, clairvoyance, X-Ray vision, and probably crystal-gazing as well. He wraps it all up in one package and calls it ESP—meaning Extra Sensory Perception."

"That," Merlini said, "is not the half of it. His psychokinesis, or PK for short, is positively miraculous—and frightening." The magician pulled several issues of the *Journal of Parapsychology* from the stack of magazines and upset the whole pile. "If the conclusions Rhine has published here are correct—if there really is a tangible mental force that can not only reach out and influence the movements of dice but exert its mysterious control over other physical objects as well—then he has completely upset the apple-cart of modern psychology and punctured a whole library of general scientific theory as well."

"He's already upset me," I said. "I tried to use PK in a crap game Saturday night. I lost sixty-eight bucks."

My skepticism didn't disturb Merlini. He went right on, gloomier than ever. "If Rhine is right, his ESP and PK have reopened the Pandora's box in which science thought it had forever sealed voodoo and witchcraft and enough other practices of primitive magic to make your hair stand on end. And *you're* growling about losing a few dollars——"

Behind me a hearty, familiar voice said, "I haven't got anything to worry about except a homicidal maniac who has killed three people in the last two days and left absolutely no clues. But can I come in?"

Inspector Homer Gavigan of the New York City Police Department stood in the doorway, his blue eyes twinkling frostily.

Merlini, liking the Cassandra role he was playing, said, "Sure. I've been waiting for you. But don't think that PK won't give you a splitting headache, too. All a murderer would have to do to commit the perfect crime——and a locked room one at that——would be to exert his psychokinetic mental force from a distance against the gun trigger." He pointed at the revolver on the desk. "Like this—"

Gavigan and I both saw the trigger, with no finger on it, move.

Bang!

The gun's report was like a thunderclap in the small room. I knew well enough that it was only a stage prop and the cartridge a blank, but I jumped a foot. So did Gavigan.

"Look, dammit!" the Inspector exploded, "how did you——"

The Great Merlini grinned. He was fully awake now and enjoying himself hugely. "No," he said, "that wasn't PK, luckily. Just ordinary run-of-the-mill conjuring. The rising Cards and the Talking Skull are both sometimes operated the same way. You can have the secret at the usual catalog price of——"

Like most policemen Gavigan had a healthy respect for firearms and he was still jumpy. "I don't want to buy either of them," he growled. "Do we have a date for dinner—or don't we? I'm starved."

"We do," Merlini said, pulling his long, lean self up out of the chair and reaching for his coat. "Can you join us, Ross?"

I shook my head. "Not this time. I've got a date just now with Andrew Drake."

In the elevator Merlini gave me an odd look and asked, "Andrew Drake? What has he got to do with ESP and PK?"

"What doesn't he have something to do with?" I replied. "Six months ago it was the Drake Plan to Outlaw War; he tried to take over UN single-handed. Two months ago he announced he was setting up a fifteen-million dollar research foundation to find a cancer cure in six months. 'Polish it off like we did the atom bomb,' he says. 'Put in enough money, and you can accomplish anything.' Now he's head over heels in ESP with some Yogi mixed in. 'Unleash the power of the human mind and solve all our problems.' Just like that."

"So that's what he's up to," Merlini said as we came out on to 42nd Street, half a block from Times Square, to face a bitterly cold January wind. "I wondered."

Then, as he followed Gavigan into the official car that waited and left me shivering on the curb, he threw a last cryptic sentence over his shoulder.

"When Drake mentions Rosa Rhys," he said, "you might warn him that he's heading for trouble."

Merlini didn't know how right he was. If any of us had had any clairvoyant ability at all, I wouldn't have taken a cab up to Drake's; all three of us would have gone—in Gavigan's car and with the siren going full blast.

As it was, I stepped out all alone in front of the big 98th Street house just off Riverside Drive. It was a sixty-year-old mansion built in the tortured style that had been the height of architectural fashion in the '80s but was now a smoke-blackened monstrosity as coldly depressing as the weather.

I nearly froze both ears just getting across the pavement and up the steps where I found a doctor with his finger glued—or frozen perhaps—to the bell push. A doctor? No, it wasn't ESP; a copy of the *A. M. A. Journal* stuck out of his overcoat pocket, and his left hand carried the customary small black case. But he didn't have the medical man's usual clinical detachment. This doctor was jumpy as hell.

When I asked, "Anything wrong?" his head jerked around, and his pale blue eyes gave me a startled look. He was a thin, well-dressed man in his early forties.

"Yes," he said crisply. "I'm afraid so." He jabbed a long forefinger at the bell again just as the door opened.

At first I didn't recognize the girl who looked out at us. When I saw her by daylight earlier in the week, I had tagged her as in the brainy-but-a-bit-plain category, a judgment I revised somewhat now, considering what the Charles hairdo and Hattie Carnegie dress did for her.

"Oh, hello, doctor," she said. "Come in."

The doctor began talking even before he crossed the threshold. "Your father, Elinor—is he still in the study?"

"Yes, I think so. But what——"

She stopped because he was already gone, running down the hall toward a door at its end. He rattled the doorknob, then rapped loudly.

"Mr. Drake! Let me in!"

The girl looked puzzled, then frightened. Her dark eyes met mine for an instant, and then her high heels clicked on the polished floor as she too ran down the hall. I didn't wait to be invited. I followed.

The doctor's knuckles rapped again on the door. "Miss

Rhys!" he called. "It's Dr. Garrett. Unlock the door!"

There was no answer.

Garrett tried the doorknob once more, then threw his shoulder against the door. It didn't move.

"Elinor, do you have a key? We must get in there—quickly!"

She said, "No. Father has the only keys. Why don't they answer? What's wrong?"

"I don't know," Garrett said. "Your father phoned me just now. He was in pain. He said, '*Hurry! I need you. I'm*——' " The doctor hesitated, watching the girl; then he finished " '*—dying.*' After that—no answer." Garrett turned to me. "You've got more weight than I have. Think you can break this door in?"

I looked at it. The door seemed solid enough, but it was an old house and the wood around the screws that held the lock might give. "I don't know," I said. "I'll try."

Elinor Drake moved to one side and the doctor stepped behind me. I threw myself against the door twice and the second time felt it move a bit. Then I hit it hard. Just as the door gave way I heard the tearing sound of paper.

But before I could discover what caused that, my attention was held by more urgent matters. I found myself staring at a green-shaded desk lamp, the room's only source of light at the overturned phone on the desk top, and at the sprawled shape that lay on the floor in front of the desk. A coppery highlight glinted on a letter-opener near the man's feet. Its blade was discolored with a dark wet stain.

Dr. Garrett said, "Elinor, you stay out," as he moved past me to the body and bent over it. One of his hands lifted Andrew Drake's right eyelid, the other felt his wrist.

I have never heard a ghost speak but the sound that came then was exactly what I would expect, a low, quivering moan shot with pain. I jerked around and saw a glimmer of white move in the darkness on my left.

Behind me, Elinor's whisper, a tense thread of sound, said, "Lights," as she clicked the switch by the door. The glow from the ceiling fixture overhead banished both the darkness and the spectre, but what remained was almost as unlikely. A chair lay overturned on the carpet, next to a small table that stood in the center of the room. In a second chair, slumped forward with her head resting on the tabletop, was the body of a young woman.

She was young, dark-haired, rather good-looking, and had an excellent figure. This latter fact was instantly apparent because—and I had to look twice before I could believe what I saw—she wore a brief, skin-tight, one-piece bathing suit. Nothing else.

Elinor's eyes were still on the sprawled shape on the floor. "Father. He's—dead?"

Garrett nodded slowly and stood up.

I heard the quick intake of her breath but she made no other sound. Then Garrett strode quickly across to the woman at the table.

"Unconscious," he said after a moment. "Apparently a blow on the head—but she's beginning to come out of it." He looked again at the knife on the floor. "We'll have to call the police."

I hardly heard him. I was wondering why the room was so bare. The hall outside and the living room that opened off it were furnished with the stiff, formal ostentation of the overly-rich. But Drake's study, by contrast, was as sparsely furnished as a cell in a Trappist monastery. Except for the desk, the small table, the two chairs, and a three-leaf folding screen that stood in one corner, it contained no other furniture. There were no pictures on the walls, and although there were shelves for them, no books. There wasn't even a blotter or pen on the desk top. Nothing but the phone, desk lamp—and, strangely enough, a roll of gummed paper tape.

But I only glanced at these things briefly. It was the

large casement window in the wall behind the desk that held my attention—a dark rectangle beyond which, like a scattered handful of bright jewels, were the lights of Jersey and, above them, frosty pinpoints of stars shining coldly in a black sky.

The odd thing was that the window's center line, where its two halves joined, was criss-crossed by two foot strips of brown paper tape pasted to the glass. The window was, quite literally, sealed shut. It was then that I remembered the sound of tearing paper as the lock had given way and the door had come open.

I turned. Elinor still stood there—motionless. And on the inside of the door and on the jamb were more of the paper strips. Four were torn in half, two others had been pulled loose from the wall and hung curled from the door's edge.

At that moment a brisk, energetic voice came from the hall. "How come you leave the front door standing wide open on the coldest day in——"

Elinor turned to face a broad-shouldered young man with wavy hair, hand-painted tie, and a completely self-assured manner. She said, "Paul!" then took one stumbling step and was in his arms.

He blinked at her. "Hey! What's wrong?" Then he saw what lay on the floor by the desk. His self-confidence sagged.

Dr. Garrett moved to the door. "Kendrick," he said, "take Elinor out of here. I'll——"

"No!" It was Elinor's voice. She straightened up, turned suddenly and started into the room.

But Paul caught her. "Where are you going?"

She tried to pull away from him. "I'm going to phone the police." Her eyes followed the trail of bloodstains that led from the body across the beige carpet to the overturned chair and the woman at the table. "She—killed him."

That was when I started for the phone myself. But I hadn't taken more than two steps when the woman in the bathing suit let out a hair-raising shriek.

She was gripping the table with both hands, her eyes fixed on Drake's body with the rigid unblinking stare of a figure carved from stone. Then, suddenly, her body trembled all over, and she opened her mouth again—But Garrett got there first.

He slapped her on the side of the face—hard.

It stopped the scream, but the horror still filled her round dark eyes and she still stared at the body as though it were some demon straight from hell.

"Hysteria," Garrett said. Then seeing me start again toward the phone, "Get an ambulance, too." And when he spoke to Paul Kendrick this time, it was an order. "And get Elinor out of here—quickly!"

Elinor Drake was looking at the girl in the bathing suit with wide, puzzled eyes. "She—she killed him. Why?"

Paul nodded. He turned Elinor around gently but swiftly and led her out.

The cops usually find too many fingerprints on a phone, none of them any good because they are superimposed on each other. But I handled the receiver carefully just the same, picking it up by one end. When Spring 7-1313 answered, I gave the operator the facts fast, then asked him to locate Inspector Gavigan and have him call me back. I gave Drake's number.

As I talked I watched Dr. Garrett open his black case and take out a hypodermic syringe. He started to apply it to the woman's arm just as I hung up.

"What's that, Doc?" I asked.

"Sedative. Otherwise she'll be screaming again in a minute."

The girl didn't seem to feel the needle as it went in.

Then, noticing two bright spots of color on the table, I

went across to examine them closely and felt more than ever as though I had stepped straight into a surrealist painting. I was looking at two rounded conical shapes each about two inches in length. Both were striped like candy canes, one in maroon against a white background, the other in thinner brilliant red stripes against an opalescent amber.

"Did Drake," I asked, "collect seashells, too?"

"No." Garrett scowled in a worried way at the shells. "But I once did. These are mollusks, but not from the sea. *Cochlostyla*, a tree snail. Habitat: The Philippines." He turned his scowl from the shells to me. "By the way, just who are you?"

"The name is Ross Harte." I added that I had had an appointment to interview Drake for a magazine article and then asked, "Why is this room sealed as it is? Why is this girl dressed only in——"

Apparently, like many medical men, Garrett took a dim view of reporters. "I'll make my statement," he said a bit stiffly, "to the police."

They arrived a moment later. Two uniformed prowl-car cops first, then the precinct boys and after that, at intervals, the homicide squad, an ambulance interne, a fingerprint man and photographer, the medical examiner, an assistant D. A. and later, because a millionaire rates more attention than the victim of a Harlem stabbing, the D. A. himself, and an Assistant Chief Inspector even looked in for a few minutes.

Of the earlier arrivals the only familiar face was that of the Homicide Squad's Lieutenant Doran—a hard-boiled, coldly efficient, no-nonsense cop who had so little use for reporters that I suspected he had once been bitten by one.

At Dr. Garrett's suggestion, which the interne second-ed, the girl in the bathing suit was taken, under guard, to the nearest hospital. Then Garrett and I were put on ice, also under guard, in the living room. Another detective ushered Paul Kendrick into the room a moment later.

He scowled at Dr. Garrett. "We all thought Rosa Rhys was bad medicine. But I never expected anything like this. Why would *she* want to kill him? It doesn't make sense."

"Self-defense?" I suggested. "Could he have made a pass at her and——"

Kendrick shook his head emphatically. "Not that gal. She was making a fast play for the old man—and his money. A pass would have been just what she wanted." He turned to Garrett. "What were they doing in there—more ESP experiments?"

The doctor laid his overcoat neatly over the back of an ornate Spanish chair. His voice sounded tired and defeated. "No. They had gone beyond that. I told him that she was a fraud, but you know how Drake was—always so absolutely confident that he couldn't be wrong about anything. He said he'd put her through a test that would convince all of us."

"Of what?" I asked. "What was it she claimed she could do?"

The detective at the door moved forward. "My orders," he said, "are that you're not to talk about what happened until after the Lieutenant has taken your statements. Make it easy for me, will you?"

That made it difficult for us. Any other conversational subject just then seemed pointless. We sat there silent and uncomfortable. But somehow the nervous tension that had been in our voices was still there—a foreboding, ghostly presence waiting with us for what was to happen next.

A half hour later, although it seemed many times that long, Garrett was taken out for questioning, then Kendrick. And later I got the nod. I saw Elinor Drake, a small, lonely figure in the big hall, moving slowly up the wide stairs. Doran and the police stenographer who waited for me in the stately dining room with its heavy crystal chandelier looked out of place. But the Lieutenant didn't feel ill at ease; his questions were as coldly efficient as a surgeon's knife.

I tried to insert a query of my own now and then, but soon gave that up. Doran ignored all such attempts as completely as if they didn't exist. Then, just as he dismissed me, the phone rang. Doran answered, listened, scowled and then held the receiver out to me. "For you," he said.

I heard Merlini's voice. "My ESP isn't working so well today, Ross. Drake is dead. I get that much. But just what happened up there, anyway?"

"ESP my eye," I told him. "If you were a mind-reader you'd have been up here long ago. It's a sealed room—in spades. The sealed room to end all sealed rooms."

I saw Doran start forward as if to object. "Merlini," I said quickly, "is Inspector Gavigan still with you?" I lifted the receiver from my ear and let Doran hear the "Yes" that came back.

Merlini's voice went on. "Did you say sealed room? The flash from headquarters didn't mention that. They said an arrest had already been made. It sounded like a routine case."

"Headquarters," I replied, "has no imagination. Or else Doran has been keeping things from them. It isn't even a routine sealed room. Listen: A woman comes to Drake's house on the coldest January day since 1812 dressed only in a bathing suit. She goes with him into his study. They seal the window and door on the inside with gummed paper tape. Then she stabs him with a paper knife. Before he dies, he knocks her out, then manages to get to the phone and send out an S.O.S.

"She's obviously crazy; she has to be to commit murder under those circumstances. But Drake wasn't crazy. A bit eccentric maybe, but not nuts. So why would he lock himself in so carefully with a homicidal maniac? If headquarters thinks that's routine I'll——" Then I interrupted myself. There was too much silence on the other end of the wire. "Merlini! Are you still there?"

"Yes," his voice said slowly, "I'm still here. Headquarters was much too brief. They didn't tell us her name. But I know it now."

Then, abruptly, I felt as if I had stepped off into some fourth-dimensional hole in space and had dropped on to some other nightmare planet.

Merlini's voice, completely serious, was saying, "Ross, did the police find a silver denarius from the time of the Caesars in that room? Or a freshly picked rose, a string of Buddhist prayer beads—perhaps a bit of damp seaweed——?"

I didn't say anything. I couldn't.

After a moment, Merlini added, "So—they did. What was it?"

"Shells," I said dazedly, still quite unconvinced that any conversation could sound like this. "Philippine tree snail shells. Why, in the name of——"

Merlini cut in hastily. "Tell Doran that Gavigan and I will be there in ten minutes. Sit tight and keep your eyes open——"

"Merlini!" I objected frantically, "if you hang up without——"

"The shells explain the bathing suit, Ross—and make it clear why the room was sealed. But they also introduce an element that Gavigan and Doran and the D. A. and the Commissioner are not going to like at all. I don't like it myself. It's even more frightening as a murder method than PK."

He hesitated a moment, then let me have both barrels.

"Those shells suggest that Drake's death might have

been caused by even stranger forces—evil and evanescent ones—from another world!"

My acquaintance with a police inspector cut no ice with Doran; he ordered me right back into the living room.

I heard a siren announce the arrival of Gavigan's car shortly after, but it was a long hour later before Doran came in and said, "The Inspector wants to see all of you—in the study."

As I moved with the others out into the hall I saw Merlini waiting for me.

"It's about time," I growled at him. "Another ten minutes and you'd have found me D.O.A., too—from suspense."

"Sorry you had to cool your heels," he said, "but Gavigan is being difficult. As predicted, he doesn't like the earful Doran has been giving him. Neither do I." The dryly ironic good humor that was almost always in his voice was absent. He was unusually sober.

"Don't build it up," I said. "I've had all the mystery I can stand. Just give me answers. First, why did you tell me to warn Drake about Rosa Rhys?"

"I didn't expect murder, if that's what you're thinking," he replied. "Drake was elaborating on some of Rhine's original experiments aimed at discovering whether ESP operates more efficiently when the subject is in a trance state. Rosa is a medium."

"Oh, so that's it. She and Drake were holding a séance?"

Merlini nodded. "Yes. The Psychical Research Society is extremely interested in ESP and PK—it's given them a new lease on life. And I knew they had recommended Rosa, whom they had previously investigated, to Drake."

"And what about the Roman coins, roses, Buddhist

prayer beads, and snail shells? Why the bathing suit and how does that explain why the room was sealed?"

But Doran, holding the study door open, interrupted before he could reply.

"Hurry it up!" he ordered.

Going into that room now was like walking onto a brightly lighted stage. A powerful electric bulb of almost floodlight brilliance had been inserted in the ceiling fixture and its harsh white glare made the room more barren and cell like than ever. Even Inspector Gavigan seemed to have taken on a menacing air. Perhaps it was the black mask of shadow that his hat brim threw down across the upper part of his face; or it may have been the carefully intent way he watched us as we came in.

Doran did the introductions. "Miss Drake, Miss Potter, Paul Kendrick, Dr. Walter Garrett."

I looked at the middle aged woman whose gayly frilled, altogether feminine hat contrasted oddly with her angular figure, her prim determined mouth, and the chilly glance of complete disapproval with which she regarded Gavigan.

"How," I whispered to Merlini, "did Isabelle Potter, the secretary of the Psychical Research Society, get here?"

"She came with Rosa," he answered. "The police found her upstairs reading a copy of Tyrrell's *Study of Apparitions*." Merlini smiled faintly. "She and Doran don't get along."

"They wouldn't," I said. "They talk different languages. When I interviewed her, I got a travelogue on the other world—complete with lantern slides."

Inspector Gavigan wasted no time. "Miss Drake," he began, "I understand the medical foundation for cancer research your father thought of endowing was originally your idea."

The girl glanced once at the stains on the carpet, then

kept her dark eyes steadily on Gavigan. "Yes," she said slowly, "it was."

"Are you interested in psychical research?"

Elinor frowned. "No."

"Did you object when your father began holding séances with Miss Rhys?"

She shook her head. "That would only have made him more determined."

Gavigan turned to Kendrick. "Did you?"

"Me?" Paul lifted his brows. "I didn't know him well enough for that. Don't think he liked me much, anyway. But why a man like Drake would waste his time——"

"And you, doctor?"

"Did I object?" Garrett seemed surprised. "Naturally. No one but a neurotic middle-aged woman would take a séance seriously."

Miss Potter resented that one. "Dr. Garrett," she said icily, "Sir Oliver Lodge was not a neurotic woman, nor Sir William Crookes, nor Professor Zoellner, nor——"

"But they were all senile," Garrett replied just as icily. "And as for ESP, no neurologist of any standing admits any such possibility. They leave such things to you and your society, Miss Potter—and to the Sunday supplements."

She gave the doctor a look that would have split an atom, and Gavigan, seeing the danger of a chain reaction if this sort of dialogue were allowed to continue, broke in quickly.

"Miss Potter. You introduced Miss Rhys to Mr. Drake and he was conducting ESP experiments with her. Is that correct?"

Miss Potter's voice was still dangerously radioactive. "It is. And their results were most gratifying and important. Of course, neither you nor Dr. Garrett would understand——"

"And then," Garrett cut in, "they both led him on into an investigation of Miss Rhys's psychic specialty—apports." He pronounced the last word with extreme distaste.

Inspector Gavigan scowled, glanced at Merlini, and the latter promptly produced a definition. "An apport," he said, "from the French *apporter*, to bring, is any physical object supernormally brought into a séance room—from nowhere usually or from some impossible distance. Miss Rhys on previous occasions—according to the Psychical Society's *Journal*—has apported such objects as Roman coins, roses, beads, and seaweed."

"She is the greatest apport medium," Miss Potter declared somewhat belligerently, "since Charles Bailey."

"Then she's good," Merlini said. "Bailey was an apport medium whom Conan Doyle considered bona fide. He produced birds, oriental plants, small animals, and on one occasion a young shark eighteen inches long which he claimed his spirit guide had whisked instantly via the astral plane from the Indian Ocean and projected, still damp and very much alive, into the séance room."

"So," I said, "that's why this room was sealed. To make absolutely certain that no one could open the door or window in the dark and help Rosa by introducing——"

"Of course," Garrett added. "Obviously there could be no apports if adequate precautions were taken. Drake also moved a lot of his things out of the study and inventoried every object that remained. He also suggested, since I was so skeptical, that I be the one to make certain that Miss Rhys carried nothing into the room on her person. I gave her a most complete physical examination—in a bedroom upstairs. Then she put on one of Miss Drake's bathing suits."

"Did you come down to the study with her and Drake?" Gavigan asked.

The doctor frowned. "No. I had objected to Miss

Potter's presence at the séance and Miss Rhys countered by objecting to mine."

"She was quite right," Miss Potter said. "The presence of an unbeliever like yourself would prevent even the strongest psychic forces from making themselves manifest."

"I have no doubt of that," Garrett replied stiffly. "It's the usual excuse, as I told Drake. He tried to get her to let me attend but she refused flatly. So I went back to my office down the street. Drake's phone call came a half hour or so later."

"And yet"—Gavigan eyed the two brightly colored shells on the table—"in spite of all your precautions she produced two of these."

Garrett nodded. "Yes, I know. But the answer is fairly obvious now. She hid them somewhere in the hall outside on her arrival and then secretly picked them up again on her way in here."

Elinor frowned. "I'm afraid not, doctor. Father thought of that and asked me to go down with them to the study. He held one of her hands and I held the other."

Gavigan scowled. Miss Potter beamed.

"Did you go in with them?" Merlini asked.

She shook her head. "No. Only as far as the door. They went in and I heard it lock behind them. I stood there for a moment or two and heard Father begin pasting the tape on the door. Then I went back to my room to dress. I was expecting Paul."

Inspector Gavigan turned to Miss Potter. "You remained upstairs?"

"Yes," she replied in a tone that dared him to deny it. "I did."

Gavigan looked at Elinor. "Paul said a moment ago that your father didn't like him. Why not?"

"Paul exaggerates," the girl said quickly. "Father didn't

dislike him. He was just—well, a bit difficult where my men friends were concerned."

"He thought they were all after his money," Kendrick added. "But at the rate he was endowing medical foundations and psychic societies——"

Miss Potter objected. "Mr. Drake did *not* endow the Psychic Society."

"But he was seriously considering it," Garrett said. "Miss Rhys—and Miss Potter—were selling him on the theory that illness is only a mental state due to a psychic imbalance—whatever that is."

"They won't sell me on that," Elinor said and then turned suddenly on Miss Potter, her voice trembling. "If it weren't for you and your idiotic foolishness Father wouldn't have been—killed." Then to Gavigan, "We've told all this before—to the Lieutenant. Is it quite necessary——"

The Inspector glanced at Merlini, then said, "I think that will be all for now. Okay, Doran, take them back. But none of them are to leave yet."

When they had gone, he turned to Merlini. "Well, I asked the question you wanted me to, but I still think it was a waste of time. Rosa Rhys killed Drake. Anything else is impossible."

"What about Kendrick's cab driver?" Merlini asked. Did your men locate him yet?"

Gavigan's scowl, practically standard operating procedure by now, grew darker. "Yes. Kendrick's definitely out. He entered the cab on the other side of town at just about the time Drake was sealing this room and he was apparently still in it, crossing Central Park, at the time Drake was killed."

"So," I commented, "he's the only one with an alibi."

Gavigan lifted his eyebrows. "The only one? Except for Rosa Rhys they *all* have alibis. The sealed room takes care of that."

"Yes," Merlini said quietly, "but the people with alibis also have motives while the one person who could have killed Drake has none."

"She did it," the Inspector answered. "So she's got a motive—and we'll find it."

"I wish I were as confident of that as you are," Merlini said. "Under the circumstances you'll be able to get a conviction without showing motive, but if you don't find one, it will always bother you."

"Maybe," Gavigan admitted, "but that won't be as bad as trying to believe what she says happened in this room."

That was news to me. "You've talked to Rosa?" I asked.

"One of the boys did," Gavigan said sourly. "At the hospital. She's already preparing an insanity defense."

"But why," Merlini asked, "is she still hysterical with fright? Could it be that she's scared because she really believes her story—because something like that really did happen in here?"

"Look," I said impatiently, "is it top secret or will somebody tell me what she says happened?"

Gavigan glowered at Merlini. "Are you going to stand there and tell me that you think Rosa Rhys actually believes——"

It was my question that Merlini answered. He walked to the table in the center of the room. "She says that after Drake sealed the window and door, the lights were turned off and she and Drake sat opposite each other at this table. His back was toward the desk, hers toward that screen in the corner. Drake held her hands. They waited. Finally she felt the psychic forces gathering around her—and then, out of nowhere, the two shells dropped onto the table one after the other. Drake got up, turned on the desk light, and came back to the table. A moment later it happened."

The magician paused for a moment, regarding the bare, empty room with a frown. "Drake," he continued, "was examining the shells, quite excited and pleased about their appearance when suddenly, Rosa says, she heard a movement behind her. She saw Drake look up and then stare incredulously over her shoulder." Merlini spread his hands. "And that's all she remembers. Something hit her. When she came to, she found herself staring at the blood on the floor and at Drake's body."

Gavigan was apparently remembering Merlini's demonstration with the gun in his office. "If you," he warned acidly, "so much as try to hint that one of the people outside this room projected some mental force that knocked Rosa out and then caused the knife to stab Drake——"

"You know," Merlini said, "I half expected Miss Potter would suggest that. But her theory is even more disturbing." He looked at me. "She says that the benign spirits which Rosa usually evoked were overcome by some malign and evil entity whose astral substance materialized momentarily, killed Drake, then returned to the other world from which it came."

"She's a mental case, too," Gavigan said disgustedly. "They have to be crazy if they expect anyone to believe any such——"

"That," Merlini said quietly, "may be another reason Rosa is scared to death. Perhaps she believes it but knows you won't. In her shoes, I'd be scared, too." He frowned. "The difficulty is the knife."

Gavigan blinked. "The knife? What's difficult about that?"

"If I killed Drake," Merlini replied, "and wanted appearances to suggest that psychic forces were responsible, you wouldn't have found a weapon in this room that made it look as if I were guilty. I would have done a little de-apporting and made it disappear. As it is now, even if the knife was propelled supernaturally, Rosa takes the rap."

"And how," Gavigan demanded, "would you make the knife disappear if you were dressed, as she was, in practically nothing?" Then, with sudden suspicion, he added, "Are you suggesting that there's a way she could have done that—and that you think she's not guilty because she didn't?"

Merlini lifted one of the shells from the table and placed it in the center of his left palm. His right hand covered it for a brief moment, then moved away. The shell was no longer there; it had vanished as silently and as easily as a ghost. Merlini turned both hands palms outward; both were unmistakably empty.

"Yes," he said, "she could have made the knife disappear—if she had wanted to. The same way she produced the two shells." He made a reaching gesture with his right hand and the missing shell reappeared suddenly at his fingertips.

Gavigan looked annoyed and relieved at the same time. "So." he said, "you do know how she got those shells in here. I want to hear it. Right now."

But Gavigan had to wait.

At that moment a torpedo hit the water-tight circumstantial case against Rosa Rhys and detonated with a roar.

Doran, who had answered the phone a moment before, was swearing profusely. He was staring at the receiver he held as though it were a live cobra he had picked up by mistake.

"It—it's Doc Hess," he said in a dazed tone. "He just started the autopsy and thought we'd like to know that the point of the murder knife struck a rib and broke off. He just dug out a triangular pointed piece of—steel."

For several seconds after that there wasn't a sound. Then Merlini spoke.

"Gentlemen of the jury. Exhibit A, the paper knife

with which my esteemed opponent, the District Attorney, claims Rosa Rhys stabbed Andrew Drake, is a copper alloy—and its point, as you can see, is quite intact. The defense rests."

Doran swore again. "Drake's inventory lists that letter opener, but that's all. There is no other knife in this room. I'm positive of that."

Gavigan jabbed a thick forefinger at me. "Ross, Dr. Garrett was in here before the police arrived. And Miss Drake and Kendrick."

I shook my head. "Sorry. There was no knife near the door and neither Elinor nor Paul came more than a foot into the room. Dr. Garrett examined Drake and Rosa, but I was watching him, and I'll testify that unless he's as expert at sleight-of-hand as Merlini, he didn't pick up a thing."

Doran was not convinced. "Look, buddy. Unless Doc Hess has gone crazy too, there was a knife and it's not here now. So somebody took it out." He turned to the detective who stood at the door. "Tom," he said, "have the boys frisk all those people. Get a police woman for Miss Drake and Potter and search the bedroom where they've been waiting. The living room, too."

Then I had a brainstorm. "You know," I said, "if Elinor is covering up for someone—if three people came in here for the séance instead of two as she says—the third could have killed Drake and then gone out—with the knife. And the paper tape could have been . . ." I stopped.

"—pasted on the door *after* the murderer left? Merlini finished. "By Rosa? That would mean she framed herself."

"Besides," Gavigan growled, "the boys fumed all those paper strips. There are fingerprints all over them. All Drake's."

Merlini said, "Doran, I suggest that you phone the hospital and have Rosa searched, too."

The Lieutenant blinked. "But she was practically naked. How in blazes could she carry a knife out of here unnoticed?"

Gavigan faced Merlini, scowling. "What did you mean when you said a moment ago that she could have got rid of the knife the same way she produced those shells?"

"If it was a clasp knife," Merlini explained, "she could have used the same method other apport mediums have employed to conceal small objects under test conditions."

"But dammit!" Doran exploded. "The only place Garrett didn't look was in her stomach!"

Merlini grinned. "I know. That was his error. Rosa is a regurgitating medium—like Helen Duncan in whose stomach the English investigator, Harry Price, found a hidden ghost—a balled-up length of cheesecloth fastened with a safety pin which showed up when he X-rayed her. X-rays of Rosa seem indicated, too. And search her hospital room and the ambulance that took her over."

"Okay, Doran," Gavigan ordered. "Do it."

I saw an objection. "Now *you've* got Rosa framing herself, too," I said. "If she swallowed the murder knife, why should she put blood on the letter opener? That makes no sense at all."

"None of this does," Gavigan complained.

"I know," Merlini answered. "One knife was bad. Two are much worse. And although X-rays of Rosa before the séance would have shown shells, I predict they won't show a knife. If they do, then Rosa needs a psychiatric examination as well."

"Don't worry," Gavigan said gloomily. "She'll get one. Her attorney will see to that. And they'll prove she's crazier than a bedbug without half trying. But if that knife isn't in her . . ." His voice died.

"Then you'll never convict her," Merlini finished.

"If that happens," the Inspector said ominously,

"you're going to have to explain where that knife came from, how it really disappeared, and where it is now."

Merlini's view was even gloomier. "It'll be much worse than that. We'll also have an appearing and vanishing murderer to explain—someone who entered a sealed room, killed Drake, put blood on the paper knife to incriminate Rosa, then vanished just as neatly as any of Miss Potter's ghosts—into thin air."

And Merlini's prediction came true.

The X-ray plates didn't show the slightest trace of a knife. And it wasn't in Rosa's hospital room or in the ambulance. Nor on Garrett, Paul, Elinor Drake, Isabelle Potter—nor, as Doran discovered, on myself. The Drake house was a mess by the time the boys got through taking it apart—but no knife with a broken point was found anywhere. And it was shown beyond doubt that there were no trapdoors or sliding panels in the study; the door and window were the only exits.

Inspector Gavigan glowered every time the phone rang—the Commissioner had already phoned twice and without mincing words expressed his dissatisfaction with the way things were going.

And Merlini, stretched out in Drake's chair, his heels up on the desk top, his eyes closed, seemed to have gone into a trance.

"Blast it!" Gavigan said. "Rosa Rhys got that knife out of here somehow. She had to! Merlini, are you going to admit that she knows a trick or two you don't?"

The magician didn't answer for a moment. Then he opened one eye. "No," he said slowly, "not just yet." He took his feet off the desk and sat up straight. "You know," he said, "if we don't accept the theory of the murderer from beyond, then Ross must be right after all. Elinor Drake's statement to the contrary, there must have been a third person in this room when that séance began."

"Okay," Gavigan said, "we'll forget Miss Drake's testimony for the moment. At least that gets him into the room. Then what?"

"I don't know," Merlini said. He took the roll of gummed paper tape from the desk, tore off a two-foot length, crossed the room, and pasted it across the door and jamb, sealing us in. "Suppose I'm the killer," he said. "I knock Rosa out first, then stab Drake—"

He paused.

Gavigan was not enthusiastic. "You put the murder knife in your pocket, not noticing that the point is broken. You put blood on the paper knife to incriminate Rosa. And then—" He waited. "Well, go on."

"Then," Merlini said, "I get out of here." He scowled at the sealed door and at the window. "I've escaped from handcuffs, strait jackets, milk cans filled with water, packing cases that have been nailed shut. I know the methods Houdini used to break out of safes and jail cells. But I feel like he did when a shrewd old turnkey shut him in a cell in Scotland one time and the lock—a type he'd overcome many times before—failed to budge. No matter how he tried or what he did, the bolt wouldn't move. He was sweating blood because he knew that if he failed, his laboriously built-up reputation as the Escape King would be blown to bits. And then . . ." Merlini blinked. "And then . . ." This time he came to a full stop, staring at the door.

Suddenly he blinked. "Shades of Hermann, Kellar, Thurston—and Houdini! So that's it!"

Grinning broadly, he turned to Gavigan. "We will now pass a miracle and chase all the ghosts back into their tombs. If you'll get those people in here—"

"You know how the vanishing man vanished?" I asked.

"Yes. It's someone who has been just as canny as that Scottish jailer—and I know who."

Gavigan said, "It's about time." Then he walked across the room and pulled the door open, tearing the paper strip in half as he did so.

Merlini, watching him, grinned again. "The method by which magicians let their audiences fool themselves— the simplest and yet most effective principle of deception in the whole book—and it nearly took me in!"

Elinor Drake's eyes still avoided the stains on the floor. Scott, beside her, puffed nervously on a cigarette, and Dr. Garrett looked drawn and tired. But not the irrepressible Potter. She seemed fresh as a daisy.

"This room," she said to no one in particular, "will become more famous in psychic annals than the home of the Fox sisters at Lilydale."

Quickly, before she could elaborate on that, Merlini cut in. "Miss Potter doesn't believe that Rosa Rhys killed Drake. Neither do I. But the psychic force she says is responsible didn't emanate from another world. It was conjured up out of nothing by someone who was—who had to be—here in this room when Drake died. Someone whom Drake himself asked to be here."

He moved into the center of the room as he spoke and faced them.

"Drake would never have convinced anyone that Rosa could do what she claimed without a witness. So he gave someone a key—someone who came into this room *before* Drake and Rosa and Elinor came downstairs."

The four people watched him without moving— almost, I thought, without breathing.

"That person hid behind that screen and then, after Rosa produced the apports, knocked her out, killed Drake, and left Rosa to face the music."

"All we have to do," Merlini went on, "is show who it was that Drake selected as a witness." He pointed a lean forefinger at Isabelle Potter. "If Drake discovered how Rosa produced the shells and realized she was a fraud, you might have killed him to prevent an exposure and save face for yourself and the Society; and you might have then framed Rosa in revenge for having deceived you. But Drake would never have chosen you. Your testimony wouldn't have convinced any of the others. No. Drake would have picked one of the skeptics—someone he was certain could never be accused of assisting the medium."

He faced Elinor. "You said that you accompanied Rosa and your father to the study door and saw them go in alone. We haven't asked Miss Rhys yet, but I think she'll confirm it. You couldn't expect to lie about that and make it stick as long as Rosa could and would contradict you."

I saw Doran move forward silently, closing in.

"And Paul Kendrick," Merlini went on, "is the only one of you who has an alibi that does not depend on the sealed room. That leaves the most skeptical one of the three—the man whose testimony would by far carry the greatest weight.

"It leaves you, Dr. Garrett. The man who is so certain that there are no ghosts is the man who conjured one up!"

Merlini played the scene down; he knew that the content of what he said was dramatic enough. But Garrett's voice was even calmer. He shook his head slowly.

"I am afraid that I can't agree. You have no reason to assume that it must be one of us and no one else. But I would like to hear how you think I or anyone else could have walked out of this room leaving it sealed as it was found."

"That," Merlini said, "is the simplest answer of all. You walked out, but you didn't leave the room sealed. You see, *it was not found that way!*"

I felt as if I were suddenly floating in space.

"But look——" I began.

Merlini ignored me. "The vanishing murderer was a trick. But magic is not, as most people believe, only a matter of gimmicks and trapdoors and mirrors. Its real secret lies deeper than a mere deception of the senses; the magician uses a far more important, more basic weapon— the psychological deception of the mind. *Don't believe everything you see* is excellent advice; but there's a better rule: Don't believe everything you *think*."

"Are you trying to tell me," I said incredulously, "that this room wasn't sealed at all? That I just thought it was?"

Merlini kept watching Garrett. "Yes. It's as simple as that. And there was no visual deception at all. It was, like PK, entirely mental. You saw things exactly as they were, but you didn't realize that the visual appearance could be interpreted two ways. Let me ask you a question. When you break into a room the door of which has been sealed with paper tape on the inside, do you find yourself still in a sealed room?"

"No," I said, "of course not. The paper has been torn."

"And if you break into a room that had been sealed but from which someone has *already gone out*, tearing the seals—what then?"

"The paper," I said, "is still torn. The appearance is—"

"—*exactly the same!*" Merlini finished.

He let that soak in a moment, then continued. "When you saw the taped window, and then the torn paper on the door, you made a false assumption—you jumped naturally, but much too quickly, to a wrong conclusion. We all did. We assumed that it was you who had torn the paper—when you broke in. Actually, it was Dr. Garrett who tore the paper—when he went out!"

Garrett's voice was a shade less steady now. "You forget that Andrew Drake phoned me——"

Merlini shook his head. "I'm afraid we only have your own statement for that. You overturned the phone and

placed Drake's body near it. Then you walked out, returned to your office where you got rid of the knife—
probably a surgical instrument which you couldn't leave
behind because it might have been traced to you."

Doran, hearing this, whispered a rapid order to the
detective stationed at the door.

"Then," Merlini continued, "you came back immediately to ring the front-door bell. You said Drake had called
you, partly because it was good misdirection; it made it
appear that you were elsewhere when he died. But equally
important, it gave you the excuse you needed to break in
and find the body without delay—*before Rosa Rhys should
regain consciousness and see that the room was no longer
sealed!*"

I hated to do it. Merlini was so pleased with the neat
way he was tying up all the loose ends. But I had to.

"Merlini," I said. "I'm afraid there is one little thing
you don't know. When I smashed the door open, I heard
the paper tape tear!"

I have seldom seen the Great Merlini surprised, but
that did it. He couldn't have looked more astonished if
lightning had struck him.

"You—you *what?*"

Elinor Drake said, "I heard it, too."

Garrett added, "And I."

It stopped Merlini cold for a moment—but only a
moment.

"Then that's more misdirection. It has to be." He
hesitated, then suddenly looked at Doran. "Lieutenant, get
the doctor's overcoat, will you?"

Garrett spoke to the Inspector. "This is nonsense.
What possible reason could I have for—"

"Your motive was a curious one, Doctor," Merlini
said. "One that few murderers——"

Merlini stopped as he took the overcoat Doran

brought in and removed from its pocket the copy of the A. M. A. *Journal* I had noticed there earlier. He started to open it, then lifted an eyebrow at something he saw on the contents listing.

"I see," he said, and then read: "*A Survey of the Uses of Radioactive Tracers in Cancer Research* by Walter M. Garrett, M.D. So that's your special interest?" The magician turned to Elinor Drake. "Who was to head the fifteen-million dollar foundation for cancer research, Miss Drake?"

The girl didn't need to reply. The answer was in her eyes as she stared at Garrett.

Merlini went on. "You were hidden behind the screen in the corner, Doctor. And Rosa Rhys, in spite of all the precautions, successfully produced the apports. You saw the effect that had on Drake, knew Rosa had won, and that Drake was thoroughly hooked. And the thought of seeing all that money wasted on psychical research when it could be put to so much better use in really important medical research made you boil. Any medical man would hate to see that happen—and most of the rest of us, too.

"But we don't all have the coldly rational, scientific attitude you do, and we wouldn't all have realized so quickly that there was one very simple but drastic way to prevent it—murder. You are much too rational. You believe that one man's life is less important than the good his death might bring—and you believed that sufficiently to act upon it. The knife was there, all too handy, in your little black case. And so—Drake died. Am I right, Doctor?"

Doran didn't like this as a motive. "He's still a killer," he objected. "And he tried to frame Rosa, didn't he?"

Merlini said, "Do you want to answer that, Doctor?"

Garrett hesitated, then glanced at the magazine Merlini still held. His voice was tired. "You are also much too rational." He turned to Doran. "Rosa Rhys was a cheap fraud who capitalized on superstition. The world would be a much better place without such people."

"And what about your getting that job as the head of the medical foundation?" Doran was still unconvinced. "I don't suppose that had anything to do with your reasons for killing Drake?"

The doctor made no answer. And I couldn't tell if it was because Doran was right or because he knew that Doran would not believe him.

He turned to Merlini instead. "The fact still remains that the cancer foundation has been made possible. The only difference is that now two men rather than one pay with their lives."

"A completely rational attitude," Merlini said, "does have its advantages if it allows you to contemplate your own death with so little emotion."

Gavigan wasn't as cynical about Garrett's motives as Doran but his police training objected. "He took the law into his own hands. If everyone did that, we'd all have to go armed for self-protection. Merlini, why did Ross think he heard paper tearing when he opened that door?"

"He did hear it," Merlini said. Then he turned to me. "Dr. Garrett stood behind you and Miss Drake when you broke in the door, didn't he?"

I nodded. "Yes."

Merlini opened the medical journal and riffled through it. Half a dozen loose pages, their serrated edges showing where they had been torn in half, fluttered to the floor.

Merlini said, "You would have made an excellent magician, Doctor. Your deception was not visual, it was auditory."

"That," Gavigan said, "tears it."

Later I had one further question to ask Merlini.

"You didn't explain how Houdini got out of that Scottish jail—nor how it helped you solve the enigma of the unsealed door."

Merlini lifted an empty hand, plucked a lighted cigarette from thin air and puffed at it, grinning.

"Houdini made the same false assumption. When he leaned exhaustedly against the cell door, completely baffled by his failure to overcome the lock, the door suddenly swung open and he fell into the corridor. The old Scot, you see, hadn't locked it at all!"

3

At the thought of sealed, locked rooms any true American sets his mind to Houdini and his mysterious world of chains, shackles, cells, and death-defying escapes.

Author Clayton Rawson was almost certainly inspired to write "From Another World" by Houdini's lucky escape in Edinburgh. The fact that the "King of Escape" was all but defeated by an unlocked door is not the only inglorious moment in his varied career. On one occasion in London, Harry Houdini's wife, Bessie, had to plead with journalists for the key needed to release her husband. It was on this occasion that Bessie with her cute figure, dazzling eyes, and long eyelashes trickling with tears performed a feat of magic that even the great Houdini with all his years of study could not match.

In the story that follows you will be introduced to Colonel Clay, the first great rogue of mystery fiction; a swindler who, to quote Mr. Ellery Queen, "playfully pilfered, purloined, and pluck-pigeoned his way to pecuniary profits."

The larcenous Colonel first glimpsed the glitter of gold in 1897 when Grant Richards, London, published *An African Millionaire: Episodes in the Life of the Illustrious Colonel Clay.*

The book was written by Grant Allen, who was born in Canada and educated in England and who probably would have spent the rest of his life as a professor of mental and moral philosophy at a Jamaican college for blacks if the school hadn't folded because of lack of funds.

Allen returned to England in 1876 and spent the remainder of his life writing works on evolution, the philosophy of aesthetics and, happily, for the devotees of crime, many stories.

There have been many scoundrels in detective fiction—Raffles, Arsene Lupin, The Infallible Godohl, and Simon Templar. Now meet the first, as Colonel Clay proves that the hand is, indeed, quicker than the eye.

The Episode of the Mexican Seer

by Grant Allen

My name is Seymour Wilbraham Wentworth. I am brother-in-law and secretary to Sir Charles Vandrift, the South African millionaire and famous financier. Many years ago, when Charlie Vandrift was a small lawyer in Cape Town, I had the (qualified) good fortune to marry his sister. Much later, when the Vandrift estate and farm near Kimberley developed by degrees into the Cloetedorp Golcondas, Limited, my brother-in-law offered me the not unremunerative post of secretary; in which capacity I have ever since been his constant and attached companion.

He is not a man whom any common sharper can take in, is Charles Vandrift. Middle height, square build, firm mouth, keen eyes—the very picture of a sharp and successful business genius. I have only known one rogue impose upon Sir Charles, and that one rogue, as the Commissary of Police at Nice remarked, would doubtless have imposed upon a syndicate of Vidocq, Robert Houdin, and Cagliostro.

We had run across to the Riviera for a few weeks in the season. Our object being strictly rest and recreation from the arduous duties of financial combination, we did not think it necessary to take our wives out with us. Indeed,

Lady Vandrift is absolutely wedded to the joys of London, and does not appreciate the rural delights of the Mediterranean littoral. But Sir Charles and I, though immersed in affairs when at home, both thoroughly enjoy the complete change from the City to the charming vegetation and pellucid air on the terrace at Monte Carlo. We *are* so fond of scenery. That delicious view over the rocks of Monaco, with the Maritime Alps in the rear, and the blue sea in front, not to mention the imposing Casino in the foreground, appeals to me as one of the most beautiful prospects in all Europe. Sir Charles has a sentimental attachment for the place. He finds it restores and refreshens him, after the turmoil of London, to win a few hundred at roulette in the course of an afternoon among the palms and cactuses and pure breezes of Monte Carlo. The country, say I, for a jaded intellect! However, we never on any account actually stop in the Principality itself. Sir Charles thinks Monte Carlo is not a sound address for a financier's letters. He prefers a comfortable hotel on the Promenade des Anglais at Nice, where he recovers health and renovates his nervous system by taking daily excursions along the coast to the Casino.

This particular season we were snugly ensconced at the Hotel des Anglais. We had capital quarters on the first floor—salon, study, and bedrooms—and found on the spot a most agreeable cosmopolitan society. All Nice, just then, was ringing with talk about a curious impostor, known to his followers as the Great Mexican Seer, and supposed to be gifted with second sight, as well as with endless other supernatural powers. Now, it is a peculiarity of my able brother-in-law's that, when he meets with a quack, he burns to expose him; he is so keen a man of business himself that it gives him, so to speak, a disinterested pleasure to unmask and detect imposture in others. Many ladies at the hotel, some of whom had met and conversed with the Mexican Seer, were constantly telling us strange stories of his doings. He had disclosed to one the present whereabouts of a runaway husband; he had pointed out to another the numbers that would win at roulette next evening; he had shown a third the image on a screen of the man she had for years adored without his knowledge. Of course, Sir Charles didn't believe a word of it; but his curiosity was roused; he wished to see and judge for himself of the wonderful thought-reader.

"What would be his terms, do you think, for a private *séance?*" he asked of Madame Picardet, the lady to whom the Seer had successfully predicted the winning numbers.

"He does not work for money," Madame Picardet answered, "but for the good of humanity. I'm sure he would gladly come and exhibit for nothing his miraculous faculties."

"Nonsense!" Sir Charles answered. "The man must live. I'd pay him five guineas, though, to see him alone. What hotel is he stopping at?"

"The Cosmopolitan, I think," the lady answered. "Oh no; I remember now, the Westminster."

Sir Charles turned to me quietly. "Look here, Seymour," he whispered. "Go round to this fellow's place immediately after dinner, and offer him five pounds to give a private *séance* at once in my rooms, without mentioning who I am to him; keep the name quite quiet. Bring him back with you, too, and come straight upstairs with him, so that there may be no collusion. We'll see just how much the fellow can tell us."

I went as directed. I found the Seer a very remarkable and interesting person. He stood about Sir Charles's own height, but was slimmer and straighter, with an aquiline nose, strangely piercing eyes, very large black pupils, and a finely-chiselled close-shaven face, like the bust of Antinous in our hall in Mayfair. What gave him his most characteristic touch, however, was his odd head of hair, curly and wavy like Paderewski's, standing out in a halo round his high white forehead and his delicate profile. I could see at a glance why he succeeded so well in impressing women; he had the look of a poet, a singer, a prophet.

"I have come round," I said, "to ask whether you will consent to give a *séance* at once in a friend's rooms; and my principal wishes me to add that he is prepared to pay five pounds as the price of the entertainment."

Señor Antonio Herrera—that was what he called himself—bowed to me with impressive Spanish politeness. His dusky olive cheeks were wrinkled with a smile of gentle contempt as he answered gravely——

"I do not sell my gifts; I bestow them freely. If your friend—your anonymous friend—desires to behold the cosmic wonders that are wrought through my hands, I am glad to show them to him. Fortunately, as often happens when it is necessary to convince and confound a sceptic (for that your friend is a sceptic I feel instinctively), I chance to have no engagements at all this evening." He ran his hand through his fine, long hair reflectively. "Yes, I go," he continued, as if addressing some unknown presence that hovered about the ceiling; "I go; come with me!" Then he put on his broad sombrero, with its crimson ribbon, wrapped a cloak round his shoulders, lighted a cigarette, and strode forth by my side towards the Hotel des Anglais.

He talked little by the way, and that little in curt sentences. He seemed buried in deep thought; indeed, when we reached the door and I turned in, he walked a step or two farther on, as if not noticing to what place I had brought him. Then he drew himself up short, and gazed around him for a moment. "Ha, the Anglais," he said—and I may mention in passing that his English, in spite of a slight southern accent, was idiomatic and excellent. "It is here, then; it is here!" He was addressing once more the unseen presence.

I smiled to think that these childish devices were intended to deceive Sir Charles Vandrift. Not quite the sort of man (as the City of London knows) to be taken in by hocuspocus. And all this, I saw, was the cheapest and most commonplace conjurer's patter.

We went upstairs to our rooms. Charles had gathered together a few friends to watch the performance. The Seer entered, wrapt in thought. He was in evening dress, but a red sash round his waist gave a touch of picturesqueness and a dash of colour. He paused for a moment in the middle of the salon, without letting his eyes rest on anybody or anything. Then he walked straight up to Charles, and held out his dark hand.

"Good evening," he said. "You are the host. My soul's sight tells me so."

"Good shot," Sir Charles answered. "These fellows have to be quick-witted, you know, Mrs. Mackenzie, or they'd never get on at it."

The Seer gazed about him, and smiled blankly at a person or two whose faces he seemed to recognize from a previous existence. Then Charles began to ask him a few simple questions, not about himself, but about me, just to test him. He answered most of them with surprising correctness. "His name? His name begins with an S I think:—You call him Seymour." He paused long between each clause, as if the facts were revealed to him slowly. "Seymour—Wilbraham—Earl of Strafford. No, not Earl of Strafford! Seymour Wilbraham Wentworth. There seems to be some connection in somebody's mind now present between Wentworth and Strafford. I am not English. I do not know what it means. But they are somehow the same name, Wentworth and Strafford."

He gazed around, apparently for confirmation. A lady came to his rescue.

"Wentworth was the surname of the great Earl of Strafford," she murmured gently; "and I was wondering, as you spoke, whether Mr. Wentworth might possibly be descended from him."

"He is," the Seer replied instantly, with a flash of those dark eyes. And I thought this curious; for though my father always maintained the reality of the relationship, there was one link wanting to complete the pedigree. He could not make sure that the Hon. Thomas Wilbraham Wentworth was the father of Jonathan Wentworth, the Bristol horse-dealer, from whom we are descended.

"Where was I born?" Sir Charles interrupted, coming suddenly to his own case.

The Seer clapped his two hands to his forehead and held it between them, as if to prevent it from bursting. "Africa", he said slowly, as the facts narrowed down, so to speak. "South Africa; Cape of Good Hope; Jansenville; De Witt Street. 1840."

"By jove, he's correct," Sir Charles muttered. "He seems really to do it. Still, he may have found me out. He may have known where he was coming."

"I never gave a hint," I answered; "till he reached the door, he didn't even know to what hotel I was piloting him."

The Seer stroked his chin softly. His eye appeared to me to have a furtive gleam in it. "Would you like me to tell you the number of a bank-note inclosed in an envelope?" he asked casually.

"Go out of the room," Sir Charles said, "while I pass it round the company."

Señor Herrera disappeared. Sir Charles passed it round cautiously, holding it all the time in his own hand, but letting his guests see the number. Then he placed it in an envelope and gummed it down firmly.

The Seer returned. His keen eyes swept the company with a comprehensive glance. He shook his shaggy mane. Then he took the envelope in his hands and gazed at it fixedly. "AF, 73549," he answered, in a slow tone. "A Bank of England note for fifty pounds—exchanged at the Casino for gold won yesterday at Monte Carlo."

"I see how he did that," Sir Charles said triumphantly. "He must have changed it there himself; and then I changed it back again. In point of fact, I remember seeing a fellow with long hair loafing about. Still, it's capital conjuring."

"He can see through matter," one of the ladies interposed. It was Madame Picardet. "He can see through a box." She drew a little gold vinaigrette, such as our grandmothers used, from her dress-pocket. "What is in this?" she inquired, holding it up to him.

Señor Herrera gazed through it. "Three gold coins," he replied, knitting his brows with the effort of seeing into the box: "one, an American five dollars; one, a French ten-franc piece; one, twenty marks, German, of the old Emperor William."

She opened the box and passed it round. Sir Charles smiled a quiet smile.

"Confederacy!" he muttered, half to himself. "Confederacy!"

The Seer turned to him with a sullen air. "You want a better sign?" he said, in a very impressive voice. "A sign that will convince you! Very well: you have a letter in your left waistcoat pocket—a crumpled-up letter. Do you wish me to read it out? I will, if you desire it."

It may seem to those who know Sir Charles incredible, but, I am bound to admit, my brother-in-law coloured. What that letter contained I cannot say; he only answered, very testily and evasively, "No, thank you; I won't trouble you. The exhibition you have already given us of your skill in this kind more than amply suffices." And his fingers strayed nervously to his waistcoat pocket, as if he was half afraid, even then, Señor Herrera would read it.

I fancied too, he glanced somewhat anxiously towards Madame Picardet.

The Seer bowed courteously. "Your will, señor, is law," he said. "I make it a principle, though I can see through all things, invariably to respect the secrecies and sanctities. If it were not so, I might dissolve society. For which of us is there who could bear the whole truth being told about him?" He gazed around the room. An unpleasant thrill supervened. Most of us felt this uncanny Spanish American knew really too much. And some of us were engaged in financial operations.

"For example," the Seer continued blandly, "I happened a few weeks ago to travel down here from Paris by train with a very intelligent man, a company promoter. He had in his bag some documents—some confidential documents:" he glanced at Sir Charles. "You know the kind of thing, my dear sir: reports from experts—from mining engineers. You may have seen some such; marked *strictly private.*"

"They form an element in high finance," Sir Charles admitted coldly.

"Pre-cisely," the Seer murmured, his accent for a moment less Spanish than before. "And, as they were marked *strictly private*, I respect, of course, the seal of confidence. That's all I wish to say. I hold it a duty, being intrusted with such powers, not to use them in a manner which may annoy or incommode my fellow-creatures."

"Your feeling does you honour," Sir Charles answered, with some acerbity. Then he whispered in my ear: "Confounded clever scoundrel, Sey; rather wish we hadn't brought him here."

Señor Herrera seemed intuitively to divine this wish, for he interposed, in a lighter and gayer tone——

"I will now show you a different and more interesting embodiment of occult power, for which we shall need a somewhat subdued arrangement of surrounding lights. Would you mind, señor host—for I have purposely abstained from reading your name on the brain of any one present—would you mind my turning down this lamp just a little? . . . So! That will do. Now, this one; and this one. Exactly! that's right." He poured a few grains of powder out of a packet into a saucer. "Next, a match, if you please. Thank you!" It burnt with a strange green light. He drew from his pocket a card, and produced a little ink-bottle. "Have you a pen?" he asked.

I instantly brought one. He handed it to Sir Charles. "Oblige me," he said, "by writing your name there." And he indicated a place in the center of the card, which had an embossed edge, with a small middle square of a different colour.

Sir Charles has a natural disinclination to signing his name without knowing why. "What do you want with it?" he asked. (A millionaire's signature has so many uses.)

"I want you to put the card in an envelope," the Seer replied, "and then to burn it. After that, I shall show you your own name written in letters of blood on my arm, in your own handwriting."

Sir Charles took the pen. If the signature was to be burned as soon as finished, he didn't mind giving it. He wrote his name in his usual firm clear style—the writing of a man who knows his worth and is not afraid of drawing a cheque for five thousand.

"Look at it long," the Seer said, from the other side of the room. He had not watched him write it.

Sir Charles stared at it fixedly. The Seer was really beginning to produce an impression.

"Now, put it in that envelope," the Seer exclaimed.

Sir Charles, like a lamb, placed it as directed.

The Seer strode forward. "Give me the envelope," he said. He took it in his hand, walked over towards the fireplace, and solemnly burnt it. "See—it crumbles into ashes," he cried. Then he came back to the middle of the room, close to the green light, rolled up his sleeve, and held his arm before Sir Charles. There, in blood-red letters, my brother-in-law read the name, "Charles Vandrift," in his own handwriting!

"I see how that's done," Sir Charles murmured, drawing back. "It's a clever delusion; but still, I see through it. It's like that ghost-book. Your ink was deep green; your light was green; you made me look at it long; and then I saw the same thing written on the skin of your arm in complementary colours."

"You think so?" the Seer replied, with a curious curl of the lip.

"I'm sure of it," Sir Charles answered.

Quick as lightning the Seer rolled up his sleeve. "That's your name," he cried, in a very clear voice, "but not your whole name. What do you say, then, to my right? Is this one also a complementary colour?" He held his other arm out. There, in sea-green letters, I read the name, "Charles O'Sullivan Vandrift." It is my brother-in-law's full baptismal designation; but he has dropped the O'Sullivan for many years past, and, to say the truth, doesn't like it. He is a little bit ashamed of his mother's family.

Charles glanced at it hurriedly. "Quite right," he said, "quite right!" But his voice was hollow. I could guess he didn't care to continue the *séance*. He could see through the man, of course; but it was clear the fellow knew too much about us to be entirely pleasant.

"Turn up the lights," I said, and a servant turned them. "Shall I say coffee and benedictine?" I whispered to Vandrift.

"By all means," he answered. "Anything to keep this fellow from further impertinences! And, I say, don't you think you'd better suggest at the same time that the men should smoke? Even these ladies are not above a cigarette—some of them."

There was a sigh of relief. The lights burned brightly. The Seer for the moment retired from business, so to speak. He accepted a partaga with a very good grace, sipped his coffee in a corner, and chatted to the lady who had suggested Strafford with marked politeness. He was a polished gentleman.

Next morning, in the hall of the hotel, I saw Madame Picardet again, in a neat tailor-made travelling dress, evidently bound for the railway-station.

"What, off, Madame Picardet?" I cried.

She smiled, and held out her prettily-gloved hand. "Yes, I'm off," she answered archly. "Florence, or Rome, or somewhere. I've drained Nice dry—like a sucked orange. Got all the fun I can out of it. Now I'm away again to my beloved Italy."

But it struck me as odd that, if Italy was her game, she went by the omnibus which takes down to the *train de luxe* for Paris. However, a man of the world accepts what a lady tells him, no matter how improbable; and I confess, for ten days or so, I thought no more about her, or the Seer either.

At the end of that time our fortnightly pass-book came in from the bank of London. It is part of my duty, as the millionaire's secretary, to make up this book once a fortnight, and to compare the cancelled cheques with Sir Charles's counterfoils. On this particular occasion I happened to observe what I can only describe as a very grave discrepancy—in fact, a discrepancy of £5,000. On the wrong side, too. Sir Charles was debited with £5,000 more than the total amount that was shown on the counterfoils.

I examined the book with care. The source of the error was obvious. It lay in a cheque to Self or Bearer, for £5,000, signed by Sir Charles, and evidently paid across the counter in London, as it bore on its face no stamp or indication of any other office.

I called in my brother-in-law from the salon to the study. "Look here, Charles," I said, "there's a cheque in the book which you haven't entered." And I handed it to him without comment, for I thought it might have been drawn to settle some little loss on the turf or at cards, or to make up some other affair he didn't desire to mention to me. These things will happen.

He looked at it and stared hard. Then he pursed up his mouth and gave a long low "Whew!" At last he turned it over and remarked, "I say, Sey, my boy, we've just been done jolly well brown, haven't we?"

I glanced at the cheque. "How do you mean?" I inquired.

"Why, the Seer," he replied, still staring at it ruefully. "I don't mind the five thou., but to think the fellow should have gammoned the pair of us like that—ignominious, I call it!"

"How do you know it's the Seer?" I asked.

"Look at the green ink," he answered. "Besides, I recollect the very shape of the last flourish. I flourished a bit like that in the excitement of the moment, which I don't always do with my regular signature."

"He's done us," I answered, recognising it. "But how the dickens did he manage to transfer it to the cheque? This looks like your own handwriting, Charles, not a clever forgery."

"It is," he said. "I admit it—I can't deny it. Only fancy him bamboozling me when I was most on my guard! I wasn't to be taken in by any of his silly occult tricks and catch-words; but it never occurred to me he was going to victimize me financially in this way. I expected attempts at a loan or an extortion; but to collar my signature to a blank cheque—atrocious!"

"How did he manage it?" I asked.

"I haven't the faintest conception. I only know those are the words I wrote. I could swear to them anywhere."

"Then you can't protest the cheque?"

"Unfortunately, no; it's my own true signature."

We went that afternoon without delay to see the Chief Commissary of Police at the office. He was a gentlemanly Frenchman, much less formal and red-tapey than usual, and he spoke excellent English with an American accent, having acted, in fact, as a detective in New York for about ten years in his early manhood.

"I guess," he said slowly, after hearing our story, "you've been victimized right here by Colonel Clay, gentlemen."

"Who is Colonel Clay?" Sir Charles asked.

"That's just what I want to know," the Commissary answered, in his curious American-French-English. "He is a Colonel, because he occasionally gives himself a commission; he is called Colonel Clay, because he appears to possess an india-rubber face, and he can mould it like clay in the hands of the potter. Real name, unknown. Nationality, equally French and English. Address, usually Europe. Profession, former maker of wax figures to the Musée Grevin. Age, what he chooses. Employs his knowledge to mould his own nose and cheeks, with wax additions, to the character he desires to personate. Aquiline this time, you say. *Hein!* Anything like these photographs?"

He rummaged in his desk and handed us two.

"Not in the least," Sir Charles answered. "Except, perhaps, as to the neck, everything here is quite unlike him."

"Then that's the Colonel!" the Commissary answered,

with decision, rubbing his hands in glee. "Look here," and he took out a pencil and rapidly sketched the outline of one of the two faces—that of a bland-looking young man, with no expression worth mentioning. "There's the Colonel in his simple disguise. Very good. Now watch me: figure to yourself that he adds here a tiny patch of wax to his nose—an aquiline bridge—just so; well, you have him right there; and the chin, ah, one touch: now, for hair, a wig: for complexion, nothing easier: that's the profile of your rascal, isn't it?"

"Exactly," we both murmured. By two curves of the pencil, and a shock of false hair, the face was transmuted.

"He had very large eyes, with very big pupils, though," I objected, looking close; "and the man in the photograph here has them small and boiled-fishy."

"That's so," the Commissary answered. "A drop of belladonna expands—and produces the Seer; five grains of opium contract—and give a dead-alive, stupidly-innocent appearance. Well, you leave this affair to me, gentlemen. I'll see the fun out. I don't say I'll catch him for you; nobody ever yet has caught Colonel Clay; but I'll explain how he did the trick; and that ought to be consolation enough to a man of your means for a trifle of five thousand!"

"You are not the conventional French office-holder, M. le Commissaire," I ventured to interpose.

"You bet!" the Commissary replied, and drew himself up like a captain of infantry. "Messieurs," he continued, in French, with the utmost dignity, "I shall devote the resources of this office to tracing out the crime, and, if possible, to effectuating the arrest of the culpable."

We telegraphed to London, of course, and we wrote to the bank, with a full description of the suspected person. But I need hardly add that nothing came of it.

Three days later the Commissary called at our hotel.

"Well, gentlemen," he said, "I am glad to say I have discovered everything!"

"What? Arrested the Seer?" Sir Charles cried.

The Commissary drew back, almost horrified at the suggestion.

"Arrested Colonel Clay?" he exclaimed. "*Mais*, Monsieur, we are only human! Arrested him? No, not quite. But tracked out how he did it. That is already much—to unravel Colonel Clay, gentlemen!"

"Well, what do you make of it?" Sir Charles asked, crestfallen.

The Commissary sat down and gloated over his discovery. It was clear a well-planned crime amused him vastly. "In the first place, monsieur," he said, "disabuse your mind of the idea that when monsieur your secretary went out to fetch Señor Herrera that night, Señor Herrera didn't know to whose rooms he was coming. Quite otherwise, in point of fact. I do not doubt myself that Señor Herrera, or Colonel Clay (call him which you like), came to Nice this winter for no other purpose than just to rob you."

"But I sent for him," my brother-in-law interposed.

"Yes; he *meant* you to send for him. He forced a card, so to speak. If he couldn't do that I guess he would be a pretty poor conjurer. He had a lady of his own—his wife, let us say, or his sister—stopping here at this hotel; a certain Madame Picardet. Through her he induced several ladies of your circle to attend his *séances*. She and they spoke to you about him, and aroused your curiosity. You may bet your bottom dollar that when he came to this room he came ready primed and prepared with endless facts about both of you."

"What fools we have been, Sey," my brother-in-law exclaimed. "I see it all now. That designing woman sent round before dinner to say I wanted to meet him; and by the time you got there he was ready for bamboozling me."

"That's so," the Commissary answered. "He had your name ready painted on both his arms; and he had made other preparations of still greater importance."

"You mean the cheque. Well, how did he get it?"

The Commissary opened the door. "Come in," he said. And a young man entered whom we recognized at once as the chief clerk in the Foreign Department of the Crédit Marseillais, the principal bank all along the Riviera.

"State what you know of this cheque," the Commissary said, showing it to him, for we had handed it over to the police as a piece of evidence.

"About four weeks since——" the clerk began.

"Say ten days before your *séance,*" the Commissary interposed.

"A gentleman with very long hair and an aquiline nose, dark, strange, and handsome, called in at my department and asked if I could tell him the name of Sir Charles Vandrift's London banker. He said he had a sum to pay in to your credit, and asked if we would forward it for him. I told him it was irregular for us to receive the money, as you had no account with us, but that your London bankers were Darby, Drummond, and Rothenberg, Limited."

"Quite right," Sir Charles murmured.

"Two days later a lady, Madame Picardet, who was a customer of ours, brought in a good cheque for three hundred pounds, signed by a first-rate name, and asked us to pay it in on her behalf to Darby, Drummond, and Rothenberg's, and to open a London account with them for her. We did so, and received in reply a cheque-book."

"From which this cheque was taken, as I learn from the number, by telegram from London," the Commissary put in. "Also, that on the same day on which your cheque was cashed, Madame Picardet, in London, withdrew her balance."

"But how did the fellow get me to sign the cheque?" Sir Charles cried. "How did he manage the card trick?"

The Commissary produced a similar card from his pocket. "Was that the sort of thing?" he asked.

"Precisely! A facsimile."

"I thought so. Well, our Colonel, I find, bought a packet of such cards, intended for admission to a religious function, at a shop in the Quai Masséna. He cut out the centre, and, see here——" The Commissary turned it over, and showed a piece of paper pasted neatly over the back; this he tore off, and there, concealed behind it, lay a folded cheque, with only the place where the signature should be written showing through on the face which the Seer had presented to us. "I call that a neat trick," the Commissary remarked, with professional enjoyment of a really good deception.

"But he burnt the envelope before my eyes," Sir Charles exclaimed.

"Pooh!" the Commissary answered. "What would he be worth as a conjurer, anyway, if he couldn't substitute one envelope for another between the table and the fireplace without your noticing it? And Colonel Clay, you must remember, is a prince among conjurers."

"Well, it's a comfort to know we've identified our man, and the woman who was with him," Sir Charles said, with a slight sigh of relief. "The next thing will be, of course, you'll follow them up on these clues in England and arrest them?"

The Commissary shrugged his shoulders. "Arrest them!" he exclaimed, much amused. "Ah, monsieur, but you are sanguine! No officer of justice has ever succeeded in arresting le Colonel Caoutchouc, as we call him in French. He is as slippery as an eel, that man. He wriggles through our fingers. Suppose even we caught him, what could we prove? I ask you. Nobody who has seen him once can ever swear to him again in his next impersonation. He is *impayable*, this good Colonel. On the day when I arrest him, I assure you, monsieur, I shall consider myself the smartest policeofficer in Europe."

"Well, I shall catch him yet," Sir Charles answered, and relapsed into silence.

Unfortunately, not all magical scoundrels have been contained between the pages of pulp magazines. In 1966 an English magician by the name of Charles Cobeck, with a rather more elaborate stage name of The Mysterious Mr. E, made a magical killing, financially speaking.

While presenting his evening magic show in clubs and private homes, Cobeck performed his original escape from chains and trunk. As they say in all good books, 'twas here where the dirty work was afoot! Instead of battling with his restraints for the full ten minutes as the audience imagined, Cobeck quietly freed himself in less than thirty seconds and disappeared backstage through the false panel of the trunk, riffled through any valuables in the vicinity, and returned to the stage in time to reenter the trunk and—sweating and flushed from his excursions—receive an ovation.

Sadly for the mysterious one, during the fifth performance of this amazing miracle the illusion was destroyed. That fine juggler and prestidigitator, Her Majesty's Government, saw fit to include Cobeck in one of its magical entertainments and he disappeared for two years (with remission). One can hardly say, but perhaps he entertained his fellow ill-doers and earned himself the nickname of the "Wandsworth Wand Waver" or, more simply, "The Mysterious AD 176542."

4

The zany tales of John Novotny have graced the pages of *Esquire*, *Playboy*, and *The Magazine of Fantasy and Science Fiction* for more than a quarter century. Mr. Novotny, an engineer at Sperry Gyroscope, lives on Long Island with his wife, Marie, and his son, Roger, and, when time permits, indulges his passion for photography, painting, and leather working. Regrettably, all these activities leave little time for the typewriter, so such stories as "The Angry Peter Brindle," "On Camera," and "A Trick or Two" must be doubly prized.

Funk and Wagnalls Standard Dictionary defines the noun *trick* as "a peculiar skill or knack," and the fate that befalls our hero Jesse Haimes in "A Trick or Two" is a peculiar one indeed.

A Trick or Two

by John Novotny

At nine that evening Laura walked beautifully into the apartment.

"Hello, Jesse," she said softly. "For some reason I thought you had given up."

"You underestimate me, Laura," he said, removing her coat. "And yourself. You never looked lovelier."

"Thank you, Jesse," she smiled, accepting a glass of champagne. "I've never been in better shape. I'm ready to go ten rounds, if necessary."

"That was uncalled-for, darling," he said, hurt. "You make me sound crude. Perhaps in other days . . . but now I'm of a different mind."

"Fine," Laura applauded, laughing gayly. "Don't tell me what role you're playing tonight. It will be more fun if I have to guess."

Jesse had a wonderful dinner waiting and they ate by candlelight. Later they sipped benedictine by the picture window overlooking the river.

"You make it seem so worthwhile, Jesse," Laura murmured. "There are moments when I almost feel like giving the devil his due."

"That's what I'm planning on," Jesse said casually.

"Oh?" Laura answered questioningly. "You expect me to succumb, to offer myself to you, out of the goodness of my heart?"

"Or the badness," Jesse added.

"I wish you luck."

"Thank you," Jesse said. "Then you agree that should you stand before me unclothed, I might assume, rightfully, that I have won the game?"

"Unclothed—by force?"

"No, my dear. No force," he smiled.

"I agree that under those circumstances you'd have a pretty good assumption," Laura said. "When do you expect me to go into this disrobing act?"

"Most anytime," Jesse said. "To hasten your decision, let me show you a few little presents I have for you."

Jesse kept himself from hurrying as he led her to the two closet doors. He opened one and pointed to the furs hanging inside.

"My choice?" Laura asked.

"All of them," Jesse said. "Look them over."

She stepped inside the closet and Jesse smiled. His mind raced over the events of the past week.

Jesse Haimes sipped his Scotch pensively, then placed the glass decisively on the table and leaned toward his friend.

"Mind you, Tom," he said, "it isn't that I haven't tried. Lord knows, I've played the gentleman, the brother, and the man-of-the-world. I've been patient, impatient, persuasive."

"Generous?" Tom inquired.

"Abundantly," Jesse insisted. "I even bought her a poodle."

"And through it all," Tom Casey smiled, "Miss Laura Carson remains unconquered, unsullied, unbowed."

"Disgustingly so," Jesse admitted.

"Let's have another drink," Tom suggested, signaling the waiter. "Or do you have a conference this afternoon?"

"Nothing," Jesse said. "A few letters to get out and some desks must be moved. We're changing the accounting room to the Forty-eighth Street side."

"Dry work," Tom Casey said. "Another scotch is definitely in order."

They sat back, waiting for the drinks, and pondered the enigma of Miss Laura Carson. Tom watched Jesse light a cigarette. As Jesse brought his hand down to drop the match in the ash tray, Tom reached forward and snapped his fingers.

"Abra-ca-dabra," he said. The ash tray vanished. Jesse's hand froze and he stared at the spot where the glass container had rested. Finally he smiled foolishly.

"Well done, Tom," he said. "How did you do it?"

"Magic," Tom said, self-consciously. "I don't usually fool around in public, but I just had the urge."

"I didn't know that was your hobby."

"It's not," Tom laughed. "That's my trick. Nothing else."

"Bring it back," Jesse said.

"I can't," Tom confessed. "I can make small items disappear. Where they go, I have no idea."

Jesse stopped smiling and began to frown. He restrained himself as the waiter approached and served the drinks. He watched the man walk away; then he turned hurriedly back to Tom Casey.

"Are you trying to tell me that this business is on the level?" he demanded, gesturing aimlessly at the center of the table. Tom nodded foolishly.

"I don't believe it," Jesse said. "After all . . . come now, Tom."

"Put your swizzle stick out there," Tom said.

Jesse slowly pushed the plastic stirring rod to the spot indicated. Tom snapped his fingers at the stick.

"Abra-ca-dabra," he said. The object disappeared.

"Good Lord," Jesse breathed. "And to think I doubted Dunninger."

The two men sat silently until Jesse called the waiter.

"Two more scotches," he ordered, "and an ash tray."

The waiter brought the drinks and the ash tray, surveyed the table and its occupants suspiciously, and departed.

"Can you teach me?" Jesse asked.

"I don't think so," Tom explained. "An old proofreader out in Denver told me about it. Everybody has one trick he can do. The proofreader could change water into whisky. That was his trick and a very handy one."

"Do you mean I have some bit of magic I can do?" Jesse asked excitedly.

"Everyone has," Tom said. "Mine you just saw."

"How does a person find out his trick—if that's what you call it?"

Tom shrugged.

"Most people never do, I guess," he said. "I just stumbled on mine."

"Maybe mine is the same as yours," Jesse suggested.

"Try it," Tom said, isolating the ash tray. Jesse replaced it with a swizzle stick.

"The waiter would raise hell about another ash tray," he explained. He took a deep breath, snapped his fingers, and intoned the necessary phrase. The stirrer remained.

"Did I do something wrong?" Jesse asked hopefully. Tom shook his head.

"Perfect technique," he said. "Negative result."

"I guess I have a different talent," Jesse murmured. "Damn it! How am I going to find out what it is?"

"It's not that important," Tom Casey said. "Unless it's

the water and whisky deal, of course."

The waiter was summoned again and soon Jesse was glaring balefully at a glass of water.

"No luck," Tom said. "I wouldn't worry about it. As I said, I hardly ever use mine. It's embarrassing when people ask questions. I can't explain the trick, so I automatically am classified as a stinker or a drunken bum. I'd just forget about it if I were you."

Jesse shook his head. The two men finished their drinks and left the restaurant. As they parted at Madison and Forty-ninth, Jesse smiled at his companion.

"First time in weeks I've been able to think about something other than Laura Carson," he said. "See you next week."

"These letters, Mr. Haimes———"

Jesse smiled at the slim brunette.

"Yes, Carol?"

"They're ready for your signature. And Mr. Wigmann would like to have two more cabinets in Accounts Payable."

"Fine," Jesse said, accepting the papers. "Tell Wiggy he'll have his cabinets in a few days."

He watched his secretary walk to her desk in the far corner of the large, tastefully decorated office they shared. After the girl settled at the desk and was busy calling Wigmann's secretary, Jesse drew his hand out from under his own desk. He looked down expectantly at the hat he held.

"Abra-ca-dabra," he muttered. No rabbit materialized.

"Thank God," he whispered. "I wasn't particularly anxious to have that ability."

Carol finished her call and came across the office.

"Yes, Carol?"

"Mr. Wigmann requests that if the cabinets are among

the surplus items in the next room, could he look at them, in order to plan where they will be placed."

"Tell him to come over in five minutes. We may have to move a few things."

The girl returned to the phone and then joined Jesse as he unlocked the door to the small office next to his. It had been pressed into use as a storage area during the reorganization period and was filled with varied pieces of office equipment. Jesse pointed.

"As I suspected," he said. "Damn! All the way in the back. I'll push these desks aside if you'll move the lamps and chairs."

After a few moments of cooperative endeavor Carol and Jesse Haimes stood before the two cabinets. Each was two and a half feet wide by seven feet tall. The cabinets had no shelves and were intended to hold clothing. Jesse opened one of the metal doors and looked inside.

"Wiggy will have to arrange for shelves," he said, closing the door. "He can call Griswold and——"

Jesse stopped and looked at the cabinet. Dimly he recalled a vaudeville act he had once enjoyed.

"Carol," he said, hesitantly. "Would you—well, this may seem odd——"

"Yes, Mr. Haimes?"

Jesse decided that wording was less important than results.

"Would you mind stepping into this cabinet for one moment?"

Carol smiled.

"Into the—cabinet?"

"Yes. Into the cabinet."

"I don't understand."

"In all probability," Jesse said, "there will be nothing to understand. If there is I will explain later."

"I hope so," Carol said, still smiling. She lifted the hem

of her skirt slightly and stepped up into the locker-like affair.

"Thank you," Jesse said. He closed the door and stepped back. With squared shoulders he faced the cabinet.

"Abra-ca-dabra," he said, softly enough so that Carol couldn't hear. He opened the cabinet and smiled in assuringly. Jesse swallowed hard as he looked at the empty space. Hurriedly he leaped to the remaining cabinet and opened the door.

"Don't be alarmed, Car—Oh, Lord!"

Carol stood framed in the cabinet. She was nude and she was angry. Jesse looked away and then, deciding the hell with it, he looked back.

"What have you done with your clothes?" he asked.

"What have *I* done?" Carol said, ominously. She pushed one bare foot forward, then pointed to her neck. "From pumps to my black choker ribbon. *Whsst.* You've never been better."

She stepped carelessly from the cabinet and sank into one of the surplus swivel chairs.

"You said you'd explain," she said. "This had better be good. Your apartment is one thing, the office is entirely different. I've always insisted———"

She stopped and looked at the cabinet she had just vacated.

"That's not the one I—Oh brother, you better start talking. I think I'll scream."

She opened her mouth and Jesse leaped forward to cover it with his hand.

"I can explain!" he said quickly. Carol relaxed and Jesse took his hand away.

"OK," she said. "Explain."

Jesse looked at the two cabinets and then back at Carol.

"I can't," he said unhappily. Carol opened her mouth wide.

"Wait!" Jesse pleaded. "I mean I don't know how it happened. Passing you from one cabinet to another just happens to be my trick."

"Oh," Carol said, raising her eyebrows. "Your trick, eh? Do you mind if your naked little secretary says you certainly have a fine collection. And may I ask what you intend to do right now?"

She swiveled in the chair and made a complete circle.

"Not very much room in here," she said tersely.

"Carol, I——"

"Apartments are apartments. Offices are offices. And I don't care for that trick. If you——"

"*Mr. Haimes. Mr. Haimes.*"

They both leaped up as Mr. Wigmann's voice floated in from Jesse's office.

"Wait there!" Jesse shouted.

"Oh, I can come in and——"

"No," Jesse shouted frantically. "Just wait a moment. Until I get things—straightened out."

"Very well," Wiggy answered. They could hear his steps as he wandered about the office.

"Get in the cabinet," Jesse whispered to Carol.

"Like hell," Carol whispered. "Never again."

"Carol," Jesse pleaded. He leaned down and kissed her full on the lips. "Ten dollars a week raise. The Winter Garden and the Stork Club one evening next week. A new gown."

Carol melted.

"Mr. Haimes. That isn't necessary."

"It certainly is," he said. "I've done you an injustice. Offices are offices. I promise to remember."

She threw both bare arms around his neck and kissed

him. Drawing away, she smiled, "Into the cabinet." As she stepped in, Jesse permitted himself one light pat on Carol's pert rump and closed the door.

"Wiggy," he called. "Now you can come in. I've finally located them."

Mr. Wigmann walked into the smaller room and approached the cabinets.

"Excellent, perfect," he said. "Good of you, Haimes, to go to the trouble. Heavens, you're perspiring something fierce. I assure you I could have waited."

"Not at all," Jesse assured him, leading him away.

"But the insides——"

"Nothing. Bare," Jesse coughed on the last word. "You'll have to arrange for shelves. See Griswold."

He ushered Wiggy to the door, shook hands, and propelled the little man into the hall. Jesse then went to the phone and dialed.

"Miss Devins? Jesse Haimes," he announced. "No, don't call B. J. I want to speak to you. I have a favor to ask. My club is putting on a show and we're missing one outfit—a girl's. I'd have asked Carol but she is out on business at the moment.—You will? Fine.—Size?—Oh, about Carol's size. One each of the following: dress . . ."

A little later he returned to the small office and released Carol.

"Don't worry about your clothes," he said. "I've sent down for a complete new outfit."

"Who?"

"B. J.'s secretary. Miss Devins," he told her.

"Good," Carol smiled. "She has excellent taste and is very conscientious. She'll take at least an hour."

Hand in hand they returned to Jesse's office.

Three days later he completed the construction work in his apartment. The two cabinets were built in flush with the wall and looked like nothing else than closet doors. Jesse put his tools away and prepared the final test. He took the small kewpie doll and placed it on the floor of closet number one. Carefully he patted the lace dress in place and rearranged the tiny cap. Finally he stood up, closed the door, and backed off.

"Abra-ca-dabra," he said, waving a few fingers negligently. He strode to cabinet number two, opened the door, and smiled as he picked up the shiny little plastic body.

"Excellent," he murmured. "Now to call Miss Laura Carson."

Jesse silently closed the cabinet door behind Laura as she hummed through the furs. Quickly he stepped back and raised his arm.

"Abra-ca-dabra," he sang.

The room was quiet except for the soft music Jesse had playing in the background. He walked to cabinet two and opened the door. Laura stood there and Jesse drew a deep breath even though he was prepared. She smiled, unflustered and completely calm, as she stepped from the cabinet. Her body was flawless, perfect, warm, and soft. Graceful movements shadowed ivory-tan skin as she walked in the soft lights. Her dark hair was long and lay tantalizingly on exquisite shoulders. Jesse was forced to lock his hands behind his back. Laura walked halfway across the room, then turned and looked at the two doors.

"You're naked," Jesse said hoarsely. Laura looked down at herself.

"Never more so," she laughed. As her body moved in laughter Jesse was forced to remove his tie. Laura walked to the big window where moonlight crept across her body. Jesse removed his shirt.

"You seem very much at ease," he remarked. "No surprise?"

Laura shook her head as he continued undressing.

"It's quite obvious that you have discovered your trick," she said.

For a moment Jesse stopped, balancing on one leg.

"Even so," he said, determined not to lose the advantage, "the circumstances have worked out."

"That's true," Laura said, "but please do me a favor."

"Yes?"

"Will you hold that fire iron out at arm's length?"

Jesse walked wonderingly to the fireplace, picked up the poker, and held it out. Laura raised a long slender forefinger and pointed at the brass tool; and in Jesse's hand the poker became pliable, soft, and wilted like wax before a flame. He stared at it in horror.

"Jesse," Laura said. "I discovered my trick long ago."

5

Count Alessandro Cagliostro, born in Palermo in 1743, heads our list of real-life criminous conjurors.

Alchemist and impostor, Cagliostro fled from Sicily to escape punishment for a series of ingenious crimes and visited in succession Greece, Egypt, Arabia, Persia, Malta, Rome, London, and Paris, where he sold love philtres, elixirs of youth, and various alchemistic powders.

He was finally tried and condemned to death for heresy, but his sentence was commuted to life imprisonment. He died in the fortress prison of San Leo in 1795.

Chelsea Quinn Yarbro, who delves into the mysteries of the Count's powers in the following tale, is another unique individual.

Author, singer, voice teacher, composer, and student of the Renaissance, Quinn utilizes all of her most unusual talents in painting a vivid picture of the scheming Cagliostro and the jaded aristocracy of France in the latter part of the eighteenth century.

In addition to writing many works of science fiction and winning a Mystery Writer's of America award for "The Ghosts at Iron River" from the anthology *Men and Malice,* Quinn has published two novels: *Ogilvie, Tallant and Moon* (New York: Putnam, 1976), a novel of suspense, whose detective-protagonist, Charlie Moon, is one of the most unusual and likeable characters in mystery fiction, and *The Time of the Fourth Horseman* (New York: Doubleday, 1976) a novel of science fiction.

Lammas Night

by Chelsea Quinn Yarbro

Inside the circle that held the pentagram the air shimmered and in the dark, cold room, Giuseppe felt he was staring into great distances.

The shimmer broadened, and now it was time to speak the final summons. Giuseppe cleared his throat and took a firmer grip on the sword he carried, though he knew it was useless against the forces he called. "Io te commandar . . ." he began in his Sicilian accented Italian. "I command thee. I, Count Alessandro Cagliostro . . ." There was a sudden popping sound, like the breaking of glass or a burst keg and the air was still once more.

Giuseppe flung down his sword in disgust. He should have known better. He could not use any but his real name, and although his title was self-awarded and therefore, he felt, certainly as valid as the unpretentious name his parents had given him, he knew that the demon would not respond to anything but plain Giuseppe Balsamo.

Of course he couldn't do that. No one in Paris knew he was not a nobleman, and he could not admit it now, particularly with the threat of prosecution for fraud hanging over him. He had already had trouble in England. He could not afford to fail here in France. He had promised to raise a demon, and he would have to do it.

The demon would not come to any name but his baptismal one.

Giuseppe sank onto the cold floor, the stones pressing uncompromisingly against his naked buttocks. The sweat which had run off him so freely grew clammy and smelled sour. He touched the old ceremonial sword he had picked up in Egypt six years before. The old sorcerer had guaranteed that sword, and Giuseppe knew now that the mad old man had not spoken idly.

One of the candles set at the point of the pentagram guttered and the hot wax ran through the edge of the chalked circle. In spite of himself, Giuseppe flinched. If the demon had still been there, the circle would not have bound it any longer. If that had occurred when the ceremony was under way, no one would have been safe. A shudder gripped him that had little to do with the cold.

In three days it would be Lammas Night, and it would be then that the jaded aristocrats expected him to give them the thrill of seeing a demon. Cynically Giuseppe considered handing out mirrors and taking his chances in a coach with a team of fast horses. But he could not risk it. There was too much at stake. For one thing he needed money. For another there were few places he could run. England was out of the question—he did not want to be sent to prison for fraud. He had to be very cautious if he returned home to Sicily, for the Inquisition took a dim view of self-confessed devil-raisers. Spain was even worse, for the Holy Office was stronger there than elsewhere. Germany would not welcome him, besides the question of debt. He could flee to the New World, but that took money unless he wanted to be stranded in New Orleans without contacts or possibilities. He could go East, but what little he had seen of the Ottoman Empire convinced him that it would be safer with an unbound demon than he would be in Istanbul.

Reluctantly he pulled himself to his feet. He was in a lot of trouble, and he would have to deal with it immediately. There really were no alternatives.

The salon glowed in the light of four hundred candles on six huge crystal chandeliers. One wall was mirrored and it reflected back the brilliant light and the grand ladies and gentlemen who crowded about the long gambling tables. The rustle of fine, stiff silks combined with the susurrus of talk and the clink of glasses of wine and piles of gold louis.

Giuseppe stood on the threshold of this splendid room, a sudden sinking feeling making him pause and tug at the three cascades of Michlin lace at his throat. He covered this nervousness with a finicky movement as he adjusted the pearl and sapphire stickpin that nestled there. He congratulated himself mentally on that stickpin. Even the English Duchess had admired it and had never suspected that it was a fake.

"Count?" said a lackey at his shoulder.

"Yes?" Giuseppe asked. He assumed his most charming manner. He knew how important the good opinion of servants could be. If he found later that he needed help to flee, servants would be of more use to him than anyone else.

"DeVre has asked for you." The lackey assumed his wooden expression again. "He is in the second salon, sir. With Martillion and Gries."

Giuseppe nodded reluctantly. "I will be with them directly. Thank you for the message." Assuming his best manner he strolled into the salon, happily acknowledging the greetings of the glittering people as he went toward the second salon.

"Count," called Countess Beatrisse du Lac Sainte Denis. She held out a rounded white arm dripping with diamonds below the fall of lace at her elbow.

Giuseppe stopped and bent to kiss her hand. "Countess," he murmured and gave her a wide, warm smile. His expressive, large eyes rested on her face, full of unspoke promise. He was suprised at how unruffled he was, how little his fear effected his behavior.

"I vow I will be with your party on Lammas Night," the Countess said archly. In her tall wig, diamonds sparkled like the sea foam, and the confection was crowned with a model of a full-rigged ship.

Giuseppe smoothed the gold Milanese brocade of his coat, "It may be dangerous, Countess. I would hate to see anyone as lovely as you at the mercy of a demon."

Countess Beatrisse laughed, but Giuseppe saw a strange light in her face. "You are too late, my dear Count. I have been at the mercy of my husband for seven years and your demon cannot fighten me."

As his inner chill deepened, Giuseppe kissed her hand and passed on. He had assumed, obviously wrongly, that his special service would be secret, that only a few would know of it or attend. He glanced around as he walked into the second salon, and heard a brief hiatus in the sound of conversation. It boded ill. He nodded in answer to the wave of DeVre, and made his way through the crowd to the buffet table where DeVre, Martillion, and Gries waited, their elegant, vicious faces showing their eagerness.

"Ah, Cagliostro," DeVre said as Giuseppe came up to him. "We are all agog with anticipation. You tell me how your preparations are going." He smiled to disguise the order.

"I have begun my calculations. But I must warn you, we cannot have more than thirteen at the service." He reached automatically for a glass of wine as a lackey bowed at his arm.

"Of course, of course," said DeVre at his most soothing, which Giuseppe knew meant nothing.

Desperately, he tried again. "You have not seen a demon before." He remembered what the Countess du Lac Sainte Denis had said a moment before. Perhaps she was right, and these were the faces of demons.

But Gries was talking, his saturnine face masklike in the scintillating light. "It's all very well for you to build up this meeting, Cagliostro. Theatrics are part of it, are they not? But you cannot expect us to keep this secret. Not in Paris. *Nom du nom,* it is not possible." He half turned to wave at Madame du Randarte, who hesitated before acknowledging his greeting. "There's a rare piece for you," he said to Martillion when he turned back once more. "She's vain, though; doesn't want her breasts bitten."

Giuseppe nodded uncomfortably. He did not like the venality of these men, and he now regretted his boast as a binder of demons. Somewhat startled, he realized he had finished the wine. As he put down the glass he reminded himself that he would need a clear head for what he had to do here.

"Not drinking, Count?" Martillion asked, one ironic brow raised. He almost sneered as he took another glass and drank eagerly.

"I cannot. I am preparing for the ceremony, you will recall." He saw a certain flicker in Martillion's eyes and took full advantage. "As I have said, this is a dangerous matter, and only those of us who have been initiated into the rites may undertake this ordeal. But there are conditions. I must meet those conditions if the ceremony is to go successfully."

Although the three laughed, Giuseppe had the satisfaction of knowing that this time they were uneasy, and that he had frightened them. He pressed on, speaking more forcefully now. "I have come because you did not specify the form you would want the demon to appear in. As you may know, demons can be charged to present themselves in guises other than their own."

"More chicanery," Gries scoffed.

"If you wish to think so . . ." Giuseppe pulled himself up to his full, if modest height. "So that you will have the choice," he went on, "I will tell you that I may conjure the demon to appear as a monster, although that is the greatest danger, and I am not certain this is wise."

Martillion tittered uneasily. "Oh, I have no fear of monsters," he said as he took another glass of wine.

Giuseppe set his jaw. "Monsters can occasionally break the protective circle, and then nothing I, or anyone else save an uncorrupted priest can do will save you."

"Mountebank," Gries said.

"There are other forms." Giuseppe colored his voice, made it warmer, more flattering. "Perhaps you would prefer a youth with supple limbs, or a beautiful woman . . .?" He let the suggestion hang, and saw the response in their faces.

"A beautiful woman?" DeVre mused. "A fiend from hell?"

"All women are fiends from hell," Gries laughed cynically.

Keeping hold of his calm, Giuseppe said, "You must tell me which you want." He had an idea now, a way that he could save himself. It was a greater gamble than he wanted to take, but that choice was out of his hands. He would have to risk being denounced or flee France with yet another charge of fraud hanging over him.

"If the demon were a beautiful woman," Martillion said reflectively, staring into the red heart of his wine, "could we use her?"

"There will be another woman at the ceremony for that purpose, and you may choose among yourselves for

that. But you lose your immortal soul if you have com-
merce with the demon."

"It's already lost, if the Church is to be believed." Gries
looked hungrily around the room, his quizzing glass held
up.

"You could lose your manhood as well," Giuseppe said
with asperity. "What the demon has touched it will not give
back."

For a moment those cynical men were silent. Then
Martillion laughed. "Still, to see a demon as a woman. . . .
It might be more to our purposes than to see a monster."
He glanced at the others and saw the assent in their eyes.
"A woman, then, Cagliostro. Beautiful. Nude?"

"It would not be wise," Giuseppe said after pretending
to think. "The flames of hell make strange garments." He
made an enigmatic gesture. "I will do what I can."

"What time on Lammas Night?" Gries asked, his eyes
growing bleary from the wine he had drunk.

For a moment Giuseppe pondered the time, weighing
theatricality with the forces he would fool. "Arrive on the
stroke of nine, for we must prepare you for the ceremony at
midnight. And I warn you," he said, his manner growing
grander, "that you must be prompt. I cannot admit anyone
after nine is struck, no matter who asks for admission. I
trust you will make this plain to the others."

Martillion sketched a bow. "Of course, Cagliostro."

His bow was returned with formal flourish, and then
Giuseppe turned and strode from the inner salon. As he
passed the gambling table, he turned to Beatrisse de Lac
Sainte Denis. "Madame," he said in a lowered tone, "That
information you requested, concerning an amulet?" He
knew this was a dreadful chance, and he waited in fright for
her answer.

Fleetingly her face showed surprise, then she said,
"Yes? Have you decided on a price?"

Giuseppe let his breath out, relieved. "Yes, Madame, I have. If you would be kind enough to wait on me in the morning? Say, at ten?"

There was speculation and a touch of fear in her eyes. "I will be there, Count. At ten." She turned back to the table and did not look at Giuseppe again.

It was shortly after ten when the elegant town coach pulled up outside the home of Count Alessandro Cagliostro, and the steps were let down for a beautifully dressed and heavily veiled woman. A maid followed her into the house.

Giuseppe himself met her in the foyer, extending his hands to her, and bowed punctiliously. "I am honored, Countess," he said, then added softly, "If you seek to keep your visit here secret, it would have been wiser to hire a coach. Your arms are blazoned on the doors of that one."

She shrugged. "As long as the spies of my husband's household follow me, I do not want to put them to any special effort. Besides, he knows that I come here. It was he who insisted on the veil." With these words she drew the veil aside and made a travesty of a smile. "Where is this amulet you spoke of?"

Giuseppe was prepared. He held out a strangely cut jewel on a chain. "It is efficacious in matters of the heart and children. But you must take especial care of it. Allow me to take you to my experiment room and demonstrate how you are to wear it, and what you must do with it when you do not wear it." He turned to the maid who waited inside the door. "Accompany us, please. I do not want to cast the Countess into disfavor with her husband."

The maid started forward, then hung back. She had heard much about Count Cagliostro, and none of it said he was lascivious. She bowed her head. "I will remain here, sir."

It was the answer that Giuseppe had hoped for. "As you wish. We should not be more than half an hour." He offered his arm to the Countess du Lac Sainte Denis. "Come with me, if you please," he said, and led her into the west wing of the house.

When they were safely out of earshot, Beatrisse du Lac Sainte Denis said, "What is this about, Count? You bewildered me last night. I did not know what to think, and this, with the jewel, confuses me even more."

He handed her the jewel. "Take it with you, in any case."

"Is it an amulet?"

"Yes," he said. "It is to bring you your heart's desire."

The devastation in her face upset him. "That cannot be, Count. But it is a kindness in you to offer." She took the jewel and absent-mindedly put it around her neck.

Giuseppe nodded. "You have heard of what is planned for Lammas Night?"

"My husband speaks of little else," she said more bitterly than she knew. "DeVre's set are expecting wonders of you. They are in an ugly mood."

In spite of himself Giuseppe shuddered. "I gathered that. And it is a pity that I will have to disappoint them."

Her brows rose. "You daren't," she said, lowering her voice as if she feared an eavesdropper. "You must not. They will not allow that."

"Yes, I realize this."

Impulsively she put her hand on his arm. "Is it that you cannot? Or that you will not?"

Giuseppe grimaced. "Some of both, Countess. I can summon certain demons, but I will not bring them to do the bidding of those men. You understand why, Madame. I need not tell you why."

"But you must." She turned her lovely, haunted face toward him. The light from the tall windows at the end of the gallery made her fine unpowdered curls glow bright chestnut. The jewels at her throat were alive with their garnet fire, and the stiff silk of her billowing skirt glowed with light. "I know what these men can be. None knows better than I. They permit no one to cross them, and if they suspect fraud, they will show no mercy to you. You will be imprisoned, either by Louis' courts or by the Church. There is no way to escape them, Alessandro," she used his name in a sudden rush of intimacy. "They are too many and too strong."

Giuseppe took her hand and kissed it. "Madame, I believe you. And that is why I have taken you into my confidence. I know something of your marriage, and I have wondered if perhaps you would like to be revenged on Jean Gabriel Louis Martillion, Count du Lac Sainte Denis?" He thought of the Count's younger brother, and realized that Martillion's vice was small beside the Count's.

Her hands closed convulsively on his. "You cannot know how dearly I would treasure revenge, even one little revenge."

With a profound nod, Giuseppe said, "If you are willing to take a risk I am sure that you may have it. There is a saying in Italy—that revenge is a dish best served cold. It will take cold blood to do what I suggest."

Beatrisse du Lac Sainte Denis turned away. "My blood was frozen long ago, Count. What do you want of me?"

Giuseppe smiled, and felt relief run through him. "When I summon the demon, it will be you."

She turned to him again. "What? How can you . . ."

"That is my concern," he said, raising her hand to his lips. He found it easier to deal with women who trusted his confidential manner and charm than with those who were attracted by his handsomeness. He was pleased to see excitement kindle in the Countess's amber eyes. "You must listen to me, and I will outline what I have done. And if you are afraid, remember that you will be heavily disguised by the lights and by the strange garments you wear. And," he added as he saw her falter, "I will paint your face as they do for the theatre. No one will suspect that Beatrisse Countess du Lac Sainte Denis is the embodiment of a demon."

She looked bewildered. "But if this is as you say, how will I be revenged?"

"That, Madame, is where the risk occurs."

It was Lammas Night. The Maytime moon rode low in the sky over Paris, and rode the echos of church bells as they tolled the hour of eight. The streets were already quiet, for when darkness descended it was not wise to be found out of doors.

The sedan chair which arrived at the servants' entrance to the home of Count Alessandro Cagliostro was run-down, and the two chairmen who carried it were not the sort most aristocrats would put their trust in. They collected their fee from the plainly dressed young woman who had hired them and watched her go into the dark passage by the kitchens. They assumed she was to be part of the celebration that would occur later. Cagliostro's summoning of a demon had given most of Paris food for speculation, and the chairmen were glad to have their own tidbit to add to the chatter. Servant girls at demon raisings were something of a surprise.

They would have been more surprised yet had they known that the kitchen door was opened by Cagliostro himself, and that he bowed over the disguised Countess' hand as formally as if she had been in all her court finery.

"Is it ready?" she whispered, somewhat taken aback by his strange white robe with the silver embroidery on it.

"Yes, just as I described it to you. But come quickly, Madame. There is not much time and I want you to practice the trick just once before I dress you."

She hung back. "You are certain that the candles will be out when I appear? I do not want anyone to see the trapdoor."

"No one will see it," he assured her as he opened the hidden door into a secret passage which led to his own austere quarters located over the room where the materialization would take place.

The garment, when he showed it to her, delighted her, though it was shockingly indecent. She touched the flame-like tongues of sheer silk which moved with every draught. Giuseppe pointed out the mechanism of the dress and she laughed at the simplicity of it. "Even if they suspect trickery," she said as she fitted the garment over her, "they would not think of this. They will look for tricks of the theatre, of strange engines." She started across the room, and stopped, suddenly modest, as the silk fell back to reveal the length of her thigh.

"No, no, Madame," Giuseppe assured her. "No demon would behave so. And in a moment I will paint your legs with red, and paste jewels on them. You must not notice your manner of dress." He pointed to the mirror near his worktable. "See? this is not Beatrisse du Lac Sainte Denis, this is some hellish vision."

The thought seemed to strike her, for she rose on her toes and turned gracefully so that the silk drifted about her. "This way, Count?"

Remembering the hungry faces of the men coming that night, Giuseppe said, "It is lovely, Countess, but do not make it too beautiful. A demon may lure, but only to hell."

She nodded, then followed him into the withdrawing room which had been cleared of furniture, and there, by the light of three candles, he showed her what she would do. "Do not let the darkness or the incense frighten you. It will be no different than the way we have done it now. I will always stand just here, and you will know by the candles by the door and by the mantle when you are in the right position. I will not fail you, Countess."

"Nor I you," she promised him, her long hands clenched.

DeVre did not like the fit of his robe, and complained bitterly that it was not seemly for him to be wearing such outlandish things.

"That is up to you," Giuseppe said coldly. "But if you are not protected, I cannot save you from the demon."

Martillion chuckled unpleasantly and looked toward his older brother, the Count du Lac Sainte Denis. "It's a masquerade," he said lazily.

This was much too close to the truth, and Giuseppe did what he could to turn their minds from the idea. "Of course it is a masquerade, gentlemen. Hell is clothing its own in flesh." He gave Gries a robe and warned him not to drink any more.

Henri Valdonne studied the others, thinking himself above all this. His position as the aristocratic head of shippers who traded in China gave him a certain world-wise reputation. He did not comply with Cagliostro's orders immediately, but made a show of inspecting the garment. "I have heard that such garments must be without seam," he challenged as he pulled off his brocaded waistcoat.

"In some rites this is so. But we are not concerned with virgins tonight, Chevalier. Only when a virgin is sacrificed must the robes be of seamless cloth." And seeing the faces of the nine men and four women around him, Giuseppe was deeply grateful that he was not subjecting a virgin to any such as these.

When all were dressed in their robes, Giuseppe led the way to the rear withdrawing room. None of the halls were lit and there were no servants in the house. Giuseppe moved quickly and was pleased that the others went clumsily in their unfamiliar robes and unlighted passages.

The pentagram and circle were already on the floor, and the sword, chalice, wand, wafers, and salt stood at each point of the pentagram outside the circle. Giuseppe went quickly to the bay of heavily curtained windows and made a show as if to adjust the curtains against prying eyes. He saw that the concealed levers were set and ready. He turned back to the others who stood, uncertainly glancing about them, in the dim light. He put his foot over a spring which worked the concealed bellows.

"Kneel!" he told them, and his generally pleasant voice was stern as a field commander. "Go to the pentagram and kneel."

He watched while the white-robed figures sorted themselves out. In a moment they were ready, and had begun to whisper among themselves.

"You must be silent!" Giuseppe pulled a diamond medallion from around his neck and hung it in front of the nearest branch of candles. A flick of his finger set it to swinging. "We call on the Forces of Darkness," he intoned, garbling the invocation so that he would not inadvertantly summon an unexpected Power. "We suppliants call the Forces of Darkness on this, Lammas Night, when they have sway in the darkness."

Martillion tittered and his hands strayed toward the chalk marks.

"Do not touch that!" Giuseppe's voice cut like a knife. "That is all that will protect you from the fires of hell. If any one of you break it, none are safe."

There was a pause and Martillion drew back. The others moved back, too.

"We summon you," Giuseppe went on, "in the Glory of your Power." He moved toward the circle and reached first for the chalice. "Here we call you with the call of blood." He elevated the chalice. Then, like a priest, he went from one kneeling figure to another, tilting the red-colored liquid into their waiting mouths. He did not tell them that what they drank was salted mead in which he had steeped Persian hashish. The color was nothing more than dye, but Giuseppe could see the concealed revulsion on the faces of his ill lot of initiates. Good. If they were revolted, they would not be too critical of the taste of what they drank, and the salt was enough to make most of them believe.

Returning to the window bay, he said, "I summon you, demons of the pit, I call on one of your number. I tell you that there is work for you here, that the souls wait for you. I, Alessandro Cagliostro call you. I call you."

The figures waited, but nothing happened. Giuseppe came forward again, and picked up the wand. With this he tapped all the others on the forehead, and when that was done, he drew blood from their fingertips with his sword. When that was over, he took the wafers, and marking each with the print of a cloven hoof, he passed these to each of his celebrants. They were a paste made with poppy syrup, and they took strong effect.

Sure now that the thirteen before him were muzzy in thought, he began the call again. He touched a loose board with his foot and hidden bells rang. A wind from nowhere chilled the room as the concealed bellows began to work, and extinguished one branch of candles. Then Giuseppe pulled one of the hidden levers and the room was plunged into darkness.

A moan came from the group, and in the next instant, the niches with their candles had revolved back as the false hearthstone returned to its proper place, and in the circle stood a blazing female demon, alive with fire and with smoke in her hair.

Giuseppe almost smiled as he saw his acolytes draw

back from this apparition. He waited until the whole effect had sunk in, and then he cried out: "Demon! I, Alessandro Cagliostro charge you. Identify these who kneel before you. Tell us the names of those who kneel. Tell us the secrets of their souls. What are the abominations that will condemn them to perdition on the Day of Wrath?"

There was a pause, and the Beatrisse du Lac Sainte Denis began to recite the vices and crimes of those gathered before her, calling up every lewd boast of her husband, every shoddy bit of gossip she had heard, every detail that had caused her shame and embarrassment. The list was a long one, and it frightened the thirteen kneeling around the pentagram.

Gradually the room grew darker as Giuseppe once more pulled the lever which controlled the candle niches. One of the initiates was breathing hard and Giuseppe knew he would have to give the Count a composing drug before he let him leave the house.

At last the long catalogue of debauchery was over. Again the bells rang and the room went dark. In the returning light the figure of the demon was seen shimmering before them. Giuseppe forced the bellows into greater breath.

Giuseppe clapped his hands three times. "Depart! Depart! Depart!" he commanded. Suddenly the air was very still.

And the demon shriveled, became a single flame, and then disappeared entirely in the center of the circle.

"Are they gone?" Beatrisse du Lac Sainte Denis asked when Giuseppe came into his quarters a little more than an hour later.

"They are gone." He held out his hand. In it lay a wired dress of red silk which trailed a long thin thread. "Perhaps you might want this, Countess."

She touched it, a secret smile on her face. Then, with a decisive nod of her head, "No. There is always the slim chance that my husband might find it. That must not happen." She paused "I pulled the thread when the bellows stopped."

"I think you will find that your husband is not well. When he left his pulse was very rapid and he had a look about his eyes that was not good."

"Did he?" she asked, disinterested. "I left the bath water, as you said. It is quite red. The servants may see it."

"The powder removed it all from your skin?" he asked. He knew his servants would never see the reddened water.

"Yes." She pulled her maid's dress about her more tightly. "Do you think he will ever suspect?"

Giuseppe laughed outright. "Madame, after they had drunk wine tainted with hashish and eaten wafers of poppy, you could have come in there in your most famous toilette, and if I had told them you were a demon, they would have believed it."

She nodded. "A bellows and a wired dress. How simple to make a demon."

"You are troubled, Countess?" Giuseppe took her hand solicitiously.

"It is just that I do not know when you will betray me," she said after a moment.

"I might say the same of you," he said easily. "Come, this is our secret. You know what I did to make the demon, and I know the demon is you. If you cannot trust me out of faith, remember that we both have a hold on the other."

The Countess nodded once more. "I must return home," she said.

Giuseppe stood aside, "I have ordered a hack for you, Madame. It will take you home, if not in fashion, at least in victory."

At that she smiled. "I saw his face, you know, as I told

him all the dreadful things he had done. His eyes were like an animal in a trap. He could not move." She went to the door. "I will always remember his eyes, Cagliostro. It will give me strength."

"You have the amulet as well, Countess. It is for your heart's desire."

"Surely you don't expect me to believe that?" she asked incredulously. "When you are nothing more than a charlatan?"

When the door closed behind the Countess, Giuseppe Balsamo, known to the world as Count Alessandro Cagliostro, went into his withdrawing room to remove the chalk marks from the floor. And to remove the holy water and Host that had protected that venal gathering from the perils of Lammas Night.

Yarbro based Giuseppe's materialization of the demon on an actual stage illusion invented by The Great Dante.

For many years Dante toured the world with his magic show featuring the materialization of a demon ghost. When he first introduced this novelty into his act, the relatively unsophisticated audiences of the 1920's reacted to the weird dress and bellows with a frenzy that audiences of the 1970's reserved for *Jaws* and *The Exorcist*.

6

"The Shadow Knows!"

These words appeared on the cover of *The Shadow—A Detective Magazine* in April 1931. The lead story was "The Living Shadow," and it introduced a depressed and entertainment-hungry public to one of the most popular characters in American literature.

The Shadow novels were written by Walter B. Gibson, an inexhaustible juggernaut of a man who wrote 282 of them under the pen name of Maxwell Grant. Twice a month he turned out a sixty-thousand word novel—a staggering total of more than sixteen million words.

Gibson was also an accomplished magician, and he used his knowledge of conjuring and prestidigitation to add color and variety to his stories.

"During my period of fact writing I dealt considerably with magic," he wrote. "It was a hobby that I turned into a business sideline. I was completing the second volume of magical secrets from Houdini's notes at the time I turned to fiction. I applied much that I had learned about a magician's technique when I came to devise situations in mystery fiction. I think that every writer can work a hobby or adapt specialized knowledge to fiction uses."

At the present time Mr. Gibson lives in New York State in a twenty-two room house next to a two-story barn that houses much of The Great Raymond's magic show.

We hope he has plenty of bookcases in which to display the novels and books on magic he has written, the stories he ghosted for Houdini, Thurston, and Blackstone, the tales he adapted for "The Twilight Zone," and the anthologies he compiled on the fine arts of murder, robbery, spying, and swindling.

1. The Shadow novels appeared as being "From The Shadow's Private Annals, as told to Maxwell Grant." Twenty-two of the novels, however, were written by Theodore Tinsley and fifteen of the later ones by Bruce Elliott, himself a magician of note.

The Man of Mysteries

A Magic Story
by Walter B. Gibson

He appeared mysteriously in my office. A moment before I had been alone, but now I was surprised to see a quiet, well-dressed, middle-aged man seated in a chair beside my desk.

"Who are you?" I asked. "Your card was not sent in to me. Didn't you speak to the girl in the outer office?"

"You have my card," was his reply. "I always send in my card, wherever I call."

I looked on the desk. There was no card there.

"Look in the lower drawer on the right," suggested the stranger.

The drawer he mentioned was locked, and I had the only key. It was where I kept my best cigars and other articles of value. I was angry, for I felt sure the stranger was bluffing me. He had never been in my office before—so how could his card be in there?

I decided to call his bluff, I reached in my pocket, brought out the key, unlocked the drawer and yanked it open. Then came my amazement. On my box of cigars lay an engraved calling card which read:

Professor Anthony
The Man of Mystery

I looked at my strange visitor. He was smiling.

"Is this your card?" I asked.

He nodded.

I was perplexed. Here was a mystery in my own office. How came the card in my locked drawer? I decided to question the professor further.

"What's it all about?" I probed.

"Just this," he replied. "I am the man of mystery. People are interested in what I do. You are interested because I have given you a problem to solve—and you can't solve it. So I'll give you another. Have you a pack of cards?"

It happened that I had. I reached in another drawer and took out a pack. I threw the case on the desk, and the professor picked it up leisurely, holding it between his long, well-shaped fingers.

He raised the case to the level of my eyes, and said: "Would you mind thinking of a card—any card in the pack—the first one that occurs to you?"

He laid the case on the desk. I had thought of a card instantly—the ace of spades.

"I have the card," I said.

He looked into my eyes for a few seconds, while his hands drew the pack of cards from the case. He dropped the case on the desk, turned the faces of cards toward himself and ran through the pack. Then he removed a card and placed it face down on the desk.

"What was your card?" he asked.

I kept my eyes on that single card. This looked like a trick. I was sure he could not fool me.

"The ace of spades," I said.

"Turn over the card," was his answer.

I turned up the card. There was the ace of spades staring at me. My own card, from my own pack! It appeared incredible.

"How did you do it?" I demanded, somewhat awed in spite of myself.

The professor smiled. "It is purely a matter of mental analysis," he explained. "I can do it with anyone, and anyone who knows my method can do it, too. I shall—if you wish—attempt the same thing in a more elaborate form, step by step, to demonstrate this principle. Suppose you name a color—either red or black."

"Red," I said, now thoroughly intrigued by this amazing fellow.

"There are two red suits," continued the professor. "Hearts and diamonds. Name one."

I thought for a second, then I said: "Diamonds."

"We know," said the professor, "that there are spot cards and court cards. We must eliminate one or the other. Which do you choose?"

"The spot cards," I said, without hesitation.

"You have chosen to eliminate the spot cards. Very well. That leaves the court cards, which we will divide into two groups—the jack, queen, and the ace, king. Again choose a pair, so that we may eliminate."

"I will take the jack and queen."

"Very well, sir. We now have the jack and the queen. We must eliminate one of these. Name the card you want."

"I want the jack!"

Professor Anthony pointed to the card case, which was within easy reach of my hand. He had not touched it since removing the deck.

"Look in that case," he requested.

Doubtingly I opened the card case. A single card was there. I took it out and looked at it. *It was the jack of diamonds!*

I sat back and puffed on my cigar. In my eyes this strange intruder had taken on the aspect of a superman. He had entered my office as if by magic; I had found his calling card within my impregnable drawer; and twice had he read my mind amazingly.

"Tell me frankly," I asked, "have you hypnotized me?"

The professor laughed. "No, no," he said. "I have told you it is no more or less than mental analysis. You can do it as well as I, if you know the method."

"I'd give ten dollars to know how you did that last one," I said. "That is, if I knew I could do it, too."

"All right," said the professor, obligingly.

I produced the ten-dollar bill and laid it on the desk. The professor returned the pack of cards to the case and began his explanation.

"In taking the cards from the case," said he, "I leave one card behind. The last time it happened to be the jack of diamonds. This time it is the three of clubs.

"Now, everything you say is used against you—but you don't realize it because I do it artfully. You name a color. If you say 'Black,' I say 'Very good'; if you say 'Red,' I reply—'That leaves black.'"

"Then I ask you to name either clubs or spades. By the same process of interpretation, I decide upon clubs as the desired suit. If you pick the spot cards, fine—if you take the court cards, the spots are left. Then I ask if we shall eliminate the low spot cards or the high ones. If you say high, I take it to mean that you eliminate them. If you say low, I interpret it that you have chosen them. Then we divide the low cards into two, three, and four, five. By my method you are bound to take the two and three. Then I ask which we shall take. If you say 'Two,' I reply: 'That leaves the three. Look in the card case.' If you say 'Three,' I point to the case and say: 'There it is.'"

He folded up the ten-dollar bill and tucked it in his vest

pocket. Mumbling to myself, I went over everything he had said. It worked. No doubt about it.

"But how," I asked, "did you know that I thought of the ace of spades? Tell me that!"

"That is another story," he replied.

"And another ten spot?" I asked.

"Well, no," said the professor. "It doesn't always work. But when it does, it is good. So five dollars would——"

I brought out the five dollars and gave it to him. He pointed to the card case.

"Just a bit of psychology," he explained. "That card case, and many others, happens to have a large spade printed on it. If you hold it momentarily before a person's eyes and ask him to think of a card, the chances are about ninety-nine to one that the ace of spades will be the card he thinks of. You can tell immediately if your hunch is right. If it isn't, drop it, and go on with the trick I just showed you."

"Very, very good! That explains everything, except how your calling card came in my drawer. Only hypnotism will account for that, I should think, but perhaps there's a trick to it, too—"

"No," said the professor. "That is not for sale. It is my own peculiar method of introduction. I don't care to part with it, just to satisfy curiosity."

"You gave me half price on one explanation," I said. "Here is double price for the one I want. Put this twenty dollars in your pocket and relieve my troubled mind. How on earth can you put your calling card in that locked drawer?"

The professor was thoughtful. Then he took the money. He deliberately opened a wallet and extracted a calling card.

"That drawer," he said, "is tightly locked. But it is no different from any other desk drawer. It has a slit in the top, between the top of the drawer and the solid desk. Just a tiny crack—but enough."

He slipped the card into the crack until just the end of it still protruded. Then a flip of his finger and the card disappeared. I unlocked the drawer. There was the card, on top of the cigar box, well back in the drawer.

"I didn't flip it too far for you." said the professor, "because I wanted you to see it right away. But with less violent customers, I have sent the card way back to the end of the drawer into a pigeon-hole or between two packages. Sometimes it takes them a minute or two to find it. When they do—well, they're surprised, to say the least."

When I looked up again, Professor Anthony was gone, with his well-earned thirty-five dollars. I had been flipping my own calling cards into every drawer in the desk with astonishing results. I had been interrupted by the girl from the outer office. She was looking at me with a puzzled expression on her face.

"Mr. Roberts to see you, sir——"

"Tell him to come in. By the way, did you see a middle-aged gentleman go out of here a few minutes ago?"

"No, sir."

"And you didn't see him come in, either?"

"No, sir," said the girl, more bewildered than before.

"All right, I'll see Mr. Roberts."

In came Roberts, and sat down beside me. The girl lingered at the doorway.

"About that big contract with the Boston Company——" Roberts began.

"That can wait a minute," I said. "Here's a pack of cards. I want to show you something——"

The girl was back in the outer office. The partition is a thin one. I heard her talking to another girl from the next room.

"The boss is going cuckoo," she was saying. "Says a

man came in and went out without my seeing him. Has a whole stack of calling cards on his desk, and he's got one in every desk drawer. He's playing cards with that man Roberts, who's bringing him a big contract. Now, the last place I worked——"

I heard it all; but I didn't mind. Roberts had just found the ten of spades in the card case.

You are now approaching the halfway mark in our crash course of crime and conjuring. At this point, you know a little about the detectives in mystery, but not as much about the art of deceiving. We must alter this shortcoming forthwith. Go and fetch a deck of cards and count them. Are there fifty-two? Yes? Good! Using these fifty-two cards you are ready to perform . . .

The Blackstone Poker Deal
(or the Curse of Vegas!)

Arrange twenty cards on the top of the deck. (The suits are abbreviated to diamonds = D, hearts = H, clubs = C, and spades = S. Similarly face cards are jack = J, queen = Q, king = K, and Ace = A.) The cards should be placed in this order:
3D, 9H, 9C, AS, AD, 10D, 6C, 10C, KC, 8D, 4C, 10S, KD, JC, AC, 10H, KH, 7H, QC, AH.

Give the deck a false cut. How? Let me explain. Hold the deck in your left hand ready for dealing. Cut a third of the deck from the top of the pack and place it on the table. Cut half of the remainder of the deck and place it on the table to the right of the first stack.

Finally, place the remaining cards in the left hand on the table to the right of the two piles. Reassemble the cards from right to left, and you have completed a simple, but very deceptive false cut.

Now, carefully deal four poker hands, and turn the

hands face up! The first hand receives three kings, the second hand a straight, the third a flush, and the fourth a full house.

Drop the fourth hand face up on the third hand, and drop both face up on the second hand, and all face up on the first hand. Replace the cards on the top of the pack. Repeat the false cut and deal the cards.

The fourth hand will now receive four aces, but hand three wins with a king high flush! This is a real puzzler of a trick. Try it for yourself, but not in Las Vegas!

"The Man of Mysteries" has an interesting angle. The conjuror in the tale was based on a real-life magician named Salo Ansbach, who used this approach to interest businessmen in learning magic. He would give them personal lessons, then go on to another town.

According to Gibson, "On one occasion he actually skinned the card into a cigar box that was slightly open. The client was dumfounded. So, to some degree, was Ansbach."

7

"Death by Black Magic," which first appeared in the magazine *Ten Detective Aces,* was written by Joseph Commings, a transplanted New Yorker now living in Maryland, who once was regional vice president of The Mystery Writers of America.

In "Death by Black Magic" Commings introduces Brooks U. Banner, an unusual and clever man who is not only a magician and a detective—but a United States Senator, as well. Senator Banner has found the time to solve more than twenty magical murders over the years, and the "impossible murder" of The Great Xanthe in "Death by Black Magic" is one of the best.

Because of the unique position of Brooks U. Banner in the hierarchy of magician-detectives, we have prevailed upon Commings to provide us with the biography of the Senator, that appeared in *Detective Who's Who.*

FROM *Detective Who's Who*

Banner, Brooks Urban, U.S. Senator; b. Utica, N. Y., 1894; s. Orson and Griselda B.; m. Minnie Waycross (now deceased); no children. Orphaned at age of four, raised in orphanage; grad. Cornell U., Albany Law School. Sec. Lieut., Infantry, World War I. Hobo; furniture salesman; auctioneer; barker for sideshow spiritualist; ward boss; county sheriff of Manhattan; U. S. Senator. Recreations: Tinkers with old locks and mechanical toys; collects childish magic tricks, such as banana with zipper on it; has wide basic knowledge of magical illusions; reads comic books; sporting enthusiast; has trunk full of press clippings covering quarter-century of crime; delights in solving locked-room murders. Organizations: Sphinx Club (magicians); Criminal Bar Ass'n. Address: 91 Morningside Drive, New York City.

Death by Black Magic

by Joseph Commings

Pelting rain shrouded the old Abbey Theater on West Forty-sixth Street on the night that the Great Xanthe was strangled. But U. S. Senator Banner had no foreboding of murder as he scurried under the dripping marquee and out of the rain that was hitting the sidewalk like .45's. The capacious wrap-rascal hung soggily on his titanic shoulders as he pounded on the boarded-up panels of the lobby doors. When he took his fist away there were no sounds save those of the punishing rain and the thin distant bleat of a taxi horn on Broadway.

A light flickered behind the crack. "Who is it?" asked a voice.

"The Clutching Claw!" said Banner with a jovial laugh.

"Oh," said the voice, recognizing the familiar chuckle.

The light blinked out and Banner heard the racket of a metal bar being removed and the rasp of a key in a long-unused lock. The lobby door creaked back and he saw Xanthe Oberlin's white face and white hair against the velvet blackness. It looked like a disembodied head.

Banner moved in out of the wet and turned on his own pocket flashlight. Xanthe rebarred the door and locked it with a snick of the tarnished key.

Banner said, "You're keeping the place tighter than the cork on a champagne bottle."

Xanthe showed his pearly smile. "Why should we be disturbed?" His leanness, his dark clothes, and the shadows made him look six-and-a-half feet tall. He loomed over Banner's own six-feet-three.

Banner drew out a kettle-sized hunting-case watch. "Eight forty-five. Right on the button."

They walked past musty plush drapes hanging in tatters on brass rails and down the aisle of the theater.

Banner was at once overcome by the eerie atmosphere of decay. The great chandelier was grim with dust and looked down with a thousand eyeless sockets. The whole place needed an airing.

The footlights and the overhead stage lights were the only illumination. The stage was bright with a canary-yellow backdrop and side curtains. The house was empty except for one girl sitting in an aisle seat in the orchestra. When they reached her row she looked up at them and smiled. She was knitting an afghan and she was so quiet you could hear a stitch drop.

She was Xanthe's daughter, Konstanz. She was twenty-one. Her hair was a black cloud and she had her father's eyes. But while his eyes were merely piercing, hers were great round black-centered orbs. They disturbed you. Her small red mouth, against a lime-white skin, disturbed you, too.

Banner greeted her with relish and seated himself down beside her. The chair squeaked rustily. Then he unbuttoned his wrap-rascal and dumped a bundle of yellowed newspapers tied with an old shoelace on the rat-chewed upholstery. Konstanz stared in astonishment at the fifteen-year-old date-line. Banner flung off his coat, spattering raindrops like a Saint Bernard shaking itself.

Xanthe said in his smooth beguiling voice, "Shall we look at the cabinet, Senator?"

"I'm raring to go, X. Where is it? Backstage?"

"Yes." Xanthe took long strides toward the ramp that led to the stage. Banner followed him, brushing a cobweb off his jowl. "Give me a hand, please, Senator. It isn't very heavy, but it's too awkward for one man."

It was just inside the wings. Together they carried it to mid-stage. It was a plain wooden cabinet, seven feet tall. It stood on four stout legs, lifting it a foot off the floor. The top was open. The side that faced the audience was curtained. The curtain was drawn back revealing a lot of nothing inside.

Xanthe grinned. "We shall try it for the first time tonight. The Chinese Cabinet of the Great Xanthe!"

Konstanz had joined them on the stage. Banner rapped the sides of the cabinet, then the back and bottom. He was certain there were no sliding panels or trick openings.

Xanthe was still grinning. "Next, Senator, I'll show you its possibilities. Do you mind sitting in the audience?"

Banner clambered off the stage. Xanthe turned to Konstanz. "When I go inside the cabinet, I want you to pull the curtain across, my child. Then step back about ten feet. Are you all set, Senator?"

Banner had lowered himself into a groaning seat in the thirteenth row. "Shoot the works, professor," he said.

Xanthe bowed his head at Konstanz and stepped firmly inside. He stood there with plenty of room on all sides. He waved a hand through the open top. "Do nothing till I give the word." Konstanz took hold of the cabinet curtain and yanked it sharply.

There was a tinkle of silver rings and a red dragon breathing flame appeared embroidered on the fully exposed curtain.

Konstanz turned and walked to the footlights. Slim and bedeviling, she stood motionless in a brown wool dress, dainty black suède pumps, and prettily filled nylons. She had left her knitting on her seat and her arms hung naturally at her sides. *She has stage presence,* thought Banner, *just like her old man.* Her profile was to Banner, his eyes glued to the drawn curtain.

Banner glanced at his watch. Eight fifty-five.

There was a long silence. Banner heard the rats scuttling behind the scenery and the lash of the rain on the roof. Somewhere a leak dripped stealthily.

Then he heard whisperings come from the stage— from the cabinet—swift whisperings. There were other small sounds, but that might have been the rats.

There was silence again.

Konstanz had never moved. The cabinet had her magnetized.

Banner got weary of waiting. He looked at his watch again. It was almost five past nine. He got up and trudged toward the stage. Konstanz turned her head and looked at him with puzzled amusement and casually shrugged her shoulders.

Banner said, "Ready or not, X, we're opening up."

There was utter silence from the box.

Banner reached his hand across the red dragon and the curtain shot back on its silver rings.

Xanthe was in there, but he was crumpled on the floor and his face was as purple as a ripe grape. Konstanz' silence made Banner glance once quickly over his shoulder to see if she was still with him.

Banner eyed the livid lump on Xanthe's temple. He reached in and lifted Xanthe's chin. He saw the deep red marks of thumbs on either side of the windpipe. He stooped, listened for heart beats, and felt for a pulse. There wasn't any.

He spun around to face Konstanz.

Her eyes were huge. "Daddy?"

"Honey," he said, "there's nothing we can do. He's dead. Strangled."

It really started late that morning in the dining room of the Sphinx Club on Fifth Avenue. As you step through its black oak doors, the past masters of necromancy frisk you with their eyes from portraits on the walls: Houdini, Herman the Great, Thurston, Blackstone, Keller. Banner was the focus of these painted canvas eyes as he trotted into the dining room shod in soiled white sneakers. He was at once hailed to a table at which four people sat.

Banner's sapphire-blue eyes gleamed. "How have you been, X?" The magician's eloquent hands with the silver wishbone ring rose to shake his. "Konstanz! How come you do to me like you do?" She was entrancing in a woolly pull-over and a pencil-slim gray skirt.

"Sit down, Senator," invited Xanthe. He was clean and comfortable in loose English-made tweeds. Four hundred years ago he would have been burned at the stake as a sorcerer. Today he earned a healthy living doing the same job. "Had breakfast? No? Have it with us."

Banner shanghaied a chair from another table and joined them. He ordered a slice of ham as big as a life raft, fried eggs with their eyes shining, and coffee fresh enough to talk back to you. While this was going on he was being introduced to the other two people.

Nedra Russell was in her middle twenties. She sat very erect and tall. She had olive-green eyes, crocus-blond hair, and one of those thin haggard faces that can be made tormentingly attractive. She nervously twisted a rhinestone bracelet on her left wrist. For a living she designed costumes.

Konstanz said, "I've known Nedra ever so long."

"Four years," smiled Nedra.

The man with them was Lawrence Creek. He was as heavy as Banner, but he didn't have the reach. He dressed like a chief pallbearer and wore a scarab tie-pin in his foulard. As soon as Banner got his nose into action he ticketed Creek as "the man with the nice stink." Creek wore *Tzigane,* a perfume that cost forty-five dollars an ounce.

Xanthe said, "Mr. Creek is a magician, too."

Banner grinned at him. "How's tricks, cousin?"

Creek took ten seconds before replying, and all the while he stared at Banner as if the family honor of the Creeks had been dragged through the muck. Banner was to learn that Creek always gave a delayed action response, no matter what you said to him. This time his answer was something incoherent.

"Senator," said Xanthe as Banner sliced a wedge of ham, "you're vitally interested in magic, aren't you?"

"Interested! I have been ever since I first broke down the secret of taking off a shirt with a vest still on. Did you ever see my cocktail shaker? I fill it with water, but if you call for beer, it pours beer, if you call for wine, it pours wine. And so forth."

He paused and stuck his hand into the bulging, junk-filled pocket of his sack-like frock coat. He searched for a minute, then held up a banana. With a childishly gleeful chuckle he peeled the banana by pulling down a zipper.

"I like to startle people by dipping my hand in water, then shaking their hand. Mine'll be as dry as a mummy's. It's been dusted with lycopodium, of course. I'll say I'm——"

Xanthe interrupted politely. "Senator, you're known to be much more than that. You've solved murders by your shrewd observation of tricks. You're keen to catch an error. I want you to see my Chinese Cabinet. It'll be featured in my new show at the Abbey Theater next month."

Banner paused in his eating. "The Abbey?"

Xanthe smiled his professionally superior smile. "You know the Abbey, don't you, with its haunted reputation? There hasn't been a performance of any kind on its stage in fifteen years. Well, it's an ideal background for magic, isn't it? I'm keeping it just as it is. Cleaning away the dust, that's all. I'm leaving all the spiders and the rust and the old programs on the floor and the general appearance of rot."

"That is a brainstorm," said Banner.

"Is the Abbey authentically haunted?" asked Creek. "I mean ghosts."

Xanthe nodded earnestly. "Yes. There's a weird murder connected with its closing."

"Tell us," said Nedra. "We'll have time for the story." There was a queer tightness in her voice and her jaded eyes were boring into the wizard's smooth placid face. Konstanz gazed at her father with great devotion.

Xanthe said in a low emotionless voice, "Fifteen years ago *Othello* was enjoying a run at the Abbey. Remember the Simmondses? They were a man-and-wife starring team. Simmonds played the Moor and his wife Desdemona. In every way they lived the parts created by Shakespeare. Simmonds was jealous, just as Othello was. He was suspicious of her. He thought she was in love with another actor in the cast, the one who played Iago.

"The final fatal performance was on a raw blustery night in early December. In the last act, you remember, Othello is so convinced of his wife's infidelity that he strangles her on her couch before the audience. Simmonds got his hands on her throat in this scene and it looked too damn real. He held her longer than the action called for. Then he rose laughing and stared out at the audience like a madman. At that moment all the stage lights went out. They were out for about twelve seconds, then they all came on again. Simmonds wasn't on the stage. *He had vanished into thin air!*"

"A trap door?" suggested Banner.

"No," said Xanthe. "The stage has a grave-trap, but at a rehearsal one of the players fell through it, injuring himself, so it had been nailed up from underneath because there was no use for it. These nails had never been tampered with.

"Now! The wings were jammed with players, scene shifters, prop men. They all swore that Simmonds did not pass through the wings. The man stationed at the stage door was positive that nobody left the theater by that exit. Ushers were in all the aisles in the audience. There was a faint glow from the fire exit lights. Simmonds never came up the aisles. Several people were standing in the lobby. They took oath that he never passed out that way. He couldn't have gone far unnoticed. He still wore the black robes of Othello.

"When they found Mrs. Simmonds strangled, every door was doubly guarded. Every person in the audience and every actor backstage left the theater in single file through a sieve of police. Simmonds never left disguised as someone else. When the police searched each nook and cranny later there was no trace of him. He was not in the theater, yet he had never left it. He literally dissolved into thin air during the twelve seconds the lights were out."

Creek said, "There was no hint of him in later years?"

Xanthe shook his white head. "None. Not the slightest trace. Every time the police think of the case they have the shudders."

"The Simmondes had a child, hadn't they?" said Nedra. "What became of it?"

"I'm not sure," said Xanthe. "I believe it was adopted by some professional family." He turned his sharp black eyes to Banner. "All this brings me to my Chinese Cabinet. It's never been worked quite like this before. I do it entirely without assistance of any kind. I want you to see its first rehearsal tonight at the Abbey. If it has a flaw, you'll spot it. How do you stand, Senator?"

Banner picked his teeth with his raccoon-bone tooth-pick. "Abracadabra is my meat."

"Konstanz will be there." Xanthe turned to Creek. "And you, my friend?"

Creek took his customary ten seconds before replying. "Sorry, Xanthe. I'm putting on a show myself tonight. Some amateur magicians in a loft . . ."

"I'll come," said Nedra enthusiastically.

Xanthe smiled and shook his head. "Must I remind you of your own work, Nedra? The costume designs for the Raja stunt. They must be ready tomorrow at the latest."

Nedra frowned. "How utterly disappointing."

"Before you go to the studio, Nedra, you'd better give it a ring and see if everything's ready for you. The number is Ravenswood 7-1149."

"Yes," she said.

"There'll only be three of us?" said Banner.

Xanthe nodded slowly. He seemed to be watching Creek the way a starved robin watches a worm.

Nedra got up and gathered her things. "I'll call the studio now," she said. "All right?"

"Yes," said Xanthe. And he repeated the phone number.

That's what had happened this morning at the Sphinx Club. Now they were in the empty theater staring in bewilderment at the magician's dead body. Banner drew the curtain on the conjurer.

"Dead!" cried Konstanz with a dry sob. "But there was nothing the matter with him. He can't be."

"He was strangled," repeated Banner grimly, "while I sat there watching. Someone got into that box and I haven't the least idea how." He took her arm and led her to the wings. She was quivering, her muscles taut. "How did your dad operate the cabinet, Konstanz?"

"I don't know, Senator. It was his secret. Nobody knew."

"Wait." He trotted back to the cabinet and returned with two tarnished keys on a bright new ring. Hooking her arm, he guided her behind the scenes.

He used his flashlight against the dark. A fuzzy spider landed on his sleeve and he flipped it off. He peered through a jungle of fly-ropes at a large prop table cluttered with magical apparatus. Among the objects was a nickel-plated revolver. On the floor beside the table lay an aluminum ladder; it had black felt pads on both ends. Banner hefted the ladder. It weighed next to nothing.

The flashlight illumined a railing eaten up with iron mould, and several concrete steps. There was a sign saying in cracked paint:

DRESSING ROOMS

Konstanz followed him up the steps and along a passage to the first door. It was christened *Dressing Room 1*. A gold paper star had been pasted on the door a long time ago; its rays were curling up like a starfish with the cramps. The brass doorknob was green with neglect. Banner turned it and the door went back silently—oiled hinges.

They walked in and listened to the rain hammering furiously at the window. Banner tried the light switch, but the results were sterile.

He played the flash over the mirrored make-up table, seeing himself looming in it and a pallid-faced girl peeking over his shoulder. The cold cream, the eyebrow pencil, and the grease-paint of fifteen years ago were still there. There was also a dusty-looking rabbit's foot. In a corner of the dressing room was a Punch and Judy outfit. The puppets were flung over the lip of the stage. Punch in the act of strangling Judy, and the Hangman over to one side watching them.

"This was Mr. Simmonds' room," said Konstanz with shocking unexpectedness.

Banner gasped. "Were those dolls like that the night Simmonds——?"

"Dad did that," she said hoarsely.

"Great sense of humor."

A drop of water sparkled on the floor. Banner's light followed other drops to a clothes closet. He trotted to it and wrenched it open. Clothes hung in there; clothes with a fresh smell as if they had just been worn. A raincoat, a soft hat, a jacket, a pair of pants. The raincoat glistened. Banner stretched out and touched it. It was wet.

The clothes were big enough to fit an average sized man. The hat was soggy and the cuffs of the pants damp.

"Someone took off his clothes in here," said Konstanz.

"For what reason? To walk around in these drafts in his ectoplasm?"

Konstanz didn't answer.

Banner closed the closet. They went to *Dressing Room 2*. Except for the remains of occupation years ago, there was nothing for them. From the floor of *Dressing Room 3* Banner picked up a program with heel marks stamped on it. He read the names of the cast with some curiosity. He stopped for a long time at the line:

IAGO . . . . *Xanthe Oberlin*

He shoved it at her. "Did you know that?"

She shook her head dumbly. Then she said, "Simmonds strangled his wife and disappeared. Tonight my father was strangled." Her breast heaved and her teeth chattered. "*Simmonds has come back!*"

He threw his arm about her shoulders to steady her. "I

heard whispering in the cabinet after your father went in. I couldn't make it out. Could you?"

"I'm sure I heard him say, 'My God, what are you doing here?'"

Banner wheeled suddenly. "I'm going to look at the stage doors."

They found first the loading door, through which scenery was brought into the theater. It was locked and rusted tight. At the end of a streaky walled passage they found the regular stage door. It was locked and bolted from the inside.

Returning to the stage, Banner let his eye speculate on the dim steel frame outline of the bridge or catwalk that ran above the stage, masked from the audience by the teaser curtain.

He said, "It would be better if you didn't go near the cabinet, Konstanz, while I'm gone."

"Where are you going?" she questioned, panicky.

"To try all the doors."

He went up one side of the auditorium, trying the fire exits, and down the other. All were fastened with rusty iron chains on the inside. He had left Konstanz sitting by the footlights in a rickety chair, listening to his footfalls trail away in the balcony as he proceeded, rattling chains like a big fat ghost. He entered the lobby, following the beam of his flashlight. The lobby doors were locked and barred, as Xanthe had left them.

"By thunder," he muttered, "nobody has used any of the exits. This is giving me the willies."

He bumped open the door of the manager's office and fell over furniture undermined by termites. A phone was on a desk and he prayed it was in working order. The phone number uppermost in his mind was the one Xanthe had mentioned that morning, Ravenswood 7-1149.

He put the receiver to his ear and heard the hum. He

dialed the number. In a moment he heard a woman say, "Hello?"

It was Nedra Russell.

"This is Senator Banner," he said. "Still working at the studio?"

"Yes," she answered. "Is the show over? Where are you calling from, Senator?"

"The Abbey Theater. We've seen an act tonight that wasn't on the program. Somebody killed Xanthe."

The wire went dead. Then: "Who killed him?"

"I don't know."

"Who else is there?"

"Only Konstanz and myself. Just the two of us. We're as lonesome as a pair of polecats. Drop whatever you're doing and join us."

"Of course I'll be there." She hung up.

Banner dialed again and got a loft building.

A man answered. "Lawrence Creek?" "No," said the man, "he can't come to the phone. He's performing. How long? Since eight-thirty. Of course he's been on the stage all the time. He's got three hundred people to prove it. Disappearing acts? No, he hasn't disappeared. He's been doing card-and-coin tricks and mind reading. Penny ante stuff . . . The Abbey Theater? I don't know about that. What? All right, all right! Don't get your liver in an uproar. I'll tell him it's the cops."

Banner dialed a third time—Police Headquarters.

He was in the motion of hanging up when he heard pistol shots pound the dank air four times and then Konstanz' voice hysterically calling him.

Banner charged down the center aisle. Konstanz stood in the orchestra pit, shivering and holding the nickel-plated revolver in her hand. Its muzzle smoked.

"Hey, June bug! No fair packing a pistol."

"Look!" she cried, pointing at the stage. "Look!"

Banner raised his eyes. A yellow human skull with a jagged crack in its cranium leered at him over the footlights from in front of the cabinet.

"Lawsy!" he bellowed. "How'd that come there?"

Konstanz swallowed several times. "After you left me," she said shakily, "I sat near the wings. Then I thought I heard a muffled voice somewhere backstage. I felt riveted to the chair, but finally I got up and peeked into the wings. I gathered enough courage to slip up to the prop table and pick up the pistol. It was very quiet then. I had begun to think my ears were misbehaving when suddenly at the top of those concrete steps I saw the flicker of a light crawl along the wall. I knew it wasn't you. I fired I don't know how many times. I don't know whether I hit——"

Banner had taken the gun out of her limp hand. He ejected two remaining rounds. "You didn't hit anything. These're blanks."

"The next thing I heard," she hurried on, "was a thump on the stage. I rushed back. That horrible skull was rolling to a stop, wheeling its hollow eyes at me. I screamed for you." She tore at his sleeve with pink nails. "Take me home, Senator, please, please. I can't stand it any longer."

"Leave?" he said. "When things are beginning to make sense?"

"Sense!" she cried.

"Come here and Uncle Remus'll read you a bedtime story." He let her follow him to the seat he had dumped his old newspapers on. He picked up the top one. "I spent the afternoon at a half-dozen press offices cudgeling editors to let me have fifteen-year-old newspapers containing accounts of the Simmonds murder. First, there's a description of Simmonds. He's one hundred and fifty pounds, five feet ten, tow-headed, gray-eyed, athletic."

"Those wet clothes in the dressing room would fit him," murmured Konstanz.

"I think so. Listen to what the chief electrician named

Rock has to say: 'Before the last show Simmonds came to me and told me he was going to include a new effect in the night's performance. He gave me ten dollars for my part. And when a big star like that gives orders, you snap to. Even if you think it sounds screwy. He told me to pull the master switch on the control board so as to black the stage for about fifteen seconds as soon as he rose from the couch after strangling Desdemona. He gave me a song and dance about a psychological wrinkle he was working into the act. I realize now that he wanted darkness so that he could escape after murdering his wife. Please believe that I was in no way his accomplice knowingly. . . .'

"The inspector asked him if he noticed anything unusual during the interval the lights were out. 'Something that turned out to be no account, inspector. I thought I heard a noise of something landing lightly behind my switchboard. But when I looked later all that was there were some sandbags at the end of a rope.'"

Banner let the paper slide out of his hand. There was a satisfied smirk on his face. He jogged onto the stage again and wrestled one of the baby spotlights out of the wings. He aimed it straight up at the vaulting roof above the stage and flicked the switch.

The spot cut a swath in the blackness. He swept the dome as if hunting for enemy aircraft. Then he grunted. "Back in the limelight, brother. Konstanz!"

She stood close and squinted up at what was spot-lighted.

The wood-beamed gridiron was a hundred feet above the stage. High up among a tangle of rigging and flies hung something else. It was like a huge black bat, sleeping feet upward.

"Oh, my gosh!" she gasped. "What's that?"

"That," said Banner, feeling a chill, "is the murderer."

Then someone began to thump the lobby doors.

Konstanz clung to Banner like a barnacle while he unlocked the way for Lawrence Creek.

"What's going on?" snapped Creek, bringing in with him a gust of weather and a whiff of expensive *Tzigane*.

"We're opening a chamber of horrors. You're welcome, Creek."

As they went down the aisle, Banner told him the story in headline phrases. Creek was rattled by the time he saw the way the stage was set. Then he remembered he should show dignity and poise and he took Konstanz aside to comfort her.

The lobby doors got a rubdown with nightsticks. Banner let in the police. Captain Roberts, a walking gingersnap, was in charge of the homicide detail. Banner told him to put men at the lobby and stage doors before he did anything else. He added that a woman named Nedra Russell would show up at any time and to let her in.

When Roberts saw the thing hung away up on the gridiron, he ordered it taken down.

"How, captain?" asked a detective.

"Easy," said Banner. "Stand clear."

He went behind the switchboard. There were four sandbags there, each weighing about fifty pounds. These were tied to the end of a rope that stretched upward into nothingness. Banner's large claspknife began to hack the rope. It came asunder. The rope, released from the sandbags, shot upward out of sight. He heard a yell from those on the stage and a loud crash of something loose falling heavily.

Banner viewed the junk heap of half rotted clothes and yellow bones. "Put up your handcuffs, Roberts. Othello's in no condition to resist arrest. . . . *Simmonds never left the stage after he killed Desdemona!*"

He's been hanging there for fifteen years?" gasped Roberts.

Banner nodded. "Simmonds planned to escape all

right. He rigged up that rope, a pulley, and some sandbags that outweighed him. He tipped the beam at one hundred and fifty. The bags are at least two hundred. The bags were balanced somewhere up above so that they would pitch downward at a yank from the rope. The other end of the rope reached to the floorboards of the stage. Simmonds concealed it among the drapes. When the lights went out he dived for the rope and stuck his foot in a loop. In his rush, he missed his grip and the upgoing rope flipped him over backwards. Stunned, he shot up feet first. When he came to, everyone was searching for him. He couldn't untangle himself without help. He couldn't cry for help or they'd nab him for murder. So he hung there till he died."

"Heavens," breathed Roberts.

"Tonight," said Banner, "the disturbance produced by the sound of the four shots that Konstanz fired jarred the skeleton's skull loose."

"That's all fine and dandy," said Roberts. "You've solved a mystery that's been plaguing us for years. But what about tonight? Simmonds' *ghost* didn't kill Xanthe!"

Nedra Russell came down the aisle from the lobby. She wore a dull black Persian lamb wrap over a black evening gown. Her eyes roved excitedly. Banner had her meet Captain Roberts, then he had them all take front row seats. In the meantime Xanthe's body had been removed from the cabinet by the medical men.

"First of all," said Banner, "I'll want a man who knows how to fly scenery. Somebody who's had experience in it. It looks complicated."

Roberts urged a blue-coated sergeant forward.

Banner sent the sergeant up to the fly floor, then he himself disappeared behind the scenes. Next they heard his voice saying, "You can't see me. I'm behind the teaser curtain on the catwalk above the stage. I'm going to lower the aluminum ladder I'm carrying down through the open top of the cabinet."

They saw one end of the ladder slowly descend until it rested on the floor of the Chinese Cabinet. Banner appeared from above, like an untidy archangel, coming down the ladder. Half-way down he stopped.

"I've instructed the sergeant to experiment with the drops. Okay, Chuck, I'm ready!"

A Spanish patio scene started to come down in front of Banner's nose.

Banner sneezed. "Not that, Chuck. Try again."

Several more varied scenes were lowered.

Captain Roberts was getting restless. "This ain't even funny," he snorted.

He heard Banner shout, "This is it!" And he looked up to find Banner without a head. Slowly dissolving, Banner became only the lower half of a man. Then only his shoes were left. Then the rest of the ladder vanished and there was nothing left but the Chinese cabinet and the canary-yellow drapes.

"My gosh!" howled Roberts. "I'm seeing things!"

Banner stepped into sight out of the cabinet.

He said, "It's done with a drop that's a huge mirror. The top of the mirror is tilted at an angle enough to reflect the drapes on the upper front of the stage. These drapes are identical with the ones hanging behind the cabinet. The murderer was hidden behind that looking-glass drop-scene when he entered the cabinet!"

Roberts dashed onto the stage to examine the mirror, front and back. "Amazing," he muttered. "Yet easily rigged up with a winch."

Banner went down into the audience and whispered to Konstanz in a voice that did not carry more than six inches, "Go to the manager's office, wait five minutes, then call this number." He gave her the number.

Puzzled, she left her seat and walked up the aisle.

"Captain," said Banner, "have those two men who're guarding front and back doors come to *Dressing Room One* toot sweet. Better leave replacements."

Roberts issued orders. He was on the Senator's coattail when Banner reached the dressing room.

"It's still raining," said Banner.

"There's been no letup."

Banner frowned at the phone on the make-up table. The number on the handset dial was Longacre 4-3281.

As Roberts' two men entered, the phone bell sounded with a purr so muffled that it could not be heard outside the room. Banner looked at the bell box. The bell's hammer had been padded with felt. Banner snatched up the receiver. He heard: "This is Konstanz Oberlin speaking. Senator Banner told me to—"

"That's enough, lambsy," said Banner. He replaced the phone. He swung on the nearer cop. "Were you watching the lobby door?"

"Yes, sir."

"Have you let in a woman in black?"

"I have not."

Banner wheeled on the other. "Did she get in through the stage door."

"No, sir."

"I didn't think so," said Banner. "Her coat would have glistened, even if she'd only crossed the sidewalk from a taxi. Instead it was dull. *She hadn't been out in the rain!*"

Roberts was standing flat-footed. "What's this?"

Banner tried to be patient. "Arrest Nedra Russell! She killed Xanthe! And don't ask her why she wore an evening gown to work. Look at the shoes its skirt is covering up."

"In a way," said Banner later, "both crimes were alike. The killer escaped by going *up.* . . . You've got to understand Xanthe; the vanity of the supreme artist. He wanted to foster the illusion that the trick of the cabinet depended on him alone. He didn't want us to know that he needed someone's help, so he prepared the alibi for Nedra. That was the purpose of the hocuspocus about the phone number—her alibi. What's more, he knew that if he could dupe *me*, he'd really be pulling off something.

"He went about it painstakingly, the way he performed his stunts. That little skit about Nedra's staying at the 'studio' to design costumes was put on for my benefit. Xanthe repeated the Ravenswood number twice so that it would stick in my mind in the event I wanted to check on Nedra's not being in the theater. If I called that number, she would answer—seemingly from her studio—and I wouldn't know she was helping Xanthe.

"Sometime before I arrived tonight, Xanthe secretly let Nedra in through the stage door, locking and bolting it after her. Her wrap and evening gown were in *Dressing Room One*. She was wearing a man's suit under a raincoat, and a soft hat. This was necessary, for she had to have suitable clothing to climb around the rigging backstage in order to get that aluminum ladder down to X in the cabinet.

"Okey-doke. The trick was working beautifully. Nedra operated the winch that let down the screening mirror and Xanthe was ready to vanish from the cabinet—all of which was supposed to leave me dumfounded in my seat. Nedra appeared on the catwalk above him and lowered the ladder, blocking his exit. We heard them whispering. X was annoyed. She had some excuse about something going wrong.

"Then she brained him and, dropping into the cabinet, strangled him. You don't have to be strong to strangle somebody who's unconscious. Prolonged pressure is enough. When she was sure he was dead she skinned up the ladder again, pulled it up after her, carted it backstage, and worked the winch to raise the mirror into the drops, where it hung concealed. She darted back to *Dressing Room One* and changed clothes, putting on her gown and wrap. She had to keep out of our way as we prowled around in the rooms. But that wasn't very hard.

"The only time she was nearly caught was when I phoned the 'studio,' really *Dressing Room One*. The Ravenswood number changed to Longacre was more of X's foresightedness. He had written that phony number on the dial to throw me off about Nedra's whereabouts during the act. Konstanz heard her answer my ring and fired a blank pistol at her as she left the dressing room. After the police came, Nedra pretended to enter through the lobby. It looked so obvious that she thought we'd never question the cop on guard."

Captain Roberts said, "You were right about her shoes. She was wearing rubber-soled sports. Not the kind at all that goes with an evening gown."

"There were no shoes in the closet. I knew that although the killer changed clothes, he was still wearing the same shoes. Has Nedra told you about the motive?"

Roberts shook his head. "She's as mum as that skull."

Banner chuckled. "That's no more than likely. The skull belongs to her *father*. She's the Simmondses' child that was left parentless by the Abbey murder fifteen years ago. By coincidence she became chummy with Konstanz. She didn't know that Xanthe was the Iago who instilled the jealousy in her father until she came here a few days ago to help prepare the theater for the show. She saw X's name billed on a program. She said to herself, 'That's the man who made my father kill my beloved mother.' The same murderous streak that was in her father was in Nedra. . . . You'll see if I'm not right!"

Perhaps this story by Joseph Commings best sums up some of the varied and valid reasons that have made magic such a universally popular form of entertainment. "Death by Black Magic" points up the possibility that not all magic is quite as deceptive as you imagine.

In this half of the twentieth century, scepticism runs riot and belief in magic is considered to be naive and childish. However, psychics and mind readers still continue to create controversy wherever they perform their feats of magic (or is it telepathy?). Maybe tomorrow or next year another Houdini, Thurston, Dante, or Robert-Houdin will come along who will challenge people's beliefs and make them wonder: "Is it Magic?"

Next time you watch a magician on television saw a pretty young lady in half, analyze your feelings. Do you not find that buried within you is a little edge of fear for her safety?

INTERMISSION

A Pictorial Glimpse into the Magicians' World of Magic and Illusion

The Ballyhoo

THE RENAISSANCE OF PRESTIDIGITATION

An early example of a bill-board size Carter the Great lithograph. Charles J. Carter was one of America's great showmen; he made eight world tours and traveled with more than thirty tons of baggage. Magician Harry Kellar once told him, "Never change your show, Charlie. Just keep it big as hell, and paint it once a year!"

PROGRAMME.

CARTER THE MYSTERIOUS
The World's Inimitable Magician
ENGAGED ON A TOUR OF THE WORLD !!

Presenting an Entertainment of Modern Miracles
Unparalleled in this or any other time.

OVERTURE
Part I.

Forty-five minutes with the Inimitable
CARTER, in

A BOUQUET OF MYSTERIES

A. Rapid Transit.
B. Digital Manipulation.
C. A Mystery from Luxor.
D. Aerial Cards.
E. Metamorphosis.
F. The Astral Hand.
G. Inexhaustive Bottle.
H. The Nest of Boxes.
I. **Levitation.**—The opposite to gravitation.

The First Part concludes with

J. **THE MAGICAL DIVORCE**
which is literally and metaphorically "Out of
Sight." A Novel Conceit, in
which a human being is made to instantly vanish

INTERMISSION: Entr'acte.

OVERTURE
Part II.

A WEIRD SEANCE from SIMLA
OR
THE MYSTERIES of the YOGI
in which the pet theories of Theosophists and
Spiritualists are exploited. "Can such
things be and o'eroome us like a summer cloud?"

SPECIAL NOTICE.
You are politely requested to kindly sign your
name in full to questions written, to enable Miss
Price to better identify the questioner.

INTERMISSION: Entr'acte.

OVERTURE
Part III.

Carter, assisted by **Corinne** impersonating the
famous Chinese Court Magician
Ching Ling Foo

wherein the wonderful sorcerers of China are
imitated and impersonated—Immense objects
produced from nothingness, Space annihilated,
Marvels in Space with the latest discoveries and
innovations of science.

Advance Manager	Mr. Harry P. Lyons.
Chief Mechanic	Mr. Fred Besnah.
Personal Assistant	Mr. Chas. Hugo.
Treasurer	Mr. James Reid.
Assistant	M'll'e Maxwell.

NOTICE.

Here on Saturday after-
noon at 4 o'clock there
will be a special Matinee
for Ladies and Children.

*CHILDREN WILL BE ADMITTED
TO ANY PART OF THE HALL
AT HALF PRICE.*

CHAS. J. CARTER.

At the **Matinee on Saturday** afternoon
Miss PRICE (Mrs. Carter) will devote more time than
ordinarily to the answering of **Ladies Questions** only,
and they are specially invited to bring all the questions
desired. Special tricks will also be shown for the
little ones.

(Miss Price) CORINNE CARTER
who unfolds a marvellous chapter from the supernatural, in an exhibition of
thought transference, or mental telepathy. The
result of years of study and research.

A program from Carter's First World Tour.

Theater facade for a matinee performance.

Carter on tour in India.

The Magicians

Carter the Great and assistants.

On March 16, 1910, at Digger's Rest, a field near Melbourne, Harry Houdini made the first successful airplane flight on the Australian Continent. Upon landing he made a prediction to Carter the Great, who had accompanied him to Australia. Houdini said, "If anyone remembers me in the future, Charlie, it will be as an aviator—not as a magician!"

The flight.

Harry Kellar and Ching Ling Foo, two great turn-of-the-century magicians.

One of the earliest photographs of magician William "Billy" Robinson in his vaudeville days. Years later, using the pseudonym of Chung Ling Soo, Robinson became famous by impersonating the oriental magician Ching Ling Foo. On March 23, 1918, at the Wood Green Empire Theater in London, he was shot to death on stage while "Catching a Marked Bullet"!

Allan Shaw, the "King of Coins," Carter the Great, and Harry Houdini at the grave of William Henry Davenport, whose spirit cabinet seances brought him international fame.

The Show

(*Above*)   "The   Lion's
Bride,"   a   massive   and
complex   stage   illusion
performed as the finale of
Carter's   show   for   more
than twenty years. (*Right*)
Carter the Great and his
assistant   in   a   publicity
still taken for "The Iron
Maiden of Nurenberg," an
effect in which the young
lady   is   impaled   on
seventy-two   solid   steel
spikes.

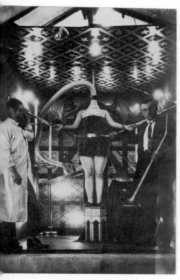

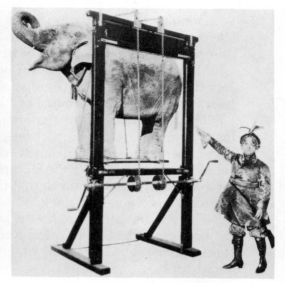

"The Headless Lady," a typical side-show gimmick from the 1920s.

Another publicity still. This time it's for the illusion "The Vanishing Elephant."

Carter the Great performing "Levitation."

8

One day in 1932 a young man wearing a black mask delivered a lecture on mystery writing at The Columbia University School of Journalism in New York. His name was Manfred B. Lee, and he was one-half of the partnership that was to gain preeminence in the mystery and detective field under the name of Ellery Queen.

The other half of this symbiosis of sagacity and skulduggery was Lee's cousin, Frederic Dannay, and if their flip of the coin had been heads instead of tails Dannay would have had to deliver the lecture, for Queen fans were not aware of the dichotomy at that time, and the gambit of the mask was a good gimmick.

Three years earlier in 1929 the first Ellery Queen novel had been published. It was *The Roman Hat Mystery*, and from that moment the team of Lee and Dannay never looked back.

They published thirty-five novels as Ellery Queen, four Drury Lane novels as Barnaby Ross, more than seventy-five short stories, and editorial and critical works that are among the finest in the genre. Not to mention that singlehandedly they have kept the detective short story alive by publishing the best work in the field in *Ellery Queen's Mystery Magazine* for more than thirty-five years.

"The Adventure of the Hanging Acrobat," which appeared in *The Adventures of Ellery Queen* (Stokes, 1934), is one of their earliest short stories and makes one long for the good old days of the big top, when Professor Vassar and his Trained Pigs made you laugh until your sides hurt, and Jonathan Highler, The Aeronautical Human Bomb, made you very much aware that the circus surely was "The Greatest Show on Earth"!

The Adventure of the Hanging Acrobat

by Ellery Queen

Long, long ago in the Incubation Period of Man—long before booking agents, five-a-days, theatrical boarding houses, subway circuits, and *Variety*—when Megatherium roamed the trees, when Broadway was going through its First Glacial Period, and when the first vaudeville show was planned by the first lop-eared, low-browed, hairy impresario, it was decreed: "The acrobat shall be first."

Why the acrobat should be first no one ever explained; but that this was a dubious honor every one on the bill—including the acrobat—realized only too well. For it was recognized even then, in the infancy of Show Business, that the first shall be last in the applause of the audience. And all through the ages, in courts and courtyards and feeble theatres, it was the acrobat—whether he was called buffoon, *farceur*, merry-andrew, tumbler, mountebank, Harlequin, or *punchinello*—who was thrown, first among his fellow-mimes, to the lions of entertainment to whet their appetites for the more luscious feasts to come. So that to this day their muscular miracles are performed hard on the overture's last wall-shaking blare, performed with a simple resignation that speaks well for the mildness and resilience of the whole acrobatic tribe.

Hugo Brinkerhof knew nothing of the whimsical background of his profession. All he knew was that his father and mother had been acrobats before him with a traveling show in Germany, that he possessed huge smooth muscles with sap and spring and strength in them, and that nothing gave him more satisfaction than the sight of a glittering trapeze. With his trapeze and his Myra, and the indulgent applause of audiences from Seattle to Okeechobee, he was well content.

Now Hugo was very proud of Myra, a small wiry handsome woman with the agility of a cat and something of the cat's sleepy green eyes. He had met her in the office of Bregman, the booker, and the sluggish heart under his magnificent chest had told him that this was his fate and his woman. It was Myra who had renamed the act "Atlas & Co." when they had married between the third and fourth shows in Indianapolis. It was Myra who had fought tooth and nail for better billing. It was Myra who had conceived and perfected the dazzling pinwheel of their finale. It was Myra's shapely little body and Myra's lithe gyrations on the high trapeze and Myra's sleepy smile that had made Atlas & Co. an "acrobatic divertissement acclaimed from coast to coast," had earned them a pungent paragraph in *Variety*, and had brought them with other topnotchers on the Bregman string to the Big Circuit.

That every one loved his Myra mighty Brinkerhof, the Atlas, knew with a swelling of his chest. Who could resist her? There had been that baritone with the dancing act in Boston, the revue comedian in Newark, the tap-dancer in Buffalo, the adagio in Washington. Now there were others—Tex Crosby, the Crooning Cowboy (Songs & Patter); the Great Gordi (Successor to Houdini); Sailor Sam, the low comic. They had all been on the same bill together now for weeks, and they all loved sleepy-eyed Myra, and big Atlas smiled his indulgent smile and thrilled in his stupid, stolid way to their admiration. For was not his Myra the finest female acrobat in the world and the most lovely creature in creation?

And now Myra was dead.

It was Brinkerhof himself, with a gaunt suffering look about him that mild spring night, who had given the alarm. It was five o'clock in the morning and his Myra had not come home to their theatrical boarding-house room on Forty-seventh Street. He had stayed behind with his wife after the last performance in the Metropole Theatre at Columbus Circle to try out a new trick. They had re-hearsed and then he had dressed in haste, leaving her in their joint dressing room. He had had an appointment with Bregman, the booker, to discuss terms of a new contract. He had promised to meet her back at their lodgings. But when he had returned—*ach*! no Myra. He had hurried back to the theatre; it was locked up for the night. And all the long night he had waited. . . .

"Prob'ly out bummin', buddy," the desk-lieutenant at the West Forty-seventh Street station had said with a yawn. "Go home and sleep it off."

But Brinkerhof had been vehement, with many ges-tures. "She never haf this done before. I haf telephoned it the theatre, too, but there iss no answer. Captain, find her, please!"

"These heinies," sighed the lieutenant to a lounging detective. "All right, Baldy, see what you can do. If she's piffed in a joint somewhere, give this big hunk a clout on the jaw."

So Baldy and the pale giant had gone to see what they could do, and they had found the Metropole Theatre locked, as Brinkerhof had said, and it was almost six in the morning and dawn was coming up across the Park and Baldy had dragged Brinkerhof into an all-night restaurant for a mug of coffee. And they had waited around the theatre until seven, when old Perk the stagedoor man and timer had come in, and he had opened the theatre for them, and they had gone backstage to the dressing-room of Atlas & Co. and found Myra hanging from one of the sprinkler pipes with a dirty old rope, thick as a hawser, around her pretty neck.

And Atlas had sat down like the dumb hunk he was and put his shaggy head between his hands and stared at the hanging body of his wife with the silent grief of some Norse god crushed to earth.

When Mr. Ellery Queen pushed through the chattering crowd of reporters and detectives backstage and convinced Sergeant Velie through the door of the dressing room that he was indeed who he was, he found his father the Inspector holding court in the stuffy little room before a gang of nervous theatrical people. It was only nine o'clock and Ellery was grumbling through his teeth at the unconscionable inconsiderateness of murderers. But neither the burly Sergeant nor little Inspector Queen was impressed with his grumblings to the point of lending ear; and indeed the grumblings ceased after he had taken one swift look at what still hung from the sprinkler pipe.

Brinkerhof sat red-eyed and huge and collapsed in the chair before his wife's dressing table. "I haf told you everything," he muttered. "We rehearsed the new trick. It was then an appointment with Mr. Bregman. I went." A fat hard-eyed man, Bregman the broker, nodded curtly. "Undt that's all. Who—why—I do not know."

In a bass sotto voce, Sergeant Velie recited the sparse facts. Ellery took another look at the dead woman. Her stiff muscles of thigh and leg bulged in rigor mortis beneath the tough thin silk of her flesh tights. Her green eyes were widely open. And she swayed a little in a faint dance of death. Ellery looked away and at the people.

Baldy the precinct man was there, flushed with his sudden popularity with the newspaper boys. A tall thin man who looked like Gary Cooper rolled a cigaret beside Bregman—Tex Crosby, the cowboy-crooner; and he leaned against the grime-smeared wall and eyed the Great Gordi—in person—with flinty dislike. Gordi had a hawk's beak and sleek black mustachios and long olive fingers and black eyes; and he said nothing. Little Sam, the comedian, had purple pouches under his tired eyes and he looked badly in need of a drink. But Joe Kelly, the house manager, did not, for he smelled like a brewery and kept mumbling something drunken and obscene beneath his breath.

"How long you been married, Brinkerhof?" growled the Inspector.

"Two years. *Ja.* In Indianapolis that was, *Herr Inspektor.*"

"Was she ever married before?"

"*Nein.*"

"You?"

"*Nein.*"

"Did she or you have any enemies?"

"*Gott, nein!*"

"Happy, were you?"

"Like two doves we was," muttered Brinkerhof.

Ellery strolled over to the corpse and stared up. Her ropy-veined wrists were jammed behind her back, bound with a filthy rouge-stained towel, as were her ankles. Her feet dangled a yard from the floor. A battered stepladder leaned against one of the walls, folded up; a man standing upon it, he mused, could easily have reached the sprinkler pipe, flung the rope over it, and hauled up the light body.

"The stepladder was found against the wall there?" he murmured to the Sergeant, who had come up behind him and was staring with interest at the dead woman.

"Yep. It's always kept out near the switchboard light panel."

"No suicide, then," said Ellery. "At least that's something."

"Nice figger, ain't she?" said the Sergeant admiringly.

"Velie, you're a ghoul. . . . This *is* a pretty problem."

The dirty rope seemed to fascinate him. It had been wound tightly about the woman's throat twice, in parallel strands, and concealed her flesh like the iron necklace of a Ubangi woman. A huge knot had been fashioned beneath her right ear, and another knot held the rope to the pipe above.

"Where does this rope come from?" he said abruptly.

"From around an old trunk we found backstage, Mr. Queen. Trunk's been here for years. In the prop-room. Nothin' in it; some trouper left it. Want to see it?"

"I'll take your word for it, Sergeant. Property room, eh?" He sauntered back to the door to look the people over again.

Brinkerhof was mumbling something about how happy he and Myra had been, and what he would do to the *verdammte Teufel* who had wrung his pretty Myra's neck. His huge hands opened and closed convulsively. "Joost like a flower she was," he said. "Joost like a flower."

"Nuts," snapped Joe Kelly, the house manager, weaving on his feet like a punch-drunk fighter. "She was a floozy, Inspector. You ask *me*," and he leered at Inspector Queen.

"Floo-zie?" said Brinkerhof with difficulty, getting to his feet. "What iss that?"

Sam, the comic, blinked his puffy little eyes rapidly and said in a hoarse voice: "You're crazy, Kelly, crazy, Wha'd'ye want to say that for? He's pickled, Chief."

"Pickled, am I?" screamed Kelly, livid. "Aw right, you as' *him*, then!" and he pointed a wavering finger at the tall thin man.

"What is this?" crooned the Inspector, his eyes bright.

"Get together, gentlemen. You mean, Kelly, that Mrs. Brinkerhof was playing around with Crosby here?"

Brinkerhof made a sound like a baffled gorilla and lunged forward. His long arms were curved flails and he made for the cowboy's throat with the unswervable fury of an animal. Sergeant Velie grabbed his wrist and twisted it up behind the vast back, and Baldy jumped in and clung to the giant's other arm. He swayed there, struggling and never taking his eyes from the tall thin man, who had not stirred but who had gone very pale.

"Take him away," snapped the Inspector to Sergeant Velie. "Turn him over to a couple of the boys and keep him outside till he calms down." They hustled the hoarsely breathing acrobat out of the room. "Now, Crosby, spill it."

"Nothin' to spill," drawled the cowboy, but his drawl was a little breathless and his eyes were narrowed to wary slits. "I'm Texas an' I don't scare easy, Mister Cop. He's just a squarehead. An' as for that pie-eyed sawback over there"—he stared malevolently at Kelly—"he better learn to keep his trap shut."

"He's been two-timin' the hunk!" screeched Kelly. "Don't b'lieve him, Chief! That sassy little tramp got what was comin' to her, I tell y'! She's been pullin' the wool over the hunk's eyes all the way from Chi to Beantown!"

"You've said enough," said the Great Gordi quietly. "Can't you see the man's drunk, Inspector, and not responsible? Myra was—companionable. She may have taken a drink or two with Crosby or myself on the sly once or twice—Brinkerhof didn't like her to, so she never drank in front of him—but that's all."

"Just friendly, hey?" murmured the Inspector. "Well, who's lying? If you know anything solid, Kelly, come out with it."

"I know what I know," sneered the manager. "An' when it comes to that, Chief, the Great Gordi could tell you somethin' about the little bum. Ought to be able to! He swiped her from Crosby only a couple o' weeks ago."

"Quiet, both of you," snapped the old gentleman as the Texan and the dark mustachioed man stirred. "And how could you know that, Kelly?"

The dead woman swayed faintly, dancing her noiseless dance.

"I heard Tex there bawl Gordi out only the other day," said Kelly thickly, "for makin' the snatch. An' I saw Gordi grapplin' with her in the wings on'y yest'-day. How's 'at? Reg'lar wrestler, Gordi. Can he clinch!"

Nobody said anything. The tall Texan's fingers whitened as he glared at the drunken man, and Gordi the magician did nothing at all but breathe. Then the door opened and two men came in—Dr. Prouty, Assistant Medical Examiner, and a big shambling man with a seared face.

Everybody relaxed. The Inspector said: "High time, Doc. Don't touch her, though, till Bradford can take a look at that knot up there. Go on, Braddy; on the pipe. Use the ladder."

The shambling man took the stepladder and set it up and climbed beside the dangling body and looked at the knot behind the woman's ear and the knot at the top of the pipe. Dr. Prouty pinched the woman's leg.

Ellery sighed and began to prowl. Nobody paid any attention to him; they were all pallidly intent upon the two men near the body.

Something disturbed him; he did not know what, could not put his finger precisely upon the root of the disturbance. Perhaps it was a feeling in the air, an aura of tension about the silent dangling woman in tights. But it made him restless. He had the feeling . . .

He found the loaded revolver in the top drawer of the

woman's dressing-table—a shiny little pearl-handled .22 with the initials *MB* on the butt. And his eyes narrowed and he glanced at his father, and his father nodded. So he prowled some more. And then he stopped short, his gray eyes suspicious.

On the rickety wooden table in the center of the room lay a long sharp nickel-plated letter opener among a clutter of odds and ends. He picked it up carefully and squinted along its glittering length in the light. But there was no sign of blood.

He put it down and continued to prowl.

And the very next thing he noticed was the cheap battered gas burner on the floor at the other side of the room. Its pipe fitted snugly over a gas outlet in the wall, but the gas tap had been turned off. He felt the little burner; it was stone cold.

So he went to the closet with the oddest feeling of inevitability. And sure enough, just inside the open door of the closet lay a wooden box full of carpenter's tools, with a heavy steel hammer prominently on top. There was a mess of shavings on the floor near the box, and the edge of the closet door was unpainted and virgin-fresh from a plane.

His eyes were very sharp now, and deeply concerned. He went quickly to the Inspector's side and murmured: "The revolver. The woman's?"

"Yes."

"Recent acquisition?"

"No, Brinkerhof bought it for her soon after they were married. For protection, he said."

"Poor protection, I should say," shrugged Ellery, glancing at the Headquarters men. The shambling red-faced man had just lumbered off the ladder with an expression of immense surprise. Sergeant Velie, who had returned, was mounting the ladder with a penknife clutched in his big fingers. Dr. Prouty waited expectantly below. The Sergeant began sawing at the rope tied to the sprinkler pipe.

"What's that box of tools doing in the closet?" continued Ellery, without removing his gaze from the dead woman.

"Stage carpenter was in here yesterday fixing the door—it had warped or something. Union rules are strict, so he quit the job unfinished. What of it?"

"Everything," said Ellery, "of it." The Great Gordi was quietly watching his mouth; Ellery seemed not to notice. The little comedian, Sam, was shrunken in a corner, eyes popping at the Sergeant. And the Texan was smoking without enjoyment, not looking at any one or anything. "Simply everything. It's one of the most remarkable things I've ever run across."

The Inspector looked bewildered. "But, El, for cripe's sake—remarkable? I don't see——"

"You should," said Ellery impatiently. "A child should. And yet it's astounding, when you come to think of it. Here's a room with four dandy weapons in it—a loaded revolver, a letter cutter, a gas burner, and a hammer. And yet the murderer deliberately trussed the woman with the towels, deliberately left this room, deliberately crossed the stage to the property room, unwound that rusty old rope from a worthless trunk discarded years ago by some nameless actor, carried the rope and the ladder from beside the switchboard back to this room, used the ladder to sling the rope over the pipe and fasten the knot, and strung the woman up."

"Well, but——"

"Well, but why?" cried Ellery. "Why? Why did the murderer ignore the four simple, easy, hand methods of murder here—shooting, stabbing, asphyxiation, bludgeoning—and go to all that extra trouble to *hang* her?"

Dr. Prouty was kneeling beside the dead woman,

whom the Sergeant had deposited with a thump on the dirty floor.

The red-faced man shambled over and said: "It's got me, Inspector."

"What's got you?" snapped Inspector Queen.

"This knot." His thick red fingers held a length of knotted rope. "The one behind her ear is just ordinary; even clumsy for the job of breakin' her neck." He shook his head. "But this one, the one that was tied around the pipe—well, sir, it's got me."

"An unfamiliar knot?" said Ellery slowly, puzzling over its complicated convolutions.

"New to me, Mr. Queen. All the years I been expertin' on knots for the Department I never seen one like that. Ain't a sailor's knot, I can tell you that; and it ain't Western."

"Might be the work of an amateur," muttered the Inspector, pulling the rope through his fingers. "A knot that just happened."

The expert shook his head. "No, sir, I wouldn't say that at all. It's some kind of variation. Not an accident. Whoever tied that knew his knots."

Bradford shambled off and Dr. Prouty looked up from his work. "Hell, I can't do anything here," he snapped. "I'll have to take this body over to the morgue and work on it there. The boys are waiting outside."

"When'd she kick off, Doc?" demanded the Inspector, frowning.

"About midnight last night. Can't tell closer than that. She died, of course, of suffocation."

"Well, give us a report. Probably nothing, but it never hurts. Thomas, get that doorman in here."

When Dr. Prouty and the morgue men had gone with the body and Sergeant Velie had hauled in old Perk, the stagedoor man and watchman, the Inspector growled:

"What time'd you lock up last night, Mister?"

Old Perk was hoarse with nervousness. "Honest t' Gawd, Inspector, I didn't mean nothin' by it. On'y Mr. Kelly here'd fire me if he knew. I was that sleepy——"

"What's this?" said the Inspector softly.

"Myra told me after the last show last night she an' Atlas were gonna rehearse a new stunt. I didn't wanna wait aroun', y'see," the old man whined, "so seein' as nob'dy else was in the house that late, the cleanin' women gone an' all, I locked up everything but the stage door an' I says to Myra an' Atlas, I says: 'When ye leave, folks,' I says, 'jest slam the stage door.' An' I went home."

"Rats," said the Inspector irritably. "Now we'll never know who could have sneaked back without being seen or waited around in hiding until——" He bit his lip. "You men there, where'd you all go after the show last night?"

The three actors started simultaneously. It was the Great Gordi who spoke first, in his soft smooth voice that was now uneasy. "I went directly to my rooming house and to bed."

"Anybody see you come in? You live in the same hole as Brinkerhof?"

The magician shrugged. "No one saw me. Yes, I do."

"You, Texas?"

The cowboy drawled: "I moseyed round to a speak somewhere an' got drunk."

"What speak?"

"Dunno. I was primed. Woke up in my room this mornin' with a head."

"You boys sure are in a tough spot," said the Inspector sarcastically. "Can't even fix good alibis for yourself. Well, how about you, Mr. Comedian?"

The comic said eagerly: "Oh, I can prove where I was, Inspector. I went around to a joint I know an' can get twenny people to swear to it."

"What time?"

"Round midnight."

The Inspector snorted and said: "Beat it. But hang around. I'll be wanting you boys, maybe. Take 'em away, Thomas, before I lose my temper."

Long, long ago—when, it will be recalled, Megatherium roamed the trees—the same lop-eared impresario who said: "The acrobat shall be first," also laid down the dictum that: "The show must go on," and for as little reason. Accidents might happen, the juvenile might run off with the female lion tamer, the ingénue might be howling drunk, the lady in the fifth row, right, might have chosen the theatre to be the scene of her monthly attack of epilepsy, fire might break out in Dressing Room A, but the show must go on. Not even a rare juicy homicide may annul the sacred dictum. The show must go on despite hell, high water, drunken managers named Kelly, and The Fantastic Affair of the Hanging Acrobat.

So it was not strange that when the Metropole began to fill with its dribble of early patrons there was no sign that a woman had been slain the night before within its gaudy walls and that police and detectives roved its backstage with suspicious, if baffled, eyes.

The murder was just an incident to Show Business. It would rate two columns in *Variety*.

Inspector Richard Queen chafed in the hard seat in the fifteenth row while Ellery sat beside him sunk in thought. Stranger than everything had been Ellery's insistence that they remain to witness the performance. There was a motion picture to sit through—a film which, bitterly, the Inspector pointed out he had seen—a newsreel, an animated cartoon. . . .

It was while "Coming Attractions" were flitting over the screen that Ellery rose and said: "Let's go backstage. There's something——" He did not finish.

They passed behind the dusty boxes on the right and

went backstage through the iron door guarded by a uniformed officer. The vast bare reaches of the stage and wings
were oppressed with an unusual silence. Manager Kelly,
rather the worse for wear, sat on a broken chair near the
light panel and gnawed his unsteady fingers. None of the
vaudeville actors was in evidence.

"Kelly," said Ellery abruptly, "is there anything like a
pair of field glasses in the house?"

The Irishman gaped. "What the hell would you be
wantin' *them* for?"

"Please."

Kelly fingered a passing stagehand, who vanished and
reappeared shortly with the desired binoculars. The
Inspector grunted: "So what?"

Ellery adjusted them to his eyes. "I don't know," he
said, shrugging. "It's just a hunch."

There was a burst of music from the pit: the overture.

"*Poet and Peasant*," snarled the Inspector. "Don't they
ever get anything new?"

But Ellery said nothing. He merely waited, binoculars
ready, eyes fixed on the now footlighted stage. And it was
only when the last blare had died away, and grudging
splatters of applause came from the orchestra, and the
announcement cards read: "Atlas & Co.," that the Inspector lost something of his irritability and even became
interested. For when the curtains slithered up there was
Atlas himself, bowing and smiling, his immense body
impressive in flesh tights; and there beside him stood a tall
smiling woman with golden hair and at least one golden
tooth which flashed in the footlights. And she too wore
flesh tights. For Brinkerhof with the mildness and resilience of all acrobats had insisted on taking his regular turn,
and Bregman the booker had sent him another partner,
and the two strangers had spent an hour rehearsing their
intimate embraces and clutches and swingings and nuz-

zlings before the first performance. The show must go on.

Atlas and the golden woman went through an intricate series of tumbles and equilibristic maneuvers. The orchestra played brassy music. Trapezes dived stageward. Simple swings. Somersaults in the air. The drummer rolled and smashed his cymbal.

Ellery made no move to use the binoculars. He and the Inspector and Kelly stood in the wings, and none of them said anything, although Kelly was breathing hard like a man who has just come out of deep water for air. A queer little figure materialized beside them; Ellery turned his head slowly. But it was only Sailor Sam, the low comic, rigged out in a naval uniform three sizes too large for his skinny little frame, his face daubed liberally with grease-paint. He kept watching Atlas & Co. without expression.

"Good, ain't he?" he said at last in a small voice.

No one replied. But Ellery turned to the manager and whispered: "Kelly, keep your eyes open for——" and his voice sank so low neither the comedian nor Inspector Queen could hear what he said. Kelly looked puzzled; his bloodshot eyes opened a little wider; but he nodded and swallowed, riveting his gaze upon the whirling figures on the stage.

And when it was all over and the orchestra was executing the usual *crescendo sustenuto* and Atlas was bowing and smiling and the woman was curtseying and showing her gold tooth and the curtain dropped swiftly, Ellery glanced at Kelly. But Kelly shook his head.

The announcement cards changed. "Sailor Sam." There was a burst of fresh fast music, and the little man in the oversize naval uniform grinned three times, as if trying it out, drew a deep breath, and scuttled out upon the stage to sprawl full-length with his gnomish face jutting over the footlights to the accompaniment of surprised laughter from the darkness below.

They watched from the wings, silent.

The comedian had a clever routine. Not only was he a travesty upon all sailormen, but he was a travesty upon all sailormen in their cups. He drooled and staggered and was silent and then chattered suddenly, and he described a mythical voyage and fell all over himself climbing an imaginary mast and fell silent again to go into a pantomime that rocked the house.

The Inspector said grudgingly: "Why, he's as good as Jimmy Barton any day, with that drunk routine of his."

"Just a slob," said Kelly out of the corner of his mouth.

Sailor Sam made his exit by the complicated expedient of swimming off the stage. He stood in the wings, panting, his face streaming perspiration. He ran out for a bow. They thundered for more. He vanished. He reappeared. He vanished again. There was a stubborn look on his pixie face.

"Sam!" hissed Kelly. "F'r cripe's sake, Sam, give 'em 'at encore rope number. F'r cripe's sake, Sam——"

"Rope number?" said Ellery quietly.

The comedian licked his lips. Then his shoulders drooped and he slithered out onto the stage again. There was a shout of laughter and the house quieted at once. Sam scrambled to his feet, weaving and blinking blearily.

"'Hoy there!" he howled suddenly. "Gimme rope!"

A papier-mâché cigar three feet long dropped to the stage from the opposite wings. Laughter. "Naw! Rope! Rope!" the little man screamed, dancing up and down.

A blackish rope snaked down from the flies. Miraculously it coiled over his scrawny shoulders. He struggled with it. He scrambled after its tarred ends. He executed fantastic flying leaps. And always the tarred ends eluded him, and constantly he became more and more enmeshed in the black coils as he wrestled with the rope.

The gallery broke down. The man *was* funny; even Kelly's dour face lightened, and the Inspector was frankly grinning. Then it was over and two stagehands darted out of the wings and pulled the comedian off the stage, now a helpless bundle trussed in rope. His face under the paint was chalk-white. He extricated himself easily enough from the coils.

"Good boy," chuckled the Inspector. "That was fine!"

Sam muttered something and trudged away to his dressing room. The black rope lay where it had fallen. Ellery glanced at it once, and then turned his attention back to the stage. The music had changed. A startling beautiful tenor voice rang through the theatre. The orchestra was playing softly "Home on the Range." The curtain rose on Tex Crosby.

The tall thin man was dressed in gaudiest stage-cowboy costume. And yet he wore it with an air of authority. The pearl-butted six-shooters protruding from his holsters did not seem out of place. His big white sombrero shaded a gaunt Western face. His legs were a little bowed. The man was real.

He sang Western songs, told a few funny stories in his soft Texan drawl, and all the while his long-fingered hands were busy with a lariat. He made the lariat live. From the moment the curtain rose upon his lanky figure the lariat was in motion, and it did not subside through the jokes, the patter, even the final song, which was inevitably "The Last Round-Up."

"Tinhorn Will Rogers," sneered Kelly, blinking his bloodshot eyes.

For the first time Ellery raised the binoculars. When the Texan had taken his last bow Ellery glanced inquiringly at the manager. Kelly shook his head.

The Great Gordi made his entrance in a clap of thunder, a flash of lighting, and a black Satanic cloak, faced with red. There was something impressive about his very charlatanism. His black eyes glittered and his mustache-points quivered above his lips and his beak jutted like an eagle's; and meanwhile neither his hands nor his mouth kept still.

The magician had a smooth effortless patter which kept his audience amused and diverted their attention from the fluent mysteries of his hands. There was nothing startling in his routine, but it was a polished performance that fascinated. He performed seeming miracles with cards. His sleight-of-hand with coins and handkerchiefs was, to the layman, amazing. His evening clothes apparently concealed scores of wonders.

They watched with a mounting tension while he went through his bag of tricks. For the first time Ellery noticed, with a faint start, that Brinkerhof, still in tights, was crouched in the opposite wings. The big man's eyes were fixed upon the magician's face. They ignored the flashing fingers, the swift movements of the black-clad body. Only the face . . . In Brinkerhof's eyes was neither rage nor venom; just watchfulness. What was the matter with the man? Ellery reflected that it was just as well that Gordi was unconscious of the acrobat's scrutiny; those subtle hands might not operate so fluidly.

Despite the tension the magician's act seemed interminable. There were tricks with odd-looking pieces of apparatus manipulated from backstage by assistants. The house was with him, completely in his grasp.

"Good show," said the Inspector in a surprised voice. "This is darned good vaudeville."

"It'll get by," muttered Kelly. There was something queer on his face. He too was watching intently.

And suddenly something went wrong on the stage. The orchestra seemed bewildered. Gordi had concluded a trick, bowed, and stepped into the wings near the watching men. Not even the curtain was prepared. The orchestra had swung into another piece. The conductor's head was jerking from side to side in a panicky, inquiring manner.

"What's the matter?" demanded the Inspector.

Kelly snarled: "He's left out his last trick. Good hunch, Mr. Queen . . . Hey, ham!" he growled to the magician, "finish your act, damn you! While they're still clappin'!"

Gordi was very pale. He did not turn; they could see only his left cheek and the rigidity of his back. Nor did he reply. Instead, with all the reluctance of a tyro, he slowly stepped back onto the stage. From the other side Brinkerhof watched. And this time Gordi, with a convulsive start, saw him.

"What's coming off here?" siad the Inspector softly, as alert as a wren.

Ellery swung the glasses to his eyes.

A trapeze hurtled stageward from the flies—a simple steel bar suspended from two slender strands. A smooth yellow rope, very new in appearance, accompanied it from above, falling to the stage.

The magician worked very, very, painfully slowly. The house was silent. Even the music had stopped.

Gordi grasped the rope and did something with it; his back concealed what he was doing; then he swung about and held up his left hand. Tied with an enormous and complicated knot to his left wrist was the end of the yellow rope. He picked up the other end and leaped a little, securing the trapeze. At the level of his chest he steadied it and turned again so that he concealed what he was doing, and when he swung about once more they saw that the rope's other end was now knotted in the same way about the steel bar of the trapeze. He raised his right hand in signal and the drummer began a long roll.

Instantly the trapeze began to rise, and they saw that the rope was only four feet long. As the bar rose, Gordi's lithe body rose with it, suspended from the bar by the full length of the rope attached to his wrist. The trapeze came to a stop when the magician's feet were two yards from the stage.

Ellery squinted carefully through the powerful lenses. Across the stage Brinkerhof crouched.

Gordi now began to squirm and kick and jump in the air, indicating in pantomime that he was securely tied to the trapeze and that not even the heavy weight of his suspended body could undo the knots; in fact, was tightening them.

"It's a good trick," muttered Kelly. "In a second a special drop'll come down, an' in eight seconds it'll go up again and there he'll be on the stage, with the rope on the floor."

Gordi cried in a muffled voice: "Ready!"

But at the same instant Ellery said to Kelly: "*Quick!* Drop the curtain! This instant. Signal those men in the flies, Kelly!"

Kelly leaped into action. He shouted something unintelligible and after a second of hesitation the main curtain dropped. The house was dumb with astonishment; they thought it was part of the trick. Gordi began to struggle frantically, reaching up the trapeze with his free hand.

"Lower that trapeze!" roared Ellery on the cut-off stage

now, waving his arms at the staring men above. "Lower it! *Gordi, don't move!*"

The trapeze came down with a thud. Gordi sprawled on the stage, his mouth working. Ellery leaped upon him, an open blade in hand. He cut quickly, savagely, at the rope. It parted, its torn end dangling from the trapeze.

"You may get up now," said Ellery, panting a little. "It's the knot I wanted to see, *Signor* Gordi."

They crowded around Ellery and the fallen man, who seemed incapable of rising. He sat on the stage, his mouth still working, naked fear in his eyes. Brinkerhof was there, his muscular biceps rigid. Crosby, Sailor Sam, Sergeant Velie, Bregman. . . .

The Inspector stared at the knot on the trapeze. Then he slowly took from his pocket a short length of the dirty old rope which had hanged Myra Brinkerhof. The knot was there. He placed it beside the knot on the trapeze.

They were identical.

"Well, Gordi," said the Inspector wearily, "I guess it's all up with you. Get up, man. I'm holding you for murder, and anything you say——"

Without a sound Brinkerhof, the mighty Atlas, sprang upon the man on the floor, big hands on Gordi's throat. It took the combined efforts of the Texan, Sergeant Velie, and Manager Kelly to tear the acrobat off.

Gordi gasped, holding his throat: "I didn't do it, I tell you! I'm innocent! Yes, we had—we lived together. I loved her. But why should I kill her? I didn't do it. For God's sake——"

"*Schwein,*" growled Atlas, his chest heaving.

Sergeant Velie tugged at Gordi's collar. "Come on, come on there. . . ."

Ellery drawled: "Very pretty. My apologies, Mr. Gordi. Of course you didn't do it."

A shocked silence fell. From behind the heavy curtain voices—loud voices—came. The feature picture had been flashed on the screen.

"Didn't—do—it?" muttered Brinkerhof.

"But the knots, El," began the Inspector in a bewildered voice.

"Precisely. The knots." In defiance of fire regulations Ellery lit a cigaret and puffed thoughtfully. "The hanging of Myra Brinkerhof has bothered me from the beginning. Why was she *hanged?* In preference to one of four other methods of committing murder which were simpler, more expedient, easier of accomplishment, and offered no extra work, as hanging did? The point is that if the murderer chose the hard way, the complicated way, the roundabout way of killing her, then he chose that way *deliberately.*"

Gordi was staring with his mouth open. Kelly was ashen pale.

"But why," murmured Ellery, "did he choose hanging deliberately? Obviously, because hanging offered the murderer some peculiar advantage not offered by any of the other four methods. Well, what advantage could hanging conceivably offer that shooting, stabbing, gassing, or hammering to death could not? To put it another way, what is characteristic of hanging that is not characteristic of shooting and the rest? Only one thing. *The use of a rope.*"

"Well, but I still don't see——" frowned the Inspector.

"Oh, it's clear enough, dad. There's something about the rope that made the murderer use it in preference to the other methods. But what's the outstanding significance of this particular rope—the rope used to hang Myra Brinkerhof? *Its knot*—its peculiar knot, so peculiar that not even the Department's expert could identify it. In other words, the use of that knot was like the leaving of a fingerprint. Whose knot is it? Gordi's, the magician's—and, I suspect, his exclusively."

"I can't understand it," cried Gordi. "Nobody knew my knot. It's one I developed myself——" Then he bit his lip and fell silent.

"Exactly the point. I realize that stage magicians have developed knot-making to a remarkable degree. Wasn't it Houdini who——?"

"The Davenport brothers, too," muttered the magician. "My knot is a variation on one of their creations."

"Quite so," drawled Ellery. "So I say, had Mr. Gordi wanted to kill Myra Brinkerhof, would he have deliberately chosen *the single method that incriminated him*, and him alone? Certainly not if he were reasonably intelligent. Did he tie his distinctive knot, then, from sheer habit, subconsciously? Conceivable, but then why had he chosen hanging in the first place, when those four easier methods were nearer to his hand?" Ellery slapped the magician's back. "So, I say—our apologies, Gordi. The answer is very patently that you're being framed by some one who deliberately chose the hanging-plus-knot method to implicate you in a crime you're innocent of."

"But he says nobody else knew his confounded knot," growled the Inspector. "If what you say is true, El, somebody must have learned it on the sly."

"Very plausible," murmured Ellery. "Any suggestions, *Signor?*"

The magician got slowly to his feet, brushing his dress suit off. Brinkerof gaped stupidly at him, at Ellery.

"I don't know," said Gordi, very pale. "I thought no one knew. Not even my technical assistants. But then we've all been travelling on the same bill for weeks. I suppose if some one wanted to . . ."

"I see," said Ellery thoughtfully. "So there's a dead end, eh?"

"Dead beginning," snapped his father. "And thanks, my son, for the assistance. *You're* a help!"

"I tell you very frankly," said Ellery the next day in his father's office, "*I* don't know what it's all about. The only thing I'm sure of is Gordi's innocence. The murderer knew very well that somebody would notice the unusual knot Gordi uses in his rope-escape illusion. As for motive——"

"Listen," snarled the Inspector, thoroughly out of temper, "I can see through glass the same way you can. They all had motive. Crosby kicked over by the dame, Gordi . . . Did you know that this little comedian was sniffin' around Myra's skirts the last couple of weeks? Trying his darnedest to make her. And Kelly's had monkey business with her, too, on a former appearance at the Metropole."

"Don't doubt it," said Ellery sombrely. "The call of the flesh. She was an alluring little trick, at that. Real old Boccaccio melodrama, with the stupid husband playing cuckold——"

The door opened and Dr. Prouty, Assistant Medical Examiner, stumped in looking annoyed. He dropped into a chair and clumped his feet on the Inspector's desk. "Guess what?" he said.

"I'm a rotten guesser," said the old gentleman sourly.

"Little surprise for you gentlemen. For me, too. The woman wasn't hanged."

"What!" cried the Queens, together.

"Fact. She was dead when she was swung up." Dr. Prouty squinted at his ragged cigar.

"Well, I'll be eternally damned," said Ellery softly. He sprang from his chair and shook the physician's shoulder. "Prouty, for heaven's sake, don't look so smug! What killed her? Gun, gas, knife, poison——"

"Fingers."

"Fingers?"

Dr. Prouty shrugged. "No question about it. When I took that dirty hemp off her lovely neck I found the distinct marks of fingers on the skin. It was a tight rope, and all that, but there were the marks, gentlemen. She was choked to death by a man's hands and then strung up—why, *I* don't know."

"Well," said Ellery. "Well," he said again, and straightened. "*Very* interesting. I begin to scent the proverbial rodent. Tell us more, good leech."

"Certainly is queer," muttered the Inspector, sucking his mustache.

"Something even queerer," drawled Dr. Prouty. "You boys have seen choked stiffs plenty. What's the characteristic of the fingermarks?"

Ellery was watching him intently. "Characteristic?" He frowned. "Don't know what you mean—— Oh!" His gray eyes glittered. "Don't tell me . . . The usual marks point upward, thumbs toward the chin."

"Smart lad. Well, these marks don't. They all point *downward*."

Ellery stared for a long moment. Then he seized Dr. Prouty's limp hand and shook it violently. "Eureka! Prouty, old sock, you're the answer to a logician's prayer! Dad, come on!"

"What is this?" scowled the Inspector. "You're too fast for me. Come where?"

"To the Metropole. Urgent affairs. If my watch is honest," Ellery said quickly, "we're just in time to witness another performance. And I'll show you why our friend the murderer not only didn't shoot, stab, asphyxiate, or hammer little Myra into Kingdom Come, but didn't hang her either!"

Ellery's watch, however, was dishonest. When they reached the Metropole it was noon, and the feature picture was still showing. They hurried backstage in search of Kelly.

"Kelly or this ole man they call Perk, the caretaker," Ellery murmured, hurrying his father down the dark side-aisle. "Just one question . . ."

A patrolman let them through. They found backstage deserted except for Brinkerhof and his new partner, who were stolidly rehearsing what was apparently a new trick. The trapeze was down and the big man was hanging from it by his powerful legs, a rubber bit in his mouth. Below him, twirling like a top, spun the tall blonde, the other end of the bit in her mouth.

Kelly appeared from somewhere and Ellery said: "Oh, Kelly. Are all the others in?"

Kelly was drunk again. He wobbled and said vaguely: "Oh, sure. Sure."

"Gather the clans in Myra's dressing-room. We've still a little time. Question's unnecessary, dad. I should have known without——"

The Inspector threw up his hands.

Kelly scratched his chin and staggered off. "Hey, Atlash," he called wearily. "Stop Atlash-ing an' come on." He swayed off toward the dressing-rooms.

"But, El," groaned the Inspector, "I don't understand——"

"It's perfectly childish in its simplicity," said Ellery, "now that I've seen what I suspected was the case. Come along, sire; don't crab the act."

When they were assembled in the dead woman's cubbyhole Ellery leaned against the dressing table, looked at the sprinkler pipe, and said: "One of you might as well own up . . . you see, I know who killed the little—er—lady."

"You know that?" said Brinkerhof hoarsely. "Who is——" He stopped and glared at the others, his stupid eyes roving.

But no one else said anything.

Ellery sighed. "Very well, then, you force me to wax eloquent, even reminiscent. Yesterday I posed the question: Why should Myra Brinkerhof have been hanged in preference to one of four handier methods? And I said, in demonstrating Mr. Gordi's innocence, that the reason was that hanging permitted the use of a rope and consequently of Gordi's identifiable knot." He brandished his forefinger. "But I forgot an additional possibility. If you find a woman with a rope around her neck who has died of strangulation, you assume it was the rope that strangled her. I completely overlooked the fact that hanging, in permitting use of a rope, also accomplishes the important objective of *concealing the neck*. But why should Myra's neck have been concealed? By a rope? Because a rope is not the only way of strangling a victim, because a victim can be *choked* to death by fingers, because choking to death leaves marks on the neck, and because the choker didn't want the police to know there *were* fingermarks on Myra's neck. He thought that the tight strands of the rope would not only conceal the fingermarks but would obliterate them as well—sheer ignorance, of course, since in death such marks are ineradicable. But that is what he thought, and that *primarily* is why he chose hanging for Myra when she was already dead. The leaving of Gordi's knot to implicate him was only a secondary reason for the selection of rope."

"But, El," cried the Inspector, "that's nutty. Suppose he did choke the woman to death. I can't see that he'd be incriminating himself by leaving fingermarks on her neck. You can't match fingermarks——"

"Quite true," drawled Ellery, "but you *can* observe that fingermarks are on the neck *the wrong way*. For these point, not upward, but downward."

And still no one said anything, and there was silence for a space in the room with the heavily breathing men.

"For you see, gentlemen," continued Ellery sharply, "when Myra was choked she was choked *upside down*. But how is this possible? Only if one of two conditions existed. Either at the time she was choked she was hanging head down above her murderer, or——"

Brinkerhof said stupidly: "*Ja.* I did it. *Ja.* I did it." He said it over and over, like a phonograph with its needle grooved.

A woman's voice from the amplifier said: "But I love you, darling, love you, love you, love you . . ."

Brinkerhof's eyes flamed and he took a short step toward the Great Gordi. "Yesterday I say to Myra: 'Myra, tonight we rehearse the new trick.' After the second show I see Myra undt that *schweinhund* kissing undt kissing behind the scenery. I hear them talk. They haf been fooling me. I plan. I will kill her. When we rehearse. So I kill her." He buried his face in his hands and began to sob without sound. It was horrible; and Gordi seemed trans-fixed with its horror.

And Brinkerhof muttered: "Then I see the marks on her throat. They are upside down. I know that iss bad. So I take the rope undt I cover up the marks. Then I hang her, with the *schwein's* knot, that she had once told me he had shown to her——"

He stopped. Gordi said hoarsely, "Good God. I didn't remember——"

"Take him away," said the Inspector in a small dry voice to the policeman at the door.

"It was all so clear," explained Ellery a little later, over coffee. "Either the woman was hanging head down above her murderer, or her murderer was hanging head down above the woman. One squeeze of those powerful paws . . ." He shivered. "It had to be an acrobat, you see. And when I remembered that Brinkerhof himself had said they had been rehearsing a new trick——" He stopped and smoked thoughtfully.

"Poor guy," muttered the Inspector. "He's not a bad sort, just dumb. Well, she got what was coming to her."

"Dear, dear," drawled Ellery. "Philosophy, Inspector? I'm really not interested in the moral aspects of crime. I'm more annoyed at this case than anything."

"Annoyed?" said the Inspector with a sniff. "You look mighty smug to me."

"Do I? But I really am. I'm annoyed at the shocking unimaginativeness of our newspaper friends."

"Well, well," said the Inspector with a sigh of resignation. "I'll bite. What's the gag?"

Ellery grinned. "Not one of the reporters who covered this case saw the perfectly obvious headline. You see, they forgot that one of the cast is named—of all things, dear God!—Gordi."

"Headline?" frowned the Inspector.

"Oh, lord. How could they have escaped casting me in the role of Alexander and calling this The Affair of the Gordian Knot?"

The big top is a home of glamour, mystery, humor, danger, and expertise. No wonder that magic has always had such an affinity with the sawdust strewn floors of these canvas playhouses.

Watch a circus performer fail in a difficult stunt, brace himself, attempt it again and fail again, only to succeed to a thunderous ovation on his third attempt. This is one of the many tricks of the trade that magical and circus performers share in common.

Siegfried and Roy, unquestionably the greatest contemporary magical entertainers in the world today, perform an act where they produce, vanish, change, and levitate not sequined girls but ferocious, snarling lions and tigers! This act provides a combination of carnival and theater that thrills audiences night after night.

9

Weird Tales magazine for September 1937 was an all-star issue. It had a lovely art-deco cover by Margaret Brundage, stories by Seabury Quinn, August Derleth, Clark Ashton Smith, and verse by H. P. Lovecraft and Henry Kuttner. It also contained the story "School for the Unspeakable" by Manly Wade Wellman. We read the story in 1947 and have been a fan of his ever since.

Manly Wade Wellman was born in Portuguese West Africa, came to America as a child, and traveled widely until he settled in North Carolina after the Second World War. He began writing full-time in the '30s, and his works include mystery novels, mainstream fiction, regional histories, science-fiction, and the fantastic and haunting tales of John, the wandering balladeer of the Southern Mountains. The stories of John were collected in one volume and published in 1963 by Arkham House under the title *Who Fears the Devil* and in 1973 Carcosa House published a collection of his best fantasy tales, *Worse Things Waiting*, which received the Best Book Award at the 1975 World Fantasy Convention.

"Murder Among Magicians" was published in the December 1939 issue of *Popular Detective*. The pulp magazines were in their heyday, and scores of them—and thousands of stories—were published every month. Most of them cost a dime, had a "damsel devoured by demon" on the cover and were filled with advertisements for kidney-flushing devices, mail-order detective schools, and sex-education books that were mailed to you in a plain brown wrapper. But always they were full of stories that were *fun* to read; that's the key. Heroes bigger than life, lovely ladies who were never allowed to be more than just lovely ladies, and arch-villains who were the epitome of everything evil and malignant.

Murder Among Magicians

by Manly Wade Wellman

Secutoris, foremost stage magician and escape artist of his day, flashed white teeth between spiky beard and spiky moustaches at his guests. Full-bodied, vigorous, ungrayed despite his fifty-odd years, in the flame-colored evening suit he affected, he dominated the living room of Magic Manor, his sea-girt miniature castle.

The five guests, four men and a woman, were magicians like himself—four of them the best in the profession after him. Three of the men wore formal black; the fourth wore tweeds. The slender woman wore a sheathlike low-cut evening frock of lemon silk.

"*If* there is a life after death, and *if* my spirit returns," Secutoris was continuing a discussion, "it will speak a word for you to recognize."

"What word?" asked Hugh Drexel.

Young Drexel was a newspaperman; not a professional magician. But his sleight-of-hand hobby had gained for him the job of ghostwriting Secutoris' memoirs, which in turn won the tall, light-haired, strong-featured young man the entree to such gatherings as this.

"I'll say the word 'free.' 'Free!'" Secutoris' sonorous voice tossed the word exultantly, and he added sardonically

"Of course, Wiggins here will sell the information to some skulking medium the day I die. It will be up to you others to expose him, if he does."

Few would have had the nerve so to gash the feelings of Arouj, finest fire-juggler in America, a hot-tempered, swarthy man who claimed Arab descent, though rumor had it that he was a New York waif, born Wiggins. He it was who had not bothered with formal attire.

"How many times," Arouj demanded shrilly, "have I asked you not to call me Wiggins?"

"Hundreds," Secutoris chuckled, unabashed. "Isn't it your name?"

"You changed your name for the stage, didn't you?" challenged Arouj. "What if I called you—Delivuk, isn't it?"

"I wouldn't mind in the least, Secutoris suavely assured. "Delivuk, is an honored name in my native Hungary."

A sudden puff of wind whined around the house, and then came the sound of big waves tugging at the rock in Bennington Harbor on which Magic Manor stood.

"That wind heralds a storm," commented old Roheim, in his cultured voice.

Skeleton-lean, bald, and grim as a mummy, Roheim always spoke with deliberation and precision. Some said that he had served his apprenticeship in magic under Robert-Houdin in France. His friendship with Secutoris brought more comment, however, for the black-bearded "Handcuff King" had married, then divorced Roheim's daughter, who had since died.

"If it should storm," said Secutoris, smiling hospitably, "you may all have to stay the night. It would not be safe to trust a launch on that sea in the dark."

"We'd crowd you," murmured Stefan Delivuk, Secutoris' half-brother.

Known professionally as Stephano, Delivuk was thin

and mousegray, and appeared shabby even in evening dress. A critic had once called him more skilful than Secutoris, though overshadowed by his brother's spectacular showmanship.

"We men could sleep anywhere, of course," he went on, "but Cassa——"

He smiled at the woman in the lemon gown, who smiled back at him and shook her head.

Cassa, as she was known professionally, had been born Zita Lewissohn. She was a gypsy beauty, with her cloud of storm-black hair. Hugh Drexel could not keep his eyes from her. Neither, it seemed, could Secutoris. Old Roheim's burning gaze sometimes rested on her, as well.

"I mustn't stay," she said quickly. "I must leave before it's late. Lend me the launch now, Secutoris."

Secutoris shrugged slightly.

"Oh, it may clear off—it's only the shank of the evening," he said. "Half an hour to witching midnight. Have a drink?"

He snapped his fingers toward a dark alcove. A fringe of tiny lights blazed up around the opening, and a figure materialized behind them—Roget, Secutoris' bald manservant, with a tray of cocktails. He stepped into the room amid applause.

"The old black-art gag," Arouj sniffed disdainfully, though he accepted a drink. "Lights to keep us from seeing in, and a panel drawn back to reveal Roget."

"Quite true," Secutoris acknowledged readily. "But here *is* a new one."

He took a deck of cards from a sideboard and quickly selected the kings and aces.

"Don't draw one," he said. "You'll say I forced it. Think of a card, Wiggins—only think."

Shuffling the eight cards, he laid them face down on the center table.

"Now touch four," he said.

Scornfully Arouj did so. Secutoris discarded the pasteboards he indicated.

"Now two more," urged Secutoris, and two cards were left. "One," he said next, and a third time removed the card Arouj touched.

A single pasteboard remained.

"What was your choice?" he asked.

"Ace of hearts," muttered Arouj.

Slowly and impressively, Secutoris turned the remaining card face up. It was the ace of hearts.

"Ten dollars for that trick," Stephano offered quickly.

"I wouldn't give a dime for it," sneered Arouj.

"Wiggins wouldn't give a dime to see the Supreme Court play marbles," observed Secutoris, chuckling, then shook his head at Stephano. "No sale, old boy. I've willed you all my effects—including my magic. Wait until I die."

"Stephano needs new tricks badly in his act," Drexel murmured to Cassa, "but Secutoris won't help, not even with that little ruffle."

"And he has been speaking of dying," she whispered back. "Why doesn't he do it?"

"You don't like him, do you?" said Drexel.

She shook her head.

"I quit his show because he got too—friendly. Now he's starting it again."

In her lovely dark eyes was scornful distaste.

Secutoris, blandly unconscious that he was the subject of discussion, was unlocking a closet door.

"Want to see my apparatus for next season's show?" he invited, and stepping inside, began to lift glittering paraphernalia from a shelf.

With a quick, taunting laugh, Arouj scuttled forward, and slammed the closet door, turning the key hurriedly. In his eyes gleamed impish delight.

"There, Secutoris!" he cried. "You are the escape artist—let's see you escape from that!"

Insistent rapping came from inside.

"Open up," called Secutoris in a muffled voice.

"No, *you* open it!" Arouj grimaced joyfully at the others.

"I'll make you sweat for this, Wiggins!" Secutoris promised balefully, thumping louder.

"Look here," interposed Stephano. "I've an interest in my brother's tricks. I don't want you others to see how he escapes."

"Should he escape," said Roheim.

"I'll escape, all right!" growled Secutoris from within.

"Suppose we give him ten minutes," said Roheim, in his carefully enunciated tones.

"Hear that, Secutoris?" crowed Arouj, taking the key from the lock. "You've got ten minutes to get out—if you can."

They went into the adjoining study and the little fire-juggler tossed the key on a desk. Interested mainly in their profession, shop talk was quickly under way again. They were deep in a discussion of illusions, audiences, triumphs—when abruptly the room was plunged into darkness.

"Every heavy sea jams those light wires," groaned Stephano. "Why did he build out here in mid-ocean, anyway?"

Groping toward the wall of the blackened study to the light switch, Drexel rammed the desk and his hand touched the key Arouj had laid down. For a moment he was tempted to creep noiselessly into the living room and free Secutoris, for a joke. But why help Secutoris, who was annoying Cassa? Drexel stepped back from the desk, pocketing the key. As good a joke one way as the other, he decided.

Behind Drexel someone clicked vainly at the switch. Voices were mumbling complaints about the darkness when at last a glow appeared, touching faces into strange live masks. Roget was entering with two candles in sticks.

"How long do you suppose the lights have been out?" Cassa asked at Drexel's elbow.

Roheim produced a watch, his hawklike profile bending close above it.

"I should judge that Secutoris has been locked in for at least fifteen minutes now," he pronounced weightily. He took a candlestick from Roget. "Where is the key?"

"I have it," responded Drexel, and Roget led the way into the living room.

The candle made strange shadows dance on wall and ceiling as the group clustered around the closet door. It was shut and locked, as they had last seen it.

"Give up, Secutoris?" called Arouj maliciously.

No answer came from inside the closet.

"He's probably out of there, lying in wait for you in the shadows," suggested Stephano.

Arouj looked hurriedly behind him, as the others all laughed. But there was a slight nervousness in the laughter.

"He's not in sight," said Drexel. "Let's open up."

He put the key in the lock, turned it—and like a great red bottle tumbling from a shelf Secutoris pitched out, thudded down on his face, and lay still . . .

When the harbor police boat arrived from Bennington, it stopped at the very front door, for the tide covered the rocks up to the foundations of Magic Manor. The occupants of the miniature castle, gathering at the entry, could barely make out the lights of the mainland, for a heavy rain fell, whipping the waves to a black snarl.

A giant figure emerged from the cockpit and strode in, water streaming from a huge slicker and a soaked felt hat.

"Grinstead—Homicide detail," the rain-soaked man introduced himself tersely. "Who owns this place?"

"It belonged to Secutoris, the magician," answered Stephano. "He's the dead man I telephoned the police about."

Grinstead doffed his wet hat and they got a better view of his wide mouth, heavy brows and broken nose.

"Any of his family here?" he asked crisply.

Roget turned and walked silently into the back of the house.

"I suppose I'm next of kin," Stephano volunteered. "I'm his half-brother."

Grinstead stalked into the candlelit parlor and lifted the sheet from the still form in the corner. He studied the distorted, bearded features, the purple weal around the throat, the rumpled red garments.

"Strangled," he grunted.

Drexel handed him a joined pair of metal rings that lay on the center table.

"These were leg irons from the display in his study," he explained. "Stuff he used in his act. One of them was clamped around his neck to choke him."

Grinstead snatched the irons.

"And you took them off?" he roared.

"Of course I took them off," Drexel said stoutly. "I tried to revive him—gave him artificial respiration."

"And everybody else pawed these irons, of course," the huge detective growled. "Covered 'em with prints. How do you expect me to catch the murderer?"

"Murderer?" echoed Cassa, shuddering. "He was—murdered?"

"Of course not, lady," Grinstead said witheringly. "This shackle just sneaked up all by itself and coiled lovingly around his neck."

Cassa's wide eyes were fearstricken.

"I thought perhaps suicide——" she began faintly.

"Not a chance." Kneeling ponderously, Grinstead touched the dead man's crown with his huge forefinger. "See that bruise? He couldn't have done it himself without diving headfirst onto something. No, somebody biffed him right on top of the head, then clamped the ring around his throat and let him choke."

He covered the body again.

"You, half-brother," he addressed Stephano. "Tell me about it."

As Stephano talked, the officer wrote hurriedly in a notebook. Then he made a heavy-footed tour of the castle, peering into all corners of the living room, the study, the kitchen-workshop, and the room where Secutoris and Roget sometimes slept. Finally he motioned Drexel into the study.

"I'll start with you," he announced gruffly.

The door closed, they sat down. Grinstead took the telephone from the desk and dialed a number.

"Murder, Chief," he said into the transmitter, when he got his call. "Won't be back till tomorrow. It's drowning weather."

He hung up and then turned to face Drexel.

"That half-brother said you were a newspaper reporter. What are you doing here?"

Drexel explained, and Grinstead nodded.

"So Secutoris was the Handcuff King?" he said at last. "Was this strangling shackle some kind of a phony?"

Drexel took it from the desk between them, studied it and shook his head.

"Hardly," he said. "Secutoris didn't need fake irons. The real ones just fell off of him when he wanted them to. He must have been completely knocked out, as you say, or he'd have shucked this one."

"How long does it take a magician to pick a lock?"

Drexel thought. "Two minutes and up, depending on how good he is. And Secutoris was the best, since the death of Houdini."

Grinstead digested the information.

"How long between the time the lights blinked out and the time the candles were brought in?" he asked then.

"About eight minutes," guessed Drexel.

"During which somebody unfastened the door, laid Secutoris out, put the iron to him, locked up again, and came back in here," Grinstead summed up. He pursed his wide, hard lips. "Could anybody besides Secutoris pick that lock, do the job, and unpick it again, in the dark, as quick as that?"

"I can't say."

Drexel did not volunteer the information that Cassa had once been Secutoris' stage assistant.

"Where did you get the key to unlock the closet?"

"Why, off this desk, where Arouj put it down," said Drexel.

Grinstead changed the subject.

"This Stephano, now. With his brother's tricks he'd be a big success instead of just getting by, eh?"

"He would."

Grinstead made notes in his book.

"You can go now," he said, and as he opened the door he called to Stephano: "Come in here, you, half-brother."

Drexel sat down beside Cassa as Stephano entered the study. Everyone tried not to look at the sheeted corpse in the corner, and faces were pale and strained in the candlelight. Bits of small talk trailed off awkwardly, with long silences between.

Finally Grinstead opened the door again.

"Give me the little guy who locked Secutoris in," he called, and Arouj got up and went forward.

More silence followed Arouj's departure.

"Have you seen my new cigarette-case illusion?" asked Roheim irrelevantly, and the others sighed with relief, thankful for any distraction from their gloom-ridden thoughts.

With one claw-hand the withered old magician drew a silver case from a side pocket, passing it around for examination.

"Will someone lend me a cigarette?" he asked calmly.

Cases or packages were proffered. Roheim accepted from Cassa a long, violet-tinted cigarette with gold lettering. He clipped the butt end between the two halves of the case, and touched the tip to the candle that stood on the table.

"Now puff," he ordered, and the cigarette case expelled a cloud of smoke. "Puff," he repeated, and again it obeyed.

"Clever," cried Stephano, forgetting his horror in his professional interest. "I'll give you five dollars for the trick."

"And I accept," Roheim said cordially. "I shall diagram the case for you, showing the secret bellows. But will you not have all the effects you need, better than this, since your brother has left his secrets to you?"

"Thunder, that's so!" said Stephano.

Drexel wondered if he had really forgotten that.

"Come in, Roheim," growled Grinstead as he released Arouj.

Fired by the old conjuror's example, Cassa took Roheim's place and entertained with legerdemain, and Arouj took his turn when Grinstead summoned her.

Idly, Drexel picked up the cigarette case Roheim had laid on the table. He studied it for a hint of its mechanism, then scrutinized the violet cigarette. It seemed as smart, exotic and distinctive as the girl herself. He tried a puff. The tobacco was subtly flavored with rose perfume.

Grinstead called in Roget, the manservant, last of all.

"Miss me?" asked the girl, trying to be cheerful as she sat down beside Drexel.

"Terribly." He squashed out the coal of the cigarette in an ash tray.

"Don't you like my fancy cigarettes?" she asked, then laughed. "To tell the truth, I don't, either. They're just swank."

Drexel caught Roheim's hostile sideward stare, and the sudden flash of enmity he saw startled him. Was Roheim jealous of him? Old men's love was sometimes fiercest, he knew, because most hopeless.

Again Grinstead emerged from the study, an envelope in his hand.

"Gather around," he commanded. "Here is Secutoris' will. Might as well read it now as wait for any lawyers. I've got to solve this case."

His voice was gruffly official as he seated himself at the candlelighted table. The two flickering flames of the candles made distorted figures on the walls, as though stealthy specters had also gathered.

"Roget got this out of the safe for me," Grinstead informed, displaying the envelope. On it was written:

IN THE EVENT OF MY DEATH, THE TERMS OF MY WILL, HEREIN ENCLOSED, ARE TO BE READ ALOUD TO MY HALF-BROTHER STEFAN DELIVUK, MY CONFIDENTIAL SERVANT AARON ROGET, AND MISS ZITA LEWISSOHN, WITH RESPONSIBLE WITNESSES ATTENDING.

"What's his will doing out in this sea-going coop?" put in Drexel.

"It's a copy, sir," volunteered Roget. "The original is, of course, with his New York attorneys."

Grinstead tore open the envelope and extracted a folded sheet of typewriting.

Drexel, settling in his chair beside the half-open closet door, happened to glance downward into the gloomy niche where Secutoris had met death. A pale speck on the floor caught his eye. He looked around quickly. The others were all listening as Grinstead read the will's formal opening. His hand reached down, his fingers clipped the object and brought it out.

It was the butt of a cigarette—gold-lettered, violet-tinted, rose-perfumed!

He dared not look at Cassa or the others. Grinstead was reading in a mechanical tone from the copy of the will:

"'All of my property, with the exception of specific bequests hereinafter mentioned, I bequeath to my half-brother Stefan, known professionally as Stephano; and in particular do I give him all apparatus used in my magical and escape illusions on the stage, with my sealed notebooks describing their use'."

Drexel still held the cigarette butt that Roheim had used in his cigarette case trick. Stealthily he compared it with the one he had found in the closet. They were identical, save that the one from the closet floor was flicked with raspberry lipstick—Cassa's.

She had smoked it, and it had been dropped in the closet where Secutoris had died. And Cassa knew many of Secutoris' lock-forcing tricks!

A chill wave swept over Drexel as he thrust the stubs into his coat pocket. He hardly heard Grinstead's voice rasping on until one phrase suddenly startled him.

"'I bequeath to Zita Lewissohn, professionally known as Cassa, my house Magic Manor located on a rock in the harbor of——'"

"Wait!" Stephano sharply interrupted. "Why, Cassa, should my brother leave you this place?"

"As if you had to ask that!" jeered Arouj.

"I resent that!" cried Cassa hotly, and Drexel started to get up from his chair.

"Take it easy, you people!" Grinstead bleakly overrode them. "Get this: 'To Aaron Roget I bequeath the sum of five hundred dollars, and should he make further claim against my estate, alleging kinship or other right, I direct that the enclosed sealed paper be opened and its contents made public. Should he agree to the terms of this, my will, then I direct that said paper be burned unopened."

"Where's the paper?" inquired Arouj officiously.

"Probably with the original will," said Grinstead. "We'll get hold of it later."

"No!" Roget had sprung to his feet. He was white as milk, all the way to the top of his bald skull. "I call everyone to witness that I accept the terms! Let the paper be burned."

"If I was you," said the detective, "I wouldn't try to hold anything out."

"I'll tell this much, then," chattered Roget breathlessly. "That sealed document concerns my birth. It's a secret, and Secutoris always could make me do whatever he wanted by threatening to tell." His voice rose hysterically. "My mother has suffered enough without——"

"That sounds like a murder motive," sniffed Stephano, and Roget, breaking off, glared at him.

"Let me make my own pinches," Grinstead snapped, folding the document. "Well, that's all the will. Anybody got anything to say?"

"I have," said Roheim, rising to his gaunt height. He leveled a skeleton forefinger at Drexel, his eyes glittering. "Search that man!"

Everybody whipped around to stare.

"I saw him pick up something from the closet floor and hide it in his pocket," accused the old man coldly. "Secutoris died in that closet, If Mr. Drexel found anything, he should produce it."

Drexel rose from his chair.

"You're dreaming," he protested lamely.

"If you found anything, turn it over," commanded Grinstead.

Drexel let the big detective probe in his pocket and bring out the two stubs. Roheim's eyes glittered.

"They are Cassa's," contributed Arouj, craning his thin neck to see.

Drexel made a feeble effort to defend his action.

"——well, I admire Cassa," he said, feeling foolish. "I wanted a souvenir——"

"I think he took that one from Roheim's case," Stephano informed Grinstead, pointing to one stub. "The other has lipstick on it. She must have been smoking it."

"Then she must have dropped it in the closet," Roheim charged austerely.

Cassa's cheeks were glowing.

"I did nothing of the sort!" she snapped. "I've been smoking all over the place, but I wasn't once near the closet. Only when Secutoris went in, and when he"—she faltered—"came out."

"You actually think she could overpower a strong man like Secutoris?" demanded Drexel loyally.

"He was stunned," reminded Grinstead. "She could have swung those irons hard enough to knock out Joe Louis." He peered into the closet. "Funny I didn't notice that butt in there."

"Why did my brother will this house to you?" Stephano again demanded of Cassa.

"He and I were friends once." Cassa sounded exasperated. "He wanted a quiet place where he could work out new effects, rest, and give a few parties. I helped him plan Magic Manor. As he was out of ready cash at the time, I lent him enough to start building. He couldn't pay me back at once—you know how money slipped through his fingers—so he put me in his will for protection."

"If you were his friend, why did you leave his act?" insisted Stephano, his eyes glaring.

"He——" Her voice stumbled, as if in confused rage at

the memory. "Well, he was always suggesting—he tried to force me to marry——"

"Don't insult my dead brother!" Stephano shouted furiously. He whirled toward Grinstead. "Why don't you put her under arrest?"

Drexel's last thread of restraint snapped. He bounded at Stephano, hurled his right fist to the chin. Cassa's accuser went reeling, then recovered and charged back. But he missed a swing, and floundered on his knees before a second smashing right from Drexel. As he rose, Grinstead sprang in, caught the two men by their collars like fighting terriers, held them, struggling at arm's length.

"Drexel's her accomplice," panted Stephano. "He was jealous——"

"You cheap grifter!" yelled Hugh Drexel. "You're hanging it on Cassa because she told the truth about your chiselling brother!"

"Bottle it!" roared Grinstead. With a sudden effort he shoved them in opposite directions. "Another outbreak like that, and I'll lick you both—and don't think I can't!"

He turned heavily to Cassa.

"Unless you can explain this cigarette business," he said flatly, "I'll have to hold you."

"Don't say a word, Cassa," counseled Drexel hurriedly. "Let a lawyer do all the talking for you. Grinstead, you feel sure that the closet door couldn't be opened without a key?"

"That's the way it looks." Grinstead nodded. "Why?"

"Well, I picked up the key as the lights went out. I never let go of it until it was in the lock again. If you have to arrest someone, arrest me!"

Drexel thought it over when Grinstead, weary after an hour of fruitless questioning, left him alone in the study. Sitting at the desk, he stared at the shelves of manacles and other apparatus, at the framed photographs of Houdini,

Harry Kellar and Bautier de Kolta, at the fluttering flame-point of the candle on the desk before him.

He had not admitted guilt, nor had he been too emphatic in protesting innocence. He would give Cassa some hours, at least, to marshal her defences before he set about clearing himself.

But how, he kept asking in his mind, could the door have been opened and Secutoris killed, save by someone who forced the lock quickly and blindly? There had been only one way to reach him.

Or was that true?

"Fool!" Drexel accused himself.

This was a magician's house. If Secutoris had designed it, undoubtedly it had been built like a glorified trick cabinet full of secret traps, masked exits, and the like. That shadowy nook where Roget had appeared with the cocktails should have been clue enough.

Drexel rose, lifted the candle, and approached the wall that divided the study from the living room.

It sounded solid to his tappings until he came to the rear of Secutoris' closet. There, of course, it rang hollow. Drexel examined the wall at that point, first closely, then from two paces' distance.

The wall paper, he saw, was arranged in vertical strips about forty-five inches wide. He resumed his tapping across the particular strip which backed the closet. The hollow ringing sound answered him all the way from edge to edge—no further, and no less far. He fingered the edges. The paper did not overlap the strips to left and right, but showed a hairline of clearance, like a black line drawn with ink.

Opening his penknife Drexel thrust its point into one of the hairlines. It entered to the depth of a quarter of an inch. Then he prodded the substance beneath the paper. It was not plaster but wallboard—wallboard that, in all probability, covered a wooden framework, designed to move in one piece.

Here, Drexel was satisfied, would be a back door to the closet. It was a device right out of a crime thriller. Only a conjuror would think of building it. Through it the murderer . . . But who was the murderer?

Cassa had helped design Magic Manor. She must know of this secret panel. But Drexel resolutely banished the thought. Roget knew, of course. Probably Stephano; perhaps Roheim. Arouj may have shared the secret, or may have guessed it as he, Drexel, had done.

He turned his attention to the panel again, searching in vain for a button, a projection that might house a spring, or a crack wide enough to pry into. The only marks were two irregular dark spots or stains, such as might come from the frequent pressure of naked, sweaty palms. They were just inside the two edges of the panel, at shoulder height. Drexel pressed upon them, but there was no movement.

The living room door opened and he pivoted to confront Grinstead and Roheim.

"What are you up to?" demanded the detective.

Drexel beckoned him eagerly. "Look, here's how the killer worked without a key! See how the panel is set in? Secutoris was going to come out this way. But someone knew and was waiting for him. Whoever it was biffed Secutoris, let him fall back against the front closet door, and then used the iron to choke him."

He spoke excitedly, forgetting that he was suspected of the very crime he outlined.

Grinstead bent close, stared and nodded.

"You know all about this family entrance, huh?" he commented very shrewdly, and Drexel's forgetfulness was banished.

"I know," he groaned in disgust. "I suppose I shot Lincoln, too."

Roheim laid a bony hand on the detective's huge shoulder.

"If Mr. Drexel knows, might not others?" he purred. "Let me try my plan."

"This old guy says he's a hypnotist," Grinstead explained to Drexel, "and says that anybody under his spell will tell the truth. Want to take a whack at it to show if you're innocent or not?"

"Certainly not," said Drexel disdainfully.

"Others have consented," Roheim said to the detective pointedly. "Allow me to begin with Cassa."

"Okay," mumbled the big man.

Drexel started to protest, then subsided, glaring silently at the angular shadows in the corners of the study. What foolishness had prompted Cassa to submit to hypnosis? What made Roheim so anxious to offer his assistance? Drexel could think of no answer.

In a few moments Cassa entered on the arm of Roheim. Her slow, mechanical movements and fixed expression showed that she was in a trance. At the heels of the pair came Grinstead, with Arouj and Stephano close behind.

"Cassa," murmured Roheim monotonously, "are you able to understand?"

"Yes," she whispered.

"Are you acquainted with this house?" droned the hypnotist.

"I helped to design it."

"You know the closet where Secutoris' body was found?"

"I know it."

"How many ways lead into that closet, Cassa?"

"Two," she replied, in a voice no louder than a sigh. "One visible—one hidden."

Someone gasped. Grinstead motioned for silence.

"You know the hidden way, Cassa?" was Roheim's next soft, insistent suggestion.

"Yes."

"Show us."

Slowly she faced the wall where the panel was, and walked haltingly toward it. Roheim kept pace with her. She put her slim hands upon the stained spots, and pushed upward. The panel rose like a window sash, vanishing into a recess above the level of the ceiling. The interior of the closet stood exposed.

Roheim snapped his twiglike fingers at Cassa's ear and whistled shrilly. She breathed deeply, as if waking. Then she stared into the black recess. She screamed and wilted to the floor, eyes closed and face as pallid as wax. Roheim pivoted triumphantly to face Grinstead.

"Well?" he smiled. "Is she not guilty?"

Drexel had sprung forward and was lifting Cassa. With her in his arms, he glared at the hypnotist.

"Still framing," he shot out, then laid Cassa on a divan.

Arouj caught a carafe of wine from a table and Drexel forced some between Cassa's lips. She moaned and stirred, then opened her eyes. Drexel turned to Roheim, his wrath exploding like a bomb.

"Your howl about cigarette stubs couldn't railroad her, so you put her into a trance," he accused. "Of course she fainted when she woke up looking into that dark closet! Any overwrought woman would. If you knew she'd tell the truth under hypnosis, why didn't you ask her outright if she killed Secutoris?"

He advanced menacingly. Roheim faced him, his old body tense but unafraid.

"You knew she'd clear herself," Drexel raged on, "and you can't afford that, Roheim. Because you killed Secutoris yourself!"

Roheim shook his head. "No," he said in slow, exact defiance.

Cassa sat up. "Look," she muttered weakly. "The body's gone."

Every eye sought the corner where the dead Secutoris had lain. Only a crumpled sheet remained.

"Free!" came a sudden, exultant cry. "Free!"

From the darkened back of the house strode a figure—robust, swaggering, clad in flame-colored evening clothes.

"May I come in? That's a good one, asking to come into my own living room."

Then they knew. It was Secutoris' voice coming from the lips of that flame-attired apparition. Teeth flashed between spiky mustache and spiky chin-tuft. Glowing eyes mocked.

Chilled, all who saw, shrank back before the apparition. Drexel caught Cassa's hand and held it tightly. Roheim began to mutter prayers.

"You wonder why I'm here," went on the voice of Secutoris. "You wonder, too, who killed me. No, one of you doesn't have to wonder. Won't that one confess—before I drag the story out?"

A pause. Nobody broke the silence. The brilliant eyes singled out Arouj.

"Don't you wish you hadn't locked me up, Wiggins? Your evening's been ruined, and you didn't humiliate me, after all. I've made the most spectacular escape of my career. But you wouldn't give a dime for this trick, either, would you, Wiggins?"

"Don't call me Wiggins!" wailed Arouj.

A quiet taunting chuckle mocked him. The pale, bearded face floated toward Drexel, who steadied his own gaze.

"Shaky?" inquired the voice of Secutoris. "Were you

really trying to help me with your artificial respiration? Or only—shall we say—stalling?"

"I did my best," Drexel forced himself to say through dry lips. "It wasn't much."

"No, it wasn't much." The eyes slid to Cassa. The voice was caressingly gentle. "Still afraid, my dear?"

"Never afraid of you, Secutoris." Cassa spoke bravely, but she gripped Hugh Drexel's hand with desperate strength. "Only repelled."

"Repelled?" He seemed to wish that she would unsay that. "Do you hold ill will against me?"

"Not against the dead," she replied, her voice steady.

A slow, sad smile revealed the teeth under the mustache. The brilliant eyes left Cassa and fastened upon Roheim.

"You're old," came the soft voice. "Are you ready to lay life down?"

"I did not kill you," said Roheim, tightly and defiantly.

"Why did you do your best to make Cassa seem guilty?"

Roheim made his stare meet that of Secutoris.

"I tried because—let me say it this way. My daughter died because you left her. Could I have any good will toward this other woman whom you wanted?" Pulses throbbed in the bony temples. "I tried to make her seem guilty by planting the cigarette butt, and by sending her, hypnotized, to reveal the secret of the closet." The old man's voice began to shake. "I—I hated her. I tried—to hurt her. But I did not kill you, I say."

Now the eyes were on Stephano.

"Brother, are you glad to have inherited my tricks?"

"N-no," mumbled Stephano wretchedly. "Not when——"

"Enough of this comedy."

Secutoris' voice lost its tone of mockery and took on a

steely hardness. The brilliant eyes swept commandingly over the group. As though assailed by a gust of icy wind, that group huddled closer. Secutoris brought his right hand from behind his back. It held two metal rings.

"These irons failed once tonight. They won't fail again."

One ring sprang open in his hand, gaping like a pair of lean, starved jaws.

"I know the killer, and the killer knows I know!" rang out Secutoris' voice. "That killer shall strangle—and shall not return from the dead!"

The very candle flame trembled, the shadows on wall and ceiling writhed.

"Now!" bawled the thing in flame-colored garments.

The hand lifted the yawning iron. Secutoris took a step forward. Another.

Then a scream tore the drum-taut air. Limbs struggled in the press of horrified bodies. Grinstead grunted in satisfaction, and shoved forward into the open. Writhing and fluttering in his grip was Arouj.

"No, no!" shrieked the frantic fire-juggler. "Don't give me to him!"

"Then you did it," accused Grinstead.

"I couldn't stand his insults!" Arouj twisted around, clawing the detective's coat. "Once he locked me in that closet for an hour, then let me out through the panel, laughing. He forgot—I remembered." His words gushed over each other in his hysteria. "After locking him in tonight, I knew he'd turn off the lights with a hidden switch inside. When he did, and came out into the room back of the panel I was waiting for him with a blackjack, and then I put the iron——"

He collapsed, half-fainting. Grinstead eased him into a chair.

"My job is over," said the man in flame-colored

clothes, in a new voice. He plucked away beard and mustache and lifted the bushy wig from his bald pate.

"Roget!" came the chorus.

"Right." Grinstead nodded. "He told me how he'd doubled for his master in escape tricks and such, with makeup, costume, and voice. So I got him to help. When he came at the bunch with that iron, I watched from behind. All of you were scared almost screwy—but only this little Arouj guy tried to run. And I grabbed him."

Everyone began to chatter and gesticulate. Everyone but Cassa and Drexel. They moved toward the front window, his arm around her shoulder, and saw that, as the dawn came, the storm was ceasing.

Perhaps Harry Houdini, in his desire to hear a special code word from beyond the grave, inspired Secutoris. Bessie Houdini, Harry's widow, waited six years to hear her mother-in-law's maiden name spoken by a spirit medium. She never did.

Magic Manor seemed to harbor a peculiar bunch of characters, but any gathering of magicians is a little frightening to a non-magically oriented onlooker. Just ask a hotel manager who has been host to a magicians' convention! Next time you see a lone figure swaddled in a strait-jacket, struggling bravely to free himself while suspended head down from a rope attached to your local Safeway Store, this is a sure sign that a magicians' meeting is in town. Avert your eyes, take a side street, and remember Secutoris—there might be a "Murder Among Magicians"!

10

The Golden Age of detective fiction dawned in the mid-twenties with the publication of Agatha Christie's tour de force *The Murder of Roger Ackroyd.* In America S. S. Van Dine, John Dickson Carr, and Ellery Queen began to bewilder readers with highly complex puzzle-plots, while in Great Britain Christie, Freeman Wills Crofts, Dorothy Sayers, and a young man by the name of Philip MacDonald did the same.

MacDonald was born in the early 1890s, served with a cavalry regiment in Mesopotamia during the First World War, and in 1924 introduced Colonel Anthony Gethryn, one of fiction's great detectives, in his classic novel *The Rasp.*

The Wraith, The Link, Murder Gone Mad, and *The Rynox Murder Mystery* followed and firmly established Gethryn as one of the most popular fictional detectives of the day alongside Hercule Poirot, Philo Vance, and Lord Peter Wimsey. In 1963 his novel *The List of Adrian Messenger* was filmed with George C. Scott in the role of Colonel Gethryn.

"The Green-and-Gold String" was the second prize winner in *Ellery Queen's Mystery Magazine's* Third Annual Contest and was the lead story in the October 1948 issue. It was the first recorded adventure of that magnificent charlatan and clairvoyant extraordinary, Dr. Alcazar, who is both deductive sleuth and debonair rogue.

The Green-and-Gold String

by Philip MacDonald

The banner hung over the entrance of a small, square tent of pitch-black canvas, which was sandwiched between a shooting gallery and the beflagged pitch of the Weight-Guesser. The banner read, "DOCTOR ALCAZAR, *Clairvoyant Extraordinary—What Does the Future Hold For YOU? General Reading—50¢. Special Delineation—$1.00.*"

All down the midway the lights blazed, and the evening air was heavy with the odd, distinctive odor which comes from the blending of humanity and peanuts, popcorn and circus. Over everything was wrapped a heavy veil of sound—laughter, shouts, the roaring of barkers, asthmatic music from the merry-go-rounds, the crack of firearms, shrieks from the Dodge-'Em and the Loop-a-Loop . . .

In the doorway of the small black tent, Doctor Alcazar—who had no right to the name and less to the title—was receiving his second client of the past twenty-four hours.

Doctor Alcazar was tall and graceful and lean. His face was of extraordinary pallor, his dark eyes large and lustrous and glowing. His black, well-tended hair, impressively gray at the temples, surmounted an Olympian brow and he wore, over evening clothes and a pleated shirt in whose faintly yellowish bosom sparkled an enormous ruby-red stud, a long black cloak which hung gracefully from his wide shoulders.

"Good evening, madame," said Doctor Alcazar in his rich and flexible voice. "You wish to consult me?"

He loomed over his visitor as he bowed, and his lustrous eyes took in every detail of her from head to foot.

Thirty-fiveish. Doesn't look American. Expensive suit, hardly worn. Too tight. Too short. Not hers.

The woman was very nervous. She twisted her bag around in her hands and looked up at Doctor Alcazar's face and then quickly away again.

She said, "Ow, well—maybe I do . . ."

Aha! British. Cockney. But lived some time in U. S.—hence "maybe" not "p'raps."

"Then step this way," said Doctor Alcazar, and having ushered his client into the tent, let fall the canvas doorway, upon the outside of which large white letters announced IN CONSULTATION.

It was dark inside the tent, which was hung with dusty black draperies, but a nimbus of soft, orange-colored light came from a lamp over the table and chairs which were the only furnishings.

Doctor Alcazar seated his client at one side of the table, placing her chair with courtly precision. Throwing back his cloak, he then took the other chair to face her.

"And now, madame," said Doctor Alcazar, "do you wish a General Reading? Or—as I myself would recommend in your case—a Special Delineation?"

His visitor's nervousness seemed to be increasing. She sat on the edge of her chair (which disturbed Doctor Alcazar) and said:

"Well, now, I couldn't hardly sye." Her homely face was drawn and puckered with indecision. "Y'see, sir, it's a private matter—and—and—" Words failed her, and her hands fluttered nervously—to her hat, to her hair, to the cheap brooch at the throat of the ultra-expensive but overtight blouse.

H'mm. Seamstress's fingers. "Sir." Possible housekeeper. More likely lady's maid.

"Madame," said Doctor Alcazar, "anything you tell me—anything I may discern about you—is in the highest degree confidential." He leaned forward, fixing his compelling gaze upon her. "May I first suggest that you relax, madame. Any undue tension or nervousness disturbs and obfuscates your aura."

An uncertain titter came from the woman. She said, "I know I'm all upset-like—but I'll try," and she sat back in her chair and rested her hands on the arms, leaving her purse on the table.

Doctor Alcazar was relieved. He said, "Excellent!" and then, "We will begin, please, by your giving me some personal possession to hold." He reached out a hand, palm uppermost. "It is a matter of attaining close contact with your psyche."

She said, "Ow, I see," and put both hands up to her throat, as if to unpin the cheap brooch.

This would never do—and Doctor Alcazar said smoothly, "Anything except personal jewelry, madame. Its intrinsically counteractive density tends to adumbrate the necessary metaphysic radiations."

"Ow—I see . . ." she said again, and picked her purse off the table, set it on her lap, and opened it.

She was in perfect position beneath the mirror which hung above her, so unobtrusively, in the drapery festooned from the tent top. Doctor Alcazar leaned back in his chair and through half-closed, mystic eyes saw the contents of the purse in the mirror as her fingers rummaged in it. There were, to his experienced gaze, several items of possible use among the usual feminine litter:

An open change purse from which protruded the end

of a long roll of stamps; half a candy bar with its wrappings carefully folded back; a crumpled, postmarked envelope addressed to Miss Lily Something-or-other-which-began-with-M; and a small, neatly-folded piece of violet-colored wrapping paper tied around with curious string of interwoven green-and-gold strands.

Doctor Alcazar's client picked out a compact and laid it in his still outstretched hand, and closed her bag.

Doctor Alcazar murmured, "Thank you . . . Thank you . . ." and as his long fingers caressed the small enameled case, he began to speak in a remote and vibrant monotone.

"You have," said Doctor Alcazar, "a most highly sensitized *anima,* and are therefore a sympathetic subject . . . You are named for a flower—yes, a *lily!* . . . You are a foreigner by birth, but have resided in this country for a considerable time . . . You have a generous, impulsive nature, but are somewhat handicapped by shyness . . . Your life is bound up with that of a person of wealth—I *think* a woman . . . A great deal of your time is taken up by the traditionally feminine occupation of sewing . . ."

As the General Reading proceeded, its effect upon Doctor Alcazar's client grew more and more marked, and when he reached the point at which he informed her that she had "a fondness for candy, a sweet tooth," she could contain her astonishment no longer.

"Well, I never!" she gasped.

Doctor Alcazar sat upright and fully opened his eyes. He said, "And that, madame, is the General Reading. . . . In the Special Delineation we can go deeper—much deeper. Do you wish to proceed?"

"Ow, *yes!*" said his client, and now Doctor Alcazar assumed a more expansive position, fixing his unusual gaze firmly upon her face.

"You are troubled about something," said Doctor

Alcazar. "A matter about which you would like to consult me."

"That's right," breathed his client.

"Then, madame," said Doctor Alcazar, "tell me your problem."

But he had wrought too well.

"Do I 'ave to?" asked his client. "Don't you *knaow* what it is?"

"Hell!" said Doctor Alcazar to himself. "A boomer!" Aloud he said, with noticeable coldness, "I regret that madame feels it necessary to test me further. However. . . ."

He put one hand to his brow—and watched the woman from its shadow—and thought.

Stamps. Paper and string.

He said, "I seem to see letters—correspondence. . . ."

No reaction.

He said, "—but then you are a great letter writer. Ah! There is something else—a piece of material, is it? No. It's paper—wrapping paper. And it's a strange color—almost violet. . . ."

Ah! On the nose!

He said, ". . . Strange—I have lost sight of this paper . . . Something else is taking its place . . . I can't quite distinguish it—but there are two colors, interwoven . . . Green-and-gold, green-and-gold. . . ."

"Coo-*er!*" breathed his client, and Doctor Alcazar noted that her astonishment was mixed with something else—something very much like fear.

"Now, madame!" Doctor Alcazar was stern. "You have had proof of my powers—and my time is limited. If you wish my advice, state your problem."

The woman, intensely nervous, was on the edge of her chair again, but now it didn't matter. She said:

"It's abaout my mistr—my sister. . . ." Her tongue

182 • Sleight of Crime

came out and moistened her lips. "It's abaout my sister—
and her 'usband . . . Y'see, sir, I've jest found aout 'e's
deceivin' 'er like, an' I'm the only person what knows." She
gathered impetus now she was fairly launched. "But the
funny thing is—an' it's why I don't rightly knaow what to
do—the funny thing is that what 'e's doin' to deceive 'er is
mykin' 'er 'appy . . . Naow, my problem, like you call it, is
did I oughter tell my sister? Or did I oughter leave well
alone. I'm fair bewildered-like, tryin' to think what to
do. . . ."

"You are entangled, madame," said Doctor Alcazar,
placing his elbows on the table and making an arch of his
hands, "in a most unusual psychotic web. . . ." His hands
slowly raised themselves and covered his eyes. His voice
became the throbbing monotone again.

"There are widely differentiated *Kamas* here," said the
monotone. "There are twisted skeins ahead . . . Two paths
before you . . . They are clouded . . . I see you taking
one—then the other . . . But what is this? At the end of
each path is the same figure, awaiting you . . . And in this
figure lies the solution . . . You need make no decision—
you may follow either path—for the result is the
same. . . ."

Doctor Alcazar took his hands from his eyes, sat back
in his chair, and rested the hands on its arms. It was a
decisive, final attitude, and hardly ever failed to denote the
end of a delineation.

But this client was unusual. She stared at Doctor
Alcazar, and her mouth began to tremble. She said, "Is
that *all*, sir?" and Doctor Alcazar, bowing in assent, rose to
his feet.

He stepped to the entrance of the tent and raised the
door flap. He cast a glance outside—and saw two possibilities and allowed them to see him.

His current client rose slowly from her chair as he

waited for her. She fumbled with her purse, pulling out a crumpled dollar bill. She said, "But couldn't you tell me what's going to '*appen*, sir? I mean each way-like. . . ."

There were tears in her eyes and somewhat to his surprise Doctor Alcazar felt faintly sorry for her. He relieved her of the bill and led her to the entrance to the tent.

"Madame," he said, "I could advise you more fully if you told me the truth, instead of pretending your dilemma concerned your sister." He checked interruption with an upraised hand. "No accurate reading of the future can be based upon falsehood. Why not return later for another consultation—after you have decided upon frankness?"

She continued to gaze up at him raptly, an excellent advertisement. She breathed, "Oh, thank you, sir! That's jest what I'll do!"

And then she said, "I'm sorry abaout not tellin' the truth, reely I am!" and hurried away, to be swallowed immediately in the crowd which jammed the midway more thickly than ever.

Doctor Alcazar looked after her. He wondered, idly, whether he would ever see her again.

He never did.

But three days later, and two hundred miles farther up the coast, he saw a picture of her.

It was a big photograph on the front page of the morning paper, and over it dark heavy letters spelled out MURDER VICTIM.

Doctor Alcazar raised his eyebrows and read:

BEVERLY HILLS MURDER
NEW DEVELOPMENT
Gloria Druce Offers $5,000
Reward for Capture of Slayer

Gloria Druce, former luminary of stage and screen and now Mrs. Clinton de Vries, today expressed dissatisfaction with police progress in investigating the brutal murder last Saturday night of her personal maid, Lily Morton.

"The murderer *must* be brought to justice!" Miss Druce declared. "Lily had been with me for years, ever since my first visit to London. She was more than a maid, she was my constant friend and companion . . ."

It was at this point in his reading that Doctor Alcazar's friend and luncheon host, the Weight-Guesser, jogged him in the ribs and said, "Wanna 'nother barker, Doc?"

Doctor Alcazar didn't look up, but he said, "Thanks Avvie," and devoured the remains on his plate and went on reading.

He came to an end several minutes later, and folded the paper and put it down on the counter by his coffee cup. He stared at it vacantly, then searched in the pocket of his checked sports shirt, found a crumpled cigarette, put it in his mouth—and forgot to light it.

The little man called Avvie could restrain himself no longer. He said, "What's eatin' you, Doc?" and reached out and picked up the paper and unfolded it. "Somep'n here?"

"Um-hmm!" said Doctor Alcazar. "To my ears, Avvie, has come a far-off, delightful crackling of moola. And," he added, "I mean moola."

"Huh?" Avvie's quick brown eyes scurried over the page. "This?" His finger pointed to "$5,000 Reward."

"Ye-es," said Doctor Alcazar. "Maybe. But it's a general scent I'm getting. . . ."

A frown wrinkled Avvie's small face, and he pointed to Lily Morton's picture. "Mean ya know who blotted this dame?"

"No," said Doctor Alcazar. "No, I don't. But—well, listen to me a minute. . . ."

They reached Los Angeles late that night and took up residence at the Hollyhock Motel. They had a working capital of eighty-two dollars and seventeen cents, seventy-five dollars of which had been supplied by Avvie and the balance by Doctor Alcazar.

They went to bed. They waked early, and made for Hollywood, where Avvie set out for the Public Library and the newspaper files, and Doctor Alcazar went about other business. . . .

By two in the afternoon they were on their way to Beverly Hills. They traveled in style this time—in a big, black, shiny, Cadillac sedan, the rental of which had grievously reduced their capital.

Avvie was driving, still in his nondescript gray suit, but with a dark-blue, shiny-visored cap surmounting his squirrel-like little face.

Doctor Alcazar sat in the back seat at regal ease, a credit to the Western Costume Company and a very different picture from the beslacked and sport-shirted figure of the early morning. Doctor Alcazar, to whose lean cheeks the interesting pallor seemed to have returned, wore a loose, dark, expensive-looking suit of faintly old-fashioned cut; around his neck, in place of collar and tie, an elaborate stock of black silk pinned with a single pearl-like stone. And his unfathomable eyes looked out at the world from beneath a wide-brimmed hat of deep-napped black felt, indescribably dashing.

The big car purred up and around the steep curves of Coldwater Canyon to Mulholland Drive, then swooped majestically down towards Beverly while the sun shone in a pleasant Californian manner and the laurel-covered hills gave way to lawns and trees and gardens.

Turning into the quiet magnificence of Fairbanks Drive, Avvie slowed the pace, and leaned out of the window. The house he was looking for was Number 347—but suddenly, opposite the neo-Spanish portico of Number 345, Doctor Alcazar leaned forward and tapped him on the shoulder.

"Hold it," said Doctor Alcazar.

"This ain't it," Avvie said. "Next one up."

"Stop, will you!" said Doctor Alcazar and then, when Avvie obediently pulled into the curb, "Those notes you made at the Library? Still got 'em on you?"

"Sure." Avvie produced a small black notebook and handed it over. "The address is first—then the dope on this Druce——"

"No, no," said Doctor Alcazar, flipping over the pages. "I want the newspaper stuff—finding the body—all that . . . Ah! Here it is . . ." He read rapidly, and then shook his head and looked at Avvie. He said, "I'm going to ask you once more. Are you *sure* there was nothing, anywhere, about what she had in her pocketbook?"

"Sure I'm sure!" Avvie was aggrieved. "All it said any place was it wasn't robbery because there was still dough in it."

Doctor Alcazar shrugged. "Okay," he said slowly. "Okay." And he gave the notebook back.

Avvie slid it into his pocket. He looked thoughtfully at Doctor Alcazar and said, "Jeez, you're a rum potato, Doc! . . . An' me—well, maybe I'm screwy; seventy-five smackers in the kitty—and I *still* don't know what's on the agenda!"

Doctor Alcazar smiled. "Neither do I, Avvie," he said. "At least, not yet. . . ."

Avvie shrugged, and drove on to the entrance of Number 347, and through big, wrought-iron gates, and up to the front of a large, white, opulently haphazard house.

Doctor Alcazar descended from the car, looked around him with lordly approval, and ascended the steps.

He pressed a bell and turned again to survey the gardens.

The door opened behind him, and he slowly revolved to impel the force of his presence upon a white-coated, vaguely European manservant.

"Mrs. de Vries?" said Doctor Alcazar, with Olympian glance. "Is she at home?" He produced a card, only slightly oversized, one side of which bore in blackest copperplate the two words *Doctor Alcazar.* He took a pen from his pocket and wrote upon the reverse side of the card, *Concerning Lily Morton.*

He handed the card to the servant. He said, "If you would give this to Mrs. de Vries . . ."

The man looked at the card, then at Doctor Alcazar again. "Will you come in, sir," he said, and held the big door wider and led Doctor Alcazar across a hallway and ushered him into a long pleasant room, with French windows which looked out upon a flower-framed terrace and a tree-framed pool. It was a charming room, and it exuded, tastefully, an aura of wealth which delighted Doctor Alcazar.

Left alone, he took it all in with a slow and comprehensive sweep of his eyes, and then, as the door opened again, turned to meet the woman who was coming towards him.

She was small and slim and straight, and in the slacks and shirt and sandals she was wearing, her body might have belonged to a girl. But the close-cut hair which lay in tight curls all over her small well-shaped head was iron-gray, and underneath it was a lined and impish little face which made no pretense of disguising what must have been its more than fifty years.

Doctor Alcazar bowed, and unobtrusively his eye swept over her.

H'mm. Friendly. Forceful. Intelligent. But difficult to start. Watch it.

Doctor Alcazar straightened. He said, "Miss Druce . . ." and caught himself. "I beg your pardon—Mrs. de Vries."

The elfin face split in an enormous, delightful smile which made the wrinkles happily part of it and seemed to bring a deeper shade of blue to the eyes.

"Don't apologize," she said. "Please!" Her voice was surprisingly deep, and ever so slightly husky. "I like to be reminded. In fact, I *love* it."

Doctor Alcazar smiled gravely. "It is hard to think of Gloria Druce by any other name. . . ."

The smile began to fade, and Doctor Alcazar became aware that the blue eyes were regarding him shrewdly.

Oh-oh! Not so good. How to start?How to start?

She said, "Thank you, Doctor. You wanted to see me about poor Lily?"

Doctor Alcazar inclined his head.

She said, "What is it, then?" and her tone was changing, not auspiciously. "If you know anything that would help them, you should really have gone direct to the police."

Bad. Try something. Anything. Maybe . . .

Doctor Alcazar raised a deprecatory hand. "No, no," he said. "Please, Miss Dr—Mrs. de Vries! I'm afraid I'm not here to give help—but to ask for it!"

Aha! Jackpot!

There was a quick softening of the blue gaze, and she said, "Oh—I'm sorry . . . But I'm afraid I don't understand. . . ."

"How could you?" said Doctor Alcazar. "And it is I who should apologize. For imposing on your kindness. . . ."

The big smile was completely friendly again as she waved him to a chair and perched herself on the arm of a settee and said, "Why not sit down and tell me all about it?"

"Thank you," said Doctor Alcazar. "Thank you." He folded his length into the chair and began.

"I should perhaps explain, Mrs. de Vries," said Doctor Alcazar, "that I am what is sometimes called a metaphysician—a sort of Professor of the Occult. . . ."

It was a fine story and confident now; he did every word of it justice. It gave his listener several firm impressions, and an extraordinary but (to her, at least) entirely believable history of the events which were supposed to have brought him here. The impressions were, first, that Doctor Alcazar was a genuine and expert prober into the *arcana*; second, that he was not now (and never had been) one to turn his gifts and knowledge to financial gain; third, that he himself was much moved and excited over the strange happenstance which had brought him here.

The story itself, freed from its bravura embellishments, ran thus:

Doctor Alcazar, while engaged on "a simple little experiment in behalf of a pupil," had received a "most unusual interruption to the *Kamic* stream." The crystal he had been using at the time had become, suddenly and disturbingly, a battleground between the images from the stream he had deliberately tapped and other images "from a stream unknown." The battle had been extraordinary, and had lasted for one crowded hour before the "outside, unknown, interrupting force" had been victorious. The images it projected were strong and persistent, and they summed up (really Doctor Alcazar must not waste more of Mrs. de Vries's time than he could help!) to the total picture of a woman in distress. A woman who was in dire danger, and seeking help. . . .

All that, ran the story, had been two weeks ago; to be precise, fifteen days. Eleven days before Lily Morton's death. Doctor Alcazar had made a full notation of the singular occurrence in his files and had then put the matter from his mind until yesterday when, at the home of friends in Del Monte, he had chanced to glance at the newspaper and had seen Lily Morton's photograph upon the front page. . . .

It was at this point that his listener interrupted Doctor Alcazar for the first time.

"And it was the same face!" she said, more in statement than question. "It was Lily's—Lily's image you'd seen in the crystal!"

Doctor Alcazar spread his hands. "That is the question, Miss Druce," he said, "which has brought me four hundred miles to see you." He paused. "My first impression, on seeing the picture, was that I had seen the same face as that in the crystal. But then"—he smiled a grave smile—"first impressions, after all, are often unreliable. And a true Metaphysician must be as sure of his facts as any Scientist. . . ."

Mrs. Clinton de Vries looked at Doctor Alcazar with wide blue eyes.

"This," she declared, "is *terribly* interesting! Absolutely fascinating!" Her gaze clouded, and a look of distress puckered the impish face. "Poor Lily!" She sighed, then gave her straight shoulders an impatient little shake and said briskly, "Well, then, Doctor, what you want are photographs of the poor girl." She stood up. "I'll go and——"

"Please!" Doctor Alcazar checked her. "What I would like to do—if you will permit me—is to recount to you, from my memory, a description of the face I saw in the crystal. Then, if I chance to hit upon some—ah—factor or factors known to you but not registered by the camera— well, then we shall be entitled to assume that it was indeed Lily Morton's *Kamic* stream which so astonishingly obtruded upon my own."

"Oh! . . . Oh, I see!" The blue eyes were concentrated, absorbed. "That's—wonderful! There couldn't be any mistake that way, could there? . . . Yes. Yes. Please do that, Doctor."

Doctor Alcazar covered his eyes with one graceful hand and said, slowly and in a dim, faraway sort of voice which was first cousin to the booming monotone so frequently heard in the small black tent:

"I saw in the crystal—a woman . . . Part of her form, but dimly. But I saw her features clearly. Clearly. . . ."

Drawing upon his memory, which was indeed prodigious, Doctor Alcazar gave a minute and detailed description, suitably intoned and punctuated for this semi-mystic occasion, of the homely English face he remembered staring at him across his table. When he had finished, he slowly lowered the hand from his eyes, shook his head slightly as if to clear it, and looked interrogatively at Mrs. Clinton de Vries.

She was staring at him, rapt and intent. She said, in a curiously low voice, "Lily! That's Lily! I think I was sure before you started, Doctor, but when you remembered things like the little mole under her ear, and the gold filling in that tooth . . ."

She didn't trouble to finish the sentence. She just went on staring at Doctor Alcazar.

Who now played the card—the dangerous, all-powerful or all-ruinous card—which he had suddenly realized was in his hand.

Doctor Alcazar slowly rose to his feet. He stood towering above the small woman, and bowed over her, and smiled his grave smile, and picked up his hat from the table where it lay.

"Miss Druce," he said simply, "you have set my mind at rest."

He said, "I cannot thank you enough for having so graciously given me your time." He bowed again. She rose slowly, but he pretended not to notice she was rising. He was already turning away, already crossing towards the door with long deliberate strides.

It was an unpleasant moment. It was a series of unpleasant moments.

His hand was actually on the door latch before she spoke.

She said, from somewhere much closer behind him than he had thought her to be, "Oh, Doctor . . ."

He turned, his hand still on the latch, and waited with stately courtesy.

She came nearer. She tilted the gray head to one side, looked up at him and said, "Doctor, will you be—what will you—I mean, aren't you going to try and find out more?"

Aha! The winner and still champion. . . .

Doctor Alcazar permitted a slightly puzzled expression to show upon his face.

He said, "'Find out?' . . . I'm afraid I don't quite follow, Mrs. de Vries."

She said, "What I really mean——" and broke off and went on looking up at Doctor Alcazar, smiling her enormous smile again.

"Now, you give *me* some time," she said. "Come back and sit down, please."

Doctor Alcazar did as he was bidden. He chose a chair nearer the French windows, and his hostess leaned against the edge of the desk nearby and looked down at him.

"Now look," she said with a sort of bright-eyed bluntness, "although I've always *wanted* to believe what Hamlet said to Horatio was right, I've met so many phoneys in my time I haven't had a chance. . . ."

She came away from the desk and crossed to Doctor Alcazar's chair. There was a tremendous earnestness about her. "They're always trying to chisel," she said. "And they never *prove* anything! . . . But you've done something in ten minutes none of them ever did—you've convinced me!"

"I am honored," murmured Doctor Alcazar.

"And I've had an idea," she said. She put her hands in her pockets and hunched her shoulders and began to pace up and down, an oddly graceful little goblin.

"Suppose," she said. "Suppose you deliberately worked at—what would you call it—*getting in touch* with Lily again! And suppose you succeeded! . . . Don't you think it's possible you might be able to find out who killed her?"

"H'mm . . ." Doctor Alcazar pondered this apparently startling question. He said, "But surely the police——"

"*Pah!*" said Gloria Druce. "They haven't got anywhere—and they never will!" She sighed. "I don't suppose we can blame them really, though. God knows this must be outside their ken! I tell you, Doctor, that poor girl didn't have an enemy in the world. Her whole life's been wrapped up in mine ever since I first employed her in London umpteen years ago. That may sound conceited, but it's true."

She stopped again, abruptly, and fixed Doctor Alcazar with a penetrating eye. She said, "Well—will you try?"

Doctor Alcazar's long white hand rubbed reflectively at his long white jaw. He said slowly, after due interval:

"It's an interesting idea, Miss Druce. . . ." He permitted a twinkle to come into the dark eyes. "In its way, too, it's a sort of challenge. . . ." He thought some more. "But I think I should warn you—it is most unlikely to succeed."

"But you'll *try!*" She beamed at him and then said briskly, "Wonderful! When do we start? And where?"

Doctor Alcazar smiled up at her from the depths of the chair. "We-ell," he said, "before I could even attempt to get in touch, I should require some—some personal belonging, constantly used, of the unfortunate Miss Morton's. Some——"

"*I* know." She couldn't wait for him to finish his sentence. "And all her things are upstairs. What would you like?"

Doctor Alcazar was still reflective. He said, "Something she used recently—the more recently the better. . . ."

"That's easy! I've got everything she had when—when it happened. The police sent them back because there weren't any fingerprints or anything."

"Oh—really?" Doctor Alcazar sternly repressed eagerness. "Would her purse—her handbag—be among these effects?"

The pretty gray head nodded vigorously. "With everything in it—even her money, poor girl."

"Then," said Doctor Alcazar, "if I could have something out of it . . . Anything. . . ." And then he said, as if in afterthought, "No, no. Perhaps it would be better if I could have the bag itself. . . ."

She said, "Of course you can!" and made a movement towards a bell-push, and then thought better of it and ran to the door like a girl, throwing, "Back in a minute," over her shoulder.

It was, actually, only fifty seconds before she was back, holding out to Doctor Alcazar, as he rose to meet her, a purse of imitation crocodile—a purse which he remembered.

He took it in his hands and said, "Thank you . . . thank you. . . ." His eyes closed, he turned it over and over, his long fingers seeming to sense its texture.

He shook his head. He murmured, "No—no . . ." and opened his eyes. He said, "You permit me . . . ?" and crossed to the desk and opened the bag and gently tipped its contents out onto the blotter.

He stood staring down at the heterogeneous litter and

picked out with his eye, first the candy bar, a good bite or two smaller than when he had last seen it; next the change purse, still with the roll of stamps projecting from it; next the envelope addressed (he could see now) to Miss Lily Morton. . . .

String and paper gone. As expected. As hoped. Something to work on. Get busy.

Doctor Alcazar picked out the small enameled compact. He said, "This might do very well," in a low, murmuring voice, and stood upright with the little case in his hand, his fingers moving constantly over its smooth surface. His remarkable eyes were closed, and his striking head flung back.

He came to, as it were. He opened his eyes, and he looked down at the compact in his hand. He said, "Yes . . . Yes . . . With your permission, Mrs. de Vries, I will take this with me," and slid it into a side pocket of his coat.

She said, "Oh! Aren't you going to stay and—No. You'll have to have your crystal, of course."

Her face had fallen like a disappointed child's—which made matters even simpler than Doctor Alcazar had expected.

"I will indeed," said Doctor Alcazar, with one of his gravest smiles. "However, I happen to have it in my car; so I could, if you really wish, make preliminary studies here and now."

"Oh—*wonderful!*" She was alight again. "I'll ring for Josef; he can get it at once."

Doctor Alcazar raised a gently protesting hand. "If you don't mind," he said, "I will go myself. I don't allow anyone else to handle it—even my own man. . . ." With a little bow he strode to the door, and opened it, and passed out of the room.

He crossed the hall and opened the big door and went

quickly down the steps towards the Cadillac. He called, "Dupois! Dupois!"—and Avvie jumped out of the driver's seat, and said, "Yes sir?"

Doctor Alcazar came up to the car and while Avvie held the door, leaned in and fumbled with the glove compartment.

Doctor Alcazar said softly, out of the side of his mobile mouth, "I'll see you get inside. I want dope on Clinton," and then straightened and stood away from the car, holding something wrapped in a chamois-leather bag.

He returned to the house. As he stepped into the hallway, he saw the man servant entering the long room with a tray upon which were glasses and decanters. He quickened his pace a little and went into the room as the man was setting down the tray on a table near the windows overlooking the drive.

His hostess came to meet Doctor Alcazar. "Suppose we have a drink?" she said.

"That," said Doctor Alcazar, "would be delightful." And then he added, with graceful hesitance, "I wonder whether I might impose still more on your kindness, Miss Druce? On behalf of my chauffeur. He has been driving all day, and——"

"But of *course!*" She turned quickly and said, "Josef, will you see that Doctor Alcazar's man has anything he wants?"

"Yes, madame," Josef said, and very soon was seen through the window by Doctor Alcazar, leading Avvie away around the corner of the house.

Much gratified with the course of events, Doctor Alcazar, having handed his hostess her glass, took a big and grateful draught from his own. . . .

It was nearly an hour later when he pushed his chair back from the desk, sighed wearily, and peered at Gloria de

Vries through the bluish dusk they had produced in the room by lowering all the blinds and pulling all the curtains.

In front of him on the desk, glittering softly in the light of the single lamp, was the small crystal globe which the chamois leather had covered. He drew a hand wearily across his brow. He said, "There's nothing—nothing. . . ."

He opened his other hand and laid down Lily Morton's compact. He said, "I am wasting your time, my dear lady . . . wasting your time. . . ."

She said, in a kind of vehement whisper, "Oh, don't give up yet! Please don't!"

"As you wish," said Doctor Alcazar bravely. He turned in his chair, picked up the compact in his left hand, shaded his eyes with his right hand, and hunched once more over the glittering ball of the crystal. . . .

And once more there was silence. . . .

But not for long this time. Suddenly, Doctor Alcazar's whole body seemed to grow tense and he said, in a hushed yet urgent voice:

"Ah! Here is something! . . . The crystal is clouding. . . ."

His left hand, gripping the dead woman's compact, raised itself from the table, seemed to hover close to his temple. He said:

"Ah! The mists are clearing . . . I see—is it a figure, a woman's figure? I cannot be sure . . . No—it is gone . . . All I see is—a big post standing in the ground. There is something coiling around the post—a serpent, is it? . . . No. It is something *being* coiled around the post, by unseen hands . . . Ah! It is a rope—a strange rope—oddly colored—with interwoven strands of green-and-gold. . . ."

No reaction. But keep on trying.

". . . The mists are clearing, clearing . . . The colors of the rope are vivid, very vivid . . . There is a strange light over everything . . . The post itself is colored—a peculiar, almost violet shade . . . The contrast between the violet of the post and the green-and-gold of the rope is striking. . . ."

A small, quickly stifled "Oh!" of astonishment came from the shadows to Doctor Alcazar's left. He bent lower over the crystal.

"The image is growing brighter. The mists have gone . . . But still I see only the rope and the post . . . Wait—wait! There is something strange about the post. It doesn't look like timber at all now. It looks—it looks—But I cannot see—the light is fading. The mists are closing in again. . . ."

Doctor Alcazar sat back in his chair, his shoulders sagging. He shook his head as if in defeat, and gently laid Lily Morton's compact down upon the desk again. He turned slowly in his chair and looked at his audience.

"I am sorry," he said wearily. "The image has faded. . . ." He smiled sadly. "But I feel impelled to tell you, Mrs. de Vries, that I think we were being—misled, shall I say?"

"Misled?" The small woman was staring at Doctor Alcazar with extraordinary intentness. "Because what you saw wasn't anything to do with Lily?"

"Exactly." Doctor Alcazar sighed again.

She jumped to her feet and came close to him. She said, "It was wonderful, all the same! It wasn't about Lily—but it *was* about me!"

Doctor Alcazar frowned. "I'm afraid I don't understand."

She said, "Wait!" and went quickly across to a corner and flipped on another light, bent down and opened a cupboard beneath a bookshelf, and took something from it, which she held behind her back as she marched towards him again.

"Look!" she said, and whipped her hand from behind

her and held under Doctor Alcazar's eyes a roll made up of
many sheets, obviously smoothed out after use, of violet-
colored wrapping paper tied around with multiple windings
of green-and-gold string.

Doctor Alcazar sat straight in his chair. He took the
roll of paper from her with a murmured, "Permit me," and
held it under the light of the desk lamp where he studied it
with wondering concentration.

"Don't you *see*?" she said. "The paper's your post—and
the string's the rope! Violet—and green-and-gold!"

Doctor Alcazar said, "Yes . . . Yes . . ." and looked at
her. He said, "Your psychic projection must be strong—
enormously strong!" He eyed the paper and string again.
"Has this any particular significance, Mrs. de Vries? Any—
emotional meaning?" He reached out and switched on the
other desk lamp, so that he could see her face.

An odd change came over it. She smiled—but it was a
different sort of smile. A shy smile, like the smile of an
embarrassed girl. She said, "Well—yes, I suppose it has. In
a way. . . ." And then she said, "I'm going to tell you all
about it. It's nothing to do with poor Lily—but it's so
amazing, so extraordinary the way it—it sort of popped
in! . . . It's all to do with George."

"George?" said Doctor Alcazar. "That is your husband's name—middle name?"

"No, no! George is—an old admirer of mine. Of Gloria
Druce's—not Gloria de Vries's. . . ."

Doctor Alcazar smiled—and waited.

"But—I've never seen him! I don't even know his
name. 'George' is just what I call him." She took the roll
from Doctor Alcazar's hand. "This paper and string is what
he always wraps my presents in. . . . It's really quite
romantic—that's all I get from him, gifts. There's no note
with them, ever; no address; nothing! Except in the very
first one—that was about two years ago—there was an old

program for *The Green and the Gold,* with a picture of me on the front when I first played it in New York. . . . That's how I knew he was an admirer. . . ."

She looked at Doctor Alcazar and her smile faded, and she said, almost somberly, "You don't know how much it means to an old actress, Doctor, when someone remembers. . . ."

"Yes," said Doctor Alcazar. "Yes. . . ." He said, "What sort of gifts does he send you?"

"Oh. . . ." She made a little gesture. "All sorts. Books—and perfume—and odd little knickknacks— everything! And they're always delightful!"

"No candy?" said Doctor Alcazar, smiling a smile which, in the circumstances, cost him effort to produce.

"Oh, *yes!* Every third or fourth package. Heavenly liqueur chocolates!" She put the paper down on the desk again and said, in quite a different voice, "But all this is keeping us from poor Lily. . . ."

Doctor Alcazar rose to his feet. He said, "I'm afraid, Mrs. de Vries, that it would be useless just now." He picked Lily Morton's compact from the table. "But I will take this, if I may—and resume my efforts tonight, alone. . . ."

In spite of his hostess's disappointment, he took his leave. He had to.

Doctor Alcazar had detected still more death in the air—and he wanted to think. . . .

It was five-thirty when the Cadillac rolled out of the imposing gates and onto Fairbanks Drive.

At five-thirty-five, in obedience to directions from Doctor Alcazar, it pulled up only two blocks away, at the far end of a road which petered out in unexpected trees and heath land.

Doctor Alcazar got out of the car, and so did Avvie who looked around him and said, "Where's this—and what gives?"

"And you're the one who reads the papers," said Doctor Alcazar. He took Avvie by the shoulder and pointed to illustrate his words. "*That* is the back fence of the de Vries property. This road, *here*, is part of the short cut Lily Morton took from Sunset Boulevard the night she was killed. *This* vacant lot, between us and the de Vrieses', is the rest of the short cut. And *that* tree"—he pointed to a lone, tall, twisted eucalyptus—"marks the spot where she was killed! . . . Now clam up—and let me alone."

Doctor Alcazar then strode away from Avvie and the car. His eyes turning this way and that, he walked all around the little strip of barren earth—and then, making his way to the tree, stood underneath it, looking up as if he were studying its branches.

And then he came back to the car. He got into it and said, "Okay," to Avvie and leaned back on the cushions.

"That's great!" Avvie turned to regard him sourly. "Where to now—the morgue?"

Doctor Alcazar seemed deep in thought. He said vaguely, "No—to eat. There used to be a little place on Pisanta Street. Mexican. Good. Very reasonable. . . ."

The little place was still there and an hour later Avvie finished his last tortilla, refilled his coffee cup, and leaned back in his chair.

"Well, Doc," he said, "when d'ya start talkin'?"

Doctor Alcazar lit a cigarette. He said, "After *you* have," and grinned at Avvie. "So—what gives with Clinton de Vries, Esquire?"

Avvie said, "Gotta lotta stuff—but I don't know if it helps. Clint's around forty—forty-five. From a picture I seen, he goes around a hundred an' sixty-two. Bin married to the dame around five years. Makes like a playboy some—but a right guy by the general concentrus. Him and the missus rub along okay, but no heartthrobs: he's got the polo horses, she's got the dough."

Avvie picked up a fork and began to probe at a

hindmost molar. But he put the fork down almost at once and looked at Doctor Alcazar again.

"Somep'n I forgot," he said. "The guy's got the varicose vein in his leg. Wears one o' them rubber socks. I seen a spare on the line an' ast about it." He began to ply the fork again. "For what it's worth," he mumbled.

Doctor Alcazar regarded him with almost avuncular pride. He said, "Avvie, you did a very nice job in the time. But," he added, "I must ask you one or two questions."

Avvie finished with the fork and set it down. He said, "Hold it, hold it—I ain't through yet. Now, as to said Clint's recent movements: he's got a cabin up to Big Bear. Went up there the morninga the day this Lily got blotted. The missus called him when they found her next day an' he come right down to help. It eventuates there's nothin' he can do—so he goes right back. Comin' home tomorra, time for dinner."

Avvie had finished now. He leaned over the table and took a cigarette from Doctor Alcazar's pack, lit it, and said through smoke:

"*Now* make with the questions."

"Avvie," said Doctor Alcazar, "I don't have a one! You've really covered the ground. But covered it!"

Avvie smiled, a trifle grimly. "It's your turn, brother," he said.

Doctor Alcazar had been smiling, but now his face was set and somber. He said, "We came down here to try and horn in on a five grand reward for finding who killed Lily Morton. . . ."

He said, "Well, I've found that out. But I've found out some more too. The same guy's going to kill somebody else. He didn't want to kill Lily Morton. But he had to. Because Lily Morton had tumbled onto something which might have stopped him getting away with the murder he was really trying for. . . ."

He said, "This guy's been working on this other woman for a couple of years—sending her presents. She doesn't think they come from him; she thinks they come from somebody who used to have a yen for her when she was ace-high on Broadway. . . ."

He said, "The guy's *established* the present-sender. The woman's even made up a name for him. She feels quite safe with anything 'George' sends her—especially candy! . . ."

He said, "But some day, Avvie, she won't be safe with that candy. Some day that candy'll be the death of her. . . ."

Doctor Alcazar paused and Avvie looked at him and said, "Aw! Quit talkin' in riddles, will ya! So the dame's the de Vries dame——"

"And," said Doctor Alcazar, "the guy's the de Vries guy!"

Avvie stared. Avvie shook his head. "Couldn'ta been," Avvie said. "He was up to Big Bear like I told you."

Doctor Alcazar regarded him with displeasure. "He couldn't have been. Because he was around that vacant lot at night, killing Lily Morton. It's easy. He starts in the morning—and then stashes his car—and lies low—and when it's dark hangs around that dead end and waits for Lily. *He* knows the way she always comes in. And after he's killed her, off he goes to the mountains, and wakes up in Big Bear in the morning."

Avvie wriggled in his chair. "How come you're so sure a yourself?" His lip curled. "Get it outa the crystal, did ya?"

"I got it," said Doctor Alcazar, "from Lily Morton herself. About two hours, I figure, *before* she was killed." He stubbed out his cigarette, and lit another.

Avvie stared at him. "How's that again?" he said.

Doctor Alcazar said, "Lily Morton wanted some advice, Avvie. She knew a woman—" now a very fair replica of the dead woman's voice came from his mouth—" 'whose 'usband was deceivin' 'er like—on'y what 'e was doin' to deceive 'er was mykin' 'er 'appy' . . . And Lily Morton was the 'on'y person what knew' . . . And Lily Morton was 'fair bewildered-like tryin' to think what she oughter do'—tell the woman, or leave well alone. . . ."

Doctor Alcazar said, "She tried to tell me the woman was her sister—but she slipped up at the beginning and started to say 'my mistress,' which is what maids in England call the women they work for."

He paused, and Avvie said, "Doc, you're reachin'!" and shook his head.

Doctor Alcazar frowned. He said, "No. Listen to this: in her purse, Lily Morton had a peculiar piece of violet-colored wrapping paper—new—tied up with a bit of peculiar string, green-and-gold. I sprung this on her—and her reaction was worried, maybe frightened. Now, what do I find this afternoon, with Druce? I work on the paper and string because it's the only real lead I've got—and pretty soon I get the whole story of 'George,' because this peculiar paper and string is the same as the kind he always uses on the presents. . . ."

He said, "And that's not all. I found out the paper and string were the only things missing from Lily's purse when they found her!"

Avvie wasn't scornful any more. "Goes somep'n like this, huh? 'George' must be Clint; when Lily found out he was, Clint blotted her. Which means he must be gonna use 'George' to blot the missus—else he wouldn'ta gone to them lengths."

He looked at Doctor Alcazar, his small brown eyes bright like a bird's.

Doctor Alcazar beamed. "Terse," he said. "And concise. And absolutely right. You've got a grasp, Avvie—definitely a grasp."

Avvie drank some coffee in silence. Then he said, "Trouble is, you got nothin' to pin on Clint. This Lily knew he was 'George'——but *she* ain't talkin'! You got no *proof!*"

"Avvie," said Doctor Alcazar, "you get better and better."

"And from where I sit," said Avvie, "we're looking worse an' worse." He put a hand in his pocket and pulled out silver and some crumpled bills, looked at them, and shook his head.

"Lay off," said Doctor Alcazar reprovingly. "What are you getting at? We couldn't quit if we wanted to. In the first place, there's the paramount question of cabbage. We're surrounded by it, my boy—and we have to pick some. . . . And what about the little Druce? You know, there's something about her, Avvie."

"So whatta we do?" Avvie was belligerent. "Pick us a park bench and sit around gettin' corns; waitin' for 'George' to make up his mind it's time to send the old lady a strychnine-flavored Popsicle!"

"No," said Doctor Alcazar slowly. "No. That's not my idea at all. . . ."

Whatever this idea may have been, it worked so well in its preliminary stages (which were conducted by telephone the next afternoon) that within twenty-four hours Doctor Alcazar was dining at Number 347 Fairbanks Drive, the only guest of Mr. and Mrs. Clinton de Vries.

Mrs. de Vries, who had no idea she had been jockeyed into the position, was plainly delighted to be Doctor Alcazar's hostess again. And Mr. de Vries, though he made no secret of the fact that he was skeptical of his wife's attempt to "trail a killer with spooks," was nevertheless a bland and genial host who, despite the fact that he seemed himself a trifle on the jumpy side, obviously did his charming best to put his visitor at ease.

Mr. de Vries was much younger seeming than his

forty-odd years. He had a fine figure, excellent clothes, a pleasing and forthright manner—and a Rhodes scholar's charming, amorphic accent. He had drunk, with no visible effect, an astonishing quantity of martinis before dinner, and at the meal was constantly having his wineglass refilled. Towards his wife his manner was courteous and comradely—and (thought Doctor Alcazar) rather carefully rehearsed.

Dinner was nearly over before Mrs. de Vries said, suddenly and with emphasis, "I can't stand all this *chattery!* I want to talk about Lily!" She looked across the table at her husband. "Clinton, I can't help it if you think it's silly: all I ask is that you don't try and be *funny!* " She looked at Doctor Alcazar. "Doctor," she said, "I can't wait any longer. You sounded so excited on the phone, I have to know what's happened!"

Doctor Alcazar smiled blandly at her and then glanced at his host.

"Perhaps Mr. de Vries," began Doctor Alcazar, and was stopped by a snort from his hostess.

"If Clinton doesn't like it," she said, "he can go talk to a horse!" She smiled her wide smile suddenly at her husband. "Sorry, Clint," she said. "But I did sort of mean it. . . ."

"My dear Gloria," said Mr. de Vries, "go ahead. Talk about anything you like. Do anything you like." He smiled at Doctor Alcazar—the merest trifle too friendly a smile. He said, "*You* understand, Doctor, I'm sure." He raised his glass to his mouth but went on looking at Doctor Alcazar over its rim—the merest trifle too steadily. "You've met plenty of skeptics in your time, I'm sure." He laughed—the merest trifle too loudly.

Doctor Alcazar laughed too—a rich and muted and mellow laugh. He said, "Mr. de Vries, skeptics are—if I may be permitted the phrase—just my meat. . . ."

He raised his own glass and sipped at it, studying Mr. de Vries.

Nervous. Might be really scared. Hopes I'm a phoney but isn't sure. Keep at him.

"May I ask," said Doctor Alcazar, looking at his hostess, "how much you have told Mr. de Vries of our experiment?"

"As much as he'd listen to. About you seeing Lily—and describing her; and then about the paper and string. . . ."

"Ah!" said Doctor Alcazar. "That string! That green-and-gold string!" He looked at Clinton de Vries, as if waiting his opinion.

De Vries hesitated. He played with his wineglass. He said, "Yes—very int'resting. Very int'resting. But . . ." He didn't go on.

He doesn't like it. Keep close, keep punching.

"Indeed, yes," said Doctor Alcazar. "*Very* interesting!" His voice had taken on a subtle shade of mysticism, and the eyes he turned on Mrs. de Vries wore the far-off look of a visionary. He said:

"You say I seemed excited when I telephoned you. I was. I had been at work on our problem and I had seen"—he paused, most effectively—"the most extraordinary thing! I had seen—perhaps to you I should say *sensed*—I had sensed something which made me realize that the green-and-gold string, and the violet paper, were *not* obtrusions of your psychotic stream, Mrs. de Vries— but truly part of Lily Morton's!"

Doctor Alcazar sat back in his chair, rested his hands on the table, and turned his striking eyes and their faraway look on his host again.

"I believe," said Doctor Alcazar, "that the unknown 'George' is the murderer of Lily Morton. . . ."

From the end of the table, the little gray-headed woman stared at him with wide, horrified eyes. She was about to speak—but her husband spoke first.

He said, "Good *God!*" very sharply—and then, too smoothly, "Now *that* is the most preposterous notion!"

"*Clinton!*" said Gloria de Vries. She turned to Doctor Alcazar. "But—but—are you *sure*, Doctor?"

Smiling, Clinton de Vries lifted his glass. But something happened—something went wrong with the movement. The glass slipped from his hand and fell to the table, tilting out a pool of wine and snapping its fragile stem.

"Oh—too bad, too bad!" said Doctor Alcazar, and was busily helpful with his napkin.

Keep close; keep punching.

Doctor Alcazar, his labors over, looked again at Mrs. de Vries. He said, "You ask, am I sure of this strange union of 'George' and Lily Morton's murderer? . . . To be frank, Miss Dru—Mrs. de Vries, I am not. Not yet. But I do feel convinced that one more evocation of the psychomantic waves will bring"—he shrugged—"either confirmation or the reverse."

"Oh, Doctor!" She leaned towards him eagerly. "Is there—can you—I mean, couldn't you do it here? . . ."

It worked—it worked!

"If you would like that," said Doctor Alcazar benignly, "I'm sure it could be arranged. . . . Unless, of course, Mr. de Vries has any objection. . . ."

Hold your breath!

"Go ahead, go ahead!" said Clinton de Vries. "Matter of fact, I think I'll sit in—if you don't mind."

A-aah!

"No, no. In fact, quite the contrary," said Doctor Alcazar.

And less than twenty minutes later, in the long and pleasant room where he had first met Mrs. de Vries, he was once again seated before the desk near the French windows, raptly concentrating upon the small crystal globe before him. Again, the only lighted lamp in the room was the one upon the desk beside him. But this time it was night, and the darkness was real darkness instead of simulated dusk. To each side of him, only just within the faintest outer fringes of the light, sat Mrs. de Vries, to his right—and Mr. de Vries, to his left.

As he sat, Doctor Alcazar's whole body seemed to grow tense, and he said, in a hushed yet urgent voice:

"Ah! Here is something! . . . The crystal is clouding. . . ."

His voice grew lower, thicker. It said, slowly, dragging out the words:

"In the mist—a tree. A eucalyptus, bent and gnarled and twisted. Its branches look like hands reaching down . . . It stands in a patch of wasteland . . . The mist is closing in and I cannot see . . . Ah! The crystal is clearing again—but the tree is changing. It is not a tree, it is a post standing upright from the ground. The post that I saw before—violet-colored, and with green-and-gold rope coiling around it . . . A figure comes up to the post, creeping and furtive. A man's figure. I can only see his back—the back of the man I have seen in the crystal before. The back of the unknown 'George.' . . ."

Doctor Alcazar paused, drawing in a deep and sighing breath. He listened, but heard nothing. No sound. No movement.

"The figure is uncoiling the rope from the post. In his hands the rope becomes cord . . . He is tearing down the post, and in his hands it becomes paper—sheet upon sheet of wrapping paper, violet colored. As he folds it, his shoulders shake. I cannot see his face, but I know that he is laughing. An evil, gloating, malevolent laugh. He is planning evil; evil to someone associated with this strangely colored string and paper. . . .

"The image is changing again. It is a room—a familiar room—*this* room! The morning sun streams through the windows. There is no one here. But on the desk—on *this* desk—is a package. A package wrapped in violet paper and tied with green-and-gold string. . . ."

Again Doctor Alcazar paused, and now he heard

movements from his audience. Little shiftings and twitchings.

He bowed lower over the glittering little globe in front of him and said, the eerie monotone deepening:

"Someone is entering the room. A woman. Gloria. She comes to the desk. She examines the package. She tears off the wrappings, delighted.

"Ah! be careful, Gloria! You think this is a gift sent with love—but it is a gift sent with cold and deadly purpose . . . A gift which is meant, like all its forerunners, to lull you into a sense of false security . . . There is a mordant, miasmic aura surrounding that package, Gloria! One day—some day, any day—a package like this will come, and you will be happy about it, and trustful—but it will spell your death. . . ."

From the shadows on the right came the sound of a woman's voice; a startled formless little sound.

". . . The image changes . . . Another room—and Lily is here, Lily Morton . . . She is staring in amazement at something she has found. String—green-and-gold string. And paper—violet-colored paper . . . They are unused; that is why she is astonished. Finding them here has shown her the identity of 'George.' . . .

"The knowledge troubles her. She doesn't know what to do. She takes a small piece of the paper, a little coil of the string. . . .

"She is gone . . . But now comes the image of 'George' again . . . Still I cannot see his face. He is staring after Lily. He knows she has discovered him. . . .

"Now he is beneath the twisted tree again. It is stark and gaunt against the night sky. He is waiting . . . He hears approaching footsteps. Lily's footsteps. He tenses. Lily approaches. He leaps at her, strikes. . . .

"Lily is motionless—a lifeless, crumpled heap upon the ground. He bends over her body, searching. He finds her handbag. He opens it—takes something from it with his gloved hands . . . What has he taken? I cannot see . . . Yes—it is the little roll of violet-colored paper, bound with the green-and-gold string."

Doctor Alcazar stopped. And waited. He had heard another movement—a sharp rustle—from his left. And a hissing intake of breath.

He's going. He's back on his heels. What to use for the knockout? . . . Ah!

Doctor Alcazar shifted in his chair. Growing excitement appeared to have seized him. His hands gripped the desktop as his eyes stared down at the globe.

". . . He is stealing away . . . If *only* I could see his face! . . . He is limping a little. His leg is paining him, aching. He puts his hand down to it, seeming to adjust something beneath his trouser leg. . . ."

An odd little cry from the right, a strangled cry of panic-stricken astonishment.

No sound from the left.

". . . Ah! He is turning! At last we are going to see his face! He——"

The click of a switch—and the room was flooded with light.

"All right, that's enough!" The voice that came out of Clinton de Vries was harsh and high-pitched. "Stay where you are. Both of you. Don't move."

He was standing—and there was a gun in his hand, squat and black and ugly. His face was a dirty gray color, and his eyes were glazed and bright. He looked at Doctor Alcazar and said, "You heard me. Keep *still*." He looked at the hunched, frozen immobility of his wife and said, "You. Get up. Open the safe and take out the money you put there this morning."

Doctor Alcazar looked at the French windows. The curtains over them billowed and Avvie stepped into the room. The coat of his noncommittal gray suit was tightly buttoned, and his brown felt hat was pulled low on his forehead. His right hand was in his side pocket, grasping a gun.

As de Vries wheeled, Avvie moved forward. "Okay, de Vries," he snapped. "That'll do. You'd better drop the pistol."

He moved steadily across the room, a courageous little man. He said, "I got a warrant for you here," in the same dry, crackling voice, and then stopped abruptly.

An extraordinary sound had come from the throat of de Vries—an insane, animal sound. His lips rolled back from his teeth and his mouth opened, wide. His hand flashed up and thrust the muzzle of his gun into his mouth, pointing upwards.

There was an oddly muffled report—and a mess—and no more Clinton de Vries. . . .

Avvie sat in the dimmest corner of the little barroom. His fingers drummed incessantly on the stained tabletop, and he kept glancing at the door. . . .

It opened for the twentieth time—and admitted the tall and lean and imposing form of Doctor Alcazar, who paced slowly towards his friend, drew up a chair, sat down, put a hand inside his coat, and slowly pulled out his wallet.

From the wallet he drew an oblong, blue-tinted slip of paper, and turned it so that Avvie could see its face.

Avvie's eyes opened, very wide. He swallowed. He said, "Ten G's!" without knowing he'd spoken.

Doctor Alcazar folded the check, put it back in his wallet, and turned and called an order to the barman. An impressive order.

Avvie said, "What we gonna do?" His voice was still hoarse with shock. "Split an' quit?"

Doctor Alcazar eyed him reprovingly. "My dear

Avvie!" he said. "Our hard-gotten gains *might*, of course, be used to found The Alcazar College of Psychic Research. . . .

"On the other hand," said Doctor Alcazar, "they *could* be used to set us up in business. . . ."

"Howzat?" Avvie said. "Whaddya mean—business?"

"The business," said Doctor Alcazar, "of Private Investigation. . . . You type a report and they give you a century—but you look in the crystal and they give you ten grand!"

Philip MacDonald did not choose a farfetched premise when he presented Dr. Alcazar, the mind-reading, fortunetelling rogue. The desire to have the unrevealable revealed has been the downfall of many. The fortuneteller is always prepared and waiting with a detailed account of the past or deep analysis of the future for the anxious client. It is, consequently, not surprising that this kindred art of magic has attracted the biggest charlatans. Many a struggling magician has traded a life of pulling rabbits from hats for that of the clairvoyant and fortuneteller, whose success is dependent on the morally debatable art of "seeing."

Magicians deceive by toying with the senses of sight, sound, and touch and with imagination. The fortuneteller plays on emotions, superstition, and fears. Little wonder that no love is lost between these rival factions.

11

In 1910 *Conjurors' Tales,* a slim, privately printed volume of seven short stories, was published in England. These "factual" narratives were written by an unknown magician, George Johnson. The book was a gamble, so to partially defray printing costs the publisher included an assemblage of mind-boggling ballyhoos for The Marvel Mart in Glasgow, Hamley Bros.—Makers of High-Class Conjuring Tricks, and a book delving into the art of chapeaugraphy, appropriately titled *Twenty-Five Heads Under One Hat.*

"Professor Swankton's Ruse," which follows, as well as the absurdly amusing advertisements, have lost little of their simple charm over the years.

Professor Swankton's Ruse

(A HOLIDAY EPISODE)
by *George Johnson*

The picturesque bridge, with its ivy-clung buttresses at the entrance to the town of Tamstock is, as every Devonshire visitor knows, the particular beauty spot of the neighbourhood, and near by I had fixed up my easel, preparatory to sketching the charming picture formed by the dancing stream, fresh from the rocky boulders of the moor.

The main road, as it enters the town, turns at rather a sharp angle, and one with an eye to the artistic is glad to remove their gaze from the ugly bill hoarding, and even the little barber's shop on the far side of the road, which form an incongruous contrast to the scene of sylvan beauty presented fifty yards or so further on.

My easel being set up in close proximity to a gate in the hedge which, excepting for a few feet of meadow land, borders the river, passers by might have the privilege of admiring the view and my efforts at portraying it on canvas at the same time. Soothed with this knowledge, and having settled myself more or less uncomfortably on that most unstable of resting places, an artist's sketching stool, it was with anything but good humour that I almost immediately rose again in response to an imperative "Hi!" from the region of the gate.

The speaker, from his apparel, seemed to be a working mason or something of the sort, very much down on his luck, judging by the general state of his appearance, and the stubbly nature of his chin.

"Were you calling me?" I asked.

"Beg yer pardon, sir, I am sorry to bother you, but——" and he hesitated.

"Oh, don't apologise, what is it you want, and hurry up."

I was anxious to get back to my canvas, near which an enquiring cow seemed to be contemplatively interested.

"Well, sir, I be going in opposite to get a shave" (the knowledge cheered me somewhat), "and I wondered if you would be so kind as to keep a heye on this yere bag o' tools for a few minutes, seeing as you're staying a bit."

"Certainly," I replied. "But why in the name of wonder cannot you take the bag in with you; it's not very large."

"No, sir, it aint that; you see—well, the fact is, the barber over there has a dog; he's a very good dog and a sort of pal of mine, and sometimes coming 'ome on a Saturday I 'ave a few scraps in the bag, left over breakfast, and he noses round for them. Well, today Mrs. Cummins up at the farm gave me a couple of puddins for the missus, and as there ain't nowhere much to rest the bag on there, 'cept the floor——"

"I see," I broke in, "your canine friend might help himself while you were being operated on. All right, leave the bag, I'll keep an eye on it"; and with profuse thanks the labourer made for the hairdressers.

While this temporary deposit business was in progress, my gaze had wandered across the road to the hoarding; the principal item of the advertisements setting forth that Professor and Madam Swankton, "The world's greatest

conjurers and thought readers," would open at the Public
Hall, Tamstock, for six nights on the Monday following.
Just beneath this advertisement a disreputable tramp had
been tinkering with an equally disreputable bicycle, these
items being mentioned as they had a considerable bearing
on what followed.

The bag of tools had been carefully placed in the
corner of the gateway, and my easel, being a few yards
away on the other side, I concluded all would be safe
pending the return of the bag's owner.

Having resumed work but a few moments, a slight
sound as though the gate was being shaken, caused me to
look in the direction of my charge; what was my horror to
find that it had disappeared? The next few moments were
somewhat exciting. I vaulted the gate just in time to see the
cyclist mount his machine and pedal rather leisurely up the
road with the tool bag dangling over his shoulder, and the
owner in hot pursuit as fast as his short legs could carry
him.

The road in the direction leading away from the town
is fairly straight for half-a-mile, and but little distance had
been covered by pursuer and pursued before a gust of wind
carried away the tramp's headgear in the shape of a much
ill-used bowler hat, revealing a head of hair carefully parted
down the centre. It struck me as curious that a tramp
should take such pains over this single part of his adorn-
ment, considering that the remainder of his attire was
négligé, to say the least of it.

As the hat fell, the cyclist seemed to put on extra
speed, and in a short time was out of sight. The mason,
giving up the chase, returned to me out of breath, and
apparently very much out of temper.

"You're a nice sort of gent," he remonstrated, gazing
ruefully at the battered felt hat which he had picked up.
"I'd no sooner got in the shop, when 'appening to look over

my shoulder I sees that sinner dart across and grab my bag; couldn't you have collared him?"

"I cannot help it, as you must have seen," I replied, rather nettled. "You had better go to the police about it; I am sorry, but it wasn't my fault." A little crowd of passers by had by this time congregated, and to a chorus of "blooming shame," and the like, the man walked away towards the town.

These events happened on the Saturday, and as I purposed putting in the following week at Tamstock, in the expectation of hearing more of the matter, I was not disappointed. The following Monday it rained solidly the whole day, and when the evening at last arrived, I bethought myself of the entertainment advertised to take place at the Public Hall; more especially as, being an amateur conjurer, the performance appealed to me. Entering rather late, I had to put up with a back seat; all accommodation being on the ground floor, and catering apparently for the popular classes, the greater part of the hall was given over to the cheaper seats.

The first part of the performance consisted of conjuring and illusions, Professor Swankton possessing no mean merit as a sleight-of-hand performer, and, after the interval, the conjurer introduced what he described as "The feats of thought transference, presented by that truly wonderful lady, Madam Swankton!" Madam, having been thus introduced, pieces of paper were distributed to various members of the audience, who were asked to write any question they pleased, afterwards retaining the paper. Madam was then placed in a mesmeric sleep and replied to the different queries, greatly to the wonder of the very provincial audience.

I had seen the whole business so many times, and knowing well how the trick was done, it had ceased to interest me, so was about to leave the building when something about a lost bag arrested my attention.

"Someone at the back of the hall," said the clairvoyant, "I think he is a mason, he is dressed in a light tweed suit, and wears a turn-down collar; he enquires about a bag of tools that was stolen from him by a man with a bicycle on Saturday last. It was near the Tamstock Bridge that the theft was committed. Tell him that the tramp was afraid to keep the tools, and that the bag is buried near the first tree after passing the second milestone on the Exeter Road."

"A Free Mason who lost a bag of tools on Saturday?" queried the professor. "Will he please stand up?"

My friend of the bridge episode immediately showed up somewhere near the back.

"Is that right sir? Did you lose some tools last week?"

"Quite right," came the reply. "But I ain't no Free Mason all the same; I'm a Buffalo, if anyone wants to know, and what I asked was where the man is that pinched my bag."

The professor apparently hastened to pour oil on the troubled waters.

"Madam Swankton does not profess to tell you everything, but should you be fortunate enough to recover your loss, may I ask you to come here tomorrow evening and say so; in any case, we should like to know the result, so will you please accept this ticket for our next performance?" At this there was considerable applause, and with the reply to a few more questions, the entertainment ended.

During the whole evening I had been haunted by some memory in connection with the professor's carefully parted hair; and it was only when the curtains finally closed that it dawned on me—the tramp with the bicycle whose hat had fallen off! "So that's their little game," I thought. "Well! if this is conjuring it *is* playing it pretty low down."

The hall had nearly emptied, when I presented myself to the pianist, who was collecting his music. "Will it be possible for me to have a word with Professor Swankton?" I asked. The pianist did not know, but would inquire. I waited a few moments, when the man of magic appeared before the curtains.

"Good evening," he remarked pleasantly enough, "You wished to speak to me?" "I do," I replied. "As an amateur conjurer, which I have been pretty well all my life, I wish to say that the way in which that poor man has been defrauded of his bag and tools, and given so much unnecessary anxiety for several days, merely that you may gain a cheap advertisement, is not conjuring, but, in my opinion, very nearly swindling."

The professor still beamed on me. "You do not fully understand——" he began, but I interrupted him. "It is quite useless arguing; when your hat blew off on Saturday, I noticed, among other things, your manner of wearing the hair. I recognise you as the cyclist who took the bag, and I have come here to say that unless, tomorrow evening, you make your wretched dupe some pecuniary compensation for this business, I shall expose the whole matter."

Professor Swankton looked rather annoyed at the beginning of my tirade, but at length he was evidently struck with some point of humour, for his features broadened into a laugh. "You assure me that you *are* a conjurer," he said, "and as such I suppose you are willing to keep conjurers' legitimate secrets?"

"Certainly," I replied, "but, do you call this sort of thing legitimate, do you consider——."

My further remarks were drowned in a roar of laughter from behind the curtain.

"Bill!" called the professor.

"Yes, guvnor," and in a state bordering on convulsions, with shirt sleeves rolled up and in another suit of clothes, appeared my labouring friend.

"You," I gasped!

"Yes, me, sir; you see it had to be worked on somebody, and you were handy," and then he added, deprecatingly, "You see, I'm a sort of combined baggage man and general assistant to this concern, I hope you don't mind?"

"But the tools," I remonstrated, "someone may go and search for them."

"That's all right, anyone may look, but we shall find them, you see the bag is buried *near* a tree, we did not say how near."

I joined heartily in the general merriment, and together with Madame Swankton, we afterwards made a merry supper party.

I saw a lot of the Swanktons during the ensuing week, and we left for town together at the end of our stay, their run having been as successful as my holiday had been a pleasant one.

Now that you have learned a card trick, here is part two of your exclusive magic course . . .

Professor Swankton's Coin Trick

The debonair performer of miracles (that is you) asks someone to volunteer to hold a dime in the palm of his hand. You then push the dime into the palm of his hand with your thumb. The accomplice closes his hand, feeling the coin. When you say the magic words, the volunteer opens his hand to find the coin has disappeared.

How is this miracle achieved? On the ball of your right thumb place a small piece of double-sided adhesive tape. Press the dime onto the tape. As you close the other's fingers over the coin, withdraw your right thumb and the coin will come with it. Because of the pressure applied seconds earlier, your accomplice still believes he is holding the coin.

12

It is appropriate that Walter B. Gibson, a most prolific writer, be represented in this anthology not once, but twice.

This time around Mr. Gibson takes us on a tantalizing trip to postwar Europe and introduces us to the dauntless derring-do and audacious sleight of hand of The Great Girard.

The Florentine Masks

by Walter B. Gibson

From the window of his hotel room, Gerard White-stone studied the reflected lights in the lazy, murky river far below, while his hand idly flipped a coin and caught it without a passing glance. After each toss, his thumb probed the coin's upper surface, establishing its "Heads" or "Tails" position solely by touch. A neat trick, that. By mastering it, Gerard was able to match coins in the dark, a valuable accomplishment on certain occasions.

Gerard was an American, the coin a British half crown, the river an Italian stream—the Arno. There was nothing too unusual about that combination to a magician of international reputation who traveled everywhere. Half crowns were precisely the right size for his coin manipulative act, and particularly attractive at the current exchange rate. As for the locale, European audiences appreciated his skill so highly that Whitestone, as the Great Gerard, was in constant demand throughout the continent and tonight was finishing a week's engagement in Florence, a city to which all artistry naturally gravitated.

Gerard's distant stare, his repeated tossing of the coin, mirrored his mood, much as the glow from the Lungarno, the quays bordering the river, was wavered by the Arno's

223

ripples. That river, too, had its moods. Once, Gerard had seen it sullen, ruddy in the glow of fires left by retreating Nazis, its reflections shivering from the explosions of bridges and buildings along the embankments.

Now, as if in recollection, the Arno seemed to gain a pinkish glow in which Gerard could picture the delicate oval of a childish, trusting face. His hand, pocketing the coin, brought out a handkerchief and began shaping it in imitation of a rabbit, long ears and all, while he watched for a smile from that imaginary face amidst the ripples. Then, suddenly the illusion was dispelled by a sound like the faint echo of a Nazi bomb, carried over from the years.

Gerard looked up as the door slammed behind a pert, vivacious blonde, her slender figure cutting off the hallway exit light that had briefly tinted the reflected waters. The smiling intruder, a half-size above tiny, was Mimi, the magician's attractive assistant, coming to warn him that he must not be late for the first night of his engagement.

"You can't possibly be expecting children in the roof garden," said Mimi, "so why sharpen up on the bunny number?"

"I was thinking back," said Gerard. "I was remembering how I felt when I was a G. I., here in Florence——"

"You've been doing that too much on this tour," interrupted Mimi, "and it could lead to trouble. You must have been generous with the free shows, the way the natives remember you."

"I was." Gerard nodded as he turned from the window. "Here in Florence, I had an audience of one—a little girl. To be precise, a very little girl. Smaller than you, Mimi, and much, much younger. All of nine or ten years old, I would say. She was lost——"

"And so you found her!"

"How did you guess?" Gerard smiled blandly as he opened the door and accompanied Mimi out into the corridor. "Yes, I found her and turned her over to her father. I told her she could thank me when I came back—in a dozen years or so."

"It's very thoughtful of you to give them time to grow up. Of course you remember her name. You didn't forget one of the others. I've watched them flocking around to thank you in every city we've passed through."

Gerard shook his head as the elevator arrived. "There's one I missed," he told Mimi ruefully, "but I still have hopes."

"At least," said Mimi, nudging his hand as they entered the lift, "she has a fair chance of finding out for herself that you're back."

Mimi's wave indicated Gerard's picture on the wall of the elevator, which included the announcement that he was appearing at the Terrazza Giardino. Then, the thoughtful magician and his petite assistant were stepping from the elevator at the roof garden itself.

Mere minutes later, Gerard, immaculate in tails, white tie, and boutonniere, was bowing to an enthusiastic audience as his fingers plucked half crowns from thin air, and dropped them into a glass bowl that Mimi carried.

Occasionally, Gerard interrupted this serious and profitable business by wryly producing a thousand lire note instead. The audience, with typical Florentine humor, accepted the gesture as comic relief. But there was one face that remained unmoved amidst the mirth. It belonged to a girl who was very beautiful, but who failed even to smile when her companions laughed.

The girl sat at a table near the rail. Against the subdued glow of the Florentine skyline, her features had the delicate aspect of an exquisite cameo, like the antique brooch that closed the V-neck of her low-cut evening gown. The brooch was evidently a family heirloom and her dress, though sleek and modern, was as conservatively jet black as her hair. So harmonious was every feature of the ensemble that she appeared to have stepped from a frame in a portrait gallery.

Gerard cued Mimi as he finished the coin act. "While I'm doing the card fans, check with the management and get the name of that girl with the party by the rail," he said. "I may need it for the mind reading act."

"If you mean that poor imitation of the Mona Lisa," said Mimi, "she's so completely not your type that I'll believe you this once when you say you're interested only in her mind."

Gerard proceeded with the card fans, a splendid exhibition interspersed with wedge shuffles that enabled him to fan two packs in double size. When Mimi returned, Gerard spun the cards in a continuous stream squarely into a waiting top hat that his agile assistant carried.

Above the snap of the cards, Mimi whispered in an undertone: "Rosa Uberti is the name. One of the first families and I don't mean the first we saw driving into town. Rosa means rose, glamor boy, and that stands for thorns in any language."

Bland as ever, Gerard was catching clusters of playing cards from nowhere, to add to those he had spun into the hat. He found a fan under Mimi's chin, and another at his own elbow. When he drew a handkerchief from his pocket and whipped it sharply, he caught a card on its far corner, repeating the surprise while the audience applauded.

"If you want to see a real smile," Gerard whispered to Mimi, "watch Signorina Uberti now."

As Mimi watched, the Mona Lisa expression widened and broke, while Rosa's eyes brightened eagerly. Mimi turned to Gerard with a startled exclamation: "Why, it must *really* be thought projection!" Then, Mimi caught herself as she noticed Gerard's handkerchief.

Instead of pocketing it, the magician had casually pulled one corner up between his right thumb and forefinger, another corner up between the last two fingers. Only someone who had seen him elaborate those folds would have recognized that he had formed a pair of huge rabbit ears.

Mimi knew and so did the solemn girl at the table by the rail. Under her breath, Mimi exclaimed: "Then she must be the—the little girl!"

"The very little girl," emphasized Gerard, "but she hasn't just come to thank me. There's obviously some new trouble on her mind."

"And being a mind reader as well as a magician," said Mimi, "I am sure you will find out exactly what it is."

Gerard smiled his appreciation of Mimi's remark. He drew a fresh pack of cards from his pocket, and fanned it as he approached the table next to Rosa's. There, he requested a lady to glance at a card and concentrate upon it.

Gerard sighted the card by following the woman's gaze and noting the exact spot at which she momentarily paused. He remembered it as the ten of clubs while he was handing the pack to a man at the same table with a whispered request that he shuffle it.

While Gerard was having the lady assure the audience that her choice was absolutely a random one, he dipped his hand in his pocket, where he had a blank card with a back like the regular pack. On the blank, he wrote with the tiny stub of a soft pencil: *"The card is the ten of clubs. Tell me when and where I can meet you alone."*

Nobody noticed the action of Gerard's hidden hand. He palmed the card from his pocket, and added it deftly but secretly to the shuffled pack as he looked for another volunteer assistant.

He spied Rosa, bowed and stated in smooth Italian:

"You and I have never met, Signorina? Or if we have, it would have been during my last visit to Florence, some ten years ago—or more."

The girl returned a solemn smile. "I would have been very young then, Signor," she said.

"Then we have no arrangement, no collusion between us?"

"Absolutely none."

"Please take this pack." Gerard handed the cards to Rosa. "Step over to the lights of the fire exit. With your back turned, go through the pack card by card and pick out the one that intrigues you most and return here without a word."

The girl nodded. She went past a pillar while the audience waited breathless. When she returned, Rosa handed Gerard the pack, retaining a single card which she pressed against the cameo that adorned her gown.

Gerard turned to the lady at the next table and inquired: "The card you thought of, please?"

"Ten of clubs," was the reply.

Rosa Uberti, her lips genuinely smiling, turned her card toward the audience. A huge gasp became a rising wave of applause as Gerard received the card from Rosa and took a bow. His face impressively serious Gerard stepped to the platform for his final number, announced by Mimi with appropriately simulated horror as "Sawing a Woman into Segments."

Mimi, of course, was the woman. She was placed in a long box, her head and feet extending from the ends. Gerard and a burly Hindu assistant named Abdul did the sawing, rapidly and efficiently cutting the box into threes. Gerard had the end closest to Mimi's head.

"So you wanted her name for the mind-reading act," taunted the recumbent blonde. "Yet you didn't call her by name. Just what *was* on your mind, Gerard my darling, other than that ten spot?"

"She might have missed the card," Gerard said, between strokes of the saw. "In that case I would have baffled her by mentally revealing her name instead."

"How clever," said Mimi, "but I've never known you to miss that card trick."

"I've never missed with the saw trick either," reminded Gerard, gently, "but you never know what may happen if you don't keep your mind on it."

That quieted Mimi.

The show ended with Mimi's restoration after the sawing ordeal. As Gerard took his final bow, he noted that Rosa had left. He hurried down to his room, ran through the pack that he had replaced in his pocket and found the card that he had penciled. Across his query was the answer in vivid red, done with the point of a lipstick: STEPHANO—VITE.

Gerard knew Stephano's, just off the Via de' Buoni. He hurriedly changed clothes, left the hotel and headed directly to the Piazza della Republica. Once the Mercato Vecchio, or Old Market, this square had later become the Piazza Vittorio Emmanuele. Now, as the Piazza della Republica, it still rated as a gathering place for Florentine night life.

Waiters served a myriad of tables, the overflow from numerous cafes, while everyone from ragged beggars to gaily garbed musicians plied their trade among the diners, in quest of the ever elusive lire. Deliberately, Gerard let himself be recognized as he skirted the *piazza,* even acknowledging the exclamations of "Il Grando Prestidigitatoro!" voiced by diners who had caught his act at the Terrazza Giardino earlier in the day.

It was Gerard's policy to make himself conspicuous, so

he adhered to it. Too much, perhaps, for as he hesitated, seeking the side street to Stephano's, there was a stir among a group of men at a table nearby. One gestured toward the departing magician and undertoned: "Now, Vincente!" The man called Vincente arose and followed.

If Gerard prided himself on his skill at navigating alleys, he should have taken lessons from Vincente. At the magician's slightest backward glance, Vincente flattened against the nearest wall or eased into a handy doorway. Between such operations, he weaved through patchy darkness, where some occasional trickle of light, too vague to reveal Vincente's full figure, caught the glint of a steel blade that protruded, unsheathed, from his tightly-clenched hand.

Gerard did not pause or look back until he came suddenly upon Stephano's, a tiny unpretentious restaurant, the only oasis of light in a desert of whispering darkness. As Gerard stopped as though to admire a doubtful Florentine statue in the window, Rosa Uberti stepped from the doorway into the light beside him.

The girl was far more beautiful in this picturesque setting, which was reminiscent of the spot where Gerard had first met her as a stray waif during the fury of a Nazi bombardment. She was out of breath and trembling a little and an eager flush had replaced her previous pallor and cameolike fixity of expression, further heightening her charm.

Yet her eyes were still secretively restless, and wary. "You are sure you are quite alone?" she asked, taking firm hold of Gerard's arm.

"I am never alone with a friend," said Gerard. Then, reminiscently: "Your father, whom I met so briefly, years ago. How is he?"

Rosa's face clouded in the glow from the cafe window, revealing more to Gerard than if she had replied to him with a sudden desperate outpouring of words. In perfecting the intuitive talents with which he supplemented his sleight-of-hand, Gerard had learned to translate facial expressions into readings, often uncannily accurate, of the thoughts and emotions behind them.

Rosa showed no resignation to indicate bereavement, nor the weariness that a family illness would almost certainly have left in its wake. Rather, her pallor seemed more to spring from an anticipation of some horror, a stark fear magnified by sheer uncertainty.

Significantly, Gerard asked: "Where is your father now?"

"The police have taken him," the girl replied, "but they will not tell me where, or why, except that he has stolen something and is in protective custody. I know, though, that Conte Castricani can give you the answer!"

"Conte Castricani?"

"Guido Castricani." Rosa pronounced the name spitefully. "He called himself Conte in the days of Il Duce. Now he is General Castricani, the people's friend. Their enemy before; their friend to be. We do not like him."

"Has he publicly accused your father?"

"He would not dare!" Though Rosa had turned with her back to the light, Gerard could see the blaze of her dark eyes. Their glow faded, and became limpid with sudden doubt as she added: "Unless he has thought up lies that people will believe. Castricani has done that before—too well."

Her eyes flashed again, their sparkle more fear-swept than before, as she voiced a frantic warning: "Look out—behind you——"

As a figure lunged from across the alley, Gerard faded into a sideward dive; then rebounded from hand and knee. He sprawled his assailant on the cobbles, a stiletto clattering to the stones ahead of him. Gerard glimpsed a narrow,

mustached face with a white scar crossing the dark forehead and heard Rosa exclaim: "Vincente!"

Then, the man had scrambled to his feet and was
loping away. By the time Gerard turned, Rosa too was
gone. The only route she could have taken was through
Stephano's, but when Gerard entered the little restaurant
he found it empty except for half a dozen octagonal tables
that looked as much museum pieces as the statuettes and
mosaics that crowded the walls.

A far door led through a Florentine garden, complete
with fountain and marble benches, with an arched passage
beyond. But before Gerard could explore that route, a
waiter entered and inquired: "Il Caffe, Signor?"

Gerard confirmed with a nod that he wanted coffee
and watched the waiter draw it from an espresso machine
that looked like the best antique in the place.

While Gerard was finishing his coffee, a trio of carabinieri stalked into Stephano's, gorgeous in multicolored
uniforms and plumes. Two gripped Gerard's arms while a
third delivered a spiel in rapid Italian, from which Gerard
gathered that he was to accompany them for questioning.

During the march, he glimpsed the frowning three
hundred foot tower of the Palazzo Vecchio, which served
as the town hall, but before they reached the Piazza della
Signorina, where it was located, the carabinieri swung into
a side street and through the doorway of a residence
imposing enough to be a palace in its own right.

Up a sweeping staircase with an ornate balustrade,
Gerard was ushered into a huge office overlooking a dark,
hushed courtyard. There, behind a tremendous desk that
even the unlamented Duce might have envied, sat a tawny
man of Gerard's approximate build, though his face was
fuller and a trifle jowled. His keen eyes flashed a greeting as
deceptive as his smile. Then, with an abrupt, authoritative
gesture he waved Gerard to an immense chair and introduced himself: "I am General Guido Castricani."

"I have heard of you," acknowledged Gerard in his smoothest Italian. "You are the people's friend."

Castricani swelled pompously, then demanded sharply: "From whom did you hear that?"

"From the people," parried Gerard. "Where else?"

"Perhaps from Signorina Uberti. You know her of course."

The name brought a blank stare from Gerard.

"Come now." Castricani's tone had the sharpness of Vincente's stiletto. "Your blonde assistant inquired the signorina's name at the Terrazza. I have the management's word for it."

An understanding smile illuminated Gerard's blankness.

"That's Mimi for you," he said. "She must have had a momentary, quite unjustified fit of jealousy when I did my mind reading. This Signorina Uberti!"—he frowned disparagingly—"would she be beautiful, perhaps, except that she has no color, no expression? A face like waxwork, but much less interesting?"

"That could describe her."

"Check the management again," suggested Gerard. "They will assure you that I perform my mental tests only with persons I have never met before—and never expect to meet again."

Elbows on the desk, Castricani doubled his chin as he cradled it on interlaced fingers. His tone poured like olive oil: "Signorina Uberti goes often to Stephano's——"

"So that's why you sent the gendarmes!" broke in Gerard. "You thought I planned to meet her there."

"But apparently, you did not." Castricani shrugged. "However, since you are here, you may meet Rosa's father, if you wish."

Castricani's unexpected switch to the name Rosa did not catch Gerard off guard. He asked: "Who is Rosa? What has her father to do with Signorina Uberti?"

Castricani arose, beaming apologies. "You would not know," he said, "that Rosa is Signorina Uberti. Her father is Carlo Uberti. You shall meet him now. Come."

The order was not for Gerard, but for the carabinieri. Two stepped forward and clamped Gerard's arms while a third slapped a blindfold about his eyes, tightening it until his temples throbbed to the bursting pitch.

They spun Gerard about, shoved him stumbling through a door, along corridors, down steps, and up again until the route seemed endless as well as hopeless. Finally, the march ended at Castricani's purred order. Gerard heard the officers tramp away; then Castricani personally removed the blindfold.

Gerard blinked in the dim light of a stone-walled passage. He saw steel bars and thought he was behind them, until he realized that he was looking into a cell of ample size, carpeted and furnished with chair, table, and cot. The cell had an occupant, a man with a thin, gaunt face and large, scholarly forehead, whose glinting, tormented eyes were strikingly like Rosa's.

Except for that forehead and those eyes, Gerard would never have recognized Carlo Uberti. True, he had met Rosa's father only once and then not long enough to learn his name. But Uberti's dynamic personality had registered so forcefully with Gerard that the man's appearance had been indelibly implanted in the magician's recollections.

The spark was still there, but not enough to fire Uberti's visage as it once had done. With passing years, Uberti had retired within his shell, becoming more and more the scholar, and losing most of the vigor that had once inspired him. His face, yellowed like parchment, had assumed the semblance of a mask in which only the eyes seemed alive. It was only when Uberti's eyes lighted with recognition that his face regained for an instant the meaningful vitality which Gerard remembered so well.

Only briefly did that flash of recognition show. Then, his gaze going suddenly blank, the prisoner turned to Castricani. "I suppose this is another of your perjured witnesses," he said bitterly, "brought here to swear he saw me take the art records from the strong room in the Pallazzo Vecchio."

Castricani shook his head sadly and turned to Gerard. "Those records," he said, "are vital to our city. They list priceless *objets d'art* that were shipped to secret storage vaults or hidden in obscure places during the war. Gradually, we have been reassembling them and checking them by the lists in the vault. Those are the records that are gone from our safe keeping——"

His voice sank to a whisper.

"Safe keeping!" interrupted Uberti vehemently. "You mean you placed them where you could keep them safe for just one man—yourself. It was a deliberate theft——"

"The committee also gave you access to the records," Castricani reminded him. "You told them you were anxious to make duplicates, to guard against a possible loss of the originals."

"Which is why you stole them!" stormed Uberti. He turned to Gerard, his voice tremulous and despairing. "Those records are a key-list, a veritable catalog, giving the details of each Florentine treasure, even to the secret markings. Now that they are gone, Castricani and his comrades can bring back spurious items and sell the genuine treasures at fabulous prices to unscrupulous art dealers anywhere in the world. Those records, attested with the signatures of Florentine officials, will convince all prospective purchasers!"

"Hear how cunningly he attributes his own schemes to me," purred Castricani. "Signor Uberti craftily avoids mentioning that he was about to leave Florence with his daughter when I detained him."

Uberti stared defiantly at Castricani. "I was going where I could safely denounce you as a thief——"

Castricani interrupted with a startlingly direct and unexpected proposal to Gerard. "If you can persuade Signor Uberti to sign a full confession admitting that he took the civic records, I shall give him twenty-four hours to leave Italy before I make the statement public.

"Sorry, General," said Gerard. "I'm only the magician playing the Terrazzo Giardino. At this moment I'm due back there for my next show."

"I shall take you there," said Castricani. "But first I have a question I want Uberti to answer." He turned to the cell. "Tell me, Signor, are there any of the carabinieri you completely trust?"

"Yes, there is Bellini for one," said Uberti, "and Letta for another. There are a few more——"

"Those two are enough. Addio, Uberti."

Castricani guided Gerard along the passage, where the carabinieri met them and replaced the blindfold. The return route was more circuitous than the original, with more ups and downs, but Gerard found himself back in Castricani's office when the bandage was again removed from his eyes.

Castricani ordered one of his men to summon Bellini. Soon, a tall carabiniere arrived and while Castricani questioned the man, Gerard studied him casually but closely.

"On the night of the eleventh," said Castricani, "you saw Signor Uberti leave the Palazzo Vecchio. Correct, Bellini?"

"He passed me as I came from the Via Castellani," said Bellini. "It was midnight. I heard the bell strike."

Castricani dismissed Bellini and conducted Gerard to the street where a shiny car took them on a roundabout trip to the hotel. They paused at a piazza to quiz Letta, who was on duty there.

"Signor Uberti walked by me on the Via Magazzini," recalled Letta. "It is the street I always take when I finish my patrol. I spoke to him but the midnight bell was striking and he did not hear me, though he looked my way. He was coming from the Palazzo Vecchio."

"What chance does Signor Uberti have?" purred Castricani, as they rode along. "When two such witnesses speak against him?"

"He has every chance," said Gerard, "if no one knows yet that the records have been taken."

"But they do know," said Castricani. "The day after the theft, I called in our civic committee and showed them the empty vault. They said I would be held accountable unless I named the real thief."

"So you named Signor Uberti?"

"I stated the simple truth, that only Uberti and I had access to those archives. The committee has granted me a week to investigate the case. Naturally, if I had Uberti's confession, to go with the testimony of Bellini and Letta——"

Castricani spread his hands eloquently, to let Gerard pick up the theme, which the magician promptly did.

"The case would be closed," summed Gerard, "and you would be clear. You could then sell off the treasures just as Uberti claims you would, letting him take the blame."

Castricani gave a pained smile at the very thought. The car was pulling up at the hotel so he timed his comment accordingly.

"After your show," Castricani told Gerard, "I shall drop you at Uberti's home. I am sure his daughter will be pleased to hear about her father—even from a total stranger. She will feel that her father's life and freedom are worth more than all the treasures of Florence. Later you may persuade him to sign that confession—for the sake of his daughter."

During the show, Castricani watched from a ringside

table, his saggy face inflexible above his wingtip collar, with never the flicker of an eyelash marring the cold sparkle of his penetrating gaze.

Mimi mentioned him to Gerard as they went into the sawing act. "That creep looks like a dealer in well-preserved, used cadavers," she said. "From the daggers in his eyes, you'd think he wanted to step up and dissect me personally."

"He would carve you into more segments than a grapefruit," warned Gerard. "So if anyone asks you about him—or about me—give them your dumbest stare. I'm going for a ride with Signor Castricani and I don't want bad news catching up."

Castricani delivered Gerard at the Uberti homestead, which was only slightly less palatial than Castricani's own. Shunted from one servant to another, Gerard finally met Rosa in a room that was obviously her father's study.

In a corner, a huge, ancient globe of the world vied in eye-catching impressiveness with a modern map of Florence hanging above Uberti's finely carved desk. The floor was a huge mosaic of Etruscan design, while the wall niches had been converted into book shelves that teemed with strikingly original specimens of the binder's art. What intrigued Gerard most was a life-size bronze bust of Signor Uberti, which stood on a black marble pedestal directly opposite the door.

"It was made from a life mask," said Rosa, "by Giacomo Amadeo, the sculptor on the Via Cherubini. It was ordered for our Florentine Hall of Fame, but its placement was postponed, by Castricani's order."

The girl gave a quick glance toward the door to make sure no servants were about. Then her expression changed. "Did you see my father? If you did, tell me what he had to say!"

"He declares he is innocent," said Gerard. "So far,

Castricani has not used strong measures to make him change his mind. He was haggard, but showed no signs of torture or drugs. But Castricani has witnesses to prove your father was at the Palazzo Vecchio the night he insists he was never there."

"Castricani's witnesses would lie to anything."

"Your father trusts two of them: Bellini and Letta, members of the carabinieri. Both told me they saw him leave the town hall."

"They told you that in my father's presence?"

"No. Castricani introduced them to me later——"

Rosa interrupted with a grim smile. From the carved desk, she brought out a photo of her father standing with a dozen carabinieri, evidently an honor guard on some important occasion.

"Pick them out," said Rosa. "Bellini and Letta."

Gerard recognized and identified the correct pair instantly.

"I thought Castricani had brought in two impostors," said Rosa, dejectedly. "That would be his style of trickery."

"Not this time." Gerard stepped to the big map and traced a route upward from the Arno. "Bellini was coming this way, from the Via Castellani, while Letta was coming along the Via Magazzini." He raised his hand toward the upper right. "That would be northeast of the Plaza Della Signorina."

Gerard halted, closing his eyes to visualize the setting. "The Palazzo Vecchio is huge, covering a few acres at least. But both Bellini and Letta heard the stroke of the midnight bell——"

"At the time they saw my father?" broke in Rosa. "That couldn't be! They were on opposite sides of the Palazzo!"

"In that case," said Gerard, "Castricani worked his trickery the other way about. He had someone impersonate your father. In fact, there were two impersonators, to clinch it, but they made the mistake of being separately at the same time."

On a sudden inspiration, Gerard draped his raglan coat about the bust of Carlo Uberti and planted his fedora on the statue's head. The effect brought a startled gasp from Rosa. She could have sworn she saw her father in the flesh.

That illusion increased when Gerard raised a lamp and brought it toward the bust. Every passing shadow or change of angle made the bronze face come more alive. From the life mask, the sculptor had captured the full detail of Uberti's striking features, even to their parchment hue.

"All they needed," said Gerard, "were replicas of the mask Amadeo used in making this statue. I know, because I have used masks often for stage impersonations and quick changes." He halted his musing tone, and added suddenly: "Can we get to the Via Cherubini in a hurry?"

As Rosa nodded, Gerard whipped his hat and coat from the bust and snapped the word "Andimo!" the urgent if slightly less colloquial Italian equivalent of "Let's go!"

On the way, Gerard learned how Rosa had appeared and vanished outside Stephano's. Her stealth at traversing narrow alleys and tiny courtyards bordered on the uncanny.

"I learned this during the war carrying messages for my father's friends," she told Gerard. "He did not know it—then."

One thing was certain. None of Castricani's clan could be trailing them along this intricate route. But Gerard's qualms on that score were suddenly renewed when they passed beneath an arch leading into the Via Cherubini.

Rosa's guiding clutch tightened frantically on Gerard's arm as she pointed with her other hand and gasped: "Look there——"

Gerard saw framed in the dim light of an upstairs window two silhouettes contorted like shapes in a shadow play. As a shadowy hand descended with a knife, the figure that received the blow crumpled all too realistically. Gerard reached an open street door with a bound and dashed up to the second floor, Rosa close behind him.

A crash came as they reached a studio and they saw the ugly face of Vincente scowling through a haze of dust from plaster casts and molds that he was wrecking with a spike-headed metal mace.

Vincente flung the metal war-club. It narrowly missed Gerard as it shattered the doorway where he was holding Rosa back. By then, Vincente had dived through a side window and was scrambling across a roof on another rapid escape. This time, he had left a victim.

Rosa, horrified, was pointing to a shaggy-haired figure in the wreckage. Gerard stooped, his eyes on a blot of blood which was spreading slowly on the man's crumpled smock. That was the way with stiletto stabs. They went deep to the heart, yet bled but little.

"Poor Amadeo," moaned Rosa. "They knew he could tell us about those masks. They did not want us to find the molds or plaster busts from which my father's bronze was made——"

She ended with a shriek as she recognized a face that glared down from at her from a closet Gerard had opened. In blind terror she seized the mace, and raised it high—but the magician halted her swing.

"It isn't Castricani," he assured her. "It's his bust, a plaster one that Amadeo must have molded from him. Castricani probably felt that he also rated the local Hall of Fame. Vincente should have destroyed it when he killed Amadeo. We can't prove that your father's masks were used to impersonate him, until we've secured further evidence. But this bust links Amadeo and Castricani."

"Then why," asked Rosa, "didn't Vincente destroy it?"

"He probably thought he did," said Gerard, gesturing to the fragments of broken plaster, "along with the rest. He will report that to Castricani and meanwhile, give us an opportunity to beat them at their own game."

Rosa's face grew less strained.

Almost tenderly, Gerard took Castricani's bust from the closet, and wrapped it in some burlap in a corner of the studio.

"Find a mask maker you know you can trust," he told Rosa. "Then notify me. We shall have him make your father's passport to freedom."

Understanding dawned in Rosa's eyes as they left the studio by a back entrance and a pathway that eventually led them to one of the Lungarno. There, Gerard turned to say goodnight, and suddenly found Rosa bundled in his arms along with Castricani's burlap-packed facsimile. Gerard hadn't planned it that way, but its miraculous inevitability assuaged his thwarted anticipation. Love made out better when it couldn't wait.

Gerard arrived back at the hotel just in time for the last show. Mimi stared at him in relief when he sauntered on to the Terrazza.

"How did you make out?" she queried. "Did Castricani show you the sights of the city—outside of himself."

"I found what I came to Italy knowing I would find." Gerard punctuated his comments by catching coins from the air in a glass bowl. "But sooner than I expected. I'd supposed it would happen in Venice—in a gondola drifting on the Grand Canal. Instead, it was in Florence on the bank of the unromantic Arno."

"And you told me," chided Mimi, "you expected to be in danger."

"I was." From his tone, Mimi realized Gerard had become deadly serious. "You know how fraudulently successful I am in predicting tomorrow's headlines?"

Mimi nodded as she caught a cluster of coins within the bowl.

"For once, I won't have to fake it," declared Gerard. "You will read of a sculptor named Amadeo, murdered in his studio."

"You mean—instead of you?"

"Only instead of me if Castricani should become convinced that I know all that the dead man knew." Gerard smiled at the strained stare his blonde assistant gave him. "But he won't, so save your horror for the sawing act, Mimi."

The next day Gerard was rising bright and early at high noon when an expected phone call came. A man was on the wire and from his polite, almost servile tone, Gerard pictured the speaker as a Uberti family retainer.

"If you wish to match your Venetian tile plaques, Signor," the caller stated, "take them to the Ponte Vecchio. I am sure someone there can accommodate you."

Soon, Gerard was carrying a large square box among the shops that lined the two-level Ponte Vecchio. You could buy an almost limitless variety of jewelry, antiquities, or trinkets in the quaint stores that literally overhung the Arno, for Florentine craftsmen specialized in everything from alabaster to zithers.

But you could not buy Venetian tile plaques. Gerard's request brought shrugs and lifted eyebrows. Why Venetian tile plaques, when the Florentine variety were all the rage, particularly in Florence? But Gerard persisted until he found a shop where the bearded proprietor observed the square box he carried, and shifted the conversation from tile plaques.

"Go to the little bookshop near the Porta Romana," he said. "Take your samples and I am sure they can duplicate the bindings."

On the way, Gerard passed the Lungarno Corsini where he had parted from Rosa the night before. He smiled at the thought that she had probably covered the same route, that very morning, making arrangements for Gerard's present reception by craftsmen who were her father's trusted friends.

The bookshop proprietor was a wizened man named Pietro who nodded at mention of bindings and conducted Gerard to a back room workshop, where he opened Gerard's box, bringing out the bust of Castricani.

"I can have the masks ready by evening," he said. "They will be thin, but full and very firm."

"Like Castricani," said Gerard. "And be sure to have them, because I must leave on the night train. You can crack up the plaster bust as soon as you are through with it."

Early evening found Rosa Uberti threading her way through Florentine alleys with Gerard in tow. At a grilled gate she gestured to a formidable lock and Gerard handled it silently, efficiently, with a pincer pick.

Easy pickings, these antique locks. They may have stopped some of the Medicis in the midst of their appointed rounds, but they were no match for modern tools. Still, Gerard had no idea where he was until Rosa conducted him through a servant's entrance and up a short flight of stairs, where he suddenly blinked in startled recognition.

They were in a passage just outside Castricani's office. Gerard edged Rosa back to the stairs, opened a small package, and brought out a pair of nested masks. He placed both on his face as one, added a suitable wig from his pocket and stepped into the light.

Rosa's shudder assured Gerard that his impersonation

of Castricani was perfect. The wig covered the hair-line, which alone could have given away the trick in average light. With a whispered "Andiamo" Gerard gripped Rosa's arm and began threading a course through intricate passages, down stairs and up, as though he knew the interior of Castricani's huge residence as perfectly as Rosa knew the byways of Florence.

Breathless, Rosa whispered: "But you were blindfolded when you were here before!"

"That didn't matter," said Gerard. "I lifted my forehead and looked down the sides of my nose, an old trick but a sure one. I checked every step, every turn by watching the floor"—Gerard gave a hollow chuckle through the fixed lips of his double mask—"as I am doing now. If I look up, I'll lose the way."

It was Rosa who looked up and stifled a gasp. Gerard knew the reason. They had come to a turn where a carabiniere was on guard.

Gerard gripped Rosa's arm and undertoned: "Steady, sweet. Play it the way we rehearsed it."

"I can't begin to thank you, General!" said Rosa, turning a forced smile upon her masked companion. "My father will be so happy to see me! We are both grateful for your kindness."

Gerard played the strong, silent Castricani, easy enough with the general's customary deadpan. He stroked Rosa's hand as he darted a glance toward the sentinel, letting his mask catch the subdued light from varied angles. The mask was the exact color of Castricani's tawn, and its lips must have appeared to twitch in the flickery glow, for Gerard could see the carabiniere suppress a responsive grin of his own.

Evidently, Rosa was not the only trusting lady that Castricani had conducted through these preserves. The guard saluted as they passed.

A few more minutes brought them to Uberti's isolated cell, where Gerard removed the two-ply mask and went to work on the lock. As he worked Rosa talked to her father, so that Uberti wasn't surprised when Gerard separated the nested masks and handed him one, along with an extra wig.

A moment later two Castricanis stood studying each other face to face just outside the cell, while Rosa darted keen looks up and down the corridor.

"You know the way back," Gerard told Rosa in a hollow whisper. "Take your father along it."

Gerard turned to Uberti. "If a guard looks at you, answer him like this." Gerard gave his chin an upward, forward thrust, and Uberti copied the act, producing the ludicrous effect of Castricani admiring himself in a mirror.

"That will do it," Gerard assured him. "I'll take the long way out, the return route they used to confuse me. I memorized it, too, and it would be disastrous to have two Castricanis seen together. We must stay apart—and in different places—as with the two Ubertis."

Gerard passed only one carabiniere on the long return trip, and the guard presented arms while the general passed. When he reached the big study, Gerard sat down at the oversized desk, where a single lamp, itself appropriately of jumbo proportions, cast an expectant glow, as though it had long awaited the grand presence of General Guido Castricani.

Masked as he was, Gerard could think of no better substitute as he worked on the locks of the desk drawers, ready to look up on an instant's notice and meet any chance visitor with a truly Castricani stare. In the third drawer, Gerard found the stolen records, with their attested signatures and meticulous descriptions of the Florentine art treasures. Rapidly satisfying himself that they were all together in a single, compact bundle Gerard took resolute possession of the documents that would insure Uberti's vindication.

It was then that Gerard leaned back to let his mask catch the full lamplight. His eyes, the only living feature of his face, became as frozen as the artificial visage through which they peered. It wasn't the sight of the revolver muzzle aimed directly at his heart that tightened the muscles of his throat. Gerard had met such threats before, and somehow laughed them off. It was the face above the looming gun——

The face was Castricani's own.

No magician wastes time on someone he cannot fool. It was that professional rule, strictly adhered to, that saved Gerard's life. His hand traveled ahead of his agile mind as it caught up the big desk lamp and let it fly, much as Vincente had hurled the mace at Amadeo's studio.

The quick, violently decisive act came too late to stop Castricani's hair-trigger shot, but it did spoil his aim. His instinctive recoil from the path of the scaling lamp caused his shot to go wild. The lamp in turn missed Castricani, but its cord yanked free, plunging the room in a darkness that swallowed the gun's echo.

Castricani fired again—this time too high. Gerard had already dived across the polished desk top. He tobogganed squarely into Castricani and they grappled, Gerard fighting to gain the gun as he reeled with Castricani out into the hallway. They reached the lighted stairway, Castricani bellowing the while: "Vincente! Vieni! Presta—presta—"

Vincente's footsteps clattered from below. Again Castricani called: "It's Gerard—il prestidigitattore—masked with my face! Don't let him fool you!"

Across Castricani's shoulder, Gerard saw Vincente dashing up the stairs, wearing a leer that indicated he had spotted the deception, for the wig was back on Gerard's head, the mask slipping from his face. In desperation, Gerard suddenly reversed his course, wheeling Castricani back into the darkened office.

There, as Castricani broke away and turned to aim, Gerard met him with a hard swing of the door. Castricani sagged with a groan, and Gerard punched him savagely in the stomach. Then, balancing his swaying adversary against the equally unsteady door, he caught the mask that was falling from his own face and planted it squarely upon Castricani's, where it stayed by virtue of the perfect fit.

Hardly could an accident have been better calculated to misguide Vincente, and give Gerard a few moments to crash his way out through the courtyard windows. To complete the bluff, Gerard shoved Castricani headlong into the hallway, and squarely into Vincente's path. Meeting Vincente, Castricani grappled groggily in the dim light from the stairway, thinking he still was struggling with Gerard.

On a chance hunch, Gerard halted. From the darkness, he watched the strange sequel to his strategy, a result that far exceeded his anticipation.

In the dim glow, Vincente recognized the mask that he had seen falling from Gerard's face and remembered Castricani's warning "Don't let him fool you!" Wrenching from the grapple, Vincente drove his stiletto deep between his adversary's ribs and stood back to watch the figure that coiled to the floor.

"Why try to trick me, magician?" he scoffed in malicious triumph. "Like Castricani, I am an old hand at this game of masks. We both passed as your friend Uberti, precisely as you now pose as Castricani!"

Vincente stopped, and whipped away Castricani's mask, expecting to see Gerard's face beneath. The lack of change left him utterly bewildered. Gerard, tense, was ready to follow that surprise with another. But before he could surge forward and take Vincente off guard, the bewildered man turned the other way. Two carabinieri were arriving from the stairs; Gerard recognized one of them as Letta.

Like Vincente, they misunderstood things. Vincente had dropped the mask aside; his hand was gripping the stiletto, to draw it from Castricani's heart. When the carabinieri raised their guns to cow the man they mistook for an assassin, Vincente didn't try to explain.

An instinctive fighter, Vincente swung about with his knife and tried to dart between the carabinieri. They took no chances with the blade he brandished. They simple blasted him in his tracks.

Vincente sprawled, came savagely to his feet again, then collapsed and gasped away his life as the carabinieri seized him. From the darkness, Gerard saw the mask flatten beneath Vincente's body; then watched the carabinieri trample it beyond recognition, never knowing what it was. The two men who could have told them—Castricani and Vincente—both were dead.

Gerard used the window route to reach the courtyard. As he circled a central fountain, a hand pressed his own. It was Rosa's. The girl guided him through a maze of passages to a corner where her father waited, still wearing Castricani's mask.

"You won't need it any longer," Gerard told him. "Castricani is dead."

In telling the full story, Gerard illustrated it by trampling the duplicate mask, the way the carabinieri had done. After Rosa and her father had watched the familiar features of Castricani vanish jowl by jowl, Gerard handed over the priceless records that he had found in Castricani's desk. Then, as he glanced at his watch, he exclaimed: "I must hurry!"

The Night Express was ready to pull from the Stazione Centrale when Gerard clambered on board a car where an excited blonde was waving from a window. As he entered Mimi's compartment, her cry "You almost missed it!" was drowned by the louder squeal of the locomotive.

"So I almost missed it," said Gerard, "but does that

excuse you for waving out the window like this?" He duplicated Mimi's action. "Why, you might lose an arm or something!"

Gerard Whitestone himself had lost nothing—not even the opportunity to wave good-bye to Rosa Uberti as she stood with her father, watching from beyond the closed train gate.

The Great Gerard was well versed in his art. Magicians the world over still search for English half crowns to utilize during their coin conjuring. Any magician reading this story will have to suppress a smile at the neat manner in which Gerard discovered his beautiful Mona Lisa's name. How many have tried that same tactic to extract information?

Gerard Whitestone has the true stamp of a magician even in his relationship with Mimi. It can not be a comforting feeling for a petite assistant enclosed in a wooden box to wonder if the magician's mind is concentrating quite fully enough on his work.

13

The illusive and enigmatic Conway Lonstar is as mysterious as the magical miracles he manipulates in "The Weapon from Nowhere." He will not answer correspondence; all business transactions are screened through his friend and confidant Simon Archer of Denver, Colorado, who maddeningly doles out tempting personal tidbits, now and then, that do nothing but increase our hunger for facts rather than diminish it.

But we have persevered, and, therefore, let it be known that Conway Lonstar is a crossword-puzzle fanatic, that he is a great fan of Nero Wolfe, Archie Goodwin, and Rex Stout, and that he is an avid reader of police-procedural novels. That is all we know.

"The Weapon from Nowhere" was first published in *Ellery Queen's Mystery Magazine.* It is a deceptive tale that should be read slowly and watchfully, for Lonstar is a writer who will take quick advantage of the careless reader.

Now, meet Maître Glenthier, a magician-detective rivaling even The Great Merlini, as he investigates a prophecy, a murder, and a miracle!

The Weapon from Nowhere

by Conway Lonstar

I was a man with a mission when I walked into Maître Glenthier's magic shop one April afternoon. Threading my way through the usual assortment of illusions with price tags—and healthy price tags at that—I spotted the proprietor-magician himself in the back room, bending over a complicated piece of apparatus I had never seen before.

Without looking around, Glenthier said, "My crystal ball tells me that Art Shores just walked in, and not merely to pass the time of day, either."

"I didn't know my walk was that distinctive," I said.

"It's not, but your face is—reflected in these mirrors." I realized then that he was working on an intricate arrangement of reflecting glass. "You look too determined for a social call. What's up?"

"Have you heard of Mrs. de Seur?"

"The housewife in the suburbs who suddenly discovered she has the gift of second sight? Who hasn't?"

"Her latest prediction," I informed him, "makes the others look like peanuts. She's predicted a murder at ten o'clock tonight—a murder in her own house!"

"What did she do—send engraved invitations to the homicide squad?"

"I don't know about that, but the wire services got an anonymous tip and passed it on to me. I'd already been approached to write her up, and this clinches it—if the murder comes off. Needless to say, I'm going out there, and equally needless to say, I'd like you to come along. If there's any hanky-panky you're the one to spot it."

Glenthier reached up and pulled a Kennedy half dollar out of the air, looking thoughtful. "What can you tell me about her?"

"Not much. I've done some research on her for this article, but all I know is she's lived quietly for years in a Westchester suburb—Scarsdale—was married to a stock-borker, and has no children. Her husband died last year and she suddenly discovered this 'gift,' in quotes. I can't find out anything about her or de Seur before they settled in Westchester, but there's a rumor they were once on the stage."

Glenthier looked interested.

"Mindreading? Clairvoyance?"

I shrugged. "Your guess is as good as mine. Not under that name, though. I've checked—no record of de Seur."

"How do we get in tonight? Journalists invited?"

"Your own mindreading isn't too bad," I grinned. "She had to be coaxed, but she agreed to let me in—and about half a dozen reporters as well. You can be my photographer."

"Just what did she predict?"

"'There will be a death,'" I quoted. "'The message is not too clear, but I hope to see more before the time comes. There is a murderer in this house who will kill at ten tonight.'"

"She's got something up her housewifely sleeve, I'll bet you a rabbit from a top hat. My engagement book happens to be clear for this evening. Let's go, and you can tell me more over dinner."

In the restaurant Glenthier was full of questions, to most of which I didn't have answers. I had one though—about the people closest to Mrs. de Seur. There was a young niece who had lived with her for a year or two, Eugenia Coyn, and a Slavic servant she had hired recently. A man named Bill Mackrae had also been on the scene a great deal since her husband's death—a good-looking man with no visible means of support.

At nine o'clock we presented ourselves at an impressive Colonial home on Merridue St. in Scarsdale. The maid, Strevna, let us in, throwing dark suspicious glances at us and muttering to herself. She ushered us into a library at the rear of the house and then marched off, a fierce bony figure.

Mrs. de Seur was sitting in a big leather chair, resting her head wearily against its back. Her eyes were half closed, but she opened them to appraise us. She was a short dumpy woman who could have profited from a course at a charm school. I'd have thought the hungriest wolf wouldn't take the slightest notice of her; yet the tall handsome man at her side was hovering attentively.

We introduced ourselves, Glenthier improvising the name of Hopper Hartog for his alias, and then we took two of the straight chairs that were scattered around, as yet unoccupied.

"Glad to meet you," Mrs. de Seur said in a voice that matched her appearance for tiredness and lack of personality. "This is Mr. Mackrae." It seemed to me that, tired or not, she looked pretty sharply at Glenthier. We had fixed him up with a camera, of course, and maybe it bothered her because she realized she wasn't photogenic.

Mackrae took drink orders from us, and brought

something for Mrs. de Seur without asking her what she wanted.

"I still say you're making a big mistake," he said to her worriedly. "Why don't we just clear the house and go somewhere? I have a feeling we're asking for trouble."

"No, Bill, I've got to see it through," she said wanly. "Otherwise I'll never feel safe."

"*I* can protect you," the tall man growled.

Further conversation was cut short by the arrival of reporters, some of whom I knew, who seated themselves in the empty chairs with mumbled greetings.

Mrs. de Seur cleared her throat. Glenthier started to reach up, then shoved his hand in his pocket. I think he was going to materialize another of those Kennedy half dollars before he remembered he was supposed to be a photographer.

"Gentlemen," the woman said in her flat grating voice, "I have been resting to conserve my strength, to devote it all to trying to——" She broke off with a sharp indrawn breath as the inner door opened. A man entered and closed the door, wordlessly. He leaned his back against the panels and nodded to her.

"He's got detective written all over him," whispered Glenthier to me, and I nodded agreement. That answered another of Glenthier's questions—whether she believed enough in her "gift" to call in the police—and whether *they* believed enough in it to be present.

"As I was saying," she continued, taking no further notice of the newcomer, "I shall try to penetrate the future, to receive a vibration . . ." She shook her head. "I can't get anything. Perhaps, if it weren't so bright——"

Mackrae turned off some lights, leaving only the dull glow of one lamp in a corner, and returned to the woman's chair, perching himself on its arm.

She closed her eyes and pressed a plump hand to her forehead. You could have heard a feather drop.

Suddenly she gasped, then sat bolt upright, her eyes wide. "A *man* will die! At ten o'clock, that was correct. But I really thought that *I* was to be the victim. How strange!"

It was now 9:30.

Some of the reporters began to fire questions, and for the sake of appearances Glenthier took a couple of pictures.

Mrs. de Seur shook her head. "That's all I can tell you. If you had kept quiet I might have learned more. But now—I get nothing." She looked drained.

Mackrae stalked across the room to the French windows and threw them open.

"I'm going to look around out there," he said grimly.

"Wait, I'll go with you," Glenthier said, and at the same time the man at the inner door yelled, "Stop!" But both of them were talking to empty air. Drapes fluttered in the breeze. Glenthier went over for a look, but came back to his seat.

"Pitch-dark out there," he murmured to me. "I couldn't tell where he went. But my own brand of prophesy says we'll discover he's involved in all this hocus-pocus, right up to his handsome dark eyebrows."

The silence in the library persisted while the minutes wore on. Mrs. de Seur rested quietly in her chair. The rest of us kept checking our watches. 9:55. 9:58. 9:59.

10:00.

Nothing.

We all glanced at each other and began to relax—until then I hadn't realized how tense I had been.

And then—*crack!*

A shot exploded outdoors. Mrs. de Seur screamed. Our eyes were fixed on the French windows where the drapes began moving back and forth in a kind of frenzy.

Then the tall figure of a man appeared. He sort of grunted, there was a light thud, and he pitched forward on his face into the room. Mrs. de Seur screamed again.

The detective at the door got there first, with Glenthier a close second and myself at the magician's elbow. When the body was turned over, we saw that it was Mackrae, and we got another shock. Protruding from his chest was a knife!

"Dead," muttered the detective. He looked at the still-smoking gun that Mackrae had dropped as he came in, which had made the thud we heard. Then he shouted out through the open French windows. When one of his men appeared, the detective gave some sharp orders, then made for the telephone.

Mrs. de Seur never moved; she sat hunched in her chair.

The detective called headquarters to send a doctor, technicians, and equipment. As soon as he hung up, he began a quick questioning—designed, so it seemed, to establish that we knew nothing, had seen nothing, and could be dismissed. It was true enough that none of us had anything helpful to offer, and the reporters hardly needed urging to leave—they had news to report with a capital N.

On the other hand, Glenthier and I were anxious to stick around, so we dropped the name of our old friend Grove Maighan of N.Y. Homicide, which worked like Grade A magic. The detective called Maighan, and was evidently informed that the detective was loaded with luck to have Maître Glenthier on the scene of the crime. When he hung up, the detective beamed at us.

"Ted Ceviet's the name, gentlemen. I don't mind saying this sort of case is a little out of my line. We wouldn't even have come out on a crank call like this, but the old girl's predictions have been making the front page, and the Chief wasn't taking any chances. But how *could* she foresee this? Maighan says you're a wizard, Glenthier, with these supernatural-looking problems. Any ideas?"

"Oh, yes," Glenthier said, reaching into the air for a Kennedy half dollar. "I have ideas. But they need crystallizing, to say the least. Mackrae fired the gun, I suppose?"

"Looks that way," nodded Ceviet. "As if he saw someone out there and fired at him, and then another guy stabbed Mackrae."

"No, sir," broke in a new voice from the doorway, followed by some commotion as two women burst in, each accompanied by a plainclothesman. It was one of the men who had spoken.

Eugenia Coyn, who could have given her aunt lessons in charm—she was a real dish to look at—glared at Mrs. de Seur. "Now see what you've done!" she said angrily. "I hope you're satisfied." Her aunt hardly looked at her.

"I quit," was Strevna's terse contribution.

"What did you mean, Mannie?" Ceviet finally got a chance to ask.

"I was with this gal here, in her room. It's right over this one. Directly after the shot I looked out the window and beamed my flashlight on that gent. There was no knife in him at that time, and no one else near him. I watched him right up to the moment he came inside."

"Could the girl have done it?" asked Ceviet.

"She wasn't near the window," was the answer, and the other plainclothesman admitted that was also true for the maid, who had been in the kitchen under his guard.

"Psychokinesis," came the flat voice from the leather chair. "They both have the power."

It took a while, after that contribution, to prevail on the two women to take Mrs. de Seur upstairs, with their guards still in attendance. "If Mannie Collspath and Mitchell Pasanno say the two women couldn't have done it, they couldn't have. They're both good men," said Ceviet. Turning to Glenthier he asked, "What's psychokinesis?"

"Manipulation of physical objects by mental means," answered the magician. "People who've studied it, like Professor Rhine and others at Duke University, claim it works. I don't believe it myself. Their research methods are a little loose in my opinion."

"Have you a better explanation of how this could have been done?" sighed Ceviet. "I had a man outside—he wasn't in the rear until too late to see anything, but I told him to search the grounds, and he reported while the two women were here. He found nothing—no footprints, except Mackrae's. And there was no one near the door on my side. I'm going to be the laughingstock of the force."

At that point his technicians arrived, and the usual hustle and bustle of fingerprinting, photographing, and so on followed. In due course the doctor pronounced that it was the knife that had killed Mackrae.

We went to talk to Mrs. de Seur, looking into the kitchen and Eugenia Coyn's room on the way. Both rooms were in the rear of the house, but there didn't seem to be any way that either woman could have stabbed Mackrae without her guard knowing. If anyone in the library had done it, we'd have known. If we ruled out psychokinesis— and Glenthier really knows what he's talking about in such matters—there wasn't much left. Suicide seemed the only answer physically possible, but that's not the way suicides happen. Whom or what had Mackrae been shooting at? How had Mrs. de Seur known in advance that it would happen? It all added up to a king-size headache.

Ceviet looked as if he were beaten. Glenthier just looked thoughtful. Nor did the magician's expression change when he stubbed out a cigarette in his closed fist, then opened an empty hand.

When we reached her, Mrs. de Seur was crying— which did nothing to improve her looks.

"I was going to marry Bill," she sobbed. "He's been so good to me since my husband died. Eugenia and Strevna are both jealous because of him. Which of them did it, Mr. Ceviet?"

"You predicted it. Don't *you* know?" he snapped.

"No," she said seriously. "It may come to me, but I feel somehow it won't. You do understand, don't you, that predicting it didn't *make* it happen?" The poor woman was rather pathetic, trying to make us understand that second sight wasn't a method of murder.

"I know how it happened," Glenthier announced suddenly, "and I know who did it. If only I could think of the name—"

"Great," grumbled Ceviet. "You know who, but you don't know the name?"

"Got it!" Glenthier was triumphant. "Alisa!"

At this apparently meaningless name Mrs. de Seur turned white as a ghost.

"You're mad! Who is this man?" she protested shrilly.

"It will be easy enough to establish that you're Alisa. Besides, microscopic examination can prove the knife was in your chair—shoved down next to or under the cushion. There's bound to be marks on the leather from the knife.

"There's your murderess, Ceviet. Her 'gift' should have told her she'd be found out."

"Damn you," she said.

Glenthier was only too happy to explain to Ceviet and me later, over refreshing Scotches in a quiet suburban cocktail lounge.

"Misdirection, as usual," he said. "The shot was meant to point to a killer *outside*—and to provide distraction. Mackrae and she were in it together—up to a point. She added a twist of her own that wasn't in *his* program. He was to go outside and fire a shot, and she was to stab anyone who took her fancy, as long as the victim wasn't near her. They probably didn't intend for her actually to kill—

an attack would have been near enough to her prediction to get her a lot of impressive publicity."

"But," objected Ceviet, "how *could* she have stabbed someone who was not near her?—to say nothing of doing it in front of witnesses without being seen."

"Art told me she'd been on the stage, and reasoning pointed to her having been a knife thrower. A thorough investigation will confirm it, but I've saved you the trouble by recalling a little lady from my circus days who was billed in the side shows as 'Alisa and Her Magic Knives.' She was so smooth and fast you hardly saw her hand move, and she was a sure shot standing or sitting.

"Tonight she was to have thrown her knife right after the shot, or when Mackrae made his entrance, the two occasions they provided to distract us—when we weren't on such a sharp lookout, when we thought it was all over after the shot. But *her* plan was to fling the knife at *him* as he fumbled with the drapes. She was lightning-quick, catching him the split second after his chest showed through the curtains—while leaving us with the impression that it had happened *before* he came in. What we thought was his grunt was the impact of the knife, which she tried to cover with a scream."

"All right," I argued. "She told us why she killed Mackrae—he was blackmailing her—maybe her husband's death also involved a little of her sleight of hand and he knew about it. But why in Houdini's name did they plan this whole rigamarole?"

"Money's the logical reason," said Glenthier, "and Mackrae wanted her to have it—I suppose he's spent whatever she had. I'd say she wanted to go on the stage as a mindreader—I wouldn't be surprised if that used to be her husband's line before he became a stockbroker; then she'd know all the tricks. But you can see she hasn't the looks; who'd hire her? But with the publicity she'd get from this stunt her looks wouldn't matter; she could choose her spots—and her fee.

"Besides," finished Maître Glenthier, "her name—and I don't mean Alisa—was a dead giveaway."

"It's so simple when you know how it's done," said Ceviet, echoing a thought I've often had. Glenthier miraculously pulled two Kennedy half dollars out of the air and left them as a tip.

———————◇◇◇———————

AUTHOR'S NOTE: Yes, anagrams again. The letters of "Mrs. de Seur" can be rearranged to spell "murderess." And "Alisa" anagrams to "alias."

Maître Glenthier should have been easily recognizable as the great magician-detective—the Great Merlini. His Watson, Art Shores, is better known as Ross Harte, and Grove Maighan of N.Y. Homicide is really Homer Gavigan of same.

Other anagrams:

Bill Mackrae = blackmailer
Ted Ceviet = detective
Eugenia Coyn = a young niece
Strevna = servant
Merridue St. = murder site
Mitchell Pasanno = plainclothesman
Mannie Collspath = plainclothesman
Hopper Hartog = photographer

And finally, of course, The Great Merlini's creator, who has been known to play his character in real life and is a mighty tricky fellow in his own right: Conway Lonstar stands for Clayton Rawson, a master of mystery legerdemain.

NORMA SCHIER

Norma Schier, who supplied the information above, has written several other short story pastiches such as this one, which have appeared in *Ellery Queen's Mystery Magazine*. Although this form is a perfect vehicle for her talents with words, it is sadly anonymous, since her name never appears in a table of contents or as a byline. She is a psychologist by profession, with interests in skiing, fine restaurants, and Reconstruction Judaism, but anyone who has ever faced her across a Scrabble board or an Anagrams set-up will remember her best as a ruthless and extraordinarily skilled opponent.

A FINAL NOTE: This anagram business was too tempting, so we indulged ourselves and included one of our own in the introduction to "The Weapon from Nowhere." Simon Archer, Lonstar's friend and confidant is, naturally, Norma Schier.

14

Thanks to those excellent BBC productions, Lord Peter Wimsey has risen from relative obscurity to unexpected popularity in a few short months, and this in turn has created a renewed interest in the novels, the short stories, and in the author, Dorothy Leigh Sayers.

Miss Sayers' "infatuation with the noble hero" (to quote Earle Walbridge) began with the publication of *Whose Body?* in 1923, which she wrote to augment an impossibly low salary as a London copywriter. The book was an immediate success and was followed by, among others, *Unnatural Death, The Unpleasantness at the Bellona Club, Clouds of Witness,* and her masterpiece *The Nine Tailors.*

Hangman's Holiday was published in 1933. It wasn't a novel this time, but a collection of short stories, six dealing with a new detective, Mr. Montague Egg, and four featuring the now famous Lord Peter. One of the best, "The Incredible Elopement of Lord Peter Wimsey," involved the monocled detective in a bewildering tale of brutality and witchcraft in the Pyrenees.

Lord Peter's critics find him "exceedingly snobbish" and his humor "self-conscious and excruciating," but in today's troubled and complex world an evening spent in the amiable company of the "affected detective" is an evening of pure joy.

The Incredible Elopement of Lord Peter Wimsey

by Dorothy L. Sayers

"That house, señor?" said the landlord of the little *posada*. "That is the house of the American physician, whose wife, may the blessed saints preserve us, is bewitched." He crossed himself, and so did his wife and daughter.

"Bewitched, is she?" said Langley sympathetically. He was a professor of ethnology, and this was not his first visit to the Pyrenees. He had, however, never before penetrated to any place quite so remote as this tiny hamlet, clinging, like a rockplant, high up the scarred granite shoulders of the mountain. He scented material here for his book on Basque folklore. With tact, he might persuade the old man to tell his story.

"And in what manner," he asked, "is the lady bespelled?"

"Who knows?" replied the landlord, shrugging his shoulders. "'The man that asked questions on Friday was buried on Saturday.' Will your honour consent to take his supper?"

Langley took the hint. To press the question would be to encounter obstinate silence. Later, when they knew him better, perhaps——

His dinner was served to him at the family table—the oily, pepper-flavoured stew to which he was so well accustomed, and the harsh red wine of the country. His hosts chattered to him freely enough in that strange Basque language which has no fellow in the world, and is said by some to be the very speech of our first fathers in Paradise. They spoke of the bad winter, and young Esteban Arramandy, so strong and swift at the pelota, who had been lamed by a falling rock and now halted on two sticks; of three valuable goats carried off by a bear; of the torrential rains that, after a dry summer, had scoured the bare ribs of the mountains. It was raining now, and the wind was howling unpleasantly. This did not trouble Langley; he knew and loved this haunted and impenetrable country at all times and seasons. Sitting in that rude peasant inn, he thought of the oak-panelled hall of his Cambridge college and smiled, and his eyes gleamed happily behind his scholarly pince-nez. He was a young man, in spite of his professorship and the string of letters after his name. To his university colleagues it seemed strange that this man, so trim, so prim, so early old, should spend his vacations eating garlic, and scrambling on mule-back along precipitous mountain tracks. You would never think it, they said, to look at him.

There was a knock at the door.

"That is Martha," said the wife.

She drew back the latch, letting in a rush of wind and rain which made the candle gutter. A small, aged woman was blown in out of the night, her grey hair straggling in wisps from beneath her shawl.

"Come in, Martha, and rest yourself. It is a bad night. The parcel is ready—oh, yes. Dominique brought it from the town this morning. You must take a cup of wine or milk before you go back."

The old woman thanked her and sat down, panting.

"And how goes all at the house? The doctor is well?"

"He is well."

"And *she?*"

The daughter put the question in a whisper, and the landlord shook his head at her with a frown.

"As always at this time of the year. It is but a month now to the Day of the Dead. Jesu-Maria! it is a grievous affliction for the poor gentleman, but he is patient, patient."

"He is a good man," said Dominique, "and a skillful doctor, but an evil like that is beyond his power to cure. You are not afraid, Martha?"

"Why should I be afraid? The Evil One cannot harm *me*. I have no beauty, no wits, no strength for him to envy. And the Holy Relic will protect me."

Her wrinkled fingers touched something in the bosom of her dress.

"You come from the house yonder?" asked Langley.

She eyed him suspiciously.

"The señor is not of our country?"

"The gentleman is a guest, Martha," said the landlord hurriedly. "A learned English gentleman. He knows our country and speaks our language as you hear. He is a great traveller, like the American doctor, your master."

"What is your master's name?" asked Langley. It occurred to him that an American doctor who had buried himself in this remote corner of Europe must have something unusual about him. Perhaps he also was an ethnologist. If so, they might find something in common.

"He is called Wetherall." She pronounced the name several times before he was sure of it.

"Wetherall? Not Standish Wetherall?"

He was filled with extraordinary excitement.

The landlord came to his assistance.

"This parcel is for him," he said. "No doubt the name will be written there."

It was a small package, neatly sealed, bearing the label of a firm of London chemists and addressed to "Standish Wetherall Esq., M.D."

"Good heavens!" exclaimed Langley. "But this is strange. Almost a miracle. I know this man. I knew his wife, too——"

He stopped. Again the company made the sign of the cross.

"Tell me," he said in great agitation, and forgetting his caution, "you say his wife is bewitched—afflicted—how is this? Is she the same woman I know? Describe her. She was tall, beautiful, with gold hair and blue eyes like the Madonna. Is this she?"

There was a silence. The old woman shook her head and muttered something inaudible, but the daughter whispered:

"True—it is true. Once we saw her thus, as the gentleman says——"

"Be quiet," said her father.

"Sir," said Martha, "we are in the hand of God."

She rose, and wrapped her shawl about her.

"One moment," said Langley. He pulled out his notebook and scribbled a few lines. "Will you take this letter to your master the doctor? It is to say that I am here, his friend whom he once knew, and to ask if I may come and visit him. That is all."

"You would not go to that house, excellence?" whispered the old man fearfully.

"If he will not have me, maybe he will come to me here." He added a word or two and drew a piece of money from his pocket. "You will carry my note for me?"

"Willingly, willingly. But the señor will be careful? Perhaps, though a foreigner, you are of the Faith?"

"I am a Christian," said Langley.

This seemed to satisfy her. She took the letter and the

money, and secured them, together with the parcel, in a remote pocket. Then she walked to the door, strongly and rapidly for all her bent shoulders and appearance of great age.

Langley remained lost in thought. Nothing could have astonished him more than to meet the name of Standish Wetherall in this place. He had thought that episode finished and done with over three years ago. Of all people! The brilliant surgeon in the prime of his life and reputation, and Alice Wetherall, that delicate piece of golden womanhood—exiled in this forlorn corner of the world! His heart beat a little faster at the thought of seeing her again. Three years ago, he had decided that it would be wiser if he did not see too much of that porcelain loveliness. That folly was past now—but still he could not visualize her except against the background of the great white house in Riverside Drive, with the peacocks and the swimming pool and the gilded tower with the roof garden. Wetherall was a rich man, the son of old Hiram Wetherall the automobile magnate. What was Wetherall doing here?

He tried to remember. Hiram Wetherall, he knew, was dead, and all the money belonged to Standish, for there were no other children. There had been trouble when the only son had married a girl without parents or history. He had brought her from "somewhere out west." There had been some story of his having found her, years before, as a neglected orphan, and saved her from something or cured her of something and paid for her education, when he was still scarcely more than a student. Then, when he was a man over forty and she a girl of seventeen, he had brought her home and married her.

And now he had left his house and his money and one of the finest specialist practices in New York to come to live in the Basque country—in a spot so out of the way that men still believed in Black Magic, and could barely splutter more than a few words of bastard French or Spanish—a spot that was uncivilized even by comparison with the primitive civilization surrounding it. Langley began to be sorry that he had written to Wetherall. It might be resented.

The landlord and his wife had gone out to see to their cattle. The daughter sat close to the fire, mending a garment. She did not look at him, but he had the feeling that she would be glad to speak.

"Tell me, child," he said gently, "what is the trouble which afflicts these people who may be friends of mine?"

"Oh!" She glanced up quickly and leaned across to him, her arms stretched out over the sewing in her lap. "Sir, be advised. Do not go up there. No one will stay in that house at this time of the year, except Tomaso, who has not all his wits, and old Martha, who is——"

"What?"

"A saint—or something else," she said hurriedly.

"Child," said Langley again, "this lady when I knew——"

"I will tell you," she said, "but my father must not know. The good doctor brought her here three years ago last June, and then she was as you say. She was beautiful. She laughed and talked in her own speech—for she knew no Spanish or Basque. But on the Night of the Dead——"

She crossed herself.

"All-Hallows Eve," said Langley softly.

"Indeed, I do not know what happened. But she fell into the power of the darkness. She changed. There were terrible cries—I cannot tell. But little by little she became what she is now. Nobody sees her but Martha and she will not talk. But the people say it is not a woman at all that lives there now."

"Mad?" said Langley.

"It is not madness. It is—enchantment. Listen. Two years since on Easter Day—is that my father?"

"No, no."

"The sun had shone and the wind came up from the valley. We heard the blessed church bells all day long. That night there came a knock at the door. My father opened and one stood there like Our Blessed Lady herself, very pale like the image in the church and with a blue cloak over her head. She spoke, but we could not tell what she said. She wept and wrung her hands and pointed down the valley path, and my father went to the stable and saddled the mule. I thought of the flight from bad King Herod. But then—the American doctor came. He had run fast and was out of breath. And she shrieked at sight of him."

A great wave of indignation swept over Langley. If the man was brutal to his wife, something must be done quickly. The girl hurried on.

"He said—Jesus-Maria—he said that his wife was bewitched. At Eastertide the power of the Evil One was broken and she would try to flee. But as soon as the Holy Season was over, the spell would fall on her again, and therefore it was not safe to let her go. My parents were afraid to have touched the evil thing. They brought out the Holy Water and sprinkled the mule, but the wickedness had entered into the poor beast and she kicked my father so that he was lame for a month. The American took his wife away with him and we never saw her again. Even old Martha does not always see her. But every year the power waxes and wanes—heaviest at Hollow-tide and lifted again at Easter. Do not go to that house, señor, if you value your soul! Hush! they are coming back."

Langley would have liked to ask more, but his host glanced quickly and suspiciously at the girl. Taking up his candle, Langley went to bed. He dreamed of wolves, long, lean and black, running on the scent of blood.

Next day brought an answer to his letter:

Dear Langley, Yes, this is myself, and of course I

remember you well. Only too delighted to have you come and cheer our exile. You will find Alice somewhat changed, I fear, but I will explain our misfortunes when we meet. Our household is limited, owing to some kind of superstitious avoidance of the afflicted, but if you will come along about half past seven, we can give you a meal of sorts. Martha will show you the way.

Cordially,
Standish Wetherall

    The doctor's house was small and old, stuck halfway up the mountainside on a kind of ledge in the rock-wall. A stream, unseen but clamorous, fell echoing down close at hand. Langley followed his guide into a dim, square room with a great hearth at one end and, drawn close before the fire, an armchair with wide, sheltering ears. Martha, muttering some sort of apology, hobbled away and left him standing there in the half-light. The flames of the wood fire, leaping and falling, made here a gleam and there a gleam, and, as his eyes grew familiar with the room, he saw that in the centre was a table laid for a meal, and that there were pictures on the walls. One of these struck a familiar note. He went close to it and recognized a portrait of Alice Wetherall that he had last seen in New York. It was painted by Sargent in his happiest mood, and the lovely wild-flower face seemed to lean down to him with the sparkling smile of life.

    A log suddenly broke and fell in the hearth, flaring. As though the little noise and light had disturbed something, he heard, or thought he heard, a movement from the big chair before the fire. He stepped forward, and then stopped. There was nothing to be seen, but a noise had begun; a kind of low, animal muttering, extremely disagreeable to listen to. It was not made by a dog or a cat, he felt sure. It was a sucking, slobbering sound that affected him in a curiously sickening way. It ended in a series of little grunts or squeals, and then there was silence.

Langley stepped backwards towards the door. He was positive that something was in the room with him that he did not care about meeting. An absurd impulse seized him to run away. He was prevented by the arrival of Martha, carrying a big, old-fashioned lamp, and behind her, Wetherall, who greeted him cheerfully.

The familiar American accents dispelled the atmosphere of discomfort that had been gathering about Langley. He held out a cordial hand.

"Fancy meeting *you* here," said he.

"The world is very small," replied Wetherall. "I am afraid that is a hardy bromide, but I certainly am pleased to see you," he added, with some emphasis.

The old woman had put the lamp on the table, and now asked if she should bring in the dinner. Wetherall replied in the affirmative, using a mixture of Spanish and Basque which she seemed to understand well enough.

"I didn't know you were a Basque scholar," said Langley.

"Oh, one picks it up. These people speak nothing else. But of course Basque is your speciality, isn't it?"

"Oh, yes."

"I daresay they have told you some queer things about us. But we'll go into that later. I've managed to make the place reasonably comfortable, though I could do with a few more modern conveniences. However, it suits us."

Langley took the opportunity to mumble some sort of inquiry about Mrs. Wetherall.

"Alice? Ah, yes, I forgot—you have not seen her yet." Wetherall looked hard at him with a kind of half-smile. "I should have warned you. You were—rather an admirer of my wife in the old days."

"Like everyone else," said Langley.

"No doubt. Nothing specially surprising about it, was there? Here comes dinner. Put it down, Martha, and we will ring when we are ready."

The old woman set down a dish upon the table, which was handsomely furnished with glass and silver, and went out. Wetherall moved over to the fireplace, stepping sideways and keeping his eyes oddly fixed on Langley. Then he addressed the armchair.

"Alice! Get up, my dear, and welcome an old admirer of yours. Come along. You will both enjoy it. Get up."

Something shuffled and whimpered among the cushions. Wetherall stooped, with an air of almost exaggerated courtesy, and lifted it to its feet. A moment, and it faced Langley in the lamplight.

It was dressed in a rich gown of gold satin and lace, that hung rucked and crumpled upon the thick and slouching body. The face was white and puffy, the eyes vacant, the mouth drooled open, with little trickles of saliva running from the loose corners. A dry fringe of rusty hair clung to the half-bald scalp, like the dead wisps on the head of a mummy.

"Come, my love," said Wetherall. "Say how do you do to Mr. Langley."

The creature blinked and mouthed out some inhuman sounds. Wetherall put his hand under its forearm, and it slowly extended a lifeless paw.

"There, she recognizes you all right. I thought she would. Shake hands with him, my dear."

With a sensation of nausea, Langley took the inert hand. It was clammy and coarse to the touch and made no attempt to return his pressure. He let it go; it pawed vaguely in the air for a moment and then dropped.

"I was afraid you might be upset," said Wetherall, watching him. "I have grown used to it, of course, and it doesn't affect me as it would an outsider. Not that you are an outsider—anything but that—eh? Premature senility is the lay name for it, I suppose. Shocking, of course, if you haven't met it before. You needn't mind, by the way, what you say. She understands nothing.

"How did it happen?"

"I don't quite know. Came on gradually. I took the best advice, naturally, but there was nothing to be done. So we came here. I didn't care about facing things at home where everybody knew us. And I didn't like the idea of a sanatorium. Alice is my wife, you know—sickness or health, for better, for worse, and all that. Come along; dinner's getting cold."

He advanced to the table, leading his wife, whose dim eyes seemed to brighten a little at the sight of food.

"Sit down, my dear, and eat your nice dinner. (She understands that, you see.) You'll excuse her table manners, won't you? They're not pretty, but you'll get used to them."

He tied a napkin round the neck of the creature and placed food before her in a deep bowl. She snatched at it hungrily, slavering and gobbling as she scooped it up in her fingers and smeared face and hands with the gravy.

Wetherall drew out a chair for his guest opposite to where his wife sat. The sight of her held Langley with a kind of disgusted fascination.

The food—a sort of salmis—was deliciously cooked, but Langley had no appetite. The whole thing was an outrage, to the pitiful woman and to himself. Her seat was directly beneath the Sargent portrait, and his eyes went helplessly from the one to the other.

"Yes," said Wetherall, following his glance. "There is a difference, isn't there?" He himself was eating heartily and apparently enjoying his dinner. "Nature plays sad tricks upon us."

"Is it always like this?"

"No; this is one of her bad days. At times she will be—almost human. Of course these people here don't know what to think of it all. They have their own explanation of a very simple medical phenomenon."

"Is there any hope of recovery?"

"I'm afraid not—not of a permanent cure. You are not eating anything."

"I—well, Wetherall, this has been a shock to me."

"Of course. Try a glass of burgundy. I ought not to have asked you to come, but the idea of talking to an educated fellow-creature once again tempted me, I must confess."

"It must be terrible for you."

"I have become resigned. Ah, naughty, naughty!" The idiot had flung half the contents of her bowl upon the table. Wetherall patiently remedied the disaster, and went on:

"I can bear it better here, in this wild place where everything seems possible and nothing unnatural. My people are all dead, so there was nothing to prevent me from doing as I liked about it."

"No. What about your property in the States?"

"Oh, I run over from time to time to keep an eye on things. In fact, I am due to sail next month. I'm glad you caught me. Nobody over there knows how we're fixed, of course. They just know we're living in Europe."

"Did you consult no American doctor?"

"No. We were in Paris when the first symptoms declared themselves. That was shortly after that visit you paid to us." A flash of some emotion to which Langley could not put a name made the doctor's eyes for a moment sinister. "The best men on this side confirmed my own diagnosis. So we came here."

He rang for Martha, who removed the salmis and put on a kind of sweet pudding.

"Martha is my right hand," observed Wetherall. "I don't know what we shall do without her. When I am away, she looks after Alice like a mother. Not that there's much one can do for her, except to keep her fed and warm and clean—and that last is something of a task."

There was a note in his voice which jarred on Langley. Wetherall noticed his recoil and said:

"I won't disguise from you that it gets on my nerves sometimes. But it can't be helped. Tell me about yourself. What have you been doing lately?"

Langley replied with as much vivacity as he could assume, and they talked of indifferent subjects till the deplorable being which had once been Alice Wetherall began to mumble and whine fretfully and scramble down from her chair.

"She's cold," said Wetherall. "Go back to the fire, my dear."

He propelled her briskly towards the hearth, and she sank back into the armchair, crouching and complaining and thrusting out her hands towards the blaze. Wetherall brought out brandy and a box of cigars.

"I contrive just to keep in touch with the world, you see," he said. "They send me these from London. And I get the latest medical journals and reports. I'm writing a book, you know, on my own subject; so I don't vegetate. I can experiment, too—plenty of room for a laboratory, and no Vivisection Acts to bother one. It's a good country to work in. Are you staying here long?"

"I think not very."

"Oh! If you had thought of stopping on, I would have offered you the use of this house while I was away. You would find it more comfortable than the *posada*, and I should have no qualms, you know, about leaving you alone in the place with my wife—under the peculiar circumstances."

He stressed the last words and laughed. Langley hardly knew what to say.

"Really, Wetherall——"

"Though, in the old days, *you* might have liked the prospect more and *I* might have liked it less. There was a time, I think, Langley, when you would have jumped at the idea of living alone with—*my wife.*"

Langley jumped up.

"What the devil are you insinuating, Wetherall?"

"Nothing, nothing. I was just thinking of the afternoon when you and she wandered away at a picnic and got lost. You remember? Yes, I thought you would."

"This is monstrous," retorted Langley. "How dare you say such things—with that poor soul sitting there——?"

"Yes, poor soul. You're a poor thing to look at now, aren't you, my kitten?"

He turned suddenly to the woman. Something in his abrupt gesture seemed to frighten her, and she shrank away from him.

"You devil!" cried Langley. "She's afraid of you. What have you been doing to her? How did she get into this state? I *will* know!"

"Gently," said Wetherall. "I can allow for your natural agitation at finding her like this, but I can't have you coming between me and *my wife.* What a faithful fellow you are, Langley. I believe you still want her—just as you did before when you thought I was dumb and blind. Come now, have you got designs on *my wife,* Langley? Would you like to kiss her, caress her, take her to bed with you—my beautiful wife?"

A scarlet fury blinded Langley. He dashed an inexpert fist at the mocking face. Wetherall gripped his arm, but he broke away. Panic seized him. He fled stumbling against the furniture and rushed out. As he went he heard Wetherall very softly laughing.

The train to Paris was crowded. Langley, scrambling in at the last moment, found himself condemned to the corridor. He sat down on a suitcase and tried to think. He had not been able to collect his thoughts on his wild flight. Even now, he was not quite sure what he had fled from. He buried his head in his hands.

"Excuse me," said a polite voice.

Langley looked up. A fair man in a grey suit was looking down at him through a monocle.

"Fearfully sorry to disturb you," went on the fair man. "I'm just tryin' to barge back to my jolly ole kennel. Ghastly crowd, isn't it? Don't know when I've disliked my fellow creatures more. I say, you don't look frightfully fit. Wouldn't you be better on something more comfortable?"

Langley explained that he had not been able to get a seat. The fair man eyed his haggard and unshaven countenance for a moment and then said:

"Well, look here, why not come and lay yourself down in my bin for a bit? Have you had any grub? No? That's a mistake. Toddle along with me and we'll get hold of a spot of soup and so on. You'll excuse my mentioning it, but you look as if you'd been backing a system that's come unstuck, or something. Not my business, of course, but do have something to eat."

Langley was too faint and sick to protest. He stumbled obediently along the corridor till he was pushed into a first-class sleeper, where a rigidly correct manservant was laying out a pair of mauve silk pyjamas and a set of silver-mounted brushes.

"This gentleman's feeling rotten, Bunter," said the man with the monocle, "so I've brought him in to rest his aching head upon thy breast. Get hold of the commissariat and tell 'em to buzz a plate of soup along and a bottle of something drinkable."

"Very good, my lord."

Langley dropped, exhausted, on the bed, but when the food appeared he ate and drank greedily. He could not remember when he had last made a meal.

"I say," he said, "I wanted that. It's awfully decent of you. I'm sorry to appear so stupid. I've had a bit of a shock."

"Tell me all," said the stranger pleasantly.

The man did not look particularly intelligent, but he seemed friendly and, above all, normal. Langley wondered how the story would sound.

"I'm an absolute stranger to you," he began.

"And I to you," said the fair man. "The chief use of strangers is to tell things to. Don't you agree?"

"I'd like——" said Langley. "The fact is, I've run away from something. It's queer—it's—but what's the use of bothering you with it?"

The fair man sat down beside him and laid a slim hand on his arm.

"Just a moment," he said. "Don't tell me anything if you'd rather not. But my name is Wimsey—Lord Peter Wimsey—and I am interested in queer things."

It was the middle of November when the strange man came to the village. Thin, pale, and silent, with his great black hood flapping about his face, he was surrounded with an atmosphere of mystery from the start. He settled down, not at the inn, but in a dilapidated cottage high up in the mountains, and he brought with him five mule-loads of mysterious baggage and a servant. The servant was almost as uncanny as the master; he was a Spaniard and spoke Basque well enough to act as an interpreter for his employer when necessary; but his words were few, his aspect gloomy and stern, and such brief information as he vouchsafed, disquieting in the extreme. His master, he said, was a wise man; he spent all his time reading books; he ate no flesh; he was of no known country; he spoke the language of the Apostles and had talked with blessed Lazarus after his return from the grave; and when he sat alone in his chamber by night, the angels of God came and conversed with him in celestial harmonies.

This was terrifying news. The few dozen villagers avoided the little cottage, especially at nighttime; and when the pale stranger was seen coming down the mountain path, folded in his black robe and bearing one of his magic tomes beneath his arm, the women pushed their children within doors, and made the sign of the cross.

Nevertheless, it was a child that first made the personal acquaintance of the magician. The small son of the Widow Etcheverry, a child of bold and inquisitive disposition, went one evening adventuring into the unhallowed neighbourhood. He was missing for two hours, during which his mother, in a frenzy of anxiety, had called the neighbours about her and summoned the priest, who had unhappily been called away on business to the town. Suddenly, however, the child reappeared, well and cheerful, with a strange story to tell.

He had crept up close to the magician's house (the bold, wicked child, did ever you hear the like?) and climbed into a tree to spy upon the stranger (Jesu-Maria!). And he saw a light in the window, and strange shapes moving about and shadows going to and fro within the room. And then there came a strain of music so ravishing it drew the very heart out of his body, as though all the stars were singing together. (Oh, my precious treasure! The wizard has stolen the heart out of him, alas! alas!) Then the cottage door opened and the wizard came out and with him a great company of familiar spirits. One of them had wings like a seraph and talked in an unknown tongue, and another was like a wee man, no higher than your knee, with a black face and a white beard, and he sat on the wizard's shoulder and whispered in his ear. And the heavenly music played louder and louder. And the wizard had a pale flame all about his head, like the pictures of the saints. (Blessed St James of Compostella, be merciful to us all! And what then?) Why then he, the boy, had been very much frightened and wished he had not come, but the little dwarf spirit had seen him and jumped into the tree after him, climbing—oh! so fast! And he had tried to climb higher and had slipped and fallen to the ground. (Oh, the poor, wicked, brave, bad boy!)

Then the wizard had come and picked him up and spoken strange words to him and all the pain had gone away from the places where he had bumped himself (Marvellous! marvellous!) and he had carried him into the house. And inside, it was like the streets of Heaven, all gold and glittering. And the familiar spirits had sat beside the fire, nine in number, and the music had stopped playing. But the wizard's servant had brought him marvelous fruits in a silver dish, like fruits of Paradise, very sweet and delicious, and he had eaten them, and drunk a strange, rich drink from a goblet covered with red and blue jewels. Oh, yes—and there had been a tall crucifix on the wall, big, big, with a lamp burning before it and a strange sweet perfume like the smell in church on Easter Day.

(A crucifix? That was strange. Perhaps the magician was not so wicked, after all. And what next?)

Next, the wizard's servant had told him not to be afraid, and had asked his name and his age and whether he could repeat his Paternoster. So he had said that prayer and the Ave Maria and part of the Credo, but the Credo was long and he had forgotten what came after *ascendit in coelum*. So the wizard had prompted him and they had finished saying it together. And the wizard had pronounced the sacred names and words without flinching and in the right order, so far as he could tell. And then the servant had asked further about himself and his family, and he had told about the death of the black goat and about his sister's lover, who had left her because she had not so much money as the merchant's daughter. Then the wizard and his servant had spoken together and laughed, and the servant had said: "My master gives this message to your sister: that where there is no love there is no wealth, but he that is bold shall have gold for the asking." And with that, the wizard had put forth his hand into the air and taken from it—out of the empty air, yes, truly—one, two, three, four, five pieces of money and given them to him. And he was afraid to take them till he had made the sign of the cross upon them, and then, as they did not vanish or turn into fiery serpents, he had taken them, and here they were!

So the gold pieces were examined and admired in fear and trembling, and then, by grandfather's advice, placed under the feet of the image of Our Lady, after a sprinkling with Holy Water for their better purification. And on the next morning, as they were still there, they were shown to the priest, who arrived, tardy and flustered upon his last night's summons, and by him pronounced to be good Spanish coin, whereof one piece being devoted to the Church to put all right with Heaven, the rest might be put to secular uses without peril to the soul. After which, the good padre made his hasty way to the cottage, and returned, after an hour, filled with good reports of the wizard.

"For, my children," said he, "this is no evil sorcerer, but a Christian man, speaking the language of the Faith. He and I have conversed together with edification. Moreover, he keeps very good wine and is altogether a very worthy person. Nor did I perceive any familiar spirits or flaming apparitions; but it is true that there is a crucifix and also a very handsome Testament with pictures in gold and colour. *Benedicite,* my children. This is a good and learned man."

And away he went back to his presbytery; and that winter the chapel of Our Lady had a new altar cloth.

After that, each night saw a little group of people clustered at a safe distance to hear the music which poured out from the wizard's windows, and from time to time a few bold spirits would creep up close enough to peer through the chinks of the shutters and glimpse the marvels within.

The wizard had been in residence about a month, and sat one night after his evening meal in conversation with his servant. The black hood was pushed back from his head, disclosing a sleek poll of fair hair, and a pair of rather humorous grey eyes, with a cynical droop of the lids. A glass of Cockburn 1908 stood on the table at his elbow and from the arm of his chair a red-and-green parrot gazed unwinkingly at the fire.

"Time is getting on, Juan," said the magician. "This business is very good fun and all that—but is there anything doing with the old lady?"

"I think so, my lord. I have dropped a word or two here and there of marvelous cures and miracles. I think she will come. Perhaps even tonight."

"Thank goodness! I want to get the thing over before Wetherall comes back, or we may find ourselves in Queer Street. It will take some weeks, you know, before we are ready to move, even if the scheme works at all. Damn it, what's that?"

Juan rose and went into the inner room, to return in a minute carrying the lemur.

"Micky had been playing with your hair brushes," he said indulgently, "Naughty one, be quiet! Are you ready for a little practice, my lord?"

"Oh, rather, yes! I'm getting quite a dab at this job. If all else fails, I shall try for an engagement with Maskelyne."

Juan laughed, showing his white teeth. He brought out a set of billiard balls, coins, and other conjuring apparatus, palming and multiplying them negligently as he went. The other took them from him, and the lesson proceeded.

"Hush!" said the wizard, retrieving a ball which had tiresomely slipped from his fingers in the very act of vanishing. "There's somebody coming up the path."

He pulled his robe about his face and slipped silently into the inner room. Juan grinned, removed the decanter and glasses and extinguished the lamp. In the firelight the great eyes of the lemur gleamed strongly as it hung on the back of the high chair. Juan pulled a large folio from the shelf, lit a scented pastille in a curiously shaped copper vase, and pulled forward a heavy iron cauldron which stood on the hearth. As he piled the logs about it, there came a knock. He opened the door, the lemur running at his heels.

"Whom do you seek, mother?" he asked, in Basque.

"Is the Wise One at home?"

"His body is at home, mother; his spirit holds converse with the unseen. Enter. What would you with us?"

"I have come, as I said—ah, Mary! Is that a spirit?"

"God made spirits and bodies also. Enter and fear not."

The old woman came tremblingly forward.

"Hast thou spoken with him of what I told thee?"

"I have. I have shown him the sickness of thy mistress—her husband's sufferings—all."

"What said he?"

"Nothing; he read in his book."

"Think you he can heal her?"

"I do not know; the enchantment is a strong one; but my master is mighty for good."

"Will he see me?"

"I will ask him. Remain here, and beware thou show no fear, whatever befall."

"I will be courageous," said the old woman, fingering her beads.

Juan withdrew. There was a nerve-shattering interval. The lemur had climbed up to the back of the chair again and swung, teeth chattering, among the leaping shadows. The parrot cocked his head and spoke a few gruff words from his corner. An aromatic steam began to rise from the cauldron. Then, slowly into the red light, three, four, seven white shapes came stealthily and sat down in a circle about the hearth. Then, a faint music, that seemed to roll in from leagues away. The flame flickered and dropped. There was a tall cabinet against the wall, with gold figures on it that seemed to move with the moving firelight.

Then, out of the darkness, a strange voice chanted in an unearthly tongue that sobbed and thundered.

Martha's knees gave under her. She sank down. The seven white cats rose and stretched themselves, and came sidling slowly about her. She looked up and saw the wizard standing before her, a book in one hand and a silver wand in the other. The upper part of his face was hidden, but she saw his pale lips move and presently he spoke, in a deep, husky tone that vibrated solemnly in the dim room:

"ὦ πέπον, εἰ μὲν γὰρ, πόλεμον περὶ τόνδε φυγόντε,
αἰεὶ δὴ μέλλοιμεν ἀγήρω τ᾿ ἀθανάτω τε
ἄσσεθ᾿, οὔτε κεν αὐτὸς ἐνὶ πρώτοισι μαχοίμην,
οὔτε κέ σε στέλλοιμι μάχην ἐς κυδιάνειραν . . ."

The great syllables went rolling on. Then the wizard paused and added, in a kinder tone:

"Great stuff, this Homer. 'It goes so thunderingly as though it conjured devils.' What do I do next?"

The servant had come back, and now whispered in Martha's ear.

"Speak now," said he. "The master is willing to help you."

Thus encouraged, Martha stammered out her request. She had come to ask the Wise Man to help her mistress, who lay under an enchantment. She had brought an offering—the best she could find, for she had not liked to take anything of her master's during his absence. But here were a silver penny, an oat cake, and a bottle of wine, very much at the wizard's service, if such small matters could please him.

The wizard, setting aside his book, gravely accepted the silver penny, turned it magically into six gold pieces and laid the offering on the table. Over the oat cake and the wine he showed a little hesitation, but at length, murmuring:

"Ergo omnis longo solvit se Teucria luctu"

(a line notorious for its grave spondaic cadence), he metamorphosed the one into a pair of pigeons and the other into a curious little crystal tree in a metal pot, and set them beside the coins. Martha's eyes nearly started from her head, but Juan whispered encouragingly:

"The good intention gives value to the gift. The master is pleased. Hush!"

The music ceased on a loud chord. The wizard, speaking now with greater assurance, delivered himself with fair accuracy of a page or so from Homer's Catalogue of the Ships, and, drawing from the folds of his robe his long white hand laden with antique rings, produced from midair a small casket of shining metal, which he proffered to the suppliant.

"The master says," prompted the servant, "that you shall take this casket, and give to your lady of the wafers which it contains, one at every meal. When all have been consumed, seek this place again. And remember to say three Aves and two Paters morning and evening for the intention of the lady's health. Thus, by faith and diligence, the cure may be accomplished."

Martha received the casket with trembling hands.

"Tendebantque manus ripae ulterioris amore," said the wizard, with emphasis. *"Poluphloisboio thalasses. Ne plus ultra. Valete. Plaudite."*

He stalked away into the darkness, and the audience was over.

"It is working, then?" said the wizard to Juan.

The time was five weeks later, and five more consignments of enchanted wafers had been ceremoniously dispatched to the grim house on the mountain.

"It is working," agreed Juan. "The intelligence is returning, the body is becoming livelier, and the hair is growing again."

"Thank the Lord! It was a shot in the dark, Juan, and even now I can hardly believe that anyone in the world could think of such a devilish trick. When does Wetherall return?"

"In three weeks' time."

"Then we had better fix our grand finale for today fortnight. See that the mules are ready, and go down to the town and get a message off to the yacht."

"Yes, my lord."

"That will give you a week to get clear with the menagerie and the baggage. And—I say, how about Martha? Is it dangerous to leave her behind, do you think?"

"I will try to persuade her to come back with us."

"Do. I should hate anything unpleasant to happen to her. The man's a criminal lunatic. Oh, lord! I'll be glad when this is over. I want to get into a proper suit of clothes again. What Bunter would say if he saw this——"

The wizard laughed, lit a cigar, and turned on the gramophone.

The last act was duly staged a fortnight later.

It had taken some trouble to persuade Martha of the necessity of bringing her mistress to the wizard's house.

Indeed, that supernatural personage had been obliged to make an alarming display of wrath and declaim two whole choruses from Euripides before gaining his point. The final touch was put to the terrors of the evening by a demonstration of the ghastly effects of a sodium flame— which lends a very corpselike aspect to the human countenance, particularly in a lonely cottage on a dark night, and accompanied by incantations and the *Danse Macabre* of Saint-Saens.

Eventually the wizard was placated by a promise, and Martha departed, bearing with her a charm, engrossed upon parchment, which her mistress was to read and thereafter hang about her neck in a white silk bag.

Considered as a magical formula, the document was perhaps a little unimpressive in its language, but its meaning was such as a child could understand. It was in English, and ran:

You have been ill and in trouble, but your friends are ready to cure you and help you. Don't be afraid, but do whatever Martha tells you, and you will soon be quite well and happy again.

"And even if she can't understand it," said the wizard to his man, "it can't possibly do any harm."

The events of that terrible night have become legend in the village. They tell by the fireside with bated breath how Martha brought the strange, foreign lady to the wizard's house, that she might be finally and for ever freed from the power of the Evil One. It was a dark night and a stormy one, with the wind howling terribly through the mountains.

The lady had become much better and brighter through the wizard's magic—though this, perhaps, was only a fresh glamour and delusion—and she had followed

Martha like a little child on that strange and secret journey.
They had crept out very quietly to elude the vigilance of old
Tomaso, who had strict orders from the doctor never to let
the lady stir one step from the house. As for that, Tomaso
swore that he had been cast into an enchanted sleep—but
who knows? There may have been no more to it than
over-much wine. Martha was a cunning woman, and,
some said, little better than a witch herself.

Be that as it might, Martha and the lady had come to
the cottage, and there the wizard had spoken many things
in a strange tongue, and the lady had spoken likewise.
Yes—she who for so long had only grunted like a beast, had
talked with the wizard and answered him. Then the wizard
had drawn strange signs upon the floor round about the
lady and himself. And when the lamp was extinguished, the
signs glowed awfully, with a pale light of their own. The
wizard also drew a circle about Martha herself, and warned
her to keep inside it. Presently they heard a rushing noise,
like great wings beating, and all the familiars leaped about,
and the little white man with the black face ran up the
curtain and swung from the pole. Then a voice cried out:
"He comes! He comes!" and the wizard opened the door of
the tall cabinet with gold images upon it, that stood in the
centre of the circle, and he and the lady stepped inside it
and shut the doors after them.

The rushing sound grew louder and the familiar
spirits screamed and chattered—and then, all of a sudden,
there was a thunder clap and a great flash of light and the
cabinet was shivered into pieces and fell down. And lo and
behold! the wizard and the lady had vanished clean away
and were never more seen or heard of.

This was Martha's story, told the next day to her
neighbours. How she had escaped from the terrible house
she could not remember. But when, some time after, a
group of villagers summoned up courage to visit the place

again, they found it bare and empty. Lady, wizard, servant, familiars, furniture, bags, and baggage—all were gone, leaving not a trace behind them, except a few mysterious lines and figures traced on the floor of the cottage.

This was a wonder indeed. More awful still was the disappearance of Martha herself, which took place three nights afterwards.

Next day, the American doctor returned, to find an empty hearth and a legend.

"Yacht ahoy!"

Langley peered anxiously over the rail of the *Abracadabra* as the boat loomed out of the blackness. When the first passenger came aboard, he ran hastily to greet him.

"Is it all right, Wimsey?"

"Absolutely all right. She's a bit bewildered, of course—but you needn't be afraid. She's like a child, but she's getting better every day. Bear up, old man—there's nothing to shock you about her."

Langley moved hesitatingly forward as a muffled female figure was hoisted gently on board.

"Speak to her," said Wimsey: "She may or may not recognize you. I can't say."

Langley summoned up his courage. "Good evening, Mrs Wetherall," he said, and held out his hand.

The woman pushed the cloak from her face. Her blue eyes gazed shyly at him in the lamplight—then a smile broke out upon her lips.

"Why, I know you—of course I know you. You're Mr Langley. I'm so glad to see you."

She clasped his hand in hers.

"Well, Langley," said Lord Peter, as he manipulated the syphon, "a more abominable crime it has never been my fortune to discover. My religious beliefs are a little ill-defined, but I hope something really beastly happens to Wetherall in the next world. Say when!

"You know, there were one or two very queer points about that story you told me. They gave me a line on the thing from the start.

"To begin with, there was this extraordinary kind of decay or imbecility settlin' in on a girl in her twenties—so conveniently, too, just after you'd been hangin' round the Wetherall home and showin' perhaps a trifle too much sensibility, don't you see? And then there was this tale of the conditions clearin' up regularly once a year or so—not like any ordinary brain-trouble. Looked as if it was being controlled by somebody.

"Then there was the fact that Mrs Wetherall had been under her husband's medical eye from the beginning, with no family or friends who knew anything about her to keep a check on the fellow. Then there was the determined isolation of her in a place where no doctor could see her and where, even if she had a lucid interval, there wasn't a soul who could understand or be understood by her. Queer, too, that it should be a part of the world where you, with your interests, might reasonably be expected to turn up some day and be treated to a sight of what she had turned into. Then there were Wetherall's well-known researches, and the fact that he kept in touch with a chemist in London.

"All that gave me a theory, but I had to test it before I could be sure I was right. Wetherall was going to America, and that gave me a chance; but of course he left strict orders that nobody should get into or out of his house during his absence. I had, somehow, to establish an authority greater than his over old Martha, who is a faithful soul, God bless her! Hence, exit Lord Peter Wimsey and enter the magician. The treatment was tried and proved successful—hence the elopement and the rescue.

"Well, now, listen—and don't go off the deep end. It's all over now. Alice Wetherall is one of those unfortunate people who suffer from congenital thyroid deficiency. You know the thyroid gland in your throat—the one that stokes the engine and keeps the old brain going. In some people the thing doesn't work properly, and they turn out cretinous imbeciles. Their bodies don't grow and their minds don't work. But feed 'em the stuff, and they come absolutely all right—cheery and handsome and intelligent and lively as crickets. Only, don't you see, you have to *keep* feeding it to 'em, otherwise they just go back to an imbecile condition.

"Wetherall found this girl when he was a bright young student just learning about the thyroid. Twenty years ago, very few experiments had been made in this kind of treatment, but he was a bit of a pioneer. He gets hold of the kid, works a miraculous cure, and, bein' naturally bucked with himself, adopts her, gets her educated, likes the look of her, and finally marries her. You understand, don't you, that there's nothing fundamentally unsound about those thyroid deficients. Keep 'em going on the little daily dose, and they're normal in every way, fit to live an ordinary life and have ordinary healthy children.

"Nobody, naturally, knew anything about this thyroid business except the girl herself and her husband. All goes well till *you* come along. Then Wetherall gets jealous——"

"He had no cause."

Wimsey shrugged his shoulders.

"Possibly, my lad, the lady displayed a preference—we needn't go into that. Anyhow, Wetherall did get jealous and saw a perfectly marvellous revenge in his power. He carried his wife off to the Pyrenees, isolated her from all help, and then simply sat back and starved her of her thyroid extract. No doubt he told her what he was going to do, and why. It would please him to hear her desperate appeals—to let her feel herself slipping back day by day, hour by hour, into something less than a beast——"

"Oh, God!"

"As you say. Of course, after a time, a few months, she would cease to know what was happening to her. He would still have the satisfaction of watching her—seeing her skin thicken, her body coarsen, her hair fall out, her eyes grow vacant, her speech die away into mere animal noises, her brain go to mush, her habits——"

"Stop it, Wimsey."

"Well, you saw it all yourself. But that wouldn't be enough for him. So, every so often, he would feed her the thyroid again and bring her back sufficiently to realize her own degradation——"

"If only I had the brute here!"

"Just as well you haven't. Well, then, one day—by a stroke of luck—Mr Langley, the amorous Mr Langley, actually turns up. What a triumph to let him see——"

Langley stopped him again.

"Right-ho! but it was ingenious, wasn't it? So simple. The more I think of it, the more it fascinates me. But it was just that extra refinement of cruelty that defeated him. Because, when you told me the story, I couldn't help recognizing the symptoms of thyroid deficiency, and I thought, 'Just supposing'—so I hunted up the chemist whose name you saw on the parcel, and, after unwinding a lot of red tape, got him to admit that he had several times sent Wetherall consignments of thyroid extract. So then I was almost sure, don't you see.

"I got a doctor's advice and a supply of gland extract, hired a tame Spanish conjurer and some performing cats and things, and barged off complete with disguise and a trick cabinet devised by the ingenious Mr. Devant. I'm a bit of a conjurer myself, and between us we didn't do so badly.

The local superstitions helped, of course, and so did the gramophone records. Schubert's "Unfinished" is first class for producing an atmosphere of gloom and mystery, so are luminous paint and the remnants of a classical education."

"Look here, Wimsey, will she get all right again?"

"Right as ninepence, and I imagine that any American court would give her a divorce on the grounds of persistent cruelty. After that—it's up to you!"

Lord Peter's friends greeted his reappearance in London with mild surprise.

"And what have *you* been doing with yourself?" demanded the Hon. Freddy Arbuthnot.

"Eloping with another man's wife," replied his lordship. "But only," he hastened to add, "in a purely Pickwickian sense. Nothing in it for yours truly. Oh, well! Let's toddle round to the Holborn Empire, and see what George Robey can do for us."

Just reading this story, you can imagine Lord Peter in his flowing robes. Here is a man with the poise, style, command, and personality to present an evening within the world of magic.

Behind most great magicians is a quiet, efficient organizer. Houdini had Stanley Collins and Lord Peter had Bunter. With Lord Peter's knowledge of psychology and Bunter's infinite capacity for details, their magical evenings must have been a delight to a more worldly audience and a fright to an unsophisticated one!

It seems a shame that Dorothy Sayers did not have enough magical background to describe in detail the illusions that took place on that evening. We have to let our imaginations do their work and visualize the illusions that took place on that far-off night.

15

We end as we began, with a tale by Stephen Leacock that is as true today as the day it was written.

A Model Dialogue

by Stephen Leacock

In which is shown how the drawing-room juggler may be permanently cured of his card trick.

The drawing-room juggler, having slyly got hold of the pack of cards at the end of the game of whist, says:

"Ever see any card tricks? Here's rather a good one; pick a card."

"Thank you, I don't want a card."

"No, but just pick one, any one you like, and I'll tell which one you pick."

"You'll tell who?"

"No, no; I mean, I'll know which it is, don't you see? Go on now, pick a card."

"Any one I like?"

"Yes."

"Any colour at all?"

"Yes, yes."

"Any suit?"

"Oh, yes; do go on."

"Well, let me see, I'll—pick—the—ace of spades."

"Great Caesar! I mean you are to pull a card out of the pack."

"Oh, to pull it out of the pack! Now I understand. Hand me the pack. All right—I've got it."

"Have you picked one?"

"Yes, it's the three of hearts. Did you know it?"

"Hang it! Don't tell me like that. You spoil the thing. Here, try again. Pick a card."

"All right, I've got it."

"Put it back in the pack. Thanks. (Shuffle, shuffle, shuffle—flip)—There, is that it?" (triumphantly).

"I don't know. I lost sight of it."

"Lost sight of it! Confound it, you have to look at it and see what it is."

"Oh, you want me to look at the front of it!"

"Why, of course! Now then, pick a card."

"All right. I've picked it. Go ahead." (Shuffle, shuffle, shuffle—flip.)

"Say, confound you, did you put that card back in the pack?"

"Why, no. I kept it."

"Holy Moses! Listen. Pick—a—card—just one—look at it—see what it is—then put it back—do you understand?"

"Oh, perfectly. Only I don't see how you are going to do it. You must be awfully clever."

(Shuffle, shuffle, shuffle—flip.)

"There you are; that's your card, now, isn't it?" (This is the supreme moment.)

"NO. THAT IS NOT MY CARD." (This is a flat lie, but Heaven will pardon you for it.)

"Not that card ! ! ! ! Say—just hold on a second. Here, now, watch what you're at this time. I can do this cursed thing, mind you, every time. I've done it on father, on mother, and on every one that's ever come round our place. Pick a card. (Shuffle, shuffle, shuffle—flip, bang.) There, that's your card."

"NO. I AM SORRY. THAT IS NOT MY CARD. But

won't you try it again? Please do. Perhaps you are a little excited—I'm afraid I was rather stupid. Won't you go and sit quietly by yourself on the back verandah for half an hour and then try? You have to go home? Oh, I'm so sorry. It must be such an awfully clever little trick. Good night!"

More Magical Mysteries:
A Reader's Guide to Longer Works of Larcenous Legerdemain

The following short list of mysteries is not for the laggard. It is provided solely for the reader who is willing to haunt used book stores, dusty attics (if any still exist), and America's last refuge of rationality—the library.

The books may be hard to track down, but as we mentioned in the introduction to this volume, finding them is the sport.

CHANCE, GEORGE—*Murder Makes a Ghost* and *The Case of the Laughing Corpse.* These novels concern the mystifying exploits of the magician sleuth, George Chance. They appeared in *The Ghost* (Summer 1940 and Fall 1940), a pulp magazine published by Better Publications.

CHESTERTON, G. K.—*Magic, A Fantastic Comedy* (Putnam, 1913). An interesting short play about a "real" magician.

CULLINGFORD, GUY—*Conjuror's Coffin* (Hammond, Hammond & Co., London). The setting of this novel is London's Soho, and it concerns murder in a run-down hotel for variety artists.

FISHER, STEVE—*Saxon's Ghost* (Sherbourne Press, 1969). An excellent and terrifying novel involving The Great Saxon, a ghost-breaker and exposer of psychic frauds.

GIBSON, WALTER B.—*The Mask of Mephisto & Murder by Magic* (Doubleday, 1975). Reprints of two early novels about "The Shadow." *Looks That Kill* (Current Detective Stories, 1948). *A Blonde for Murder* (Same as above). Mr. Gibson has written many books on the art and history of magic. We highly recommend them.

RAWSON, CLAYTON—*Death From a Top Hat* (Putnam, 1938). *The Footprints on the Ceiling* (Putnam, 1939). *The Headless Lady* (Putnam, 1940). *No Coffin for the Corpse* (Little, Brown, 1942). These four novels, which involve The Great Merlini, are nothing less than "classics." They were re-printed in paperback in 1962 by Collier Books.

TALBOT, HAKE—*Rim of the Pit* (Simon & Schuster, 1944). A novel of magic and the supernatural. It also appeared in a Dell paperback edition.

TOWNE, STUART (Clayton Rawson)—*Death out of Thin Air* (Red Star Mystery, Aug. 1940). *Ghost of the Undead* (Red Star Mystery, June 1940). *Don Diavolo Goes to the Circus* (Red Star Mystery, Oct. 1940).